THE OLD AND THE YOUNG

by

Luigi Pirandello [1867-1936]

Authorized Translation from the Italian by
C. K. Scott-Moncrieff [1889-1930]

ISBN 978-1-78139-022-1

AI MIEI FIGLI GIOVANI OGGI, VECCHI DOMANI.

LUIGI PIRANDELLO

Contents

Part I

Part II

PART I

CHAPTER I

MONSIGNORE IS QUITE RIGHT....

The rain, which had fallen in torrents during the night, had churned into a quagmire the long highroad that wound, in a succession of twists and turns, as though in search of some less laborious ascent, some less abrupt slope, over the broken surface of the vast, deserted plain.

The damage done by the storm appeared all the more depressing, inasmuch as there were already signs, here and there, of the disregard, not to say the contempt, shewn for the labours of those who had planned and constructed the road in order to give their fellow-men an easier passage over the natural obstacles of the country by means of those bends and coils, erecting now a retaining wall, now a dyke. The retaining walls had fallen, the dykes had been trampled down, where short cuts had come into being. It was drizzling still intermittently, in the pale dawn, between the icy gusts that blew over from the west. And at every gust, over that strip of countryside that was just beginning now to emerge from the wet blackness of a night of storm, a long shudder seemed to run from the town, a huddled mass of yellowish houses, standing aloft and shrouded on its height, and to pass over hill and dale, over the plain that bristled still with blackened stubble, to the boiling, crested sea beyond.

Rain and wind seemed a ruthless act of cruelty on the part of the sky that overhung the desolation of those uttermost tracts of Sicily, upon which Girgenti, amid the piteous ruins of its primeval existence, rose a silent and awed survivor in the void of a time that would bring no changes, in the abandonment of a misery beyond repair.

1

The thickset hedges of prickly pear, or of withered brambles, or of agave, and the occasiorial crumbling walls were interrupted here and there by a pair of tottering pillars supporting a crooked rusty gate, or by a rude and squalid shrine which, in the motionless solitude, watched over by the shaggy boughs of the dripping trees, instead of comfort inspired a certain sense of terror, posted there as they were to recall the Faith to wayfarers--for the most part field labourers and carters--who all too often, with overt or concealed ferocity, made it plain that they did not recall it. A wretched stray bird or two had come, fluttering timidly with drenched wings, to perch upon them; these kept watch and did not venture to titter so much as a note of lamentation in the midst of such desolation.

For some time Placido Sciaralla's aged white mare had been ploughing and splashing along this road, under the friendly encouragement of her weary rider, who sat, his hands stiff and purple with the cold, cowering beneath the wind and rain, in the gay uniform of a Bourbon soldier: red breeches and a blue greatcoat.

"Courage, Titina!"

And the tassel of his fisherman's cap, his fatigue uniform, hanging down in front, swayed from side to side, as though beating time to the poor animal's weary trot.

Of the infrequent wayfarers who passed him by, on foot or mounted upon sluggardly donkeys, any who did not know that Principe Don Ippolito Laurentano, proud and unswerving in his loyalty to the late Government of the Two Sicilies, retained on his domain of Colimbetra (to which ever since 1860 he had banished himself in shame and disgust) a bodyguard of five and twenty men in the Bourbon uniform, would turn round in amazement and stop for a while to gaze at this grotesque phantom emerging from the moist glimmer of daybreak, without knowing what to make of him.

Meeting the stupefied gaze of these ignorant fellows, Sciaralla, the captain of the aforementioned guard, notwithstanding the cold and rain that chilled and drenched him, would sit erect in his saddle, assuming an air of martial disdain; martially, were he passing one of the shrines, would he raise his hand in salute; then lowering his eyes to study the trained and trimmed points of the scanty black moustaches (most inadequate!) beneath his bold aqui-

2

line nose, would alter his friendly encouragement of the animal to an imperious "Up, there!" followed by a tug of the rein and an inward thrust of his spurs, to which as often as not Titina--the besom--finding herself treated with such violence in her torpid senility--would respond with scant courtesy.

But these encounters, so gratifying to the Captain, had become extremely rare. Everybody knew now about that bodyguard at Colimbetra, and either laughed at it or waxed indignant.

"The Pope, in the Vatican with his Switzers; Don Ippolito Laurentano, on his estate with Sciaralla and Co.!"

And Sciaralla, who, within the marches of Colimbetra, felt himself to be in his proper place, every inch a Captain, once he was outside the gates did not know what air to assume to escape from jeers and insults.

Already everybody was beginning to degrade him from his true rank, addressing him as *caporale*. Idiots! The impertinence! When he was in command of fully five and twenty men (yes, five and twenty!) and yon ought to see how he drilled them in all the military exercises and kept them on the trot. Besides.... But surely, do not all the great gentlemen keep an escort of *campieri* in livery on their estates? Quite so, but to admit that he was merely a *campiere* was something of a wrench to poor Sciaralla, who was a "man of family" and held an elementary teacher's and gymnastic instructor's certificate. He had, nevertheless, reluctantly compelled himself at times to describe his position in these terms, lest he should hear himself called by a yet more opprobrious name. A *campiere*, yes... the chief *campiere*, the *capo*.

"*Caporale?*"

"*Capo*, chief! Where d'you get the corporal from? You do admit, then, that we are a military force?"

"Whose? How? And why are they dressed like that?" Sciaralla would shrug his shoulders, screw up his eyes and heave a sigh.

"One uniform is as good as another.... One of His Excellency's whimsies, what is a man to do?"

But with others of greater credulity he allowed himself to indulge in mysterious confidences: to the effect that the Prince, whose views made him be looked at askance by the Italian Government, which--imagine such a thing--would be only too glad to

3

hear that he had been ruthlessly murdered or pillaged, did really stand in need, in this lonely part of the country, of the escort of which he, Sciaralla, was the unworthy chief. This, however, did not explain why the escort were obliged to go about dressed in that hated uniform.

"Hangmen, that's what you are!" was the retort that had more than once been made to poor Sciaralla, who would then think a trifle bitterly how easy it was for the Prince to maintain with such dignity and constancy that proud attitude of protestation, remaining always shut up within the walls of Colimbetra, whereas he and his subordinates were obliged to face the perils of the outer world and to answer there for him.

In vain, in private conversation, did he swear and forswear himself that never on any account would he, in the days of the Bourbons, have put on that uniform, a symbol, at that time, of tyranny, a symbol of the oppressors of the country; and he would add, throwing up his hands:

"But nowadays, gentlemen, why not? Now that it is you who are the masters.... You let me be! It's my daily bread, gentlemen! You don't really mean it."

In vain. They tried to turn his blood to gall, by pretending not to understand that he, after all, in his real self, was not simply a part of the dress he wore; that inside the uniform was a man, a poor man like all the rest, obliged to earn his living in some vile manner. By his smiles, by his glances, composing his features with an air of keen interest in other people's affairs, he sought in every possible way to distract their attention from his coat; after which, he would feel a fierce inward resentment of all these tricks and grimaces, because, when he looked at the coat without thinking of what it meant, why, good Lord, it seemed to him a very fine coat indeed, and one that suited him down to the ground; and he almost felt remorseful at having to pretend that it distressed him to wear it.

He had heard it said that up in town, at Girgenti, a certain official from the mainland, a bearded, bilious creature, had publicly declared with furious gesticulations that such an indecency, such insolence, so open an insult to the glory of the Revolution, the Government, the Country, Civilisation itself, would not be tolerated in any other part of Italy, nor perhaps in any other province of Sicily itself except this province of Girgenti, so... so... he had preferred not to express in words what he thought of it; with his hands he had sketched a certain gesture....

Lord, could it really be meant for him, for that Bourbon uniform of the five and twenty men of the bodyguard, all that contempt and ill-feeling? Why, oh why, did not these indignant folk turn their attention rather to His Worship the Mayor, to the Aldermen, the Municipal and Provincial Councillors, who came tumbling over one another, strutting along in their best clothes, to pay their respects to H. E. the Prince of Laurentano, who received them in his villa like a king in his royal palace? Not to mention the higher ranks of the clergy, with the Lord Bishop at their head, who, of course, might regard a Legitimist like his Excellency as his natural ally.

Sciaralla swelled with pride and joy at the sight of all these visitors; and nothing gave him greater pleasure than to stand to attention whenever they called, and present arms to them. If Monsignore came, or the Mayor, the sentry at the gate would turn out the little picket from the adjoining guardroom, and give a first salute then and there, in the best military style, with a fine clatter of arms presented and brought down to the order in quick time; another salute followed beneath the pillars of the porch outside the villa, at a shout from the second sentry by the carriage door. As for earning their pay, they had so little to do that he and his men deliberately made work for themselves, seeking whatever pretext they might find; and one of their most serious occupations was just this military salute, which was wonderfully effective in ridding them of the degrading sense that--for all their fine uniforms--they served no purpose whatsoever.

When all was said, with all these powerful protectors, Sciaralla might have laughed at the mockery he received from the lower orders, had he not, like all vain men, felt a longing to be received and greeted by everyone with, courtesy and goodwill. And so he was unable to laugh at it, indeed for some time past he had been more than a little alarmed by it, for another reason.

There was a rumour going about, which acquired greater strength every day, that all the workmen of the larger towns on the island, and the peasantry, and, nearer at hand, the workers in the sulphur pits were seeking to combine in unions, or, as they called them, fasci, to rebel not so much against the gentry as against all law and order, they said, and to overturn everything.

Over and again, when he was on duty in the ante-room, he had heard the matter discussed in the drawing-room. The Prince--of course--threw the blame on the usurping Government, which had first of all caged up and had then proceeded to starve the populace of the island by unjust and infamous taxes and appropriations; the rest of the party agreed in chorus; but the Lord Bishop seemed to Sciaralla to know better than any of them where the evil lay.

The evil, the true evil, the greatest of all the evils committed by the new Government consisted not so much in their usurpation, which still, and rightly, made the heart of H. E. the Prince of Laurentano bleed. Monarchies, civil and social institutions: these were temporary affairs; they pass away; it would be a mistake to alter or abolish them if they are just and holy; a mistake however which it might be possible to remedy. But if you abolish or obscure in the sight of men what ought to shine eternally in their spirit: their Faith, their Religion? Well, this was what the new Government had done! And how could the people remain quiet amid all the tribulations of life, if they no longer had their faith to make them accept these with resignation, or rather with jubilation as a proof and promise of reward in another life? Is there one life only? This life on earth? Will not your tribulations have their recompense in the world beyond, if they are endured with resignation? If not, what reason have we left for accepting and enduring them? Let numbers triumph then, and the bestial instinct break loose for satisfying here below all the base appetites of the body!

He was quite right, was Monsignore. The true reason of all the evil was this. No less than Monsignore, who, to tell the truth, with all the money he had could scarcely feel the tribulations of life, Sciaralla would have liked to see all the poor folk realize this reason. But he could not succeed in putting out of his thoughts a holy man, an aged mendicant, who had appeared one day at the gate of the villa, rosary in hand, and, as he stood waiting for alms and heard a long rumbling sound in his own stomach, had drawn Sciaralla's attention to it, with a sorrowful smile: "Did you hear? It wasn't I that spoke; it's the voice of hunger speaking...."

Sciaralla's consternation at this grave peril which overhung all the gentry arose more than from anything else from the calm confidence with which the Prince, there in his drawing-room, appeared to defy it. It was based, certainly, upon Sciaralla, and upon the valour and devotion of his men, this confidence on the Prince's part, and it might he good enough for him to say that he himself was not afraid, leaving all other considerations to other people.

Fortunately, up to the present at Girgenti nobody stirred a finger nor shewed any sign of proposing to stir a finger! A city of the dead. So much so--said evil tongues--that the crows reigned there, in other words the priests. An inertia, whether for good or for evil, had taken root in the most profound distrust of destiny, in the conviction that nothing could possibly happen, that every effort must prove futile to shake off the utter desolation in which were engulfed not only the souls of men but everything else as well. And Sciaralla felt that he had a convincing proof of this in the dreary spectacle presented to him, that morning, by the surrounding country and by that endless road. Courage, Titina!

He had by this time covered the section of road hewn out of the vertical face of the long brow, from which rise majestic against the sky the remains of the old Akragantine temples, and where at one time opened the Golden Gate of the ancient vanished city. Now he came stumbling down the slope that declines to the valley of Sant'Anna, through which there trickles, with an occasional obstruction, a rivulet of undrinkable water, the ancient Hypsas, now Drago, dry in summer and a source of malaria throughout the surrounding country, owing to the stagnant pools that form beneath the tangled vegetation of its banks. Swollen to a torrent by the heavy rain of the night, it surged, this morning, against the low arch of the bridge, accustomed in summer to bestride an empty bed of stones and gravel.

Indeed from that dreary tract of country, abominated by such peasants as were compelled by necessity to inhabit it, wasted, yellow, fever-ridden, there seemed to be exhaled in the murk of the frigid dawn an agonizing oppression, by which even the trees were penetrated; those centenarian, writhing olives, those almonds stripped bare by the first winds of autumn.

"Wet morning, eh?" Captain Sciaralla would hasten to say,

whenever, on this part of the road, he encountered any of the peasants or carters who knew him, to forestall jeers and insults, and would put spurs to poor Titina.

It was not without reason, though, that he chose, this morning, as a topic of conversation the rain of the past night. As he trotted along, and looked up at the black and ragged mass of drifting clouds, his thoughts turned to the rain in search of an excuse that would set his conscience at rest, he having disobeyed an express order received the evening before from the Prince's secretary: the order to set off at once with a letter to Don Cosmo Laurentano, Don Ippolito's brother, who lived in similar isolation on the other estate of Valsania, about four miles from Colimbetra.

Sciaralla had not felt inclined to venture forth at that hour of the night, and ride down the valley in such vile weather; it had occurred to him that Lisi Preola, the old secretary, having a scapegrace son who aspired to become captain of the bodyguard, would like nothing better than to dispatch Sciaralla himself into the next world; that, after all, the letter was probably not so urgent as to require him to risk his neck on a villainous road, in pitch darkness, under pelting rain, amid thunder and lightning; and that in short he might as well wait for the dawn and slip off quietly, without having to forego his evening game of briscola in the barrack-room on the crest of the Sperone, to which he retired for the night with his three chief subordinates, each of them taking his turn of three hours on guard.

Captain Sciaralla always disliked having to leave Colimbetra, but he felt that he was taking his life in his hands when he had to go to Val-sania. There he was always required to endure in patience the fury of an old fiend, the terror of all the country round, named Mauro Mortara, who, taking advantage of the easy-going nature of Don Cosmo, whose great tomes of philosophy had undoubtedly addled his brains, played the master there, refusing to take orders from anyone else.

"Courage, courage, Titina!" Sciaralla kept sighing, whenever the figure of this old man appeared to his mind's eye: of low stature, slightly bent, jacketless, wearing a thick, rough shirt of violet flannel checked with red, unbuttoned to expose his hairy chest, a huge shaggy cap on his head which he had made for himself from

8

a lambskin, the tan of which, melted by his sweat, had stained to a deep yellow his flowing locks and the untrimmed white whiskers on either side of his face: comic and savage, with a brace of big pistols always in his belt, even at night time, since he lay down to sleep fully clad on a straw mattress for a few hours only: still more alert and stronger, at seventy-seven, than a lad of twenty.

"And he won't ever die!" groaned Sciaralla. "I should think not! He has everything he wants! After all these years he is looked upon as one of the family by Don Ippolito himself, which is saying a good deal. As for Don Cosmo, the wonder is they don't call each other *tu*."

And he turned over in his mind as he rode the extraordinary adventures of this man who, in Forty-Eight, had followed into exile in Malta the old Prince, Don Gerlando Laurentano, who had shown a fondness for him ever since the time when, deprived of his place as Gentleman in Waiting, *Gold Key*, owing to some scandal at the Court of Naples, he had retired to Valsania, where Mortara had been born and bred, the son of poor peasants, and was a peasant boy himself, tending the sheep, in fact, at the time.

One in particular among the man's countless adventures arrested Placido Sciaralla's attention: the adventure that had won for Mortara the nickname *Monk*; an adventure of his earliest days, before Forty-Eight, when at Valsania, round the old Prince of Laurentano, there used to assemble in secret, from Girgenti, the section leaders of the revolutionary committee. Mauro Mortara kept guard for the conspirators at the gate of the Villa. Well, on one occasion a Franciscan friar was so ill-advised as to make his way there in search of alms. Mortara at once took him for a spy: seized him, bound him, kept him tied to a tree all day long: at nightfall he untied him and sent him packing; but the friar was unable to get over his fright, and shortly afterwards died.

This adventure remained more vivid than any of the rest in Sciaralla's imagination, not only because in it Mortara showed himself, as he liked to believe himself, a fierce man, but also because the tree to which the Franciscan had been tied was still standing there by the villa, and Mauro never failed to point it out to him, accompanying the gesture with a mute, sardonic smile and a slight nod, his face contorted with rage at the sight of that Bourbon uniform.

"Courage, Titina, courage!"

It was best to suffer in peace the insults and taunts of this old man. A man who had, indeed, met and faced dangers and mishaps of every sort in the course of his life, beyond counting; but how fortunate he was now to be serving Don Cosmo, who never took any notice of anything except those great books which kept him wandering all day in a sort of waking dream about the avenues of Valsania!

What a difference between the Prince, his own master, and this Don Cosmo! What a difference, too, between either of the brothers and their sister Donna Caterina Auriti, who lived--a penniless widow--at Girgenti!

For years past all three had been at daggers drawn with one another. Donna Caterina Laurentano, alone of the three, had been influenced by their father's new ideas; in addition to which it was said that, as a girl, she had brought shame on the family by running away with Stefano Auriti, killed later on in Sixty, as a Garibaldino, at the battle of Milazzo, while fighting side by side with Mortara and with his own son Don Boberto, who now lived in Borne and had then been a boy of twelve, the youngest soldier in the Thousand.

It may be imagined, therefore, whether the Prince could have any dealings with such a sister! Don Cosmo was another matter--why not he? He, to all appearances at least, had never taken sides with anyone. And yet perhaps he did not approve of his elder brother's protest against the new Government. Which of the two was right, though? Their father, before turning Liberal, had been a Bourbonist, a Gentleman of the Chamber and *Gold Key*: what wonder, then, if the son, deeming his father disloyal, had remained faithful to the late Government? Indeed, he was entitled to respect for showing such constancy: respect and veneration; and was in no way to be blamed if he chose that everybody should know what his views were, even by the way in which he dressed his dependents. "Yes, gentlemen, I am a Bourbonist! I have the courage of my convictions!"

"Courage, Titina!" Ohe!

At this stage a clod of earth struck Captain Sciaralla on the back, followed by a burst of mocking laughter.

The Captain started up in his saddle and turned round, furious. There was no one to be seen. From a hedge beyond the ditch, however, came the following lines of verse, declaimed in a tone of derision, very slowly:

Sciarallino, Sciarallino, sei scappato dalla storia? Dove vai con tanta boria sul ventoso tuo ronzino?

[Sciarallino, Sciarallino, have you just stepped out of the history-book? Where are you off to, so proud and stiff, on your broken-winded nag]

Captain Sciaralla recognized the voice as that of Marco Preola, the scapegrace son of the Prince's secretary, and felt his blood boil. But a moment later Preola made his appearance in such a state that the Captain's frowning brows rose to the brim of his cap, and his lips, tight pressed in anger, parted with stupefaction.

He bore no resemblance to a human being, this creature: saving the grace of Baptism, it was a hog that he suggested, fresh from his wallow, muddy and dishevelled. Standing with his legs apart, his body reeling backwards from the waist in a drunkard's balance, Preola continued to declaim from above with loose and feeble gesticulations

Dimmi, corri, Sciarallino, all'assalto d'un molino? od a caccia di lumache vai così di buon mattino con codeste rosse brache e il guibbon chiaro turchino, Sciarallino, Sciarallino?

[Tell me, are you hastening, Sciarallino, to the assault of a windmill? Or is it hunting snails that you come out like this at cockcrow with those red breeches and that sky-blue coat, Sciarallino, Sciarallino?]

"You dear fellow!" said Sciaralla, as he felt with one hand behind his back, where the clod had plastered his coat with mud. Marco Preola slid down, on the seat of his breeches, from the slimy bank of the ditch, and came up to him.

"Dear, am I?" he said. "No: I sell myself cheap! Do you like my poetry? It's fine! And there's more of it, you know? I am going to print it in next Sunday's *Empedocle*."

Captain Sciaralla continued to gaze at him, his face now contracted in a grimace in which pity was mingled with disgust. He knew that the other was liable to epileptic fits, that often he would wander about by night like a stray dog, and disappear for two or three days on end, until he was found lying like a dead animal with his face to the ground and froth on his lips, up at the Culmo delle Forche or on the Serra Ferlucchia or in the fields. He saw the man's puffy face, disfigured by a long, livid scar on the right cheek, with a thin, irregular growth of colourless hair on lip and chin; he stared at the old cap, faded and filthy, which did not come far enough down to hide the deformity of a precocious baldness; he noticed that the hair of his eyebrows had fallen out also; but he could not face the glare of those pale, greenish, impudent eyes, in which all the vices imaginable seemed to swarm. Expelled from the Military School at Modena, Preola had been in Rome for about a year on the staff of a blackmailing little paper; after serving a term of eight months' imprisonment, he had tried to commit suicide by jumping off one of the bridges into the Tiber; his life saved by a miracle, he had been sent back to his home by order of the court, and was now living at his father's expense in Girgenti.

"What have you been doing?" Sciaralla asked him.

Preola looked at his clothes and with a frigid grin replied:

"Nothing. I've made myself a bit... mucky."

He waved his hands in such a way as to indicate that he had been rolling on the ground, and added:

"A slight attack...."

All of a sudden, with a change of tone and manner, gripping Sciaralla by the arm: "Give me the letter," he shouted. "I know you have it!"

"Are you mad?" exclaimed Sciaralla, recoiling from him with a jerk.

Preola uttered a nervous laugh, then said to him:

"Out with it; I'm only going to take a sniff at it. I want to see if it smells of wedding-cake. Creature, don't you know that your master is getting married?"

Sciaralla stared at him in amazement.

"The Prince?"

"His Excellency, yes indeed! Don't you believe me? I bet that's what the letter is about. The Prince is announcing his marriage to his brother. Haven't you seen Monsignor Montoro? He's the match maker!"

Certainly Monsignor Montoro had, during the last few days, shewn his face far more often than usual at Colimbetra.

Could it be true? Sciaralla made an effort to prevent these incredible tidings, of such an astounding event, from revealing to him in a flash a vision of sumptuous entertainments, of a gay animation quite novel in that austere, vast, silent retreat; the hope of reward for the brave show that he would make with his men and the faultless service that he would render. ... But the Prince, was it possible? So serious a man... and at his age? Besides, how was anyone to believe what Preola might say? Endeavouring to hide his amazement and curiosity with an incredulous smile, he asked:

"And who is the lady?"

"If you give me the letter, I'll tell you," the other replied.

"Tomorrow! Get along with you!... I see your game."

Whereupon Sciaralla leant forward in his saddle as a signal to the mare to move.

"Wait!" exclaimed Preola, grasping Titina by the tail. "A lot I care about the wedding, or whether you believe me or not! Perhaps... now this is what I really should like to know ... perhaps the Prince is writing to his brother about the election, and their nephew's candidature. Haven't you heard about that either? Don't you know that Roberto Auriti, the 'twelve-year-old hero,' is standing for Parliament?"

"I know all I want to know, you can't take me in," said Sciaralla. "Haven't we got a Member already, Fazello?"

"Why, you're all a hundred years behind the times, at Colimbetra!" sneered Preola. "We're to have a General Election, and Fazello's not standing again, donkey, because of his son's death!"

"His son? But he's not married!"

Again Preola uttered his nervous laugh.

"And can't a bachelor, a clergyman too, have children? Idiot! We're to have Auriti, supported by the Government, against the lawyer Capolino. A fierce fight, tense excitement.... Give me the letter!"

Sciaralla thrust his spurs into Titina and jerked himself free from Preola. Whereupon the latter flung a stone after him, then a second; he was preparing to fling a third, when from round the corner came a furious voice:

"Ohe, what the... Who's that throwing stones?"

And a second voice, addressed evidently to the escaping Sciaralla:

"For shame! For shame! You dressed-up doll! Idiot! Clown!"

And from round the corner there appeared, beneath a huge, tattered umbrella, tired and travel-stained, the two inseparables, Luca Lizio and Nocio Pigna, or, as everyone had now begun to call them, *Propaganda and Co.*: the former, a pale, shock-headed lamp-post of a man, with a pair of spectacles that kept slipping to one side of his nose, hunching his shoulders with cold, and with the collar of his light summer jacket turned up; the other squat, deformed, with a crooked back, one arm dangling down almost to the ground and the other hand resting on his knee, in an attempt to establish some sort of equilibrium.

THE NAKED TRUTH!

They were the two revolutionaries of the place.

Captain Sciaralla was wrong in thinking that there was no one stirring at Girgenti.

They were stirring, Lizio and Pigna.

It must be admitted that the appearance of the pair, that morning, so drenched and numbed, under their tattered umbrella, did not suggest that there could be anything very terrible in their revolutionary enterprises.

No one could be better aware of this than Marco Preola, who, having long since abandoned to the will of destiny his own life, which he himself was the first to belittle and despise, a life in which there was no affection, no faith in anything left, unbound not only by any rule but by any force of habit, and flung to the mercy of every sudden, violent caprice, regarded everything as absurd and fatuous, and laughed at everything, finding an outlet in that laughter for the exceptional, if disordered, energies of his embittered spirit.

He knew that, three days earlier, the pair had gone down to the harbour of Porto Empedocle to catechize the porters employed in loading sulphur, the wharfingers, stevedores, lightermen, carters, checkweighmen, with a view to combining them in a *fascio*. Seeing them return at such an hour and in such a state, he wrinkled his nose, stopped in the middle of the road to wait for them and accompany them as far as Girgenti; as they drew near, he flung out his arms as though to gather up a full-sized *fiasco* of wine, and said to them:

"Come along; don't worry: I can carry it."

Pigna stopped and, drawing himself up as far as he could

15

with the support of his arm, stared contemptuously at Preola. His body was all twisted and knotted; but he had the face of a great doll, without a hair on it, cheeks burnished by the salt sweat that exuded from his skin, and a pair of black eyes, glinting and darting, the eyes of a madman, beneath a big blue bonnet, battered out of shape, which gave him the appearance of a jack in the box.

Marco Preola hailed him by a contemptuously friendly nickname, and said with a smile:

"*Nociare*, don't take on about it! It's a vile world we live in, full of ungrateful wretches. Sailors, flat-feet.... Oh, yes, and put away your umbrella, Luca! God sends us down water, and you refuse His gift? Let us give our faces a wash, like this...."

He raised his muddy face to the sky. There still spattered down from the clouds, which were reddening now at their ragged edges as they moved towards the almost risen sun, an icy, stabbing drizzle.

"What are a few pins and needles?" he cried, throwing off a shower of water like a horse, shaking his head and deliberately charging into Pigna. Filthy as he was, from head to foot, and soaked to the skin by the rain, he felt that he need no longer bother to keep himself dry and clean, and had the satisfaction, as he wallowed whole-heartedly in the mire, of being able to splash the others with impunity.

"Get away with you!" Pigna shouted at him. "Who asked you to come here? Who wants your company? Who ever told you you could take such liberties?"

Without turning a hair, Preola replied:

"I do love to see you in a rage! Mother earth, my dear fellow, mother earth! I was trying to stick some of it on you.... Nature's seal? You would run away from me, would you? And then you complain that other people are ungrateful."

"Did you ever hear such impudence..." Pigna growled, as he turned to Lizio.

But the latter was absorbed in his own thoughts, and walked on in frowning indifference. He shrugged his shoulders as who should say that he did not wish to be disturbed from his train of thought, and on he went.

Preola followed them in silence for some way, keeping his

distance, gazing at each of them in turn.

He felt himself torn by a gnawing desire to be doing something, that morning; what, he did not know. In another moment he would have begun to howl like a wolf. To keep himself from howling, he opened his mouth, gripped his lower jaw in his hand and pulled it down until he had almost dislocated it. His only relief was to vent himself on the pair of travellers; but what amusement was there in teasing Lizio? A desperate fellow like that, and one moreover whose head was always in the clouds. A twofold calamity, the suicide of his father, an excellent lawyer but of unbalanced brain, followed by that of his brother, had won him a certain sympathy in the place, in which horror blended with pity, and a certain respect to boot. He studied hard and spoke little, indeed he scarcely spoke at all. There was good reason for this: he was able to pronounce barely half the alphabet. One thing only brought him into derision, that he had found his barrel-organ in Pigna, and organ and grinder invariably appeared together on platforms. If Pigna went out of tune, he brought him back to the right pitch, with the utmost gravity, plucking him by the sleeve. Social Revolution... Brotherhood of Man... Stand Up for the Eights of the Downtrodden ... big ideas, indeed! And perhaps that was why, in his distraction, he had fastened meanwhile upon a crust of bread that others had earned for him. He was doing well, oh rather! Only, with this touch of cold in the air...

"A nice little pot of coffee, by God!" Preola burst out suddenly, waving his arms in the air. "Three lumps of sugar, a jug of cream, four slices of toast. Oh, Holy Souls in Purgatory!"

Luca Lizio turned sharply round to gaze at him. A cup of coffee was just what was in his mind at that moment, behind those knitted brows; he saw it and was almost intoxicated by it in imagination, as he inhaled its steaming fragrance; and in the force of his desire clenched the numbed fist in his pocket. Having started before dawn, and in the bitterness of defeat, from Porto Empedocle, he was starved with cold; he was longing to reach his destination. Abashed by this base need, he felt himself to be wretched, deserving of comfort, of a comfort which no one (he well knew) could provide.

A moment earlier, what with that dressed-up doll bolting off on his white mare, and Preola standing there waiting for them, his lips curved in a sneer, he had received a sudden strange impression of himself, which had penetrated to the depths of his being and stirred up a feeling that was entirely new to him, a feeling almost of stupefaction at all his red rags, all his blazing furies, which in a flash had revealed themselves to him, as though seen from outside, as foolish and vain, there in the midst of that scene of utter squalor and desolation. In the wretched emaciation of his body shivering with cold and sticky with a viscid sweat, he felt that he resembled one of those trees that rose from behind the crumbling walls, dead and dripping. He too was dripping, with cold, from the tip of his nose, and trickling from the peering, watery eyes behind his spectacles. He had huddled himself together; and, as though that impression, after plumbing the depths of his consciousness and vanishing in stupefaction, had now closed round him with a crushing grip, he felt himself a mass of aches; his narrow brows ached, and the sharp protuberance of his back, over which the stuff of his summer jacket had worn shiny, and the wrists exposed by the shortness of his sleeves, and the soaked feet in his broken shoes. And everything seemed to him now unbearable, an excess of cruelty: every fresh turn in that road, become a torrent of mud; the crude light of dawn which, notwithstanding the blackness of the clouds, struck a reflexion from the mire which dazzled his eyes; but most of all the company of that miserable scarecrow, spattered with mud from head to foot, mud without and mud within, who kept goading Pigna to speak. He, being accustomed for so many years now to remaining silent, felt a bewilderment that grew more and more confused at his own silence, which, though no one knew this, fed and waxed strong within him upon certain fantastic impressions, such as that which he had just received, which he could not have expressed in words to himself even, save at the cost of forfeiting all faith in and support of his work. Marco Preola, meanwhile, went on speaking, as though to himself:

"As for me, that's another matter; what am I? A vagabond; I deserve all this and more. But look at the weather the Lord God sees fit to send us, when two poor humanitarians are taking the road on a sacred mission, after an irreverent crowd has driven them out, at night, with a whipping!"

Pigna made as though to stop, quivering with rage; but Luca Lizio drew him on with a clutch at his sleeve and an angry growl.

18

"Whipping... just you wait!" he muttered through his teeth. "I'll give them a whipping, I will..."

"And I would take one from you, Nociare," Preola hastened to assure him with a bow, "as sure as God's in Heaven! Why, do you know, you're a hero! Stinking filth! Or is it I that am always smelling stinks.... The nose; something in the nose.... I ought not to smell them, accustomed as I am to filth.... A true hero, Nociare! The common people can't understand you. They can't understand you, because an idea, unfortunately, has no eyes or legs or mouth. What has an idea to say for itself? It speaks by the mouths of men. And the ignorant masses are incapable of distinguishing between the idea and the person who expresses it, do you follow me? You may sing like a nightingale, and yet, my Nocio, you can have no effect. Suppose you say: 'Men and women, humanity is on the march! I will teach you to march!' they are quite capable of looking at the way you throw your shanks about, and jeering: 'Just look at the fellow who wants to teach us to march!'"

"Ass!" roared Propaganda, who could contain himself no longer. "Reasoning with the feet is what you call that."

"I? The people!" retorted Preola.

"The People, let me tell you," replied Pigna, rolling his eyes like a madman; then suddenly he broke off. "Don't you dare to utter the word People; you are not fit even to name the People! The People have learned too much, my good man, let me tell you; and, first and foremost, that your *patriots* have deceived them...."

"Mine?" came with a laugh from Preola.

"Yours, the men who drove them into the Revolution of 1860, with promises of a Golden Age! Not we! Not we, as you fellows go about preaching! The patriots and the priests deceived them and are deceiving them now! We, my good man, let me tell you, prove to them, in so many words, with the proof in our hands, that (you follow me?) by virtue of their own force (you follow me?)--by virtue, I repeat, of their own force, not by any concessions from outside, they can, if they choose, improve their condition."

"By force of their own virtue would be better," Preola observed placidly, without thinking of what he was saying.

Pigna stared at him in astonishment. But the other at once

made haste to calm him:

"It's nothing, don't worry about it. It was only a joke!"

"By virtue... by virtue of their own force," Pigna went on in a low tone, none too certain of himself, turning to Lizio to read in the latter's eyes whether he had used the right words; and went on, somewhat disconcerted: "To improve, yes, Sir, this unjust economic system, under which men are living... that is to say, no... I mean, yes... some men are living without working, and others, who do all the work, cannot live! Do you follow me? We say to the People: 'You are everything! You can do anything! Unite, and dictate your own law and your own justice! '"

"Splendid!" exclaimed Preola. "Will you allow me to speak now?"

"Your own law and your own justice!" Pigna repeated, furious at the interruption. "Speak, speak."

"You won't take offence?"

"I shall not take offence: speak."

"Were you or were you not, until recently, a sacristan?"

Propaganda turned round again to gaze at him in astonishment.

"What has that got to do with it?" To which Preola, calmly:

"Yon're not to take offence! Answer me."

"A sacristan, yes, Sir," Pigna courageously admitted. "Well? What do you mean by that? That I've changed the colour of my coat?"

"Colour of your coat, indeed! That's nothing..."

"I have learned to know the priests, that is all!"

"And how to breed children," retorted Preola: "seven daughters, one after another; can you deny that?"

Nocio Pigna stopped for the third time to gaze at him. He had promised that he would not take offence. But what was the fellow driving at with this string of questions? He had lost his post in the church because one of his daughters, the eldest, and a certain Canon Landolina...

"On condition that you keep off certain topics," he warned the other, darkening and lowering his gaze.

"No, no, no," Preola broke out, placing his hand on his heart. "Listen, Nocio, I am, 'by the universal judgment of the wise,' what is commonly called a scoundrel. Is that clear? I have been eight months *in quod*... think of that! And do you see this?" he added, pointing to the scar on his cheek. "When I jumped in river, as they say in Rome.... Yes, indeed!... You can imagine, then, whether certain things can make any impression on me! Do you know, though, what has made an impression on me? The fact that you, with that poor girl..."

"I told you, we were to keep off certain topics." "My dear sir," sighed Preola, shutting his eyes. "Let me go on.... You must know that the people I fight against are the only ones for whom I feel any respect. But these same people, naturally enough, since my... let us say misfortunes, refuse to feel any for me, and would prevent me, if they could, from living. I must live! In order to live I fight against them and stand by the priests. Men do not forgive; God, on the other hand, so the priests say, has forgiven me long ago; and on that pretext they make use of me.... Look at this vast expanse, Nocio!" he went on, pushing back his hat so as to expose his brow. "And there's plenty of stuff behind it, you know! If things had gone the right way with me.... But enough of that. I, you,... everything... just look! Mud, mud, mud... Here we are, all three of us, up to our ankles in the mud of this road. Let us speak plainly, openly, Holy God, for once in a way! Let us state things nakedly and crudely, as they are, without dressing them up in fine language. The naked truth, come; let us give ourselves that pleasure! I am a swine, yes, but what are you, Nociare? What do you do? What is your work, can you tell me that? Put your hand on your heart, now, and tell the truth: you don't work at all!"

"I?" exclaimed Pigna, astonished, stupefied, rather than offended by the injustice of the remark, extending his arm and folding it over his bosom with outstretched forefinger.

"You are working for the cause? Words!" Preola was ready with his retort. "I asked you to tell me the naked truth! Instead of which you clothe it, you cover it up, as you please, to quiet your conscience. You did work... they turned you out of the church; then, from a lottery office. ... Slander, yes, I know! Still, supposing you really did pocket the half-pence of the idiots who came to bet in your shop, do you imagine that I would call that wrong? You would have been perfectly right! But now, what are you doing?

Your daughters do the work, and you eat and preach. And this other fellow here, this Saint Luke the Evangelist.... What is it you call it? Free love. Very good: words! The fact of the matter is that he has been going with another of your daughters and..."

At this point Luca Lizio, livid, speechless, quivering with rage, sprang forward with outstretched arms at Preola's throat. But the other drew back with a laugh, caught hold of his arms and thrust him away without undue violence.

"What are you doing?" he shouted at him, his eyes and teeth gleaming with malicious joy. "What is the joke? I am telling you the truth."

"Let him rip!" Pigna here interposed, holding Luca Lizio back and preparing to move on his way. "Don't you see that he makes it his business to play the gadfly?"

"A gadfly, yes..." said Preola. "What part of you did I sting? Your nakedness? Ah, we are naked and ashamed, my friends.... And in this cold weather, too.... Let us cover it up quickly with the cloak of charity! I was only trying to explain to you, dear Nocio, without offending you, why you are unable to create any effect..."

"Because the people here are carrion!" cried Pigna, turing upon him with a savage glare in his eyes.

"I quite agree!" Preola made haste to assure him. "And I myself... carrion too, don't you mean? I agree! But you don't work; your daughters do the work, and Luca eats and reads, and you eat and preach. Now the people who do work, my dear fellow, and who hear you preaching to them, 'Just look,' they say, 'who it is that wants to save us! Nocio Pigna! Propaganda! That's the man!' And they burst out laughing. You preach and you don't see your-self: you see the idea! The people, however, don't see the idea; they see the man who is preaching. You see them laugh, and you say: 'But why?'--puzzled, pained, because at that moment you identify yourself entirely with your idea, and can think of nothing else. But the audience facing you, my dear fellow, see in you the quondam sacristan, the quondam lottery clerk; they see a hunchback, a twisted cripple (it's God own truth); they rememher that you are living upon your daughters, and--let us be quite frank--how could you have any effect, my dear Nocio?"

Pigna made no reply; he shook his head several times and

once again muttered to himself:

"A lot of carrion! They ought to listen to me, if I am a hunchback or a cripple... And when have I ever said: 'I am saving you'? 'Your salvation rests with yourselves,' is what I say. But go to Aragona, a stone's throw from Girgenti; go to Favara, Grotte, Casteltermini, Campobello... Who are they? Peasants and sulphur workers, poor illiterates. Four thousand of them, at Casteltermini alone! I was there last week; I was present at the formation of the Fascio..."

"With a lamp burning before the Madonna," inquired Preola. "Wasn't there?"

"God is one thing, a priest is another, idiot!" Pigna replied haughtily.

"And the bugles sounding the royal salute?"

"Discipline! Discipline!" exclaimed Pigna. "They're doing splendidly! You ought to have seen them.... All ready and in earnest... four thousand... a solid mass... they were like the earth itself, the earth come to life, you know, moving and thinking... eight thousand eyes conscious and looking up to you... eight thousand arms.... And my heart turned in my bosom at the thought that only among ourselves, here at Girgenti, the capital, at Porto Empedocle, a sea port, open to trade: nothing! Nothing! One can do nothing! What dumb brutes they are! Worse than brutes! But do you know how they live down at Porto Empedocle? How the shipping of the sulphur is still being done? Do you know?"

Marco Preola was tired: his head drooped, as he murmured: "Porto Empedocle..."

And each of the three formed a mental image of that straggling village by the sea which had grown in a few years at the expense of the old town of Girgenti and had now become an independent *comune*. A score of huts, originally, down there on the beach, with a short loading stage of flimsy beams, known now as the Old Harbour, and a sea fortress, foursquare and frowning, in which the convicts were kept at hard labour, who subsequently, as the sulphur trade increased, had thrown out the two broad reefs of the new harbour, one on either side of the little wharf, which, by virtue of its landing stage, had retained the honour of carrying the harbour master's office and the white tower of the principal beacon. Prevented from spreading inland by the cliff of marl that overhung it, the village had extended laterally along the narrow heach, and right up to the foot of the cliff the houses were packed and squeezed together, almost on the top of one another. The loads of sulphur were piled up along the beach; and from morning to night there was a continuous rumbling of carts which came loaded with sulphur from the railway station or even direct from the nearest pits; an endless coming and going of barefooted men and animals, and a din of quarrels and curses and cries blended with the rumbling and whistling of a train which crossed the beach, making alternately for each of the two breakwaters, constantly under repair. Beyond the eastward arm the beach was fringed by the lighters, with their sails furled at half mast; at the foot of the sulphur heaps were the scales, upon which the sulphur was weighed before being loaded on the backs of the carriers, known as *men of the sea*, who, barefoot, in canvas trousers, each with a sack on his shoulders, pulled down over his head in front and twisted round the back of his neck, plunging waist-deep into the water, carried out their loads to the lighters, which then, hoisting their sails, went out to unload the sulphur into the holds of the trading steamers anchored in the harbour or outside it.

"Slave labour," said Pigna; "it makes one's heart bleed, on cold days in winter.... Bowed down under their loads, with the water up to their bellies.... Men, do you call them? Beasts is what they are.... And if you tell them that they could become men if they chose, they open their mouths in a fatuous laugh and insult you. Do you know why they are not putting landing stages on the breakwaters of the new harbour, where the loading could be done more quickly and easily from carts or trucks? Because the big pots of the place are the people who own the lighters! And all the time, in spite of the fortunes they are making out of the trade, the drains are still uncovered on the beach, and the people die of fever; with the whole sea at their feet, there is no supply of drinking water, and the people die of thirst! No one takes any trouble; no one complains of the state of things. They are like a lot of lunatics, all those men, bestialized in the war for profits, a vile and savage war."

"But do you know, you really do speak well?" Preola expressed his approval. "Do you know, you really have profited by all the sermons you had to listen to as a sacristan?"

"*Bye bye*, as the English say!" Nocio Pigna went on, stretching out his long arm with a menacing gesture. "There are three hundred thousand of us, my boy, at this very moment. And you shall hear of us again before long."

IN THE REALM OF ORCUS.

Having climbed to the summit of the road, from which the ground fell away down the slope of the valley beyond, Placido Sciaralla was now trotting along on Titina in the direction of Valsania, plunged in fresh and even more complicated considerations after what he had heard from Preola.

After a while he shrugged his shoulders and began to look about him.

There stretched out now, on his left, the smiling seaboard country, covered with almond trees and olives. He was already in sight of Seta, a hamlet of some fifty houses lining the highroad, clothes-shops and taverns for the carters, most of them, from which exuded a keen and acrid smell of must, a rich warm smell of dung, and the shops of blacksmiths, locksmiths, wheelwrights, with a tumble-down house in the centre, converted into a chapel for the Sunday services.

To avoid the gaze of these village yokels, all of whom knew him by sight, Sciaralla turned along a bridle path that crossed the fields and had soon gained the sanctuary of Valsania.

Apart from the vineyard, the object of Mauro Mortara's passionate devotion and the pride of his life, and the ancient Saracen olive grove, the almond grove and some acres of ploughland, and, in the wide ravine farther down, the orchard, all of which formed the portion reserved for Don Cosmo, all the rest was made over in small lots to poor peasant portioners, not by the Prince himself, Don Ippolito, to whom this estate belonged as well, but by subtenants of tenants, who, not content with living a life of leisure in town on the toil of these poor creatures, crushed and bled them with the most pitiless usury, and with a complicated system of customary exactions. The usury arose from the purchase of seed and various loans advanced during the year; the exactions were even more unfair, and were levied at harvest time. After toiling for a year, the so-called portioner saw carried away, heap after heap, from his steading practically the whole of his crop; the heaps for sowing, the heaps for feeding, and for the lamp, and another for the *campiere*, and another for Our Lady of Sorrows, and San Francesco di Paola, and San Calogero, in fact for almost every Saint in the Church calendar; so that as often as not he was left with only the *solame*, that is to say the few sweepings of grain mixed with chaff and dust which were left on the floors after threshing.

The sun had by this time risen, and Captain Sciaralla could see here and there, over the expanse of the fields, the glittering reflexion from some pool of rain-water or perhaps a piece of broken crockery. The whole countryside was steaming as though a veil of mist hung and quivered over it. Here and there, a group of those tumble-clown, smoke-begrimed hovels which the peasants called *roba*, house, stable, byre all in one; and the wife of one of these portioners emerging from her door to tether the grunting little pig in the open, followed by three or four fowls; outside the worm-eaten red door of the house opposite, another woman was combing the head of a whimpering little girl; while the men, with old and primitive ploughs drawn each by an emaciated mule and a slow-moving donkey that strained every muscle in the effort, barely scratched the surface of the soil, after the preliminary watering it had received in the night.

All these poor folk, seeing Sciaralla approach on his white mare, paused from their labours to salute him with reverence, as though it were the Prince in person who was passing. Captain Sciaralla responded with great dignity, raising his hand to his cap in a military salute, and received these demonstrations of respect as a compensation in advance for the humiliation that lay in store for him at the hands of that savage old beast Mortara. A secret misgiving, however, spoiled all the pleasure to be derived from these salutes: in a few minutes, when he entered the other's domain, he would be assailed by the dogs, those three mastiffs more savage than their master who had obviously taught them to give him this greeting whenever he came. And Sciaralla might shout himself hoarse while the creatures were bounding about him, leaping as high as Titina's head while she, in her turn, skipped like a sheep with terror: Mauro or the *curatelo*, Ninfa's Vanni, would appear in his own good time to call the dogs off, after the poor wretch had more than once seen death staring him in the face.

With these three mastiffs Mauro Mortara used to converse just as though they had been reasonable beings. He used to say that men did not understand dogs, but that dogs did understand men. "The trouble," he would say, "is that they, poor creatures, cannot express their meaning to us; and so we imagine that they do not understand us and do not listen."

Sciaralla however explained the phenomenon differently. These dogs understood their master so perfectly because he was more canine than themselves. And his theory seemed to receive fresh confirmation this morning.

Mauro was stationed outside the villa; his three cronies on guard round him, their noses pointing in the air. Well, on Sciaralla's arrival, this time, they remained where they were (one of them even yawned), as though they quite understood that their master would fill their part to perfection.

"What do you want here, prowling about at this hour in the morning?" was indeed all the greeting he had from Mauro, who pushed back the hood of the rough greatcoat he was wearing and revealed his head, hardened with its huge shaggy cap.

When vintage drew near, Mauro Mortara ceased to sleep at nights: he kept watch over the vines, patrolling up and down the long alleys with his three mastiffs. Perhaps he had been out there in the open all through the night of storm that had just passed: he was quite capable of it.

Sciaralla saluted him humbly, then, pointing to the dogs, asked: "Can I dismount?"

"Dismount," growled Mauro. "What have you brought?"

"A letter for Don Cosmo," replied Sciaralla as he slid from the mare's back.

Sciaralla knew that it was forbidden for him to cross the threshold of the villa, as though, with his uniform, he might desecrate that tumble-down, rambling pile of a single storey: he who came from the splendours of Colimbetra, where you could see your face reflected in the very walls! The prohibition did not come, certainly, from Don Cosmo, but from Mortara himself, who actually forbade him to tie the mare to the rings fastened to the balustrade of the rustic stair. He must hold her himself and remain standing there, outside, waiting, as though he had come for alms.

No sooner did Mauro turn to go than the three dogs stole softly up to Captain Sciaralla and began to sniff at him. The poor fellow, standing there with a sinking heart, raised his eyes in supplication to Mortara, who was climbing the stair.

"Don't you dirty your muzzles on those breeches!" said Mauro, after calling the dogs to heel: then added, turning to Sciaralla: "I'm going to send you out a mouthful of coffee, to keep your pecker up."

On reaching the landing, he prepared to give the recognized signal, namely to bring the latch down three times on the pin inside; but, as soon as he raised the latch, the door opened, and Mauro entered the house exclaiming:

"Open? Open again? Was it you opened it?" he asked through the shut door of the kitchen, which had opened for a moment to reveal the nightcapped head of Donna Sara Alaimo, the housekeeper (not the servant, oh dear no!) of Valsania.

"I?" shouted Donna Sara from inside the room. "I'm just getting up!"

And, hearing Mauro's step recede, she "made the horns," thrust out the index and little fingers of her right hand, and brandished them after him in a gesture of contempt.

Servant, nothing of the sort--not she: the idea of such a thing! neither his servant, nor anyone's else, in that house. She had the ember-fan in her hand, it was true, she was just going to light the kitchen fire, but she was a real lady, a lady horn and bred, she was; who could count eousinship with Stefano Auriti, the brother-in-law of the Laurentano, and so, why, you might say, one of the family herself.

She had been at Valsania for many years looking after Don Cosmo, who would perhaps never have felt any need of her services had not his sister, Donna Caterina, sent her to him from Girgenti, where, like a perfect lady, poor thing, she was starving decorously to death.

At Valsania her days were spent in stroking the backs of two cats (emasculated, as was proper), which followed her everywhere about the house with tails erect; in saying rosaries of fifteen decades, and endless mumbling of other prayers; but, to hear her talk, everything was going well solely because she was there--but for her all would have been at sixes and sevens! If the crops ripened, if the fruit-trees bore, if the rain came when it was wanted.... In fact, she behaved as though she ruled the universe.

Mauro could not abide her. And Donna Sara reciprocated his feeling cordially; indeed, nothing gave her greater annoyance than to lay a place for him too at table, since Don Cosmo had sunk so low as that, as to bestow so high an honour upon a son of peasants who was little better than a clodhopping peasant himself; yes indeed... while she, Donna Sara, a real lady born and bred, remained in the kitchen and was obliged to wait upon him. She went to the window and, seeing Captain Sciaralla below, heaved a deep sigh and wailed inwardly:

"Ah, Placidino, Placidino! Let us offer it to the Lord as a penance for our sins...."

Meanwhile Mauro had gone into Don Cosmo's bathroom.

Everything was old-fashioned and rustic in this old and neglected villa: cracked and uneven the rough terracotta tiles of the floor; the walls and ceilings black with smoke; the window-shutters and furniture paintless and worm-eaten; and everything seemed to reek with an odour of dry grain, parched straw, hay withered in the scorching heat of those sun-baked fields.

In the bathroom Don Cosmo, in woollen drawers, his hairy chest bare, his feet unstockinged in their old slippers, was preparing for his regular ablutions, with a dozen sponges, great and small, laid out on the washing stand. He sponged himself all over, every morning, even in winter, with cold water; and this was his one pleasure in life: the height of insanity, though, it seemed to Mauro who every morning, if he washed at all, would wash "just the mug," as he himself put it, meaning his face alone.

"Have you been sleeping with the front door open again?"

"Why not?" said Don Cosmo, as though surprised at such a question; and went on, scratching his short, curling grey heard: "Come, now!"

"Will you never open your eyes?" Mauro pursued the point. "What have I always said? Great baby! We'll have to find a tutor, a nurse for you.... Holy God, what sort of man are you? Didn't you read the newspaper yesterday? About those gallows birds who say they've nothing to eat and are going to overthrow everything that we've shed our blood to set up? The scoundrels!"

What with Mauro's frenzied gesticulations, Don Cosmo had not observed that he had a letter in his hand, and had quietly begun to lather his bald and highly polished scalp. Irritated by his calm, Mauro went on:

"And if they were all like you.... Gad, it's a lucky thing I'm here! Old as I am, they would have me to reckon with! Me, do you understand? Me!"

"In that case," Don Cosmo said quietly, turning to face him, "I can still sleep with the door open."

The newspapers, at Valsania, arrived only at long intervals, when already converted to their humble and possibly more useful function of wrapping parcels. Mauro used to straighten out the sheets with loving care, passing his hands over them again and again to smooth out the folds and creases; and, surmounting with monkish patience the enormous difficulty of reading them (since it was only late in life that he had taught himself to spell), would browse upon them for weeks at a time, committing their contents to memory from beginning to end. Any news was fresh to him, a distant echo of the life of the great world beyond.

In the last newspaper that had come into his hands thus by chance, he had read, the day before, of a strike of sulphur workers in a village of the province and of their forming themselves into a *Fascio di Lavoratori*.

"The vindication of the proletariat!"

Humph! He had made Don Cosmo explain these two long words, a Sibylline utterance to him, and all night long, sheltering in his hut from the pelting rain, had pondered and pondered, groaning with a holy horror at these enemies of their country.

He did not deign to reply to this last speech of Don Cosmo, who, to his mind, must have a screw loose also, but handed him Don Ippolito's letter.

"One of his mountebanks brought it here: Sciaralla the Captain."

"For me?" asked Don Cosmo in surprise, scooping up the water in the hollow of his hands. "Ippolito has written to me? Wonders will never cease.... Open it, read it to me: my hands are wet...."

"Dry them, then!" Mauro told him curtly. "You know that I don't choose to be mixed up in your brother's affairs. But it doesn't look like his writing."

"Ah, Preola," observed Don Cosmo, studying the envelope.

The letter had been written by the secretary at Don Ippolito's dictation, and was merely signed by him. As he read it, Don Cosmo knitted his brows at the opening lines, then gradually relaxed the tension of his forehead and eyes in a pained stupefaction; let his eyelids droop; let the hand droop that held the letter.

"Ah, poor fellow.... So it is true...."

"What is?" growled Mauro, stung by curiosity.

"He's done for himself, done for himself," exclaimed Don Cosmo. "If he yields that point, there's no way out of it... he's ruined...."

"Tell me what is the matter, holy devil!" repeated Mauro, growing more and more curious.

But Don Cosmo only gazed at him for a while in silence, nodding his head, as though he saw his brother standing before him and were commiserating him bitterly.

"He asks me for the villa----" he answered at length, letting the words fall from his lips one by one, "the villa, for Flaminio Salvo."

"Here?" asked Mauro, with a start, as though Don Cosmo had struck him a blow in the face. "Here," he repeated, drawing back. "Flaminio Salvo, in General Laurentano's villa?"

But Don Cosmo was not furious like Mauro at the imagined profanation of the villa: what he did feel was a pained stupefaction at what was implied by his brother's offer of hospitality to Salvo. A few days earlier a friend of his, Leonardo Costa, who came now and then to see him from the neighbouring seaport, had told him of the rumour that was going round Girgenti of a forthcoming marriage between Don Ippolito and Salvo's sister, a maiden lady of a certain age. Don Cosmo had refused to believe it: his brother Ippolito was two years his senior, a man of sixty-five;

for the last ten years he had been a widower, and had always seemed inconsolable, though he maintained his composure, for the death of his wife, that dear, good woman.... Impossible! And yet....

"You will answer no?" said Mauro menacingly, after a moment's silence. Don Cosmo threw up his arms and sighed, his eyes shut: "It would be no use! Besides..." "What?" Mauro interrupted him. "Salvo, that canting money-lender, here? I shall walk out of the house, if he comes! Good God, have you forgotten that his father went to the Te Deum when yours was banished? And didn't he, he himself as a young man, guide the Bourbon police to the house where Don Stefano Auriti was hiding with your sister, when the nobles of Palermo sent the keys of the city to Satriano in Caltanisetta? Have you forgotten all that? I remember every word of it, as if it was in a printed book! Let him come to Valsania, now, if you dare! But the General's room, no! Not that! The key of the *camerone* is in my keeping! There he shall not set foot, or I kill him, take the word of Mauro Mortara!"

Don Cosmo did not stir, nor did he seem to awake from his pained astonishment, at this long outburst. More than once he had been on the point of giving Mauro to understand that the idea of a United Italy had never entered the head of Gerlando Laurentano, his father, and that the Sicilian Parliament of 1848, in which his father had served for some months as Minister for War, had never suggested either an Italian Confederation or annexation to Italy, but a self-contained Kingdom of Sicily with a King of Sicily, that was all. This had been the aspiration of all the good old Sicilians; an aspiration which, if finally it had in certain respects been pushed farther, had never gone beyond a form of Federation, in which each separate state was to conserve its own liberty and autonomy. But he had never said anything to him about it; nor did he think of saying anything now; but rather allowed Mauro, snorting and quivering with rage, to turn his back on him and go off to shut himself in the old Prince's room, a room as sacred to him as the Country itself, the cradle of Freedom and now almost its temple.

Down below, in the meantime, outside the villa, poor Sciaralla was still waiting for the promised coffee: a sip of hot coffee, by Jove, and a good blaze to warm himself at.... Waiting, waiting: until he too forgot about them and began to worry over the delay in answering the letter. He ought to have had the answer in his pocket overnight, had he carried out Preola's instructions. He was thinking that by this time the Prince, over at Colimhetra, had perhaps risen from his bed and was asking his secretary for the answer. And here was he still waiting for it! Did it take all this time to read the letter and jot down a couple of lines in reply? Or could it be that Mortar had deliberately refrained from giving it to Don Cosmo?

And Captain Sciaralla groaned; he lost his temper, next, with Titina, who would not remain still for an instant, tormented by the flies.

"Be quiet! Be quiet! Be quiet!"

Three tugs at the bridle. Titina closed her tearful eyes with so sorrowful a resignation that Sciaralla at once repented of his ill temper.

"You're right, poor girl! They haven't given you so much as a wisp of hay either."

And he heaved a long sigh.

Finally Don Cosmo appeared at one of the windows of the villa. At the sound of opening shutters, Sciaralla turned hurriedly to look up. But Don Cosmo appeared surprised to see him still there. "Hallo, Placido! What are you waiting for?"

"Why, Excellency, the answer!" groaned the Captain, clasping his hands.

Don Cosmo knitted his brows.

"Does it need an answer?"

"What!" Sciaralla replied in exasperation. "When I've been waiting here for the last hour!"

There, he might have known it! That old ruffian had never said a word about it!

"You're right, my boy, just wait a moment," said Don Cosmo, and withdrew from the window.

He reflected that his brother attached great importance to even the most trifling formalities (stuff and nonsense, he called them), and would regard it as a deliberate insult, or, to say the least, a grave discourtesy if he did not receive an answer; he therefore took up a sheet of coarse paper yellow with age; dipped his clotted pen in a bottle of rusty ink and, without sitting down, on the marble top of the chest of drawers, set to work to frame an answer, which finally, after immense pains, found expression in these terms:

> Valsania, 22nd September, 1892.
> My dear Ippolito,
> You are perhaps not aware of the deplorable state into which this tumble-down old shanty has fallen; I myself am the only person who could possibly live in it, since I regard myself as already detached from this wicked world, nor do I make any complaint! If you consider, notwithstanding this, that there is no alternative to letting the Salvo family come and vegetate here; be so good, please, as to warn them that we have absolutely nothing here, and that they should bring with them all their household gear and such other furniture as they think they may need.
> I have more to say and would say it, did I not feel that it would be vain to hope that any argument of mine might prove effective. And so I shall add no more, but remain
> Your affectionate brother
> COSMO

He shut the envelope with a sigh and returned to the window. Captain Sciaralla ran towards the house, took off his cap and caught the letter in it.

"I kiss Your Excellency's hands!"

A spring, and he was in the saddle.

"Like the wind, Titina!"

Bow-wow-wow! The three mastiffs, startled from their sleep, ran after him for a long way, to bid him farewell after their own fashion.

Don Cosmo remained at the window: his eyes followed the galloping figure of Captain Sciaralla until it was hidden by a turn in the road; then the growling, panting return of the three mastiffs, after their futile pursuit and futile barking. When the three animals finally lay down on the ground again, at the foot of the stair, stretched out their heads over their forepaws and shut their eyes to return to their interrupted slumbers, he, as he gazed down at them, shook his head gently and smiled to hear, amid the surrounding silence, one of them heave a deep sigh. In the light of this settling down again to sleep and of this sigh, neither their barking nor their pursuit of Scia-ralla seemed to him any longer to be futile. It was like this: the three animals had protested against the coming of the man who had disturbed their slumber; now that they supposed they had driven him away, they shewed their wisdom by going to sleep again.

"For it is the wisdom of the dog," thought Don Cosmo, heaving a deep sigh in his turn, "after he has eaten and satisfied the other needs of the body, to let the rest of his time pass in sleep."

He looked at the trees that stood facing the villa: they too seemed to him to be absorbed in an endless dream, from which the light of day, the air that stirred their foliage, might try in vain to arouse them. For some time now, the long faint rustle of their leaves in the wind had wafted him a message, as though from an infinite distance, of the vanity of all things and the crushing tedium of life.

CHAPTER II

NO OFFENCE MEANT.

At the request of Flaminio Salvo, whose work at the bank, with all the other business to which he had to attend, never left him a moment's leisure, Ignazio Capolino, his former brother-in-law, and Nini De Vincentis, a young friend of the family, came down next morning in a carriage from Girgenti to Valsania to make the necessary arrangements for the flitting: a duty that was highly gratifying to both, though for different, indeed diametrically opposite reasons.

The carts, loaded up with furniture, had started some time in advance from Girgenti and must already have arrived at Valsania. The conversation between the pair in the carriage had turned to the projected marriage between Donna Adelaide Salvo, Don Flaminio's sister, and the Prince of Laurentano.

"No, no: it's too bad! It's too bad!" sneered Capolino. "Poor Adelaide, it is too bad really, after waiting fifty years! Let us be honest about it."

Nini De Vincentis kept on blinking, as though to confine within his fine, almond-shaped, velvety black eyes his distaste for such mockery. At the same time, the expression on his long sallow face was intended to shew at least an attempt to smile, to shew that he saw the joke, that he was making some response to Capolino's hilarity, immoderate and unseemly as it was.

"Yes, a marriage in name!" the latter went on, implacably, since there was no one to hear him (Nini, the good Nini, bread of angels, was less than no one). "In name only, for, whatever we may say, be it good or bad, the law is the law, my dear fellow. Religious and political views, if they count at all, what figure do they cut compared with the law? Now the Prince, as you know, makes it a *sine qua non* that there shall be a religious ceremony only; with his views, he cannot allow anything more. And so, a marriage that will not be legally binding, do you follow me? It will be a fine affair, oh! charming... it will require courage too, that I don't deny: but what about poor Adelaide?"

And Capolino gave another sardonic laugh, as though, to his mind, Adelaide Salvo was not the woman best fitted for this latter-day form of heroism, which was being demanded of her, for this bold challenge to society as lawfully constituted.

Nini De Vincentis remained silent, mumbling his lips, still stiffened in a painful smile, in the hope that his silence might stem the torrent of his companion's derision. The idea! Capolino only abounded all the more.

"Why is she doing it?" he went on, as though conducting an examination of the mature bride in question. "To get into society, with all the privileges of a lady? I should say it was the way out of society, if anything. She is going to shut herself up at Colimbetra! And, a monastic enclosure in every sense of the word, don't you know? The Prince, to say the very least, must be a man of five or six and sixty."

He broke off at a gesture of protest from De Vincentis.

"Why, my dear fellow! Oh, I know, you profess to be a perfect angel, but this is a question of marriage; and one has to think of such things, when a man has reached that age.... *Vis, vis, vis--* why, the priests say as much themselves. And so, society can be ruled out. She becomes a Princess, you say, and Princess of Laurentano: let us say, Queen of Colimbetra! Very good: but to me, to you, to all of us who regard a church marriage not merely as superior to the civil rite, but as the only real and valid rite; the rite which, being sufficient in the eyes of God, ought to be more than sufficient in the eyes of men. The rest of humanity, however, are under no obligation to recognize and respect her, outside the walls of Colimbetra, as Princess of Laurentano; Landino, for instance, the son of the former marriage, is not obliged to respect her as his mother-in-law. What else is there, then? Money... she is not doing it for that reason, certainly, seeing all the money there is in her own

with regret, that down by the sea at Valsania he would have only the rarest opportunities of going to see her. He took comfort for the moment in the thought that he would be superintending the preparation of her room, the nest which was to shelter her for the next few months.

As though Capolino had read the thoughts of his young friend, whose ingenuous aspirations he had long since and without difficulty discerned, he concluded his opening speech, after his outburst of laughter, with a "That will do!" and went on, rubbing his hands:

"We shall be there in a moment. You will be looking after Dianuccia's room, eh? I shall see to Donna Vittoriona's." Nini, plunged in confusion at finding his thoughts read like this, shewed a keen anxiety on behalf of the latter lady, who was Salvo's wife, and had been for many years insane.

"Yes, yes," he said, "we must take care, Heaven help her, that this change of scene does not upset her too much...."

"There's no fear of that!" Capolino interrupted him. "You'll see that she doesn't even notice it. She will go calmly on with her interminable knitting, which (*on dit*) is a mile long already. She knits stockings for the Almighty, you know. Night and day.... And she tries to make the two Vincentian Sisters who look after her work at them with her...."

Nini shook his head sorrowfully.

The carriage, a little way beyond the Seta, turned into the grounds of Valsania from the high road. The gate had collapsed: one half of it only, covered in rust, remained standing, fastened to a pillar; the other pillar had long since crumbled in pieces. The carriage drive running across this other part of the estate, which also was let out to portioners, was neglected like everything else, half-hidden by tufts of grass, among which might be seen the fresh ruts left that morning by the carts with the furniture.

Nini De Vincentis gazed about him upon this scene of desolation, without saying a word, but Capolino, that devil of a talker, Capolino, the inexhaustible windbag, went on talking for them both.

"The invalid," he said, with a grimace, "won't find life here very cheerful, what do you say?"

"It is pretty gloomy," sighed Nini.

"I don't mean only the place," Capolino went on, "I am thinking of the people here as well. A pair of specimens, my dear fellow! You'll see them in a minute. Mah... This country holiday is being taken more for Donna Adelaide, who is not coming down, than for Dianuceia, who may perhaps suspect as much and will bear it calmly as usual, in her love for her aunt.... Ah! He's a great man, Flaminio, whatever you may say!"

"The air here is good, though," the young man observed, seeking to attenuate, to some slight extent, his companion's harsh judgment of Salvo.

"Excellent, excellent," agreed Capolino, and, from that moment, withdrew into a frowning silence in which he remained absorbed until they reached the villa.

PHILOSOPHY? PE-EW, PE-EW, PE-EW...

The carts had just arrived, together with the basket chaise which had brought a couple of Salvo's menservants, a maid and two upholsterers. Donna Sara Alaimo, on the landing at the head of the stair, was clapping her hands in jubilation at the sight of those four mountains of finery on the carts below. "Be quick and unload them!" Capolino told the servants and drivers, as he sprang from the carriage, brandishing his cane in the air. Then, racing up the stairs, he inquired of Donna Sara, "Don Cosmo?"

And without waiting for an answer he made his way into the old barn of a house with Nini De Vincentis, who followed in his footsteps like a stray dog.

"Unload!" one of the servants echoed, mimicking, to his comrades' merriment, the tone of voice and imperious gesture of this self-appointed master.

Don Cosmo was running frantically from one to another of the rooms freshly scrubbed out by Donna Sara, who for the last twenty-four hours, ever since she had heard that the Salvo family were coming, had been making a great to-do, and had even persuaded Don Cosmo to have the rooms cleared of their decrepit furniture, so that the millionaire guests might not see such tokens of poverty in a princely house.

"Most honourable Don Cosmo!" exclaimed Capolino, running him to earth at last in one of the rooms, after he too had run all over the house in search of him. "All in disorder, eh? Perbacco!"

"No, no," Don Cosmo hastened to reply, so as to cut short any pretence of ceremony, his nostrils wrinkling at the acrid smell of mould which infested the house, still damp after its recent and unaccustomed cleansing. "I was looking for some corner where I can sit without being in anybody's way."

Capolino was about to protest; but Don Cosmo stopped him:

"Let me explain! I seek my own convenience and theirs at the same time: is that right? Keep covered, pray, keep covered!"

He raised his hand, as he spoke, to caress the trim little black tuft on the chin of Nini De Vincentis.

"You've grown into a fine man, my boy! And I, good Lord, have grown into an old one! And your brother Vincente? Still at his Arabic?"

"Still!" replied Nini, with a smile.

"Ah! Those fourteen volumes of Arabic manuscripts must be pressing like fourteen millstones, in the world beyond, on the soul of Conte Lucchesi-Palli, who insisted on presenting them to our Library to be the poor boy's ruin!"

"He has deciphered ten of them already," said Nini. "He has still four left... so big!"

"He must hurry up and finish them!" Don Cosmo concluded in a fatherly tone. "And you too, my boy, you should keep an eye on your affairs: I know things aren't going any too well. ... Use your judgment!"

Capolino, meanwhile, at the window, was making the open pane serve him as a looking-glass, and smoothing the short mutton-chop whiskers, already slightly grizzled, that adorned his cheeks. He was not handsome, but had a pair of keen and fervent eyes, which prevented one from noticing the harsh irregularity of his features, and gave a pleasing animation to the whole of his lean dark face.

Hearing a lull in the conversation between Laurentano and Nini, he pretended to be engaged in trying to settle the orientation of the villa.

"A southern exposure, this, isn't it? But you have chosen this room for yourself, perhaps, Don Cosmo?"

"Any room will do for me," replied Laurentano. "There are plenty of spare bedrooms, you'll find, but they're all like this, in the most wretched condition.... It is all old, avvocato, it is all old.... Now, if we go out by this door ... (no, you are not to stand on ceremony: really, what point is there in saying a thing is not old when it is? You have only to look at it!) I was saying, if we go out by this door, we come to this long corridor, which divides the house in two: all the bedrooms on this side face the south; those on the other side, the north. The entrance hall bisects the corridor, and splits the villa into two identical wings, except that at this end we have a big room, the door of which is behind me, and at the other end we have a terrace. It's quite simple." "Good, good, good," Capolino expressed his approval. "Then we have a big room as well?"

Don Cosmo smiled and shook his head; then proceeded to explain what this *camerone* was, what state it was in and who was its guardian.

"Good God!" exclaimed Capolino.

"It would be better, therefore," Don Cosmo concluded, "if you were to settle in the other half of the house, where you'll be undisturbed. I had chosen this room for myself on purpose..."

Capolino once more agreed; and, as the servants had already brought the first load upstairs, made off with Nini to the other wing. Don Cosmo remained in the bedroom, to which, with the help of Donna Sara, he transported all his books. The poor housekeeper, feeling the weight of all this learning, could not for the life of her understand how Don Cosmo, who had absorbed it all into his person, could continue to live in the clouds as he did. Don Cosmo, his nostrils still wrinkled, could not for his part understand why there was such a damp smell everywhere that morning. But perhaps he did not distinguish clearly between the smell and the annoyance he derived from the thought that from now onwards, by the coming of his guests, all his old lazy habits would be shattered, and for an indefinite period!

Presently Capolino returned, leaving the other wing of the house to De Vincentis, who had shewn a far greater capacity for the work in hand: so at least he declared. As a matter of fact, he came to put into execution one of the objects for which he had readily undertaken to act for Salvo: namely, that he might discover Don Cosmo's attitude with regard to his brother's marriage, or "feel his pulse" in the matter, to use his own expression.

There seemed no hope now that the marriage might come to nothing; but, knowing the discrepancy, indeed the incompatible opposition between Salvo's and Don Cosmo's thoughts and feelings, he liked to suppose that some friction, some actual conflict might arise from the former's stay at Valsania. Don Cosmo's was so abstract and solitary a spirit that the life of the world could not succeed in penetrating his consciousness with all its fictions and artifices and persuasions, which spontaneously transfigure it for most people; and often, for that reason, from the frozen peak of his stoical indifference, he let fall like an avalanche the most naked of truths.

"Oh, what a lot of books!" exclaimed Capolino as he entered the room. "But you still keep on studying... Romagnosi, Rosmini, Hegel, Kant ..."

As he read each name on the backs of the books he opened his eyes wider, as though punctuating the names with marks of exclamation that grew longer and longer. "Philosophy, eh?"

"Poetry!" sighed Don Cosmo, waving his hand vaguely in the air, and closing his eyes.

"What's that you say, Don Cosmo? I don't understand."

"Why, yes," Laurentano assured him, with a fresh sigh. "For study, my dear sir, there is little or nothing: what there is is enjoyment of the grandeur of the human intellect, which on a hypothesis, that is to say on a cloud (you follow me?) builds up castles, pinnacles and towers: all these various systems of philosophy, my dear avvocato, which seem to me... do you know what they seem to me? Churches, chapels, shrines, temples, of different styles, poised in the air ..."

"Ah yes, I see..." Capolino tried to interrupt him, fingering the back of his neck.

But Don Cosmo, who never spoke as a rule, his one responsive chord having been struck, could not restrain himself:

"Breathe, and the whole structure collapses; breathe, and all these castles which tower like mountains crumble, because there is nothing inside them: a void, my dear sir, all the more crushing the taller and more solemn the structure is: a void and the silence of the mystery..."

Capolino had withdrawn into his shell, to collect his thoughts, stimulated by the passion with which Don Cosmo spoke, to reply, to bring him down to earth; and waited anxiously for an opportunity; when it came, he broke out:

"And yet..."

"No, there's nothing to be said! Let us drop the subject!" Don Cosmo at once cut him short, laying a hand on his shoulder. "All nonsense, my dear avvocato!"

Fortunately, at that moment, Mauro Mortara down below, on the lawn that flanked the villa, on the side looking towards the vineyard and the sea, began to summon with his invariable cry of "Pe-ew, pe-ew, pe-ew" the innumerable flock of pigeons which he was in the habit of feeding twice daily.

Don Cosmo and Capolino went out on the balcony. Nini too leaned out to watch from the railings of the farthest balcony at the end of the house, while the menservants and maids and upholsterers looked down from the terrace.

The white ferment of wings invariably ended in a tremendous scrimmage, since the ration of peas had long remained unaltered, while the pigeons had multiplied beyond reckoning and lived now almost in a wild state, scattered about the estate and the surrounding fields. They knew their dinner-hour, however, and would arrive punctually, in dense whirring clouds, from all directions; cooing impatiently, in a great tumult, they would invade the roofs of the villa itself, of the peasants' houses, the straw rick, the dovecot, the barn, the mill and the wineshed; and if Mauro was at all behind time, forgetting them or absorbed in his own memories, a numerous deputation would flutter down from the roofs and go in quest of him, through the door of his well known room in the basement: the deputation would gradually swell into a crowd, until presently the whole lawn was aswarm with fluttering wings and cooing throats, while ever so many more remained hovering in the air, finding no room to alight.

"Stupendous, a stupendous sight!" Capolino kept on exclaiming.

Yes, and the only sight in which Don Cosmo took any pleasure. On hearing the clamorous whirr of all those wings he would always rise from table and go out to the balcony to watch. Besides, it was the signal for his own dinner as well. Having scattered the peas round him several times and finally emptied the basket over the pigeons, Mauro would come upstairs, and the two of them would sit down together.

Don Cosmo remembered with annoyance that on this occasion, however, Mauro would not be coming up; he had said to him overnight:

"This is the last time that I feed with you. Because you will do me the courtesy of believing me when I say that I will not sit down to table with Flaminio Salvo."

Now, on the lawn beneath, he was standing among his pigeons with lowered head. Capolino watched him from the halcony, as though he had some rare animal hef ore his eyes.

"Do I speak to him?" he whispered to Don Cosmo.

The latter made a negative sign with his hand.

"A bear, what?" Capolino went on. "But a fine type!"

"A bear," Don Cosmo repeated, as he withdrew from the balcony.

METASTASIO.

A few minutes later, in the dining-room in the other part of the house, which had meanwhile been richly furnished by the upholsterers, Capolino made a fresh attempt to "feel Don Cosmo's pulse" in the matter we know of. He certainly would not repeat the mistake of leading the conversation to the books of philosophy.

Don Cosmo was lost in admiration of the room, which had suddenly been made unrecognisable.

"A perfect miracle!" he exclaimed, bringing his hand down upon the shoulder of Nini De Vincentis. "One might be at Colimbetra!"

Capolino at once caught the ball in its flight.

"You haven't been there for years and years, to Colimbetra, eh?"

Don Cosmo thought for a moment.

"About ten..." and remained lost in meditation, without saying another word. But Capolino, baiting his question so as to force an answer:

"When your sister-in-law died there, wasn't it?"

"Yes," was Laurentano's dry response.

And Capolino sighed:

"Donna Teresa Montalto... what a lady! what a loss! A true lady of the old school!"

And, after a pause, heavy with feigned grief, a fresh sigh, of a different kind:

"Mah! *Cosa bella mortal passa e non dura*"

Donna Sara Alaimo, the housekeeper, who at the moment was waiting at table, seeking to raise herself in the eyes of the guests from her humble and unbefitting state, was tempted to interpose, and asked timidly, with a wistful smile:

"Metastasio, isn't it?"

Nini turned round and gazed at her in bewilderment; Don Cosmo shaped his lips to emit a special laugh of his own, consisting of a triple "Oh, oh, oh!" loud, deep and sombre. But Capolino, seeing that there was a risk of his breaking the eggs in his basket just at the propitious moment, retorted crossly:

"Leopardi, Leopardi..."

"Petrarch, excuse me, dear avvocato, Petrarch!" Don Cosmo protested with outspread hands. "I appeal to Nini!"

"Oh, of course, Petrarch, what a fool I am! *Muor giovine colui che al cielo e caro...*" Capolino at once continued the quotation. "I was thinking of something else.... And so you... so you have never seen your brother again since?"

Don Cosmo suddenly resumed his somnolent air; half shut his eyes; nodded his head in assent.

"Always buried alive down here!" Capolino proceeded to explain to De Vincentis, as though the latter were not aware of this. "Different tastes, I can understand... indeed, diametrically opposed, since Don Ippolito is fond of... of company, can't do without it.... And perhaps, if I may say so, after his loss, he would have greatly preferred not to be left alone, without any of his family round him.... But, with you here; his son always in Rome... and..."

Don Cosmo, who had by this time grasped, but in his own way, Capolino's purpose, to cut him short came out with:

"And so he does right to marry again, you mean? We are quite of one mind as to that! But you know," he went on, turning to Nini, "my fine fellow, haven't you made up your mind yet?"

Nini, finding himself thus suddenly drawn into the conversation, turned crimson:

"I?"

"Look how he's blushing!" exclaimed Capo-lino, and burst out laughing, in his rage.

"Then there is some one?" Don Cosmo inquired, tapping his chest with his finger, over the heart. "I should just think there was!" exclaimed Capolino, laughing louder than ever.

Nini, on pins and needles, mortified, shocked by this unseemly laughter, protested with marked emphasis:

"I assure you, there's absolutely nothing of the sort! Please don't say such things!"

"Of course not! San Luigi Gonzaga!" Capo-lino went on, prolonging his forced laughter. "Or rather... why, yes, where's Donna Sara? he is, really, Metastasio, a Metastasio hero, Don Cosmo! Or, shall we say, an angel... but not one of the angels they have at Alcamo, remember! Do you know, Don Cosmo, that at Alcamo they call the little pigs angels?"

Nini became genuinely distressed; turned pale; and said in a firm voice:

"You annoy me, avvocato!"

"I shan't say another word!" Capolino promised, recovering his composure.

Don Cosmo remained uneasy, without understanding at first what had happened; then opened his mouth to emit an "ah!" which stuck in his throat. Could it be a question, perhaps, of Salvo's daughter? Why, of course.... It had never occurred to him. He had never yet seen her. But of course! Excellent! A fortune for this dear Nini! And he could not help saying to him:

"Don't distress yourself, my boy. It's a very serious matter. You have no time to lose, in your position."

Nini was writhing in his chair, as though trying to endure without screaming the pricking of a hundred pins all over his body. Capolino held his breath and waited for the avalanche to fall. Don Cosmo was unable to account for the effect that his words had produced, and looked in bewilderment at each of the others in turn.

"Have I said something wrong?" he asked. "Forgive me. I shan't say another word either."

Nini was truly living in heaven, in a heaven lighted by a special sun of his own which was waiting there ready to rise, which had not yet risen and would perhaps never rise. He let it stay there, behind the rugged mountains of reality, and preferred to remain in the vain, roseate light of a perpetual dawn, since his sun, when it did rise, was not ever to set again, and the shadows, of necessity, remained tenuous and almost diaphanous. He had already been assailed by the doubt that Salvo, at present, might not be disposed to listen to his proposal of marriage, supposing that he were to force himself to make it. But he had always shrunk from considering and weighing that doubt, in order not to disturb the spotless dream of his whole life. And, not because this doubt had proved an obstacle, but because he did really lack the courage to translate into action an ideal which he had maintained at so lofty an altitude, that he almost feared to see it shattered by the slightest contact with reality, he had never made up his mind, not indeed to make a formal proposal, but even to come to an understanding with Dianella Salvo. And now, the suspicion that he might be doing so in view of the girl's dowry, which would re-establish his own financial position, caused him acute pain, poisoned for him all joy in this service which he had rendered for love, but which might however appear to have had a baser motive; and, as though all of a sudden his sun had fallen from the sky, all at once the world grew dark about him, and when the rooms had been put in order, and he, his throat choking with anguish, had made a final tour of inspection, he was unable to bestow, as he had intended, on the pillow on Dianella's bed his kiss of welcome, that she, unawares, might find it there, that night, when she retired to rest.

ALL FOR A PAIR OF PUMPKINS

Meanwhile Don Cosmo and Capolino, a pair of tiny black dots beneath the soaring arch of a sky that smouldered with the fire of the setting sun, had left the house and were strolling up and down the long straight avenue, forming a sort of hem on the left side of the crest from which a wide and deep ravine, known as the vallone, ran abruptly down.

It seemed as though some convulsion of the earth's surface had rent the tableland asunder at that point and poured it down towards the sea.

The estate of Valsania lay on one side, its farthest olives running down into the ravine, a gulf of ashen shadows, out of which arose mulberries, carubs, oranges, lemons, rejoicing in a rivulet of water which ran down from a spring that burst from the ground at the head of the ravine, in the mysterious cave of San Calogero.

On the other side of the ravine, at a corresponding level, were the wooded lands of Platania, which to the south towered menacingly over the railway line, where, emerging from its tunnel beneath Valsania, it followed the coastline as far as Porto Empedocle.

The band of flame and gold of the sunset broke up into a marvellous fantastic patchwork seen through the intense green of the distant trees, across the ravine. On the near side, over the almonds and olives of Valsania, the first cool shades of evening, tender, light and melancholy, were already hovering.

This twilight hour, when the things around him in the gathering dusk, retaining more intensely the last light of day, seemed almost to be enamelled in their several colours, was more sacred than any other to Don Cosmo in his solitude. He kept constantly in mind his sense of his own precarious existence in the place of his habitation, nor did he let this distress him. This feeling, which melted lightly and vaguely into the impenetrable mystery of the world around him, made every responsibility, every thought, an intolerable burden. We may imagine, then, how shattering he must have found Capolino's conversation, which kept turning with fervour to the success of Salvo's undertakings, to a great scheme which he was planning at the moment, with the manager of his sulphur pits, the engineer Aurelio Costa, for improving the conditions of the sulphur industry, which for many years past had been deplorable.

"A new kind of conscience, his," said Capolino. "Lucid, precise and complex, Don Cosmo, like a modern machine, of steel. He always knows what he is doing, and never makes a mistake!"

"Lucky fellow! Lucky fellow!" Don Cosmo repeated, with half shut eyes, and an air of resigned endurance.

"And a true believer, you know!" Capolino went on. "A religious man!"

"Lucky fellow!"

"It's a marvel how, with all his responsibilities, he manages to find time to bother about our Party. And how zealously he has embraced our cause!"

Presently, however, Capolino changed the subject, observing that Don Cosmo had ceased to listen to him. He drew closer to him, laid a hand on his arm, and said quietly, with a sorrowful air: "That poor Nini! I'm certain he's crying now, don't you know, just because we teased him a bit at table. Desperately in love, poor boy! But the girl, eh? No, alas, she's not for him...."

"Is she engaged to somebody else?" asked Don Cosmo, coming to a halt.

"No; not officially, no!" Capolino promptly assured him. "But... this is between ourselves, though, please: you mustn't breathe a word of it! My belief is, dear Don Cosmo, that the girl is really less sick in body than in mind."

"Touched, eh?"

"Touched. That is perhaps the one thing her father has done wrong. There Flaminio made a mistake... yes, there are no

54

two ways about it, he made a mistake!"

Don Cosmo stopped again, nodded his head several times and said, in his most serious tone:

"So you see that even he can be mistaken, my dear avvocato."

"Well, when the devil, you know, had him properly caught that time!" Capolino went on. "You know, of course, that Flaminio... it must be ten years ago; no, what am I saying, fifteen years ago at least; anyhow, fifteen years ago, more or less, he came within an inch of drowning.... Didn't you know that? Why, bathing in the sea, at Porto Empedocle. An absurd business, believe me, absurd and terrible at the same time! All for a pair of pumpkins...."

"Pumpkins? Tell me about it," said Don Cosmo, stirred by unwonted curiosity.

"Why, yes," Capolino went on. "He was bathing, at the Casotti. He can't swim, and, to be on the safe side, was keeping within the enclosure, where the water came more or less up to his chest. Suddenly (the devil take them!) he saw a pair of pumpkins bobbing along towards him, which some boy or other had presumably left in the sea. He took hold of them. As he stood crouching down, so that the water should come up to his neck (what a sorry figure a man cuts in the water, my dear Don Cosmo, a man who can't swim!), he had the unlucky inspiration to put the pair of pumpkins underneath him, as a support, with the string that held them together; he sat down on the string, and, as the pumpkins, naturally, floated on, and he had let go of the fence to see whether they were strong enough to keep him afloat with his feet off the bottom, suddenly, plump! he lost his balance and slipped over head downwards, under the water!"

"Oh, I say!" exclaimed Don Cosmo in alarm.

"You can imagine," Capolino went on, "how he began splashing with his feet to regain his balance. But, as ill luck would have it, his feet became entangled in the string of the pumpkins, and, struggle as he might under the water, he could not succeed in getting them free."

"Don't, please! oh dear, oh dear!" gasped Don Cosmo, with a convulsive tightening of his fists and all his features.

But Capolino went on:

"You will admit that it was really absurd for a man to be on the point of drowning in an enclosed bathing place, with crowds of people round him, who never noticed him and never came to his rescue, not suspecting for a moment that he was struggling there with death staring him in the face! And he would have been drowned, as sure as God's in heaven, had not a boy of thirteen--this Aurelio Costa, who is now a qualified engineer and manager of Salvo's sulphur pits at Aragona and Comitini--caught sight of a pair of feet kicking desperately on the surface and gone over to him, greatly amused, to set him free."

"Ah, I begin to understand," said Don Cosmo. "And now the daughter..."

"The daughter... the daughter..." Capolino chewed the word. "Flaminio, you will understand, had to discharge his debt to the boy, and discharged it in proportion to the danger he had run and the terror he had felt. They told him that the boy was the son of a poor weighman on the beach where the sulphur is loaded..."

"Costa, yes, Leonardo Costa," Don Cosmo broke in. "He's a friend of mine. He comes up here to see me sometimes, on Sundays, from Porto Empedocle."

"You know, then, that he works for Flaminio now?" Capolino went on. "Flaminio took himi from the scales and gave him a job in his big sulphur deposit on the east shore. As for his son Aurelio, he determined to make the boy's fortune, without counting the cost; not only that, but he took him away with him, brought him up in his own house, with his own children, Dianuccia and the other one, the little boy that died. That tragedy, too, must certainly have helped to increase his affection for the boy. Affection, though, I should say, up to a certain point only. For the same reason for which he would not give his daughter now to Nini De Vincentis, he would never give her, I imagine, to Aurelio Costa, his dependent, remember!"

"Mah!" Don Cosmo exclaimed, shrugging his shoulders. "With all his money, and with an only daughter..."

"Why, no... no..." replied Capolino. "I quite admit that if anything were to happen to him, all his fortune would be bound to pass to somebody, to his son-in-law, whoever his son-in-law might be. But Flaminio will take good care to choose his man first! He's not the sort of person to indulge in rosy dreams of romance. His daughter may.... Yes, and romance in the true sense of the word, mind! Because the true nature of her secret malady has come to my knowledge, through certain private channels; Flaminio knows it too, I believe, or at any rate suspects it; but the other, the engineer Costa (an excellent young fellow, remember! A solid young fellow, fully aware of his position and of all that he owes to his benefactor), knows nothing whatever about it, has not the remotest conception of it; I can be quite certain of that, because I have proof positive, evidence of an intimate nature. The engineer ..."

At this point Capolino broke off, having caught sight of a man at the far end of the avenue who came running towards them, waving his arms.

"Who's that?" he asked, stopping short and knitting his brows.

It was Marco Preola, bathed in sweat, gasping for breath and covered in dust, his stockings festooned about his broken shoes. He was dead beat.

"Here we are! Here we are!" he began to shout, as he drew near. "He's come!"

"Auriti?" inquired Capolino.

"Yes, sir," Preola went on. "For the election: there's no doubt about it! I've run all the way from Girgenti to tell you."

He removed his battered hat, and with a dirty handkerchief mopped the sweat that trickled from his matted locks.

"My nephew?" inquired Don Cosmo, rooted to the ground with astonishment.

At once Capolino, with a mortified air, set to work to inform him, first of Fazello's resignation, then of the pressure that had been put upon himself to accept the candidature, and of the rumours that were going about Girgenti as to this unexpected arrival of Roberto Auriti. Rumours... rumours which he, Capolino, refused to accept for two reasons. First of all, the respect that he felt for Auriti, a respect which did not permit him to suppose that, without an invitation, he would have come down to contest a seat which Fazello was resigning of his own free will. The Party Association, which represented the majority of the electors, as had been shewn by countless indisputable proofs, remained solid, even after Giacinto Fazello's withdrawal. The other reason was of a more private nature, and was this: that it would be a grief, a very great grief to him to have as a by no means redoubtable opponent, in an unequal contest, a man who, notwithstanding the differences of opinion in his family, was nevertheless related to the Laurentano brothers, whom he revered and by whose friendship he regarded himself as honoured. No, no: he preferred to believe that Auriti had come to Girgenti only to pay his mother and sister a visit.

"What's that you say, avvocato?" Marco Pre-ola burst forth, throwing off with a shrug of his shoulders the long and tedious speech in which Capolino had been stealthily endeavouring to give a specimen of his political views. "When a pack of rascals went to meet him at the station, students from the Technical Institute? When the Mafia an'd the Masons have come to town, led by Guido Veronica and Giambattista Mattina? There's no doubt about it, I tell you! He's come for the election...."

While Capolino and Preola were discussing the matter, Don Cosmo's eyes, nose and mouth were acting a remarkable pantomime: winking and wrinkling and twisting.... Living in exile as he did, his mind always absorbed in thoughts of eternity, his eyes turned to the stars, or to the sea at his feet, or to the deserted country round about, finding himself suddenly assailed by all these topical trivialities, he felt as though he were being stung by a swarm of irritating insects.

"Gesù! Gesù! It's unbelievable.... What foolishness..."

"And now, a glass of wine, Si-don Co'," exclaimed Marco Preola, to bring the discussion to a happy ending. "Your honour must do me the favour of a glass of wine. I'm finished! I've been all round Girgenti looking for our dear avvocato; they told me I should find him out here at Valsania, and off I dashed at once on foot by the Spina Santa. Look at me! My throat's properly burning."

"Go along, go and get something to drink at the house," Don Cosmo told him.

"And isn't Don Mauro there?" asked Preola. "I'm afraid," he added, with a laugh. "He fired a gun at me, last year it was.... He says I came here, into the grounds, to shoot his pigeons. Word of honour, Si-don Cosmo, it's not true! It was after the turtle-doves I came. Perhaps, now and then, I don't say, I may have made a bad shot. I fired, and, quick as lightning, I heard a shot come. ... Lucky

I turned round at once. Bang! In the seat of my breeches, a shower of pellets. ... May I be damned to hell, Si-don Co ', I swear to you, if it weren't for the respect I owe to the Laurentano family... I got a dose from both barrels and, my word of honour... "

From the other end of the avenue came a jingle of bells. The trio, who had drawn near to the villa, talking together, turned round to look. Capolino called out:

"Nini! Nini! Here are the carriages! They're arriving!"

Nini hurried down from the house; the menservants came down also, with Donna Sara Alaimo and the maids, who by this time were firm friends.

The carriages proved to be two victorias. In the first sat Don Flaminio with his daughter; in the second the lunatic with two nurses. Don Cosmo expected to see Donna Adelaide, the bride to be, alight from one of the carriages also: he was disappointed. Nini De Vincentis had not the courage to step forward and offer Dianella his arm. With a throbbing heart and eyes misty with emotion he caught a glimpse of her drawn white face through her thick green travelling veil, and followed her with his gaze while, leaning on Capo-lino's arm, closely wrapped in a heavy cloak, she climbed slowly up the stair, like an old woman, amid the obsequious greetings of Donna Sara Alaimo.

Donna Victoria, whose enormous girth made her alight with difficulty, stood between the two nurses, with fixed, vacant eyes in her large, pale face, framed in the humble black woollen shawl which she wore over her head; she gazed for a while like this at Don Cosmo; then parted her fleshy, almost colourless lips in a mournful smile and said, with a respectful bow:

"Signor Priore..."

One of the nurses took her by the hand, while Don Cosmo, standing by Salvo, shut his eyes in distress at the spectacle. Nini followed the mad woman.

"Thank you," said Flaminio Salvo, pressing Don Cosmo's hand. "I need not say more to you."

"No, no..." Laurentano made haste to reply, still disturbed and moved by the sad spectacle, feeling a sudden profound pity for this man who, in his enviable position of power, had in that moment conveyed to him, by that handclasp, the sense of his utter misery.

CHAPTER III

NOT EVEN A PINCH OF DUST!

"This way, Sir, this way, follow me," the gentleman who accompanied him was told by the old manservant with the splayed feet, which made him walk in all directions at once, his legs bent under him so that his knees knocked together.

They passed, on thick carpets, through three communicating rooms, in each of which the servant, as he passed, threw open the shutters inside the long windows. The rooms however remained in shadow, whether because of the thickness of the curtains or because of the lowness of the house itself, overtopped by the houses opposite which kept out the light. Having opened the shutters, the servant looked round each room and sighed, as much as to say: "You see how well furnished it is? And yet it is never used!"

At length they came to the drawing-room at the end, with its panelled walls divided by gilt mouldings.

The gentleman drew from an elegant pocket-book an armorial visiting card, turned down one corner and handed the card to the servant, who, pointing to a door which led out of the drawing-room, said: "One moment, please. Cavalier Preola's in there."

"Preola the father?"

"The son."

"Is he a Cavaliere too?"

"To me," the old man protested, making a deep bow and placing his hand on his heart, "all the gentry are Cavalieri!"

And, as he hobbled away on his splayed feet, he glanced furtively at the card, and read: *Cav. Gian Battista Mattina.*

("So this one really is a Cavaliere, it seems.")

Mattina remained standing, lost in thought, in the middle of the room; then shrugged his shoulders irritably; threw a careless glance round the room; caught sight of a mirror on the opposite wall and went across to it.

In the huge mirror, by the dim light, his own reflexion looked to him like a ghost; and he felt a vague momentary uneasiness as he gazed at it.

All the furniture, the carpet, the curtains exhaled that peculiar smell of old things that have grown stale with disuse; almost the atmosphere of another age.

Mattina looked round the room again with a strange sense of discomfort at the silent immobility of these old things which had stood there, year after year, unused and lifeless. He moved nearer to the mirror to study his reflexion more closely, turning his head slowly, screwing up under his tired, deeply shadowed eyes the ends of his thick moustaches, kept black with the help of some lotion, in contrast to the prematurely grey head which gave such an air of solemnity to his swarthy face. Suddenly a prolonged yawn made him part his lips in a grimace, and, as he let it escape, he contracted his features in an expression of boredom and disgust. He was just turning away from the mirror when, lowering his gaze to the surface of the bracket that supported it, he noticed a quantity of neat little worm-easts, arranged there as though in a pattern, and bent down, curious to examine them. They had done their work well, those worms! And yet nobody seemed to give them any credit for their labour.... The fruit of it, however, was there, plainly visible, saying: "This is done now. Take it away!" He put out his hand to one of the little heaps, took up a pinch of it and rubbed his fingers together. Nothing! Not even dust.... And, examining the balls of his thumb and forefinger, he went and sat down upon a comfortable armchair by the sofa. Having taken his seat, he shook the chair slightly, as though to test its solidity.

"Not even dust.... Nothing!"

With a grimace he picked up from the round table in front of the sofa an album on the first page of which was a photograph of the master of the house, Canon Agro.

Mattina had always felt that Canon Pompeo Agro bore a

strange resemblance to some large bird, the name of which escaped him. Certainly his nose, broad at the base and ending in a sharp point, stuck out from his face just like a beak. It was, however, in the keen little grey eyes, beneath a high and narrow forehead, that one detected all the astute, subtle and persistent malice for which Agro was notorious.

Mattina studied the face as though he were trying to discover from its lineaments the reason for the invitation he had received overnight. What the deuce could Agro want with him? Was the breach between this most gentlemanly of Canons and the Clerical Party, a breach that had created such a scandal in the town, an actual fact or was it not rather a concerted, insidious pose, with the object of hoodwinking the ingenuous Auriti, of penetrating into the enemy's camp and discovering his plan of campaign? Ah, if one trusted a fox.... This secret interview with Preola, for instance.... Was the whole thing an elaborate plot?

He raised his eyes, looked round the room again and once more felt himself disturbed by the silent immobility of those old things, so useless and lifeless, as though, now that he had laid bare their rottenness, they were watching him with greater hostility than ever.

He heard, through the chain of rooms, the old servant's voice repeating: "This way, Sir, this way, follow me."

He laid down the album and looked towards the door.

"Hallo! Veronica..."

"My dear Titta," replied Guido Veronica, advancing into the middle of the room.

He removed his spectacles, in order to polish them with the handkerchief which he held in readiness in his other hand, blinked his myopic, almond-shaped eyes, and with the thumb and forefinger of his stumpy hand rubbed the bridge of his nose, where it was scarred by the continual pressure of his glasses; and was making his way towards the sofa facing Mattina; but the latter, rising, took him by the arm and murmured:

"Wait, I want you to look at something."

And led him across to the bracelet to shew him all those little heaps of sawdust.

Veronica, not understanding what he was intended to look

at, and being extremely shortsighted, bent down until his nose was almost touching the top of the bracket.

"Worms?" he then remarked, but without any show of interest, looking indeed coldly at Mattina, as though to inquire why he had shewn him them: and went and sat down on the armchair.

Whereupon, "*Tu quoque?*" Mattina queried, feeling uncomfortable and seeking to hide his annoyance. "How are things going?"

"I don't know what it's all about," Veronica answered, with the air of a person trying to keep a secret.

"Oh, no more do I," Mattina hastened to add, in a tone of indifference.

And he let his glance rest casually on Veronica's brow, furrowed by three long scars running in different directions: trophies won on the duelling ground.

"Have you come from Rome?"

"No. From Palermo."

"Shall you be staying here long?"

"I don't know."

Veronica made it evident, by these curt responses, that he intended to keep his own counsel, so as not to give himself any importance by what he could say if he chose.

Indeed his plan for the time being was as follows: to show irritation, or rather boredom and distrust. Unfortunately for himself he had, as everyone knew, an ideal: the Country, represented by, nay bodily incarnate in the person of a famous old statesman defeated some years since in the course of a tumultuous sitting of Parliament, after a petty and disloyal campaign. For this Minister's sake he had let himself be provoked into duel after duel, and had invariably been defeated; he had hurled back, in the columns of the newspapers, in language unprecedented in its violence, the insults offered by the opposition. But now, this Minister having fallen, the country had fallen as well: the pigmy rabble were triumphant: it was not anger that he felt; it was a disgrace to be alive, in such times. He did not for a moment believe that Roberto Auriti could win, even with the support of the Government; but his revered Elder--who still entertained the most childish illusions as to the future of the country--had ordered him to go down to Girgenti and to fight for Auriti; lie knew that Auriti's reason for undertaking the campaign had been not so much the pressure put upon him by the Government as the old statesman's insistent demand; and so here he was at Girgenti. Simply that he might not fail in his duty, he was now here in response to an invitation from Agro, a Canon, he to whom priests were like a red rag to a bull. Here he was; he must resign himself. Notwithstanding, however, the misgivings with which he had allowed himself to set out upon this electoral mission, he felt a certain irritation, now, on finding himself placed on a level with a mere Mattina, associated with him as a fellow-conspirator in the little plot which Canon Agro was apparently trying to weave.

Mattina stirred in his seat, with a grunt, and assumed a different posture.

"He's keeping us waiting," he said.

"Whom has he got in there?" asked Guido Veronica, with no trace of impatience.

Mattina leaned forward and said in a whisper: "Young Preola, Ignazio Capolino's bottle-washer. The servant told me. What do you think? I ask you and I ask myself, what are we two here for?"

"We shall hear presently," sighed Veronica.

"I shouldn't like----"

Mattina stopped short, seeing the door open and the long, lean, stooping form of Canon Pompeo Agro enter the room.

I SUPPLY THE AMMUNITION.

Signalling with both hands to his guests to remain seated, Pompeo Agro began in a shrill, strident little voice:

"I ask your pardon.... Do not rise, please, do not rise. My dear Veronica; most eminent Cavaliere. Here, Cavaliere, come and sit here, beside me: I'm not afraid, as you know, of your youthful excesses."

"Youthful, yes!" smiled Mattina, pointing to his grizzled pate.

The Canon drew an old silver watch from his pocket.

"Your hair, eh... you shed your hair, you mean, but not your spots. Ten o'clock already, perbacco! I've wasted the whole morning.... Mah!"

His face clouded over; he sat for a moment undecided whether or not to speak; then, as though giving articulate form to his suspended ejaculation:

"Gratitude: there's no such thing!"

He shook his head, and went on:

"Would you two gentlemen mind coming with me for a moment?"

"Where?" inquired Mattina.

"To call on Roberto Auriti... such a dear friend of mine... we have been friends, as you know, from our schooldays. And our fathers, before us. The dearest friends; oh! closer than brothers. Comrades in arms, eh? Roberta's father fell at Milazzo; mine at Volturno. They made history. People ought to hear that in mind in the town, instead of making such a fuss about my... what do they call it, again? Desertion, eh?... my desertion. My cassock! Yes, my friends. But beneath the cassock beats a heart; and I too have some regard for the sacred ties of friendship, as well as... as well as..."

The Canon meant to imply "for my country"; he let this be understood by a wave of his hand and stemmed the torrent of his generous sentiments.

He was making an effort to speak in appropriate language, with a subtle smile on his lips, and kept on rubbing his dry, bony hands together under his chin, as though he were washing them at the fountain of his polished phrases, polished indeed, yet not limpid or continuous in their flow, but issuing almost in jerks, with frequent hesitations and odd pauses. From time to time, as he raised his drooping eyelids, he afforded a glimpse of a sidelong, fugitive glance, so different from his usual expression that at once the onlooker imagined that this man must, in his private life, when alone with himself, have more than one profoundly secret affliction, which made him astute and crafty, and that there must he ohscure workings in his mind.

"Before we start," he went on, with a change of tone, "just a word or two of explanation. I may have thought out... put together, shall I say, a little plan of campaign. I don't make it publicly known, of course. You gentlemen will do the fighting; I shall supply the ammunition. That is all. Weighing every consideration carefully, our most formidable adversary is who? Capolino? No; but the man who is behind him: Salvo, who was his brother-in-law, and is a most powerful person. Now I know from a trustworthy source that Salvo, until a few days ago, was absolutely determined not to permit this... this appearance of Capolino upon the scene."

"Quite so," Mattina agreed. "Because of the arrangements for a marriage between his sister and the Prince of Laurentano."

"Precisely!" the Canon endorsed his remark. "But Salvo went the length of promising him his support as soon as he learned that the Prince did not intend to consider Artriti as one of his family, and had ordered the Party not to pay any attention to him either. Things being so, our friend Roberto's chances become almost desperate. Let us not make any mistake about that."

"Oh, I know that!" groaned Veronica.

The Canon at once cut him short with a wave of his hand, and went on:

"But if we, now, let us suppose that we, my friends, in spite of the concession made by the Prince, were to succeed in binding the giant Salvo hand and foot... what about that? Well, that is my plan."

Pompeo Agro, having held out this bait to their curiosity, remained for a while with his hands outstretched in the air beneath his chin; then withdrew and clenched them; he shut his eyes as well, to collect his thoughts; emitted a second "Well!" as a hook to keep his hearers' attention fixed, and relapsed again for a while into silence.

"You gentlemen know the conditions in which the marriage is to be celebrated, by Laurentano's express wish. Now these conditions, as I have planned things, should become the... what shall we say? the chink in Salvo's armour."

"The heel of Achilles," Mattina suggested, his interest quickening.

"Precisely! Yes, Achilles!" Agro agreed. "And now let me explain. It must certainly be an important point with Salvo, he having agreed to these conditions, that the Prince's son, who lives in Borne (I fancy he's called Gerlando, eh? after his grandfather: Gerlandino, Landino), shall not be, or at least shall not shew himself openly opposed to his father's marriage. Indeed, I know that Salvo has definitely insisted upon the young man's being present at the marriage ceremony, as a recognition on his side of the bond and as a pledge of his honour as a gentleman for the future. I am not acquainted with this Gerlandino, but I know that he is made of quite a different stuff... of quite a different type, let us say, from his father."

"The very opposite!" exclaimed Veronica. "I know him well."

"Oh, capital!" Agro went on. "He, therefore, even admitting that he does not see eye to eye with Roberto Auriti either, if he has to choose between the two, I mean between him and a man like Capolino, will naturally prefer, I imagine, that his cousin should win."

Guido Veronica, at this point, sat up and heaved a long sigh, as though to rid himself of a momentary illusion, and said:

"Ah, no, I don't think that, you know! I don't really believe that Lando mixes himself up in that sort of thing...."

"Allow me to speak," the Canon resumed, in a harsher

tone.... "I have no desire that he should be mixed up in it: I wish only to learn from you, who have lived so long in Borne and know the young man, whether the antagonism, if we may so express it, between Don Ippolito Lauren-tano and Donna Caterina Auriti exists between their sons also."

"No, nothing of that sort!" Veronica at once rejoined. "In fact, they are great friends."

"That is enough for me!" the Canon exclaimed, slapping the back of one hand with the palm of the other. "It is more than enough for me! If the father does not intend to take into consideration the fact of Auriti's being related to himself, the son on the other hand may, or easily might. And there we have Salvo, the giant, bound hand and foot!"

Pompeo Agro wished to exult for a moment in this initial victory, and cast a sharp glance, with a slightly disdainful smile, first at Veronica, then at Mattina, who were both of them now pledged to the execution of his plan, which at least was deemed worthy of their consideration. Then, like a general not content with winning his battle upon the table only, by the rules of tactics, he came down to pointing out the material difficulties of the undertaking.

"The point," he said, "will be to persuade that dear fellow Roberto to make use of this expedient. Especially since we shall at least need a private letter from Gerlandino, which we can shew, or communicate in some way to Salvo (do you see?), a letter addressed either to Salvo himself, which will be difficult, or to Roberto or to some other of his friends: to yourself, for instance, my dear Veronica: in short, a proof, a document."

Guido Veronica did not wish to state in so many words that he could not expect to receive a letter from Lando, with whom he was not on any real terms of friendship; he did indeed consider Agro's plan ingenious, but felt it to be impracticable, perhaps, in view of the exaggerated punctiliousness of Roberto, who... who... yes, patriotic services, quite so.... "Spotless integrity!" Agro put in. "Yes," Veronica conceded, "and brains as well, if you like; but... but... as things are at present... the Prefect irritates him, and it seems that his friends irritate him as well. Anyhow, it will be a serious matter! I, for my own part, would gladly let myself be flayed alive to help him; but..."

He broke off; beat his brow with his hand, and exclaimed:

"I have it! Giulio... there's Giulio... Roberto's brother, who at this very moment is one of D'Atri, the Minister's, private secretaries: eh, perbacco! We can write to him... he is on the most intimate terms with Lando. "We can easily get anything we want out of Giulio, without letting anything out to Roberto, who would put all sorts of difficulties in the way. There, that's settled!"

"Splendid! Splendid!" the Canon kept on exclaiming, beside himself with joy.

Only Mattina was left like a vessel whose sail has not succeeded in catching the wind. Seeing the other two vessels skim so smoothly ahead, without a thought of himself left lagging in their wake, he felt crushed; he wanted to express his own opinion, and, having nothing else to say, tried the effect of a breath of contrary wind, and the interposition of a few reefs and shallows.

"Very good," he said, "but won't it be too late, my friends? Let us consider! Before the letter can be delivered in Rome, even if we act with the utmost speed, and the answer arrive here--it will take at least a week, at a moderate estimate. Salvo will have plenty of time to commit himself so deeply that he will not be able to draw back afterwards."

"Oh, I should like to see him!" exclaimed the Canon with a titter, and raised his hand as though greeting the absent Salvo, "No, I say, no! Never, ne-ver, ne-ver.... Do you mean that he is so greatly attached to Capolino?"

"But his dignity, surely!" the Cavaliere retorted, as though his own were at stake. "A fine figure he would cut! Why, don't you know that this very day, in the office of the Empedocle, the selection is to be officially announced, with the support of Salvo and all the committee of the Party? It's no laughing matter."

"In that case," Veronica hurriedly interposed, "to speed matters up, we can send Giulio an urgent telegram at once, in cipher."

"Excellent!" the Canon again expressed his approval, leaving Mattina defeated.

"Yes, yes," Veronica went on, "Roberto has a private code with his brother. Don't let us lose any more time.... Or rather... wait!... now that I think of it... Selmi... perdio!"

"Selmi?" the Canon asked, baffled by the sound of the

name, which fell thus suddenly like an insurmountable obstacle upon the path which he had made so smooth. "The Deputy Selmi?"

"Corrado Selmi, yes," answered Veronica. "I saw him at Palermo.... He has promised Roberto that he'll come here, and indeed that he will make a speech..."

"Well?" came from Agro. "Surely, a Member of Parliament of such authority, a true patriot..."

"That's all very well," Veronica interrupted, screwing up his eyes, and waving his hand in the air. "A patriot, well and good! But he's rotten to the core, my dear Canon. Debts... scandals ... rumours... and God forbid poor Roberto should suffer on his account. That is not the point, however.... It is Lando Laurentano I am thinking of..." And Guido Veronica pulled his fingers until the joints cracked, as though to cleanse them of the annoyance which he felt at the thought of Selmi.

"I don't understand..." observed the Canon. "Do you mean that between Laurentano and Sehni...?"

"I should just say so!" exclaimed Veronica. "A deadly enmity!"

"There's a lady in the case," put in Mattina, gravely, screwing up his eyes, overjoyed at this obstacle.

And the Canon, his curiosity aroused:

"Ah, indeed? A lady?"

"It's an old story," Veronica replied. "It's all over now, as far as I'm aware; but, not more than a year ago, Corrado Selmi--I tell you this because the whole of Borne knows it already--was the lover of Donna Giannetta d'Atri, the wife of the man who is now Minister."

The Canon held up his hand:

"Ugh, how disgraceful! And this... and this Donna Giannetta, who might she have been?"

"Why, a Montalto!" said Veronica. "Lando's cousin.... You know that the Prince's first wife was a Montalto."

"Ah, so that's how it is! And, I suppose, the young man..."

"As a boy, yes, in a cousinly way.... I don't really know much about that. The fact remains that Lando Laurentano challenged Selmi twice. ... And so, you can understand, if Selmi comes here now to support Roberto's candidature..."

"Quite so, quite so... now I understand!" exclaimed the Canon. "He must be stopped! Yes, he must be stopped!"

"It may perhaps not be difficult," Veronica concluded. "Because Corrado Selmi will have his own campaign to fight in his constituency. ... Anyhow, we shall see. Now let us go at once to Roberto."

The Canon rose.

"I am ready," he said. "The carriage is at the door. One moment, if you please. I must just fetch my hat and cloak."

A minute later, Veronica and Mattina saw the old splay-footed servant appear, in the garb of a Jehu, and took their places in the carriage with Agro.

As they came up from the Rabato, by the Piazza San Domenico, they at once noticed an unusual commotion along the main street. Four or five street arabs, running along and stopping at intervals, were bawling the name of the clerical newspaper, *Empedocle*, which they appeared to be selling like hot cakes.

"*L'Impiducli! L'Impiducli!*"

And everywhere groups were forming, some to read, others in an excited discussion of some article, evidently violent, that appeared in the paper. Veronica, seeing one of these vendors pass by the carriage, could not resist the temptation, and while the Canon--who, in the streets of the town, at that time, felt that he was in the midst of an enemy camp--advised: "Better wait till we get home!" he made the hoy fling a copy of the paper into the carriage. It was seized by Mattina.

"Shall I read it to you?"

And he began to read in a low tone the leading article, which was evidently what was arousing such a ferment among the populace.

It was headed *A patriot for family reasons*, and dealt (without mentioning names, but the slanderous intention was unmistakable) with the memory of Stefano Auriti, Roberto's father, distorting with the most odious, vilest calumny the romantic story of his love for Caterina Laurentano; the young couple's elopement shortly before the revolution of 1848; the part played by Stefano Auriti in that revolution "not indeed from love of his country, but for family reasons entirely, that is to say in the hope of acquiring a dowry together with the forgiveness of his involuntary father-in-law, a wealthy man and a Liberal, it is true, but a man, alas, of an inflexibility of character proof against any machination."

Gradually, as he went on reading, Mattina's voice changed to a note of contempt, fired by the indignation of Agro, who broke out from time to time, putting his hands over his ears and flinging himself back in his seat:

"Oh, the cowards! The cowards!"

At a certain stage in his reading Mattina saw the paper torn from his hands. Guido Veronica, white as a sheet, his face distorted with anger, flung open the door of the carriage, quivering with emotion, sprang out and, without heeding the Canon's appeals, first of all hurled himself into a group of people, in the midst of whom was Capo-lino, whom he then struck in the face with the newspaper, rubbing his nose in it.

The assault came as such a thunderbolt that everyone stood for a moment dazed with astonishment, before falling upon the aggressor: people ran up shouting from all sides: in the middle the fight grew furious: sticks whirled in the air, amid shouts and imprecations. Mattina had neither time nor opportunity to fly to Veronica's rescue; but presently the crowd began to dissolve: the protagonists were separated. The Canon shouted frantically from the carriage to Mattina. He heard him at length, and turned; but at that moment caught sight of Veronica, without hat or spectacles, his clothes torn and muddy, panting for breath amid a crowd of young men who were evidently defending him, and ran to join him. He returned, a moment later, to the Canon's carriage.

"It's nothing," he said; "keep calm; let us drive on; he is with friends; he has got well out of it."

The Canon was trembling all over.

"Oh Lord, oh Lord, what a scandal! But why? Disgusting creatures.... He ought not to have dirtied his hands with them.... And what is to happen next?"

"Oh," remarked Mattina with a trace of contempt in his voice, "a duel; it's quite simple ... or a prosecution, if our holy religion does not allow the scoundrel to accept responsibility for the slanders which it has not prevented him from uttering."

"We will leave out religion, if you don't mind, Cavaliere," Pompeo Agro said soothingly. "It has nothing to do with this, nor, if you will allow me to say so, has Capolino."

"How is that?"

"Let me explain. I know who wrote the article, that filthy thing. Preola, Preola who came this morning to see me--I don't know who sent him.... The ungrateful wretch! Dregs of humanity!"

"But Capolino," Mattina objected, "is the editor of the paper and must have passed the article."

"I would swear, I would thrust my hand in the flames," replied the Canon, "that he had not read it first. He is my adversary, look, yet I know him to be incapable of any such vile conduct. ... And now, what are we going to find at Roberto's?"

THE BITTER TONGUE.

Donna Caterina Auriti-Laurentano lived with her daughter Anna, also a widow, and her grandson, in an old and sombre house beneath the Badia Grande.

The house had belonged to Michele Del Re, Anna's husband, who had had nothing else to bequeath to his youthful widow and to their only son, Antonio, now about eighteen years old.

You went up to it by narrow, slippery lanes, broken up into steps, unevenly cobbled, often heaped with filth, reeking with the medley of foul smells that issued from the little shops, dark as caves, shops mostly of the spinners of maccheroni, which they hung outside to dry on poles and trestles, and from the hovels of the pauper women who spent whole days sitting on their doorsteps, days that were all alike, seeing the same people at the same hours, hearing the usual disputes bandied about from door to door by two or more shrill-tongued gossips over their brats, one of whom, as they played together, had had his hair torn out or his scalp cut open. The sole variety, now and again, was the passing of the Blessed Sacrament; the priest beneath the canopy, the tinkling bell, the choir of godly women:

Oggi e sempre sia lodato nostro. Dio sacramentato. ...

Her husband having died after barely three years of married life, Anna Auriti herself was virtually dead to the world. Indeed, since the day of her bereavement, she had never left the house again, not even to hear mass on Sundays; she had never shewn her face in public, not even through the panes of the windows that were never fully opened. Only the nuns at the Badia Grande, peering through the bars of their own windows, had caught glimpses of her from above, when she came out, towards dusk, for a breath of air in the narrow little terraced garden of the house, which rested against the dark, towering bulk of their abbey, originally the baronial stronghold of the Chiaramente. Nor indeed could those nuns have felt any envy of a woman as strictly cloistered as themselves. Like them, if not with even greater simplicity, she dressed in black, always; like them, she concealed beneath a black silk kerchief, fastened under her chin, the hair which, if it was not cropped close, was no longer tended with any care, being merely parted in two strands and twisted in a loose knot at the back of her head; those beautiful, abundant chestnut tresses which at one time, carefully arranged, had given such charm to her pale, gentle, sweet face.

Donna Caterina had scrupulously shared her daughter's seclusion, and had worn black also, ever since 1860, the date of her husband's heroic death at Milazzo. Of tall stature, rigid, thin, she had not however her daughter's air of calm and sorrowful resignation. The terrible griefs that had been her constant portion, the gnawing tooth of pride, the firmness of character which, at the cost of incredible sacrifices, she had unflinchingly maintained when faced with the most cruel vicissitudes of fortune, had so altered the lineaments of her face that it no longer preserved any trace of her former beauty. Her nose had grown long and pointed and overhung her withered lips, hollowed here and there where she had lost a tooth; her cheeks were sunken; her chin thrust forwards. But it was her eyes more than anything else, beneath her bushy black brows, that showed the ruin of her face: the eyelids had begun to droop, one more than the other; and the eye that was the more nearly hidden of the two, with its slow glance misty with intense suffering, gave to her spent, waxen face the aspect of some horrible mask of grief. Her hair, meanwhile, had remained black and glossy, as though on purpose to bring into prominence the mutilation of her other features and to contradict the popular belief that the hair turns white with sorrow.

There was nothing, literally nothing that Donna Caterina Laurentano had not endured, including the pangs of hunger, she who had been born in luxury, brought up amid the splendours of a princely house: hunger when, after the revolution of 1848 had been crushed, a girl of eighteen, with her infant son Roberto, she had had to go into exile in Piedmont with her husband, excluded with

forty-three others from the amnesty, and sentenced to the forfei-
ture of his modest fortune. Her father, Don Gerlando Laurentano,
who also was among the forty-three prescripts, had invited her at
the time to go with him to Malta, his place of banishment, but on
the condition that she would definitely abandon Stefano Auriti.
And she? She had refused the offer with scorn; and more scornfully still had afterwards refused the charity of her brother Ippolito,
who with a few other unworthy representatives of the Sicilian nobility had gone to do homage to Satriano at Palermo, and had
obtained from him the restitution of the property confiscated from
his father. And she had gone to Turin with her husband, like a pair
of blind and helpless waifs, to beg the bread of life for their child.

None of the other exiles, of the Sicilians who had migrated
there, would believe at first that she, a woman of such exalted
birth, the only daughter of the Prince of Laurentano, had brought
nothing away with her, was receiving no support from her family;
and Stefano Auriti had accordingly been hindered in every possible
way by his own companions in misfortune in his desperate search
for some minor employment that would provide him with bread,
mere bread alone for his wife and himself. And then she had fallen
seriously ill, and for five months had lain in hospital, through charitable intervention, after endless sufferings, and by charitable
intervention the little Roberto had been brought up in another institution. At length and with due compunction their fellow-exiles
had revised their judgment, and vied with one another in helping
Stefano Auriti. On coming out of hospital she had received the
news that her father, Don Gerlando Laurentano, had died by his
own hand at Burmula, by poison.

Of the twelve years spent at Turin, ending in 1860, Donna
Caterina retained now only a vague, confused memory, as of a life
that she had not actually lived but had rather imagined in some
strange and violent dream, interspersed at the same time with
bright glimpses, certain joyous, ardent moments of patriotic enthusiasm.

Ineradicably stamped upon her heart, however, was the
hour of her awakening from that dream: when the news came to
her that Stefano Auriti, who had set sail with his twelve-year-old
son from Quarto, with Garibaldi, for the liberation of Sicily, had

fallen in battle at Milazzo.

Even the favour of letting her go mad had God withheld from her at that moment! And she had been obliged to feel, almost to behold her wifely heart (stricken, dealt its deathblow out there in Sicily) crawl bleeding in the footsteps of her young son, left now without a father's protection to carry on the war.

They had collected a fund for her at Turin, and with the two little orphans, Giulio and Anna, who had been born there, she had returned to Sicily, her now liberated fatherland; but as a widow, in deep mourning, and more wretched than when she had left home: amid the universal rejoicing, she, with her two little ones, dressed likewise in black. Roberto had before this entered Naples with Garibaldi, and was now fighting beneath the walls of Caserta, side by side with Mauro Mortara.

She had been taken into the house of the Alaimo, poor relatives of Stefano Auriti. Once again her brother Ippolito, now in retreat at Colimbetra, had offered to assist her; and once again, with undi-minished scorn, she had refused his offer, to the amazement and consternation of the Alaimo family, whose guest she was. Poor people, poor in intellect and in heart as well as in purse, what bitterness of spirit they had caused her! She had been obliged to see herself regarded by them as by the bitterest enemies of her dignity, which they did not understand; thoroughly capable as they were of begging and accepting in secret the assistance that she had declined, not content with the work which she performed in the house and what she managed to procure from outside to enable her to earn a fair recompense for the trifling expense that she caused them.

She had raised her head a little from that horrible degradation on the return of Roberto, welcomed by the whole town in a frenzy of joy. Even now, when she recalled that day, that moment, a thrill would run through her poor flesh. Ah, with what exultation, with what a frenzy of love and grief she had clasped to her bosom the son who returned alone, without his father, the youthful hero of the Bed Shirt, whom the populace had borne to her shoulder-high in triumph.

The Provisional Government had granted her a monthly allowance, and to Roberto--since at his age nothing else could be done for him--a scholarship at Palermo. He had forfeited this scholarship a few years later, to follow Garibaldi to the conquest of Rome. But against the torrent of young blood which was to have replenished the dried veins of Rome reasons of state had set up, at Aspromonte, a dyke of fraternal bosoms; and Roberto, with the rest, had been taken prisoner and confined first at Spezia, then in the Forte Monteratti at Genoa. Regaining his freedom, he had returned to his books, but not for long. In 1866 he was once more following Garibaldi. Only in 1871 had he succeeded in taking his degree in Law; and at once had gone to Rome to provide, after all these tumultuous changes of fortune, for his own needs and for those of his family. Some years later, he had been joined by his brother Giulio. Anna, at Girgenti, had meanwhile found a husband, and Donna Caterina--until Roberto in Rome with the flame of his heroic spirit, with his own exceptional claims to recognition and his exceptional talents, should have forged ahead and paved the way to a splendid future, worthy of his past, and consoled her at length for all the bitter hardships she had suffered and for the degradation which had been the bitterest of all--had gone to live in the house of her son-in-law Michele Del Re.

His death, three years later, her daughter's bereavement, the poverty that once again fell upon them, seemed powerless to arouse her from a deeper and more intense sorrow into which she had sunk. Her son, that son of whom such great things were expected, her Roberto, up yonder, amid the turmoil and confusion of the new life of the Third Capital, amid the obscene babel of all the people who were tumbling over one another, clamouring for rewards, picking up honours and favours, her Roberto was lost! Regarding all that he had done for his country as nothing more than a sacred duty, he had never sought nor would he have known how to establish any claim to a reward; he had perhaps hoped, perhaps waited for his friends and comrades to remember him in his modest dignity. Perhaps also his finer feelings had conquered him and had kept him aloof. And what utter ruin had come in Sicily to all the illusions, all the fervid faith, by which the torch of revolt had been kindled! Poor island, treated as conquered territory! Poor islanders, treated as savages, who must first be civilized. And the *Continentals* had descended upon them to civilize them:

down had come the new soldiery, that infamous column led by a renegade, the Hungarian Colonel Eberhardt, who had come to Sicily first with Garibaldi and had then been one of those who fired upon him at Aspromonte, and that other, the little Savoyard subaltern Dupuy, the incendiary; down had come all the offscourings of the bureaucracy; and disputes and duels and scenes of savagery; and the Prefecture of Medici, and the courts martial, and burglaries, murders, highway robberies, planned and carried out by the new police in the name of the King's Government; and falsification and suppression of documents and scandalous political trials: all through the first government by the parliamentary Eight! And then the Left had come into power, and they too had begun with special measures for Sicily; and usurpations and frauds and extortions and scandalous favouritism and a scandalous waste of public money; prefects, delegates, magistrates pledged to the service of the ministerial Deputies, and shameless partisanships and electoral intrigues; an unfair distribution of taxation, reckless expenditure, degrading servilities; oppression of the conquered and of the workers, assisted and protected by the law, with impunity guaranteed to the oppressors....

For the last day or two--ever since Roberto's arrival at Girgenti--had been streaming from the bitter tongue of Donna Caterina Auriti this vehement flood of cruel memories, harsh reproaches, fierce accusations. As she looked at her son, from beneath her drooping eyelids, with that almost sightless eye, she emptied her heart of all the bitterness accumulated and stored up in all those long years; of all the grief with which she had fed and envenomed her heart.

"What do you hope for? What do you want?" she asked him. "What have you come here to do?"

And Roberto Auriti, overpowered by this onslaught from his mother, remained frowningly silent, with bent head and shut eyes.

He was now a man of three and forty: already bald, but vigorous, with a herculean chest, handsome in a manly way, his face sharply defined by his thick black eyebrows, that almost met above his nose, and by a short beard, black also, he sat there steeped in shame and confusion, like a feeble little boy in the presence of this mother who, albeit crushed by age and sorrow, retained so much strength of character and such ardent spirits.

He felt that he really was defeated, did Roberto Auriti. His strength of character, overstrained by the heroic efforts of his boyhood, had gradually declined when brought face to face with the new, hideous warfare, a fight for gold, a fight for the base conquest of office. And he had even asked for preferment himself, not for himself, for his brother Giulio, and had secured a berth for him in the Treasury. For himself he had relied upon the scanty, uncertain profits of the legal profession: profits which, for all that, left him often by no means at rest in his mind, not because he did not regard them as a fair reward for his work, for the zeal he shewed; but because the majority of his briefs came to him by way of his friends the Sicilian Deputies, from Corrado Selmi especially, and in more than one instance he had the suspicion that his case had been won not so much by his own talents as by their improper and by no means disinterested intervention. But he, since the death of his brother-in-law Michele Del Re, had his mother and widowed sister and nephew to support at Girgenti; apart from the fact that in Rome, for some years past, he had no longer lived alone.

His mother of course was not unaware that he was living in Rome with a woman, for whom with her old-fashioned prejudices and the puritanical strictness of her morals she could not feel any respect; she had never uttered a word to him about this; but he could feel the harsh condemnation in the maternal heart, a fresh bitterness--unjustified, to his mind--which his mother refrained from expressing to him in order not to humiliate him, not to wound him further.

But perhaps Donna Caterina, at such moments as this, did not give the matter a thought, wholly absorbed as she was in setting before her son, with an inexhaustible ardour, the painful memories of their family and the wretched condition of the place.

And it was during this fervid, black description that they were surprised by Canon Pompeo Agro and Mattina.

THINGS WERE BETTER IN THE OLD DAYS!

The warm cordiality with which Roberto Auriti welcomed him made it plain to Agro that the other knew nothing as yet of that vile article in the newspaper. He introduced Mattina, and paid his respects to his hostess.

Donna Caterina waited for the preliminary exchange of greetings and for the friends to express their joy at meeting again after so many years; then resumed, turning to Agro:

"For goodness' sake, Monsignore, do you, who are a true friend to him, tell him so too. We are all friends here. This gentleman too, since you have brought him to the house, must be a friend. I am trying to persuade my son not to undertake this campaign."

"Mamma," Roberto besought her, with a pained smile.

"Yes, yes," his mother insisted. "Do you gentlemen tell him. What has he done, and why, in the name of what cause does he come here to-day to ask for the votes of the people? In the name perhaps of all that he did as a boy, in the name of his dead father, in the name of the sacrifices and of the sacred ideals for which those sacrifices were made and that agony endured? Why, he will make people laugh at him!"

"Oh, no, Donna Caterina, but why?" Canon Agro tried to interrupt her, laying his hand on his heart, as though wounded. "Don't say that."

"Laugh at him! Laugh at him!" she went on with increasing warmth. "Perhaps you will kindly tell us, then, how those ideals have been converted to reality for the people of Sicily? What have they gained by them? How have they been treated? Oppressed, taxed, neglected, slandered! The ideals of Forty-eight and Sixty? Why, all the old people here cry: *Things were better in the old days!* And I say the same, do you hear? I, Caterina Laurentano, Stefano Auriti's widow!"

"Oh, Mamma, Mamma!" Roberto implored,' putting his hands over his ears.

To which his mother at once rejoined:

"Yes, my son: things were better in the old days, because then at least we had the hope and comfort of a better future, the hope that sustained us and made us overcome all the tribulations you may or may not remember, at Turin. ... Things were better then! You may be sure that people do not wish to hear anything more about those ideals. They paid too high a price for them, and now they have had enough! Away with you, get back to Rome. Because I will not, I cannot endure your coming here in the name of the Government that is over us. You have not been a thief, my son; you have not lent your hand to all the injustices, to the vilenesses of the unfair, one-sided administration of our communes, bound hand and foot for years past to the local cliques, which abuse them in every way under the protection of the Prefects and Deputies; you have not supported the infamous power of the gangs who are poisoning the air of our towns, as the malaria poisons our countryside! Why, then, are you here? What claim have you to be elected? Who is supporting you? Who wants you?"

At this moment Guido Veronica entered the room, clothed and in his right mind. He had gone up to the hotel, after the scuffle, to change his clothes, and had left word there that if anyone should come in search of him, he would be back by three o'clock. At once Agro and Mattina signalled to him that Roberto knew nothing of what had happened. Donna Caterina had risen to her feet to urge lier son to decline the support of the Government, which for that matter would be valueless in the coming contest, and to accept the challenge rather in the name of the oppressed populace. He would not win, of course; but at least his defeat would not be dishonouring, and would serve as a warning to the Government.

"For you will see," she concluded. "I make a safe prophecy:

before a year has passed, we shall witness scenes of bloodshed: the people can endure no more and are making their preparations, and before long they will rise in revolt."

Guido Veronica thrust out his plump hands before him, and shook his head:

"For heaven's sake, dear lady, for heaven's sake do not say such things; they sound horrible on your lips! Leave them to the instigators, to the demagogues who, without meaning it, are playing the Clericals' game! Forgive me, Canon; but that is just what is happening! A handful of ambitious rascals, who sow the seeds of discord to force their way into the municipal and provincial councils and into Parliament itself; another handful of ignoble enemies of their country who dream of a separate Sicily under British protection, like Malta! And then there is France, our beloved Latin sister, blowing on the embers and sending money to-day in the hope of reaping her reward to-morrow by some insane, hole-and-corner rebellion inspired by the Mafia!"

"Indeed?" broke out Donna Caterina, who could no longer restrain herself. "So you reassure yourself like that, do you? But these are calumnies, the same old calumnies that our Ministers repeat, echoing the Prefects and the petty tyrants of the local committees; calumnies meant to cloak thirty years and more of bad government; calumnies not so much odious, perhaps, as ludicrous! Here we have famine, my dear sir, on the farms and in the sulphur pits; here we have big estates, the feudal tyranny of the so-called *cappelli*, the so-called gentry, municipal taxes that squeeze the last drop of blood from people who have not so much as the price of a crust of bread; here we have all the extortions that can be made with impunity, by taking advantage of the appalling ignorance of these poor serfs, bestialized by their poverty. Do you hold your peace! Hold your peace!"

Guido Veronica gave a nervous smile, bowing and extending his arms; then turned to Roberto:

"Oh, by the way--excuse me, Signora!--I want to borrow your cipher-book, to send an urgent telegram to Rome."

"Of course, yes, good, good!" exclaimed Canon Agro, rousing himself from the pained attitude he had assumed during Donna Caterina's violent harangue.

Roberto left the room to fetch the cipher-book. The conversation between the three friends and the old lady died away; then Agro, to break an awkward silence, groaned:

"Ah, the conditions of life in our poor country are certainly sad indeed!"

And the conversation revived for a little, but without warmth. The three men had a secret understanding among themselves, and were also angry and appalled by the scandal of the newspaper article: they exchanged significant glances, and would have liked to be left to themselves for a moment to discuss the best way of breaking the news to Roberto. But Donna Caterina did not leave the room.

"Do you know whether Corrado Selmi," Guido Veronica asked her, "has written to Roberto that he's coming?"

"He's coming, he's coming," she replied, shaking her head with bitter scorn.

"I have been thinking," Veronica murmured to Agro and Mattina. "All the better if he does come. Indeed, I shall send him a telegram asking him to come at once, for me, you understand. In that way, Lando.... Hush, here's Roberto."

But it was not Roberto: there entered the room instead a tall, thin youth, to whom the glasses perched on the bridge of his nose, uniting his bushy eyebrows, gave an air of grim and rigid tenacity. It was Antonio Del Re, the nephew. Always extremely pale, his face at that moment seemed to be made of wax. "Have you seen the *Empedocle?*" he asked, with quivering lips and nostrils.

Canon Agro and Mattina quickly raised their hands to prevent him from saying more.

"Attacking Roberto?" asked Donna Caterina.

"Attacking grandfather!" the boy replied, quivering. "A handful of mud! And attacking you!"

"Filth! Filth!" exclaimed Agro. "For heaven's sake, don't let poor Roberto hear about it!"

"He's reading it now," said his nephew, scornfully.

"No! No!" cried Agro, springing to his feet. "Oh, Lord in heaven, we ought to have warned him! The scoundrels have already had the lesson they deserved from our friend Veronica. For heaven's sake, go to him, Donna Caterina.... Rashness, rashness, my boy!"

84

Donna Caterina hurried from the room; but it was too late. Roberto Auriti, unaware of what Veronica had just done, had dashed off--pale as death, his face contorted in a spasmodic smile, groping like a blind man--to the office of the newspaper, by Porta Atenea. He had there found the committee of the Party assembled, with Flaminio Salvo at their head, to proclaim, immediately after the assault upon him, the candidature of Ignazio Capolino. To the old porter, who stood on guard in the waiting room, outside the glass door of the editor's office, he had said--still with the same strange smile--that Roberto Auriti wished to speak to the editor. Inside the office a sudden silence had fallen; then the following excited words came to his ears:

"No, gentlemen! Let me go, it is my affair; I wrote the article, and I will answer for it!"

He had not even seen who it was that came to meet him: he had flung himself upon the man like a wild beast, had lifted him bodily in the air and hurled him with such force against the door as to burst it open, with a great crash of shattered glass.

When Veronica, Mattina, and his nephew Del Re came dashing upon the scene, amid the crowd of people that had rushed in from all parts of the building at the shouts that rose from the editor's room, Marco Preola, his face streaming with blood and a knife in his hand, was struggling frantically, shouting:

"Leave me alone, curse you, leave me alone! If you let him go now, I shall kill him next time! Leave me alone! Leave me alone!"

CHAPTER IV

GELLIAS ALONE STANDS FIRM

Inside the entrance hall, among the palms and laurels, with the coloured glass panes of the front door as a background, the precious headless statue of Venus Urania, dug up at Colimbetra from the ground on which the sumptuous villa now stood, seemed as though it were not for shame at her own nakedness that she held her arm upraised to cover the ideal face, which everyone who paused to admire her at once imagined, bent slightly forward, as though it were actually there; but in order that she might not see kneeling before her, outside the door of the chapel which opened on the right, all those men so strangely attired: Captain Sciaralla's Bourbon company.

Mass was just coming to an end. Inside the chapel, that gleamed with marbles and stucco, were only the Prince, Don Ippolito, bowed in prayer on his gilded and damask-covered faldstool before the altar; behind him, Lisi Preola, his secretary; behind him again, the women of the household: the housekeeper and two young maids. The male servants must be content with hearing mass from the hall; only Liborio, the Prince's favoured butler, in kneebreeches and silk stockings, was allowed to take his place on the threshold of the chapel, more inside than out; and this concession seemed to Sciaralla an act of sheer injustice on Preola's part.

In his capacity as Captain, he felt that he deserved a seat at least by the side of Preola himself, if not immediately next to the Prince.

Openly, no; he did not complain openly; prudence forbade; but it caused him acute annoyance. And he had confessed this as a sin of envy to Don Lagaipa, who came to Colimbetra every Sunday to say mass.

"In the sight of God at least we ought all to be equal, surely!"

All, except the Prince; that went without saying.

But was not he, Sciaralla, complaining because he wished to be favoured, brought forward, distinguished from his subordinates, in the sight of God? It wore the horns, then, the horns and hoofs of the devil, this secret desire of his, which at first sight seemed reasonable enough.

So Don Illuminato Lagaipa had stopped Sciaralla's mouth.

And Sciaralla heaved a deep sigh.

A real temptation of the devil, meanwhile, was that naked statue, standing in front of the chapel there, to all the men of the bodyguard who were obliged to remain outside. While their lips repeated the prayers, their eyes strayed towards it, and... certain heating passions! His Excellency the Prince, such a religious man as he was, ought never to have left that naked figure exposed to view. Oh dreadful! It seemed to be alive, it seemed.... The poor maidservants lowered their eyes whenever they passed by it; even Don Illuminato lowered his, the old hypocrite!

Meanwhile the marvellous form of the headless goddess smiled and bloomed, emerging from a gulf in time, begotten of a Grecian chisel, of a craftsman unconscious that his handiwork was to survive for so long and to speak to a profane race in a diabolical tongue, there at Colimbetra, the ornament now of an entrance hall, amid tubs of laurels and palms.

Mass at an end, the men of the bodyguard stood at attention on either side of the doorway, for the passage of the Prince, who made his way to the Museum.

This was the name given to the ground-floor rooms on the other side of the hall, where, among tall hothouse plants, was displayed the collection, of antiquities, of priceless value: statues, sarcophagi, vases, inscriptions, dug up at Colimbetra, which Don Ippolito had described many years before in his *Memorie d'Akragas*, together with the precious cabinet of medals to be seen upstairs, in the drawing-room of the villa.

The famous Akragantine Colimbetra of antiquity was actually much farther down, at the lowest point of the plain, where three valleys meet and the rocks divide and the line of the rugged brow, upon which the Temples stand, is broken by a wide gap. At this spot, now known as the Abbadia Bassa, the Akragantines, a century after the foundation of their city, had formed their fish-pond, a great basin of water extending to the Hypsas, its bank combining with the river to form part of the fortifications of the city.

Colimbetra had been the name given by Don Ippolito to his property because he too, up above at its western extremity, had formed a basin of water, fed in winter by the torrent that ran below Bonamorone and in summer by a lady, the creaking wheel of which was turned from morning to night by a blind mare. All round this basin was a delicious grove of oranges and pomegranates.

In the Museum Don Ippolito was in the habit of spending the whole morning intent upon his impassioned and uninterrupted study of Akragantine antiquities. He was at present engaged in tracing, in a fresh volume, the historical topography of the primitive city, with the help of long and minute investigations on the spot, since his modern Colimbetra covered the precise ground that had once been the heart of the Greek Akragas.

Beside one of the broad windows of the inner room, hung with light pink curtains, stood the massive inlaid writing table; but Don Ippolito composed as a rule mentally, as he wandered through the rooms; he would construct in the old manner two or three periods big with *laonde* and *conciossiache*, and would then go and commit them to writing on the great sheets that lay ready upon the table, often without bothering to sit down. With one hand on his chin, clasping his lordly beard, which still preserved the last traces, a faint suggestion of its original golden hue, the Prince, tall, vigorous, still extremely handsome, notwithstanding his age and his baldness, would pause before one or other of his relics, and gaze at it as though his clear blue eyes, beneath their contracted brows, were intent on the deciphering of some inscription or of the symbolical figures upon some archaic vase. At times he would wave his hand, or part his perfectly shaped lips, red with a youthful freshness, in a faint smile of satisfaction, if he thought that he had found a decisive, triumphant argument with which to defeat his topographical predecessors.

On his desk that morning a volume of the *Histories* of Polybius, in the Greek text, lay open at Book IX, Chapter 27, at the page where reference is made to the Akragantine Acropolis.

A most serious problem had been distracting Don Ippolito for some months past, with regard to the site of this Acropolis.

"Am I disturbing you?" inquired, bowing on the threshold of this inner room, Don Illuminato Lagaipa, who had meanwhile removed his sacred vestments and partaken of his usual breakfast of chocolate and biscuits.

He was a short, thickset priest, stunted in body but far from stunted in mind, with a swarthy, sunburned face in which the blue eyes, too pale for his complexion, seemed to wander helplessly. A good man, at bottom, peace-loving and no bigot; here, in the presence of the Prince, who made him stay to dinner every Sunday, he assumed, to gratify his host, an air of rigid and bellicose intransigence, at which he would afterwards laugh, discussing things philosophically with his old and faithful Fifa, the meek ass which carried him back to his bit of glebe by the graveyard of Bonamorone, a few acres of land which--even if they were conscious of the rapid passage of life--nevertheless, under this King or that, yielded their harvest year in year out, and registered the effects of rain and sunshine, ignorant of political and social changes.

"It is Sunday to-day, and we must abstain from work," he added, holding up his hand with a smile.

"It is not real work, that I do," Don Ippolito told him with a modest, graceful gesture. "No, of course not! *Otia, otia*, according to Cicero!" Don Lagaipa corrected himself. "You are right. I looked in to tell you that yesterday morning, before I went off to my glebe, Monsignore did me the honour of charging me with a message to Your Excellency."

"Monsignor Montoro?"

"Yes. He told me to warn Your Excellency that to-day, this afternoon, God willing, he is coming here, to talk, I suppose, about the coming election. Eh," he sighed, interlacing his fingers and waving his locked hands. "It seems the old enemy feels his horns smarting.... War, war ... tempest! I hear that a couple of very queer fish have arrived from Palermo, at the invitation, they say, of Canon Agro... yes, two who are well-known as bottle washers to the heads of the mafia... yes, of the infamous band of masons ... one Mattina and one Veronica...."

"Agro?" came grimly from Don Ippolito Lau-rentano, whose attention had been caught by the name and ignored the rest of the speech. "Then Agro does really intend to step down into the arena, with no sense of decency, no respect even for the cloth he wears?"

"Ah!" Don Lagaipa again sighed. "He is my superior... superior... but I am only repeating what is said... *relata refero*... he cannot get over, they say, his not having been made Bishop instead of our Most Excellent Monsignor Montero. He thinks he is saving his face with .. with the plea of the old ties of friendship that bind him to Auriti...."

"A fine friendship to boast of!" growled Lau-rentano. "For a priest!"

"But Agro..." Don Illuminato began. He shut his eyes, shook his head, emitted a third sigh: "Ah, it is a complicated business... yes, I tell you... it is becoming very delicate. ...."

"For me?" cried Don Ippolito, springing to his feet (and his polished scalp reddened). "Delicate for me? I would have Monsignor Montoro know... he should know it already; I do not own and I have never owned this Garibaldesco, Roberto Auriti, as my nephew. I do not even know him by sight: he has never been here, nor would I for that matter have allowed him to cross my threshold. And so, under orders from his Government, with no invitation from the people, he is coming here, is he, with the mad hope of taking Giacinto Fazello's place? Very good. He shall have what he deserves. Without paying any consideration to my unfortunate and in-vo-lun-ta-ry kinship, let us fight and win!"

"Ah, fight, fight, yes indeed! We shall have to fight!" said Don Illuminato, knitting his brows fiercely over his pale, watery eyes. "Even if we are fated not to win...."

"And why not?" asked Don Ippolito sternly. "What possible chance can Auriti have of winning? What does Agro matter?"

"But... people say... the Prefecture..." and Don Illuminato scratched his bristling jowl.

"It has no hold!" the Prince at once retorted. "We saw that

at the last municipal election."

"Quite so, quite so..." Don Lagaipa agreed. "Still... with the mafia taking the field, now ... the police befriending him... all the evil arts... they say... and now there's a man coming... I don't know his name, a bigwig ... a Deputy... Selmi, I think I heard some one say..."

Don Ippolito remained silent for a while, an expression of disgust on his face; then, shaking his fist, broke out:

"Filangieri! Filangieri!"

Lagaipa shook his head with a groan at this invocation, which fell frequently from the Prince's lips and was always accompanied by this gesture of furious rage.

"Filangieri!"

He knew with what veneration Don Ippolito Laurentano still cherished the memory of Satriano, the blessed represser of the Sicilian. Revolution of 1848, the far-seeing, energetic restorer of law and order after the sixteen months of the *obscene revolutionary bonfire*. The horror of those sixteen months had remained vividly in the Prince's mind, especially the brutal assaults of the populace upon hereditary privileges and religious belief. Satriano had been to him as the sun in his splendour, triumphant over that subversive storm; and like a sun, when the clouds had passed, he had blazed in the Sicilian sky from the Norman palace in Palermo, thrown open in a series of brilliant entertainments to surround his authority with a Napoleonic prestige. There, in the palace, Don Ippolito had met Donna Teresa Montalto, then a young girl, whom Satriano had afterwards condescended to give away in person at her marriage, taking great pains to secure from the King, for him, the bridegroom, the Order of San Gennaro, which his father had worn before him. The storm had broken once more in 1860: from his retreat at Colimbetra he could hear the distant rumble: from there he fought with all his might, within the small circuit of his native town: the Bourbon cause was for the moment lost; they must fight next to secure the triumph of the ecclesiastical power; Rome once restored to the Pope, anything might happen! In the meantime, they must at all costs prevent Giacinto Fazello's seat in Parliament from being usurped by Roberto Auriti.

"Besides," he went on, "Auriti has lost any standing he may

ever have had in the place. He has not been here for the last twenty years."

"Still, friendship, you know..." Lagaipa gently opposed, "he may have some friends here still..."

"Friendship counts for nothing in these days," Don Ippolito replied curtly. "Weighed against material interests, it is nothing!"

So saying, he took from the table the volume of Polybius, which was lying open, and instinctively raised it to his eyes. At once they turned to the passage which he had read and worried over so often, the *crux* about that wretched Acropolis. He lost interest in the conversation; read the passage through once again, his mind again filled with the controversy that was disturbing him; sighed; shut the book, keeping his forefinger between the pages, and, placing it behind his back, said:

"In fact, Don Illuminato, we have got to win! I, myself, look, have at this moment up against me an army of erudite Germans; topographers; historians ancient and modern, of all nations; popular tradition; yet I do not call myself beaten. The field of battle is here. Here I await them!"

He showed him the book, tapping the page with his knuckles, and went on:

"How would you translate the words: kat' autas tas therhinas anatolas?"

Under the shock of this fourfold "ass" which fell upon him like four sudden blows, poor Don Illuminato Lagaipa almost reeled. He felt that he had not deserved such treatment. Don Ippolito smiled; then, slipping his arm through the other's, went on:

"Come with me. I shall explain to you in a couple of words what I mean."

They went out upon the vast lawn in front of the villa; walked some way to the right of it; then, turning round, the Prince pointed out to the priest the wide stretch of land that rose behind the villa in a precipitous ascent, crowned at its summit by an isolated mound, iron-red, a hillock completely escarped all round.

"That, now, is the Akrean hill," he began. "The thing on the top, our famous Rupe Atenea. Very good. Polybius says: *The high part* (the citadel, the so-called Acropolis, in fact) *overhangs the city* (observe) *in the direction of the sunrise in summer.* And will you kindly tell me where the sun rises in summer? Perhaps from behind the hill on which Girgenti stands? No! It rises over there, from the Rupe. And so it was up there, if anywhere, that the Acropolis stood, and not upon the site of the modern Girgenti, as these German Doctors try to make out. I shall prove it... I shall prove it! Let them put Camicus up there... Cocale's palace... Omphax... anything they like... but not the Acropolis."

And with a wave of his hand he swept aside Girgenti, which appeared for a moment, standing up to the left of the Rock, and lower down. "There," he went on, pointing again to the Rupe Atenea and gathering inspiration, "there, to yonder sublime watchtower and sanctuary only, not an acropolis, not an acropolis, a shrine of the patron deities, Gellias climbed, quivering with rage and scorn, to the temple of the Goddess Athena, dedicated also to Zeus Atabirius, and set fire to it to save it from profanation. After a siege of eight months, reduced by famine, the Akragantines, in terror of death, abandon the aged, the children and the infirm and flee, protected by the Syracusan Daphneus, by the Gela gate. The eight hundred Campanians have withdrawn from the hill; the vile Desippus has sought a place of safety; any further resistance is useless. Gellias alone stands firm! He hopes by faith to preserve his life, and retires to the sanctuary of Athena. Its walls dismantled, its marvellous buildings in ruins, the whole city is burning here below; and he from above, gazing down at the vast and awful holocaust which raises a funeral pall of flame and smoke between land and sea, elects to perish in the fire of the Goddess."

"A stupendous description, stupendous!" exclaimed Lagaipa, his eyes starting from his head.

Below them, on the second of the three broad flowering terraces that led down to the villa like three steps of a giant staircase, Placido Sciaralla and Lisi Preola, leaning upon the marble balustrade, had broken off their conversation and now stood nodding their heads, marvelling like the priest at the fire of the Prince's utterance, albeit at that distance they had not caught a single word.

Don Ippolito Laurentano, still carried away by excitement, stood gazing with his deep blue eyes at the magnificent panorama. Where he had just been picturing the terrible fire and destruction, there reigned now the unconscious peace of the countryside; where had been the heart of the ancient city rose now a grove of almond trees and olives, the grove which for that reason still bore the name *della Civita*. The almond boughs had begun to shed their leaves, with the approach of autumn, and, among the perennial boughs of the ashen-grey olives, seemed almost ethereal, assumed a tint of roseate gold in the sunlight.

Beyond the grove, on the long brow of the hill, rose the remains of the famous temples, which seemed to have been set there on purpose, on the skyline, to enhance the marvellous view from the princely villa. Beyond the brow, the table-land, on which the ancient city had stood in its splendour and might, fell in a sheer and rocky precipice to the plain of San Gregorio, formed by the alluvial deposits of the Akragas: a calm, luminous plain, stretching out until it ended, far away, in the sea.

"I cannot abide these Teutons," said the Prince, as he returned with Don Illuminato Lagaipa to the Museum, "these Teutons who, being impotent now in the use of arms, invade us with their books and come and talk nonsense in our country, where so much nonsense is being talked and done already."

At this moment they heard the rumble of a carriage upon the sunken road behind the villa, and Don Ippolito knitted his brows. A moment later Liborio, the butler, entered the room, confused, speechless with surprise.

"Pa-pardon me, Your Excellency," he stammered. "The... the Signora has arrived from Girgenti."

"What Signora?" inquired the Prince.

"Your sister... Donna Caterina."

Don Ippolito stood motionless for a moment as though stunned by a sudden blow on the head. His nostrils twitched, he turned pale. Then, all of a sudden, the blood surged to his head. He shut his eyes, again grew pale, knitted his brows, clenched his fists, and, with his heart hammering against his ribs, asked:

"Here? Where is she?"

"Upstairs, Excellency, in the drawing-room," Liborio replied; and, after a pause, seeing that the Prince was still perplexed, inquired:

"Have I done wrong?"

Don Ippolito gazed at him for some time, as though he

had not heard; then said:

"No...." And he left the room, without so much as a glance at Lagaipa. His mind in a turmoil, he was trying to think of some possible explanation of this extraordinary visit, unwilling, incapable of admitting the explanation that had first flashed across his mind, to wit that his sister, she who in one misfortune after another had invariably refused with obstinate pride, nay with contempt, every offer of assistance, had now come to intercede on behalf of her son Roberto. But what else could she require of him?

THE TRAGIC PHANTOM.

When he had climbed the stairs, he was so burdened by anxiety, a prey to so stifling an agitation, that he was obliged to stop for a moment on the threshold. Should he go in? Present himself to her in that state? No. He must regain his composure first. And he stole off on tiptoe to his bedroom. There, instinctively, he made for the case in which were preserved a portrait of her in miniature, taken when she was a girl of sixteen, and the two letters that she had written him, letters without heading or signature, one from Turin, after the violent death of their father, the other from Girgenti, on her return from exile, after the death of her husband.

The first, the more faded sheet of the two, ran as follows:

The property confiscated from Gerlando Laurentano by the Bourbon Government, was restored to his son Ippolito by Carlo Pilangieri di Satriano. I have no further interest, therefore, in my patrimony. The wife and son of Stefano Auriti will not eat the bread of an enemy of their country.

The other was more laconic:

Thank you. For the widow and orphans, the poor relatives of Stefano Auriti will provide. From you, nothing. Thank you.

He thrust the two letters aside and fixed his gaze on the miniature, which he had removed from the drawing-room in his father's house after his sister's elopement with Stefano Auriti.

Since then--it was now forty-five years ago--he had not set eyes on her again!

How could he look again now, after all those years, after that endless succession of calamities, upon this lovely young girl whom he saw before him, blooming, in a deeply cut bodice, dressed in the quaint old fashion, with those keen, thoughtful eyes?

He shut the case again, after casting another glance at the two scornful notes; and sombre, frowning, made his way to the drawing-room.

Raising the curtain at the door, he saw, with eyes clouded by emotion, his sister standing to receive him, tall, dressed in black. He stopped just inside the threshold, overpowered by a crushing stupor at the sight of that ravaged, unrecognizable face.

"Caterina," he murmured, as he stood there, and instinctively held out his arms to her.

She did not move: she remained there, in the middle of the room, waxen-pale in her heavy widow's weeds, with drawn face and shut eyes; proud, exalted, hardened by the strain of waiting for him. She let him come to her and barely touched his hand with her own cold, lifeless hand, gazing at him now with those weary eyes of hers, clouded by grief, half-hidden and that unequally, by her drooping eyelids.

"Sit down," said her brother, lowering his eyes, as though afraid to look at her, and pointed to the sofa and armchairs by the wall on the left.

They sat down, and remained for a long time incapable of speech, in a silence that throbbed with intense, violent emotion. Don Ippolito shut his eyes. His sister, after making several attempts to swallow a lump in her throat, said finally, in a hoarse voice:

"Roberto is here."

Don Ippolito started; opened his eyes again, and, instinctively, let them range round the room, as though--bewildered amid the tumultuous flood of intimate memories--he were afraid of an ambush.

"Not here," Donna Caterina went on with a cold, bitter, barely perceptible smile, "on your alien ground. At Girgenti, since the day before yesterday."

Don Ippolito, overwhelmed, nodded his head several times to indicate that he was aware of this.

"And I know why he has come," he added in a sombre tone; then raised his head and looked at his sister with a painful effort: "What can I..."

"Nothing... oh, nothing," Donna Caterina made haste to reply. "I wish you to fight against him with all your force. It would be the last straw if you too were to support him, and he won the election by your party's votes!"

"You know quite well..." her brother attempted to interpose.

"I know, I know," Donna Caterina promptly silenced him with a wave of her hand. "But fight him, Ippolito, not knife in hand, not stealing out to dig up graves, like a hyaena, to lay bare sacred tombs from which the dead might rise and make you die of fright."

"Gently, gently," said Don Ippolito, holding out hands that trembled, not so much in protest as to placate this tragic phantom of his sister in her tremendous agitation. "I do not understand what you mean...."

"It is burning my hands," said Donna Caterina, flinging upon the little table by the sofa a much crumpled copy of the *Empedocle*. Don Ippolito picked up the sheet, opened it and began to read.

"With such dirty weapons.... Attacking a dead man..." Donna Caterina murmured, as a commentary upon her brother's reading.

Breathless with emotion, she watched him read the article and observed the expression of disgust on his face.

"Roberto," she continued, "went to the office of this paper. He met there the writer of the article, who is the son, they tell me, of one of your ... serfs here, Preola. He seized him and flung him against a door. They tore the man from him. ... Now the man, armed with a knife (which he brandishes!) threatens to kill him; and only this morning he was seen lurking outside my house. But I am not afraid of him; I am afraid that Roberto may compromise himself again and soil his hands.... Is this how you choose to fight him?"

Don Ippolito who, as he went on reading, had listened in

suspense to her story, at this last question recoiled, indignant, as though his sister had struck him in the face, by associating him with the abject creature who had written the article.

He rose stiffly to his feet; but at once controlled himself and went to ring a bell. To Liborio, who promptly appeared in the doorway, he gave the order: "Preola!"

Presently the old secretary entered bowing, obsequious, indeed crawling, as though he had been driven into the room by blows. He was wearing a long and heavy frock coat. From his low collar, which was too large for him, his huge, bald, bony, beardless head emerged like the head of a flayed calf.

"Yes, Your Excellency?"

"Send over at once to Girgenti for your son," the Prince ordered him. "He is to come here immediately! I wish to speak to him."

"Your Excellency, allow me," Preola ventured to say, bowing and scraping even lower, with his hand on his heart, while the network of veins started out on his crimson scalp, "allow me to present my most humble duty to the most excellent lady, your sister..."

"That will do, I tell you!" the Prince shouted angrily. "I know what I have to say to your son. Or rather, listen! He disgusts me so, that I do not wish either to speak to him or to see him. You shall say to him that if he dares to show his ugly face again in the streets of Girgenti, you will be turned out of the house: I shall dismiss you instantly! Is that clear?"

Preola extracted a handkerchief from the tail pocket of his coat and assented, reiterated his assent, as he mopped his scalp; then pressed the handkerchief to his eyes and sobbed until his whole body shook.

"A gallowsbird... a gallowsbird..." he moaned. "He is disgracing me, Your Excellency. ... I am sending him away, to Tunis.... I have made all the arrangements already.... Meanwhile, I shall have him fetched here at once. Forgive me, have pity on me, Your Excellency."

And he left the room, bowing and scraping, with the handkerchief to his lips.

Donna Caterina rose.

"By this," Don Ippolito told her, "I do not mean in the

least to forfeit any of my rights in the fight for my principles against your son."

Donna Caterina raised her eyes to a large portrait in oils of Francesco II, and to another of King Bomba, which had pride of place in the magnificent drawing-room, on one wall: bowed her head and said:

"That is understood. I told you so myself."

And she prepared to leave the room.

"Caterina!" Don Ippolito called after her, as she was reaching the door. "You are not going away like that? Perhaps we may never see each other again.... You came here..."

"Like a ghost from the tomb..." she said, shaking her head.

"And I should not have known you," her brother went on. "Because... wait here a moment: let me show you how I remembered you, Caterina."

He hastened to fetch the miniature from the case in his bedroom, and handed it to her: "Look.... Do you remember?"

Donna Caterina at first felt a violent shock at the sight of her own youthful image, and drew back her head; then took the miniature from his hands, went over to the balcony and began to study it. Those lifeless eyes had long had no tears left to shed, and now tears welled in them. Her brother, too, was silently crying.

"Would you like to keep it?" he asked her in broken accents.

She shook her head, wiping her eyes with her black-bordered handkerchief, and hurriedly returned the miniature to him.

"Dead," she said. "Good-bye."

Don Ippolito escorted her to the door of the villa; helped her into the carriage; pressed a long kiss on her hand; then followed her with his gaze until the carriage turned from the short avenue on the left to pass through the gate of the villa. There one of the bodyguard, in Bourbon uniform, had thought fit to take up his post, to present arms. Don Ippolito noticed him and stamped his foot with rage.

"These tomfooleries!" he growled, glaring at Captain Sciaralla, who was standing in the hall.

He retired upstairs, shut himself up in his bedroom, and from there sent his apologies to Don Illuminato for not asking him to remain to luncheon.

THE SHADES OF NIGHT.

Monsignor Montero arrived at four o'clock in his silent carriage, drawn by a pair of active mules in blinkers.

He was accompanied by Vincente De Vincentis, the Arabic scholar, who that day had forsaken the library of Itria for the adjoining Episcopal Palace, and had sought relief in speech, in speaking for all the days and months on end in which, as though he had left his tongue as a marker between the pages of those blessed Arabic manuscripts, he had remained as dumb as a fish.

He had talked in the carriage too, during their drive, in starts and bursts and dashes which convulsed all his meagre, bony, quivering little body with its lean red face always frowning, and eyes fixed and hard behind his powerful glasses.

More than once the Bishop, with his soft womanish hands or his honeyed voice, with its measured inflexions, suffused, one felt, with a pure, protecting authority, had urged him to calm himself; he was now recommending, quietly, prudence, prudence, as they passed through the gate of the villa amid the reverent salutes of the bodyguard; and once again, with a motion of his hand, "prudence," before alighting from the carriage.

The visitors were at once conducted by Liborio to the drawing-room, but passed out on to the marble terrace supported by the columns of the porch, to enjoy the magnificent outlook over land and sea.

Looking down, they could trace the whole line of the distant coast against the crude azure of the boundless sea, from Punta Bianca, to the east, which stood out like a silver spur, on and on, with bays and promontories more or less gently curving, to Monte Rossetto on the west, the ruddy glare of whose beacon was visible only at night. For a short space only, almost bisecting the gentle, sweeping curve, the coast line was broken by the mouth of the Hypsas.

Don Ippolito joined them presently, in great excitement, not yet recovered from the serious disturbance which his sister's visit had caused him.

"I've brought our friend De Vincentis with me," Monsignor Montoro at once began, "because there is something he wishes to see in your Museum, my dear Prince. If you will send some one with him, we can remain out here, in this bower of bliss: I cannot tear myself away from it. But first of all De Vincentis has a favour to ask of you."

"Yes," the other broke out, as though he had received an electric shock. "I meant to come out by myself, this morning. But Monsignore said no, he said, 'better come with me.' It is a very serious matter, very serious indeed...."

"Let us hear what it is," said the Prince, inviting him with a wave of his hand to resume his seat on the chair of woven rushes on the terrace.

De Vincentis stooped to see where the chair was; then sitting down and gripping the arms of it with his dry, hooked little hands, he burst out:

"Ruined, Don Ippolito! We are ruined!"

"No, come now... no..." Monsignore tried to correct this statement, holding out a hand burdened with his episcopal ring.

"Ruined, Monsignore, allow me to say!" De Vincentis repeated; and his hollow red cheeks turned livid. "And the cause of our ruin is my brother Nini! He has been to... to..."

Once again the Bishop's hands were outstretched; De Vincentis observed the gesture in time and caught himself up. But the Prince had already guessed his meaning.

"To Salvo," he said soothingly. "I know that you have surrendered to him..."

"Nini! Nini!" screamed De Vincentis. "Primosole ... Nini! It was he that surrendered it. ... I know nothing, I tell you; nothing at all about it; I'm in the dark, a blind man.... And he is blinder than I am, stupid, mad, lovesick. ... What is the word? A transfer of Primosole. ... Yes! I have signed the receipt... although... only the farm, you know, has been paid for, and that in a way that makes one laugh..."

"No, why?" Monsignore again interrupted him, gravely.

"Cry, then!" retorted De Vincentis, who had now completely lost his head. "Does that satisfy you? Eighty-five thousand lire, and the villa thrown in! My mother's old home, there..."

And he pointed with his hand towards the east, over the ridge of the Sperone, to the higher hill beyond known as *Torre che parla*, and shaped like a couchant lion, its coat and mane supplied by a dense growth of olives.

"Forty-two thousand," he went on, "was for bills that had fallen due: the rest, clean vanished, blown to the winds in less than two years! Where? How? Now I hear that he's talking of letting Salvo have the Milione estate as well. And what have we left? Debts to Salvo... our other debts... I know, I've heard all about it.... You are going to marry, I'm told, his sister... Donna Adelaide..."

"And what has that got to do with it?" asked the Prince, puzzled, vexed, looking at Monsignor Montero.

"I congratulate you, mind, I congratulate you...." went on De Vincentis promptly, turning as red as a lobster. "We are ruined, though, all the same!"

And he rose so that the others should not see the tears behind his gold-rimmed glasses. Don Ippolito looked again at the Bishop, in search of enlightenment.

"Let me explain," said the Bishop in a grave tone, a tone of regret at the young man's disobedience, and let droop over his clear pale prominent eyes a pair of eyelids as thin as layers of onion-skin. "Let me explain. I know that Flaminio Salvo has already made over the Primosole estate to his sister, and that he is prepared, when the time comes, to make over Milione as well. But I am distressed at the way in which our friend Vincente has expressed himself, because... because that is not the way in which to refer to people who are held in the highest esteem, people from whom perhaps, without knowing it, we may have received some benefit."

De Vincentis, who was standing with his back to them while he wiped his eyes, turned round at the Bishop's closing words.

"Benefit?"

"Yes, my son. You cannot tell, because, unfortunately, you have never taken any interest in your affairs. You now see the disastrous state they are in, and feel the need to inculpate somebody, wrongly; instead of applying a remedy. Was not that why you came here?"

De Vincentis, who was still speechless with emotion, nodded his head.

"It would be better," Monsignore went on, "if you were to go downstairs; if you will allow him, Prince. I shall explain to the Prince what it is that you want."

Don Ippolito rose and asked De Vincentis to accompany him; then, at the head of the stair, handed him over to Liborio, to whom he gave the key of the Museum, and returned to the Bishop, who greeted him with a sigh, waving his clasped hands.

"A couple of poor wretches, he and his brother! Flaminio Salvo, I assure you, Prince, has treated them like a true friend. Without taking any... don't for goodness' sake let us say usury, there was never any thought of that; without asking for interest, he first of all lent them very considerable sums; he next had an offer from themselves of an estate with which he, a banker, wrapped up in business, you can understand, does not know what to do: any other creditor would have put the place up to auction, to recover his outlay. Instead of which he has acted in a friendly spirit, and has continued to open his purse to the brothers, who spend and spend... I can't think how, upon what... they have no vices, poor fellows, that I must say; the best boys in the world; but not very much brain. The fact of the matter is that they are sailing on troubled waters."

"Do they want help from me?" Don Ippolito asked, in a tone which let it be understood that he would be perfectly willing to afford such help. "No, no," Monsignore replied anxiously. "To ask for something which, I am sure, will be refused. De Vincentis believes that Nini, his younger brother, is in love with Flaminio Salvo's daughter, and..."

"And?" the Prince echoed.

But he had understood already; and the conversation ended, Sicilian fashion, in an exchange of significant gestures. Don

Ippolito laid both hands on his bosom and asked with his eyes: "Am I expected to convey the request to Salvo?" Monsignore nodded a melancholy assent; the other first of all shook his head in refusal, then raised his shoulders and one hand in a vague gesture, as much as to say: "I shan't do it, but supposing I did?" Monsignore sighed, and that was all.

They sat for a while in silence.

Don Ippolito, for some years past, had been confusedly aware that this Monsignor Montoro was a grave burden to him, not so much in the flesh as in the spirit, as though with the dead weight of his pink, too well cared for person, he were encumbering all sorts of things round about him and dependent upon him, and preventing any development. What things, he would, to tell the truth, have found it hard to say; but obviously, with that figure, with that pink inert cumbersome flabbiness, he must be allowing any number of things to slide which another man, perhaps, in his place, more active and less effeminate, would have set in motion, would indeed have stirred up and carried to a conclusion.

Monsignore for his part was aware that between him and the Prince there existed a feeling not easy to define, which often on one side or the other shrank instinctively hack, leaving a yawning gulf between them which gave rise in each of them to a faintly gnawing bitterness.

Perhaps this gulf was created by a subject upon which Monsignore knew that he must not touch, and which was yet so intimate a part of the Prince's life: to wit, his archaeological studies, his worship of the past. He could not venture upon this subject, for fear of its furnishing Don Ippolito with an excuse for referring again to a matter of which he, a man of the world and absolutely free from superstition, did not wish to hear any more. More than once the Prince had endeavoured to persuade him to devote at least a small portion of the considerable emoluments of his See to the restoration of the old Cathedral, a splendid example of Norman art, ruined in the eighteenth century by horrible incrustations of stucco and the most vulgar gilding. He had refused, telling the Prince that, should he ever succeed in putting aside any savings, he would prefer to establish a fund with which he might bring back to the Convent of Sant'Alfonso, next door to the Cathedral, the Liguorine Fathers who had been expelled after 1860. Don Ippolito took not the slightest interest in the improvements that had been effected in his native town by the new administrations which had replaced the *decurie* and *intendenti* of his day. Albeit he allowed himself no rest from the fray and shewed a spirit resolute to attain the goal, he no longer believed in his heart of hearts that he would ever set eyes again on the town from which he had banished himself. He saw it in imagination as it had been before that fatal year, still with its *burgi* and *stazzoni*, that is to say its ricks of straw and its kilns on the marshy space outside Porta di Ponte; still with the three great crosses of the Calvary on the brow of the hill, from which year by year, on Good Friday, sermons were preached to the whole population assembled beneath, and still with the old garden which one of his devoted friends, Colonel Flores, commander of the Bourbon garrison, seeking to ingratiate the citizens, had laid out there ten years before the Revolution. He knew that this garden had been destroyed to enlarge the terrace on the side looking towards the sea; he knew that on the marshy space there now rose a huge palace, intended to house the provincial offices and to be the headquarters of the Prefecture. But this too was in his eyes an unworthy usurpation, since the foundation stone of the palace had been laid in 1858 by a philanthropic Bishop, who intended to build a great hospice there for the poor; wherefore the old people still spoke of it as the Palazzo della Beneficenza.

He would have liked the Cathedral to be restored by Monsignor Montero, because the churches... ah, those were not buildings which the new people could take any pleasure in adorning; and they were the one thing for which he felt a profound regret. There came to him, in his banishment, the sound of the bells of the nearer churches. He knew every one of them, and would say: "There, that's the Badia Grande ringing now... that's San Pietro now... that's San Francesco..."

There came, this evening, too, to break the long silence into which he and the Bishop, out there on the terrace, had drifted, the sound of the Angelus from the chapel of San Pietro. The sky, which a moment earlier had been an intense blue, was all suffused with violet light; and beneath, among the already harvested fields, in the gathering dusk, there stood out among the stripped almond trees a line of tall nocturnal cypresses, like a vigilant picket on guard over the Temple of Concord that soared majestic into the air from the crest of the hill.

Monsignor Montero removed his zucchetto and bowed his head slightly, shutting his eyes; the Prince crossed himself, and joined him in silent prayer.

After which, "Have you heard of the scandais," the Bishop inquired gravely, "which are bound, I fear, to disturb our peaceful diocese?"

Don Ippolito nodded his head, with half-shut eyes.

"My sister has been here."

"Here?" the Bishop asked in utter amazement.

Don Ippolito thereupon told him briefly of his sister's visit and of the violent shock that it had given him.

"Oh, I understand! I understand!" exclaimed Monsignore, raising his clasped, white hands and letting his own eyelids droop also.

"So altered..." Don Ippolito heaved a deep sigh.

To change the conversation, Monsignor Mon-toro, after drawing a long breath, groaned:

"And now our paladin is determined to take the field at all costs; and that will be a fresh scandal, which I should have liked to avoid if possible. ..."

"Capolino?" Don Ippolito frowned. "Is he going to fight?"

"Why, yes! He has been assaulted..."

"He? It was Preola!"

"He too! You haven't heard the whole story, then? Our friend Capolino was assaulted in the morning by one Veronica, who was then in the company of Agro, who is giving me so much trouble...."

"She never told me...." Don Ippolito's murmur was barely audible.

"Because it appears," Monsignore explained, "at least this is what people are saying in the town, it appears that Auriti knew nothing about the quarrel in the morning. It may be so. We shall have to turn a blind eye, because the insult, oh, the insult was very serious; they flung the paper in his face, on the public highway.... You know that our friend Capolino is a hot-tempered man, a regular knight-errant.... It was impossible to make him listen to reason, to make him observe the Christian precept. He has sent the challenge already...."

"I know that he is a good swordsman," said Don Ippolito grimly. "When all is said and done, it will do no harm to teach one of these fellows a lesson, and take them all down a peg. For my own part, Monsignore, I said as much to my own sister, a fight to a finish!"

"But of course! The victory, the victory is ours, beyond question," was the Bishop's conclusion.

Another spell of silence followed; then Monsignore roused himself and inquired: "Landino?" as though it had just occurred to him to put this question, which was as a matter of fact the true reason of his visit.

It was he who had planned this marriage between Donna Adelaide Salvo and Don Ippolito; he had given the latter to understand that only out of regard for him had Flaminio Salvo agreed to his sister's contracting this invalid marriage, invalid at least in the eyes of the State; but that he was anxious--and quite rightly--that the son of the first marriage should acknowledge his mother-in-law, and should be present at the religious ceremony: in dealing with a gentleman of his quality, the mere fact of his presence would be sufficient to cover all eventualities.

Don Ippolito's face darkened.

After a long inward struggle, he had written to his son, who had been brought up entirely away from home; first of all at Palermo, among his Montalto relatives, then in Rome; so that the two were not on intimate terms. He knew that his son had ideas and sentiments diametrically opposed to his own, although they had never had occasion, to discuss anything together. He was far from satisfied with the manner in which he had informed his son of his decision to make this second marriage, and with the terms in which he had expressed his desire to have his son with him at Colimbetra for the wedding. Too many excuses: loneliness, old age, the need of loving attention. ... He felt that he had degraded himself in his son's eyes. His feeling of disgust and degradation was, however, not due merely to a badly drafted letter: it sprang from a cause more intimate and profound, in his own heart.

Without having originally any deliberate intention, he had let himself be persuaded into putting into effect a plan which at first sight he had deemed impracticable; the serious obstacle of his own scruples overcome, the bride found, the marriage arranged, he had suddenly found himself bound by an engagement which he had not sufficiently weighed, and had been powerless to draw back upon any pretext. The Salvo family, even if they had no title of nobility, were nevertheless of ancient blood; the bride's age was suitable; no serious objection could be made to her appearance, in the photograph they had shewn him of Donna Adelaide; and then there was the satisfaction of the deference paid to his political and religious principles.... Yes, yes; but the cherished memory of Donna Teresa Montalto? and his humiliating consciousness of his own weakness? He had been powerless to hold out against the secret terror that had been assailing him for some time past, in his loneliness, at the thought of his old age, especially at night, when he shut himself up in his bedroom and, looking at his hands, found himself thinking that... yes, death is always hovering over all of us, children, young men and old, invisible, ready at any moment to clutch us; but, as we see drawing gradually nearer the limit set to man's life upon earth, and when already, year after year, for mile after mile of our journey, we have somehow avoided the assault of that invisible companion, then gradually, on the one hand, the illusion of a probable escape diminishes, and there grows, on the other hand, and overpowers us the cold, dark sense of the tremendous necessity of meeting him, of finding ourselves of a sudden facing him as man to man, in the narrow span of time that remains to us. And he felt his breath fail; he felt his throat tightened by an inexpressible anguish. His hands filled him with horror. His hands were the only part of him, so far, that showed signs of age: their swollen knuckles, their wrinkled skin. Yes, his hands had begun to die. Often they became numb. And he could no longer, at night, as he lay on his back in bed, bear to see them folded upon his belly. And yet this was his natural posture: he must stretch himself out thus to woo sleep. But no: he saw himself lying dead, with those hands as it were turned to stone upon his belly; and at once he would lose patience, assume another posture, torment himself far into the night....

For this reason he had expressed the desire for a more intimate companionship; and now his desire was being put into effect; but secretly it filled him with irritation and shame. He felt that this desire had acquired the power over him of a will that was no longer his own. An alien force indeed had assumed control over him and was guiding him and leading him astray, powerless any longer to resist; like a horse that has given the first impetus to a carriage upon a downward slope, now by the carriage itself, or rather by the force that he had given it, he felt himself thrust and driven on against his will.

"Has not answered?" Monsignore put in, to break the dark ring of silence into which the Prince had withdrawn. "Very well; I only wished to know He will answer. In the meantime... listen: we have talked to Flaminio about the formal introduction. It can be arranged at Valsania, I suppose? Donna Adelaide will go down to see her niece and her poor sister-in-law; you, from this house, by the road, without passing through the town, can go to call upon your brother and his guests. Is that all right? In the course of the week. You shall choose the day."

"At once," said the Prince, mastering himself with a violent effort. "To-morrow."

"Too soon..." Monsignore observed with a smile. "We shall have to warn them... to give them time.... The day after to-morrow perhaps,--no: it's a Tuesday. Women, you know, attach importance to these things. It will have to be Wednesday."

And he rose, with an effort and with due regard to his plump, pink, effeminately cared-for person, sighing: "*Bene eveniat!* That poor boy..." he went on, alluding to De Vincentis. "If we could find any way of soothing him.... I should be so glad. ... Mah!"

At the foot of the stair Monsignore Montoro stopped the Prince and, pointing to the door of the Museum, in which De Vincentis was, murmured:

"Don't let him see you. You can bid him goodbye from the terrace. Good evening."

The Prince kissed his ring and went upstairs again. A minute later, from the terrace, he bowed to the Bishop and waved his hand to De Vincentis, who took off his hat, evidently without recognising him. He remained there, sitting by the balustrade, watching, over the dead silence of the fields, the shadows gradually deepening, the ruddy streak of sunset, which became livid and seemed to smoke over the distant blue sea, above which in the background, loomed the dark olive-groves of Montelusa, to the right of the gleaming mouth of the Hypsas. High up in the sky a sickle moon was beginning to shine.

Don Ippolito gazed at the temples where they stood grouped austere and solemn in the dusk, and felt a vague sorrow for these survivors from another world and another life. Among all the famous monuments of the vanished city, to them alone had it been granted to witness this remote age: the only living things once, amid the appalling destruction of the city; the only dead things now amid all that life of the trees that throbbed, in the silence, with leaves and wings. >From the intervening hill of Tamburello there seemed to be moving up towards the Temple of Hera Lacinia, poised there aloft, almost vertically above the ravine of the Akragas, a long and dense procession of ancient, hoary olives; and one there was, in advance of the rest, bowed over its kneeling trunk, as though overpowered by the imminent majesty of the sacred columns; and perhaps it was praying for peace upon those deserted slopes, for peace from those temples, phantoms of another world and of a far different life. Hot, flaming, clamorous, the civilisation that at one time reigned upon those slopes had melted away, being founded upon sentiment and illusion: raucous with machinery, ice-cold, the civilisation of to-day, founded upon reason, came sweeping down from the north, like a sheet of snow.

Suddenly, through the darkness that had now fallen, there sounded the distant cry of a horned owl, like a sob.

Don Ippolito felt a lump gather suddenly in his throat. He looked at the stars which were now twinkling in the sky, and fancied that their bright tremor was being answered from the deserted fields by the tremulous shrill song of the grasshoppers. Then he saw, beyond the river-bed, to the east, the wavering light of four dark lanterns mount the steep ridge of the Sperone.

It was Sciaralla, who was climbing the hill with his three companions, to mount their ineffectual guard at the barrack-room above.

CHAPTER V

A CLOUDY DAWN.

As the first glimmer of dawn filtered down through the thick, leathery leaves of the wild fig-tree that overshadowed the end of the vineyard, Mauro Mortara, sitting propped against its trunk, knitted his brows, stretched his arms, straightened his back and emitted a rumbling sound from his throat and nose.

With the return of consciousness he blinked two or three times; he hungered still for the warm darkness of sleep; but at that moment he heard a cock crow from a distant farmyard, and a second cock, farther off still, crow in answer; he heard a flutter of wings close at hand, and roused himself.

The three mastiffs, crouching beneath the tree by his side, watched him with moist, anxious eyes, greeting him affectionately with their tails. But their master only stared at them, annoyed that they should have seen him asleep; then stared at his own legs, stretching out rigid upon the muddy soil of the vineyard; earth upon earth; shook his woollen cloak from his shoulders; rubbed his watery eyes with the back of his hand; last of all took from the bag that was hanging from a branch three crusts of stale bread and tossed them to the dogs; rose, with an effort, to his feet and, hanging his cloak on the tree, and shouldering his gun, set off still half asleep through the vineyard.

He could no longer manage to keep awake all night: cautiously, at a certain hour, as though someone might be watching him, he would retire to his lair under the fig-tree; for a moment only, he told himself; but the effort to arouse himself became greater every morning. His legs were no longer what they had once been; neither was the strength of his wrist.

Ah, his beautiful vineyard.... Yes, this year's vintage he might perhaps live to taste; but the next? He shrugged his shoulders, as much as to say: "Sufficient for the day..." and yawned at the first light of morning which seemed to be finding a difficulty in rousing the world to its toil; he looked out over the vast expanse of fields, over which the last shades of night were slow in scattering; then turned to look at the sea, down below, dark blue and vaporous between the bristling agaves and the fat grey stumps of prickly pear, that rose and writhed in the raw, murky air.

The setting moon, which had risen late that night, was still halfway up the sky, surprised there by daybreak, and was already fading in the crude morning light. Here and there in the fields, through that light veil of whitish vapour, smoke rose from the fires on which the almond husks were burning.

For the last two days, however, Mauro Mortara had been less worried. He still kept a dog-like watch round the villa; but then, reflecting that Flaminio Salvo set off every morning at that hour for either Girgenti or Porto Empedocle, and did not return until late in the evening, he heaved a sigh of relief, as though the aspect of the building became more agreeable to him with the knowledge that the other was not there. There remained, it was true, with their servants, his wife and daughter; but the wife, a poor lunatic, quiet and harmless; and the daughter... it seemed impossible! She, for all she was daughter to that "bad Christian," was not bad herself, no, far from it....

And Mauro unconsciously threw a glance over his shoulder, to see whether Donna Dianella had come out yet to the vineyard.

In the few days that she had spent at Valsania, she had almost completely recovered; she rose betimes every morning; waited until her father had driven off in his carriage, and then came and joined Mauro out here in the vineyard, and asked him endless questions about the country: about the olives and how they were tended; the mulberries, which in March gather fresh blood and, when they are in love, and ready to shoot, become soft as dough; then she would stop beneath the umbrella of the solitary pine down yonder, where the tableland dropped to the sea, to watch the sun rise over the heights of the Crocea, far away on the horizon, livid at first, then gradually waxing blue, aerial, almost fragile. The first thing to be gilded by the sun, every morning, was that pine, which stood out in majesty against the harsh, solid azure of the sea, the tenuous, empty azure of the sky.

In a few days Dianella had wrought a miracle: the bear was tamed. The expression on her face, the gentle and at the same time proud nobility of her bearing, the melancholy sweetness of her gaze and smile, the softness of her voice had wrought the miracle, quietly, naturally, challenging and conquering the sullen rudeness of the old savage.

While she was speaking, now and again, there would come into her voice and eyes a sudden opacity, as though her spirit vanished from time to time behind some word or expression and strayed far away, into unknown tracts; she would lose herself there and take a long time to return, would ask: "What were we saying?" and smile, because she herself could not account for what had happened to her. Often too, at the slightest contact with any harsh reality, she would feel a sudden dismay or rather the sense of a chill shadow closing in upon her, and would knit her brows. Immediately, however, she would cancel with another of her sweet smiles the involuntary, angry impulse, opening wide a pair of sparkling eyes, her spirits quite restored.

"Why should anyone seek to injure me?" she seemed to be saying to herself. "Am I not facing life, trustful and serene?"

Her trustfulness radiated from her every action, her every glance, and was irresistible.

Even Mortara's three savage mastiffs--you ought to have seen the fuss they made of her whenever she appeared. They too kept on turning, one after another, to gaze in the direction of the villa, as though they expected her. And Mauro, not to go too far away, hung about examining first one cane then another, whose clusters, jealously guarded treasures, he had already exhibited, almost grape by grape, to Dianella, with a gruff delight in the praises that she heaped upon them amid her exclamations of wonder:

"Oh, look at all these!"

"A good load, eh? And this cane, look..."

"A tree... it's like a fruit tree!"

"And here, this one..."

"Oh, there are more bunches than leaves! Can the vine bear the weight of all these grapes?"

"Yes, if we don't have bad weather...."

"That would be a pity! And this one," she would ask, noticing a vine on the ground. "Was it the wind? Oh, it has still to be tied...."

Or again, going farther afield:

"And these? Wild vines? New grafts; I see. Splendid, splendid.... Ah, it is worth while to be alive after all!"

And her voice seemed to thrill with her joy in the pure air and the sunshine, the same joy that quivered in the throats of the larks.

For this morning Mauro had promised her a visit to the General's *camerone*, to the "Shrine of Liberty." But the dogs, all of a sudden, pricked up their ears; first one then another stole across without barldng towards the footpath beneath the vineyard, along the edge of the ravine.

"Don Ma'! Don Ma'!" came presently in a breathless voice from below.

Mauro recognized the voice as that of Leonardo Costa, his friend from Porto Empedocle; and called the dogs to heel.

"Here, Scampirro! Here, Neula! Come here, Turco!"

But the dogs had recognized Costa also and had stopped at the boundary of the vineyard, wagging their tails at him from above.

Mauro appeared beside them.

"The chief? Has he gone?" Leonardo Costa panted.

He was a little man with a crisp, rusty beard and hair, a face baked by the sun and eyes scorched by sulphur dust. He wore a pair of gold earrings and a big white hat covered in dust and stained with sweat. He had come hurrying from Porto Empedocle, by the coast, along the railway; line.

"I don't know," Mauro answered crossly.

"Will you please call to him, to wait; I have something important to tell him."

Mauro shook his head.

"But, you will still catch him.... What has been happening?"

Leonardo Costa, as he ran, shouted back at him: "Trouble! Bad trouble in the sulphur pits!"

"Curse him and his sulphur pits!" Mauro muttered to himself.

Flaminio Salvo was coming down the steps from the villa to get into the waiting carriage when Leonardo Costa emerged from the path to the west, among the olives, shouting:

"Stop! Stop!"

"Who's that? What's the matter?" Salvo asked with a start of surprise.

"I kiss Your Honour's hands," said Costa, removing his hat as he approached, dripping with sweat and gasping for breath. "I am done... I meant to come last night... but then..."

"Then what? What has happened? What's wrong with you?" Salvo interrupted him sharply.

"At Aragona--Comitini--all the sulphur workers--on strike!" Costa announced.

Flaminio Salvo looked at him with cold anger, stroking the long grey side-whiskers which, with his gold spectacles, gave him something of the air of a diplomat, and said, contemptuously:

"I was aware of that."

"Yes, Sir. But late last night," Costa went on, "some people from Aragona came to Porto Empedocle and told us that the place had been like hell let loose all day...."

"The sulphur workers?"

"Yes, Sir: hewers, carriers, burners, carters, weighmen: all of them! They even cut the telegraph wire. I'm told they attacked my son's house, and that Aurelio stood up to them, as best he could...."

Flaminio Salvo, at this point, turned and looked narrowly into the eyes of Dianella, who had come out to the carriage. This strange glance, directed at the girl in the middle of their conversation, disturbed Costa, who turned likewise to look at the "Signorinella," as he called her. Her pallor changed to a crimson flush, then at once returned.

"Well?" shouted Flaminio Salvo angrily

"Yes, Sir," Costa went on, disconcerted. "The worst of it is, we've no troops handy; the whole village is in their hands. Only a couple of carabinieri, the serjeant and corporal.... What can they do?"

"And what can I do from here, will you tell me that?" Salvo cried in a fury of rage. "Your son Aurelio, what is he? The Managing Engineer, from the *Ecole des Mines* in Paris, what is he? A puppet? Does he need me to pull the string from here, to make him act?"

"Oh no, Sir," said Leonardo Costa, drawing back a pace, as though Salvo had lashed him across the face. "Your Honour may rest assured that my son Aurelio knows what to do. A strong head and a stout heart...it's not for me to say... but face to face with two thousand men, what with sulphur workers and carters, Your Honour will agree.... Besides, the real trouble is something else, outside the village. Aurelio sent word to me last night that they had waylaid on the road the eight carts of coal that were going to the pits on Monte Diesi."

"Indeed?" Salvo sneered.

"Your Honour knows," Costa went on, "that up there coal is as necessary to the pumps as bread to a starving man, and more. Your Honour is going to Girgenti? Do go at once to the Prefect and get him to send troops to Aragona station, as many as he can, to provide an escort for the coal to the pits. There are seven truck-loads there to replenish the store at the pit; the carters are on strike too; but the coal can be loaded on mules and donkeys, with an armed escort: it will take us longer, but at least we can avoid any danger of the great pit, the Cace (Heaven forbid!), flooding...."

"Let it flood! Let it flood!" Flaminio Salvo broke out, furious, throwing his arms in the air. "Let the whole show go to blazes! I don't give a damn for it! I shall close down, d'you hear? And send you all packing, you, your son, all of you, from top to bottom, all of you! A clean sweep! Drive on!" he told the coachman.

The carriage started, and Flaminio drove off without so much as turning to bid his daughter good-bye.

This extraordinary outburst had brought Don Cosmo to one of the windows, while Donna Sara Alaimo had appeared at the head of the steps. Both of them, as well as Dianella and Costa below, stood rooted to the ground. Finally Costa stirred himself, raised his head in the direction of the window and gave a bitter greeting:

"I kiss your hands, Si-don Cosmo! He's quite right: he's the master! But, by Our Lord on the Cross, believe me, Si-don Cosmo dear, believe me, Signorinella: they're not to blame! They really are starving; the distress is terrible!"

Donna Sara from the stairhead shook her bonneted head, her eyes raised to heaven.

"The Government takes its share," Costa continued, "and the Province takes its share; the Comune takes its share, and the chairman and the vice-chairman and the manager and the engineer and the foreman.... What can there be left over for the men who work underground and under everybody, and have to carry all the rest on their backs and are crushed down? Oh Lord! I am only a poor wretch, an ignorant clown is all I am, well and good: let him trample me underfoot if he likes! But my son, Lord in heaven, no, he mustn't lay a finger on my son! We owe everything to him, it is true; but even he himself, if he is still where he is, my revered master, who can give me a slap in the face, if he likes, since I get everything from him, indeed I kiss his hands; if he is still where he is, giving orders, and enjoying his wealth and prosperity, he owes it, all the same, to my son, he does: you know that, Signor-inella, and you too, perhaps, Si-don Cosmo... We're quits!"

"Quite so, quite so," Laurentano sighed from the window. "That business of the pumpkins ..."

"What pumpkins?" asked Donna Sara Alaimo, her curiosity aroused.

"Mah!" said Costa. "You must get the story another time from the Signorinella here, who knows my son well, since they were brought up together, with the other boy, her little brother, whom the Lord took to Himself, which was the undoing of them all. The poor Signora, there (whom I can remember so well, such a beauty, a ray of sunshine!), went out of her mind over it; and he, poor gentleman... anyone with children of his own can feel for him...."

Dianella, her heart wrung by her father's harshness, at this memory could contain herself no longer and, to conceal her emotion, took the path by which Costa had come and disappeared among the olives.

At once Donna Sara, and after her Don Cosmo invited Costa to come upstairs, to rest for a moment after his journey and not to expose his heated body to the morning breeze. Donna Sara would have liked to do more: to offer him a cup of coffee; but, lest she should lose a word of the voluble discourse on which Costa had at once embarked with Don Cosmo on the subject of Salvo, now that the latter's daughter was out of earshot, pretended that such an idea had not occurred to her.

"We know what we're saying, good Lord, we know what we're saying, Si-don Co'! What was he, when all's said and done? I myself, yes, have gone barefoot, and carried loads on my back, I say it and I am proud of it; on my back I've carried sulphur and coal, from the beach to the lighters. What is the Latin proverb? *Necessitas non abita legge.* Yes, Sir; and I've been a dock labourer, and I'm proud of it, a wretched weighman at the landing-stage for the customs, and I'm proud of it. But he, what was he? Of noble family, yes, Sir; but a mere broker, he was, who would come down on foot from Girgenti to Porto Empedocle, all covered in dust by the Spinasanta road, because he hadn't the money even to take a carriage or to hire a donkey, before the railway came. And his first profits, how did he come by them? God knows, and there's many a man that knows, alive and dead. Then he took on the contract for the first railways, he and his brother-in-law who lives in Rome now, the engineering gentleman, the banker, the Commendatore, Don Francesco Velia; we know him too...."

"Ah," put in Donna Sara, "he has another sister then, has he?"

"And why not?" replied Costa, interrupting the series of inclinations with which he had accompanied this string of titles, "Donna Rosa, the eldest of them all, the wife of" (here he bowed again) "Commendatore Francesco Velia, a big pot in the Railway Department now. This line here, from Girgenti to Porto Empedocle, wasn't it he that built it? Nothing like making hay when the sun shines! Hundreds of thousands of lire, sister; money in hatfuls, heaped like sand on the shore.... Two bridges and four tunnels.... Round a bend there; into a cutting here. ... Then other contracts for lines.... All his fortune came to him from that, am I not right, Si-don Co'? We know what we're talking about!"

"But the pumpkins? The pumpkins?" Donna Sara repeated

her question.

Costa was obliged to relate to her in the minutest detail the famous story of the pumpkins; and Donna Sara rewarded him with the most vivacious exclamations of stupefaction, terror, amazement that the local dialect contained, clapping her hands at intervals, to arouse Don Cosmo, who, knowing the story already, had relapsed into his habitual philosophical lethargy. He did rouse himself at length, but without opening his eyes; thrust forward his hand, saying:

"Still..."

"Ah, yes!" Costa at once rejoined, with emphasis, beating his breast with both hands. "In all conscience, we have but the one soul, before God, and I must tell the truth. But my son, oh, Si-don Cosmo----" (and Costa held up his hand with the thumb and forefinger joined, as though holding a pair of scales) "every son is a son, but mine! He's perfection! Straight as a die! The top of all his classes! As soon as he had taken his degree, off he went to compete for the scholarship to study abroad.... There were, sister, more than four hundred young engineers from all parts of Italy: he left them all behind him, every One of them! And he stayed abroad four years, in Paris, London, Belgium, Austria. As soon as he got back to Rome, without his having to breathe a word even, the Government gave him a post in the Corps of Mining Engineers, and sent him off to Sardinia, to Iglesias, where he did a piece of work all in colours about a mountain.... Sar-rubbas ... I don't remember... oh, Sarrabus, yes, that's right, Sarrabus (they speak Turkish, in Sardinia), a piece of work, sister, that would leave you gaping open-mouthed. He didn't stay there long, not much more than a year, because a French company, one of those that... sacks of money ... saw his map, and it fairly took their breath away. I'm not saying it because he's my son; but you may take all the engineers in existence, here and elsewhere, he can wipe the floor with them! However. This French company said to him, here's the key of our safe, my boy, help yourself to as much as you want. My son, while he was making up his mind whether to accept or not, came down here on a holiday--it will be six or seven months ago, now--to consult with me and the chief, his benefactor, whom he respects as his second father, and quite rightly! The chief himself advised him not to accept, because he wanted him for himself, do you understand? To look after his sulphur pits at Aragona and Comitini. Enough is as good as a feast, we say.... He consented, but at a sacrifice, upon my word! And after all this, now, now he's a puppet, did you hear?... Holy Christ!"

Leonardo Costa held up his arm, rose, heaved a nasal sigh, shaking his head, and took up his white hat from the seat. He ought to have left at once, but whenever he began talking about that son of his, the glory, the golden pillar of his house, he could never leave off.

"I kiss your hands, Si-'don Cosmo, let me be going. Donna Sara, your most humble servant." "Oh, but wait!" that lady exclaimed, pretending to have just thought of it, now that the conversation was at an end. "A drop of coffee..."

"No, no thank you," Costa fenced. "I'm in a great hurry!"

"Five minutes!" said Donna Sara, lifting her hands as though to imply: "The world won't come to an end!"

And she turned to go. But Costa, sitting down again, sighed, turning to Don Cosmo:

"There's a wicked woman, Si-don Co ', a wicked woman, who has been making mischief for some tune past between my son and Don Flaminio; I know it!"

And Donna Sara was powerless to cross the threshold: she turned back, screwed up her eyes, wrinkled her nose and asked with a little twitch of her head: "Who is she?"

"Don't tempt me to speak evil, Donna Sara dear!" groaned Costa. "I've said too much already!"

Donna Sara, however, had already guessed who the wicked woman was to whom he referred, and went indoors, exclaiming with upraised hands:

"What a world! Oh, what a world!"

LIKE A RIVULET.

Dianella was in no hurry that morning to join Mauro in the vineyard. That sharp, hard glance with which her father, in his anger, had suddenly turned upon her, while Costa was speaking of the danger that threatened his son at Aragona, had disturbed her profoundly; it had recalled to her memory in a flash a similar look which he had given her many years before, when her little brother had died and her mother had gone mad.

She had been eleven years old at the time.

And, more than her brother's death, more than her mother's terrible affliction, there had remained indelibly fixed in her mind the impression of that glare of hatred cast at her--a little girl still almost unconscious, uncertain, bewildered between play and mourning--by her father in the frenzy of his grief.

"Couldn't you have died instead?" had been its unmistakable message.

Quite so. Precisely so. And Dianella understood perfectly now why her father would not have hesitated for a moment to sacrifice her life in exchange for her brother's.

All the care and affection and caresses and presents which he had since then lavished upon her had been powerless to thaw the lump of ice into which that glance had frozen in her innermost consciousness. Often she felt ashamed of herself, conscious that the warmth of his paternal affection could no longer succeed in penetrating her heart, but was instinctively repulsed by that hard, frozen core. On what principle did he still go on working with such desperate energy? Piling up that vast fortune? Not for her benefit, certainly; was it from a spontaneous, overpowering necessity of his own nature; to acquire mastery over everyone else; to be feared and respected; or perhaps also to blunt the sharp edge of his sufferings in business or to take his revenge in his own way upon the fate that had struck him such a blow? But in certain moments of anger (as just now), or of weariness and loss of confidence, he let it be seen quite plainly that all his undertakings and his efforts and life itself had no longer any purpose for him, now that he had lost the heir to his name, him who was to have carried on the tradition of his power and fortune.

For some time past, convinced of this, Dianella, albeit incapable of even imagining her own life stripped of all the luxury by which she was surrounded, had begun to feel a secret contempt for her father's riches, to which one day (might that day be far distant!) she would be left the sole heir, of necessity and without any satisfaction to herself. How often, seeing him tired or angry, had she not felt inclined to say to him: "Stop! Give it up! Why do you go on increasing it, if this is to be the end of it all?" And something more than this, something very different would she have liked to say to him, had she been able to converse with her father heart to heart, without words, that is to say without moving her lips or hearing with her ears.

From what she had been able to gather by her superfine intuition and to penetrate with those silently watchful eyes, and from certain utterances which she could not help overhearing, she was already aware that her father's riches, if not altogether evilly acquired, had nevertheless made many victims in the neighbourhood. Cruel had fate been to him, cruel was the revenge that he took upon fate. He wanted everything for himself; to feel everything in his own grasp: sulphur pits and land and factories, the commerce and industry of the entire Province. Why? Why, if he went on working without any love left, almost without any object left to work for? Why heap upon her frail shoulders--his daughter's... a loved, yes, but not a cherished daughter, for all that she was now his only child--a crushing burden, all those riches, which many people were perhaps cursing secretly and which certainly would not bring her any happiness?

Dismay and anger too, at times, Dianella felt at the thought, foreseeing all too plainly that her heart might well remain crushed beneath that mountain of gold.

And yet she had nourished the illusion, until quite recently, that her father would leave her free to choose; that indeed he had himself helped her in her choice, by his benefaction to the man who as a boy had saved his life.

Nimble and bold, dark-skinned, like a figure cast in bronze, with black curling hair and eyes that darted fire, Aurelio Costa had seemed to her when she first saw him, as a boy of thirteen; and for years after that he had been her playmate, hers and her brother's. They were not conscious then of the gulf that lay between them. But afterwards, by degrees, Aurelio had become steadily more timid and circumspect. She had been barely twelve when he, at eighteen, had gone away to matriculate at the University of Palermo in the Faculty of Engineering; and she had wept floods of tears--still like an unconscious little girl--at their parting. What a joyful occasion had been his return, at the end of his first year! So hilarious, so full of jubilation had those holidays been that her father, as soon as Aurelio had left, had taken her aside and quietly, in the politest language, stroking her hair, had given her to understand that she would have done better to restrain herself, seeing that Costa was now a young man, and it was not proper therefore to address him any longer as *tu*. She--without at the time understanding why--had felt her cheeks flame. Good heavens, what next, then? Call him Lei? Was he not still the same Aurelio? No, he was no longer the same, not even to her; and she had been made well aware of this the year after, when he returned again; and increasingly so after his third, and fourth, and fifth years at the University, when finally he returned with a splendid degree and with the intention of winning that scholarship for study abroad. He, yes, it was he who was no longer the same; for she, on the other hand... with her lips, yes, "Signor Aurelio," but with her eyes she still continued to address him as *tu*. Before leaving the Island, he had come to thank his benefactor, to swear him undying gratitude; and to her he had scarcely known what to say, had scarcely ventured to look at her, and certainly, certainly had not noticed how pale her cheeks were nor how her hand trembled.

After his departure, she had many times heard her father speak of the really exceptional worth of this young man and of the splendid future that was in store for him, and extol himself for all that he had done for him, for having treated him as a son. Naturally these speeches had given ever fresh fuel to the hidden fire in her heart and had strengthened the ever growing hope that her father, having lost his only son, and having virtually created this other, to whom moreover he owed his own life, would prefer that to him, rather than to some comparative stranger, his wealth and his daughter should one day pass.

She had been greatly confirmed in this hope a few months since, when Aurelio, on his return from Sardinia, had been appointed manager of the sulphur pits by her father.

She had not set eyes on him since his departure for Paris. Oppressed, amid her useless luxury, by the pettiness of life in Girgenti, an old town, not indeed boorish but weary, listless in the uniformity of its long silent days; each day occupied by the same round of visits from the three or four families of her acquaintance, who vied with one another in shewing their affection for and trust in herself, who was like a little queen of the place, amid the invariable witticisms of the invariable young bloods, enervated, turned silly by their narrow and impoverished provincial life; she had felt herself quicken at the sight of him, so manly a creature, his own master henceforward, free to tread the path he had conquered by his strength, tenacity and hard work.

Her joy at seeing him again was however suddenly clouded. There happened to be calling upon her that day Nicoletta Spoto, who for the last year or so had been married to Capolino. She had noticed a curious embarrassment, a keen emotion, both in her guest and in Aurelio when the latter, on being shewn into the drawing-room, had bowed in greeting. Then, as soon as her father had carried Aurelio off to his study, Signora Capolino, breathing again, had related with fiery vivacity to her and to her aunt Adelaide how that poor fellow, without a penny to his name, had nevertheless dared to ask for her hand in marriage, immediately upon obtaining his post as a government engineer in Sardinia, remembering perhaps a few innocent glances that had been exchanged between them years and years earlier, when he was still a young student at the Institute. They could imagine the horror that she, Lelle Spoto, had felt at such a request, and how she had hastened to decline it, especially as the preliminary arrangements were already under way for her marriage to Ignazio Capolino.

Dianella had felt her heart sink in her bosom at these sudden, unexpected tidings; she had certainly turned all the colours of the rainbow and certainly she had betrayed herself to the other woman, of whose secret and illicit relations with her father she was already aware. She had not said anything to her, but when Aurelio, after his long interview with her father, had returned to the drawing-room, she, quivering with excitement, had greeted him with an exaggerated welcome, reminding him of the times they had spent together, their games, their mutual confidences. And more than once she had rejoiced to see the other bite her lip and turn pale.

Dianella hoped that Aurelio, on that occasion at least, had understood. She had at once forgiven him in her heart for a betrayal of which he could not have been conscious at the tune: yes, he could have had no thought of her, must have supposed that he could not'dare to raise his eyes to her level; but... at the same time, ah! was it really to that other woman, a woman in every respect unworthy of him, that his thoughts had turned? And the other woman's refusal of him had seemed to her almost an insult directed at herself. Still, after all, he had been in Paris; the vivacity, the capricious frivolity of Nicoletta Spoto might therefore prove a great attraction in his eyes, reminding him probably of some other woman that he had known there. Being himself of the humblest origin, he had imagined perhaps that he would be making a great stride, were he to ally himself with a family like the Spoto, extremely wealthy at one time, now impoverished, but still one of the leading families in the place.

And now, it was obvious, the lady in question, taking advantage of the power she had acquired over the father, was avenging herself for the affront she had received on that occasion. Dia-nella herself had noticed that for some time past her father no longer seemed satisfied with Aurelio Costa; and that for the last few evenings there, in the villa, in conversation with Don Cosmo Laurentano, he had laid stress upon certain demands which gave her food for thought.

She disapproved privately of this strange marriage between her aunt and the Prince Don Ip-polito, she was almost ashamed of it, suspecting her father of a hidden motive; namely, that he wished to make use of this marriage, which was certainly not honourable, to force his way into the Laurentano family and gradually absorb their fortune also. For the last few evenings, at supper, his conversation with Don Cosmo had dwelt, insistently, upon the Prince's son, Lando Laurentano, who was living in Rome. Why?

Absorbed in these reflections, Dianella had sat down under an olive on the brink of the deep ravine, and was gazing at the steep bank on the other side, on which a herd of goats were grazing that had come down from the estate of Platania.

The day after her arrival in the country, she had felt a new life suddenly spring up within her. The air of wild rusticity which the old villa had asumed in its neglected state; the profound melancholy which that neglect seemed to have diffused all around, over the avenues and the solitary paths, almost hidden in moss and rockrose, where the air--cool in the shade of the olives and almond trees or of the tall hedges of prickly pear--was steeped in fragrance, the bitter fragrance of sloes, the strong and pungent fragrance of mint and sage; and that wide precipitous ravine; and the bright and blithe proximity of the sea; and those old trees, untended, shaggy with random shoots, dreaming in the stillness of the vast solitude, were in pleasant harmony with the state of mind in which she found herself.

Now, however, those remarks by her father ... his anger with Aurelio... and this strike of sulphur workers at Aragona... the threats. ... And she, alone there, with literally no one to whom she might pour out her heart! To have a mother and not to be able to turn to her, and to see her mother before her eyes, worse than dead--alive and lifeless....

There wandered for some way, among the occasional clumps of reeds in the bottom of the ravine, a rivulet which at a certain point in its course had been dammed in the construction of the railway. She fixed her gaze on it, and immediately it occurred to her that she herself had been left precisely in the condition of that rivulet, like a rivulet whose course some unknown hand by a mischievous caprice had blocked, near its source, with huge and heavy stones; on one side the water had spread out in a stagnant pool, and on the other the stream had filtered underground among sand and pebbles. Oh, what an unquenchable thirst remained in her for a mother's love! But she flew to her mother, and that mother did not recognize her as her own daughter. A daughter's grief so close and urgent aroused no response whatever in that spent consciousness.

"Vittoria Vivona of Alessandria della Bocca," her mother would say of herself in a voice that seemed to come from far away. "A beautiful girl! A beautiful girl! She had hair that reached to the ground; it took three women to brush it.... She sang and played. She played the organ, too, in church, at Santa Maria dell' Udienza, and the little angels gathered round to hear her, on their knees with their hands clasped, so.... She was to have married a rich man in Girgenti; but she took a headache, and died...." Dianella could no longer restrain her tears, and began to weep silently, with a bitter delight in her solitude. But the silence round about her was so complete, so intense and immemorial the daydream of the earth and of everything upon it, that suddenly she felt herself somehow absorbed in it, fascinated by it. Burdened with an infinite, resigned sadness seemed to her now those trees, absorbed in their perennial dream, from which the wind sought in vain to arouse them. She perceived, in that mysterious, disturbing intimacy with unpeopled nature, the slightest movements, the faintest sounds, the vague rustle of the leaves, the hum of insects; and ceased to feel that she was living only for herself; she lived for an instant, unconscious and yet alertly wondering, with the earth, as though her soul had been diffused among and confused with all these country things. Ah, what a freshness of childhood in the grass that grew round about her! And how rose-pink her hand looked against the tender green of those leaves! Oh, look, a ladybird, a stray venturer, out of its season, running over her hand. ... How pretty it was! It glistened like a little jewel! Could the earth then, among all the sad and ugly things it bore, produce things so pretty and charming also?

It ran, as though in answer to her question, across the leaves, across her hand, light and cool as the breath of joy. Dianella sighed and waited with her hand on the grass for the insect to find its way back among the leaves, then drew back with a start at the joyous, unexpected arrival of the three mastiffs, which gathered round her, or rather sprang upon her, impatient, thrusting one another aside, eager to feel her hand caressing their heads. And they would not allow her to rise. Finally Mauro Mortara overtook them.

"Have you been feeling unwell?" he inquired, grimly, without looking at her.

"No... it's nothing..." she replied, shield-ing herself with her arms from the paws and tongues of the dogs, and smiling sadly. "A little tired...."

"Here!" Mauro shouted to the three mastiffs to leave her in peace.

And immediately they became still, as though turned to stone by his shout. Dianella rose to her feet and stooped to stroke their heads once more, as an apology for the disturbance.

"Poor things... poor things..."

"If you wish to come..." Mauro suggested.

"I'm ready. To see the General's room. I'm so curious...." She was embarrassed when speaking to him by the uncertainty whether to address him as voi or *tu*.

"Has your father gone?"

"Yes, yes," she made haste to assure him; and at once repented of her haste, which might betray the same sense of relief in herself that everyone else felt in her father's absence. "At Aragona," she said, "the sulphur workers have mutinied. We shall have to get soldiers and carabinieri sent there."

"Powder and shot!" Mauro at once expressed his approval, nodding his head vigorously. "I swear to you, old as I am, I'd enroll as a constable!"

"Perhaps..." Dianella attempted to put in.

But Mortara cut her short with one of his favourite ejaculations: "*Oh Marasantissima, lasciatevi servire!*"

He would not allow any argument, this Mauro Mortara. In his perpetual meditative wanderings through his rustic solitude, he had systematized his world for himself after his own fashion, and walked in that world, confident, like a god, stroking his long white beard, his eyes beaming at the satisfactory explanations which he had managed to find for everything. Everything that occurred to him must comply with the rules of this world of his. If anything refused to comply, he would cut it out, ruthlessly, or pretend not to notice it. Woe to any who contradicted him!

"*Oh Marasantissima, lasciatevi servire!* What do they want? I should like to know what they want! Do they reason or do they not? The Government, what is it? The Government is the Government. And we ought all to obey, from the highest to the lowest, all of us, each in his own station, and think of the community! Why should these gaolbirds, wretched ungrateful dogs that they are, come and spoil for us old men the satisfaction of seeing that community, Italy, changed by our efforts to a Power of the first rank? They find the table spread, the soup ladled out for them, and they spit in it, do you hear? But if everyone was to think only of himself, how could the ship keep afloat? Can't a man rise or fall, in these days, by his own deserts? What have you deserved? Bread and onions? Live on bread and onions! I can tell you that a man can be quite happy, living on bread and onions, I have lived on them myself. But if you honestly deserve something more, go ahead, prove your merit, you will advance! No, my friends, no.... The ass says to-day to his master: 'Down on all fours; I'm going to ride now....' And all the time, look: Tunis is over there!"

He turned towards the sea and with outstretched arm pointed, frowning, to a spot on the far horizon. Dianella turned to look, without understanding what Tunis had to do with it. She let him talk and did not once interrupt, except to shew her approval of all these patriotic utterances.

"Over there!" Mauro repeated angrily. "And the French are there, who stole it from us by fraud! And to-morrow we may have them here on our own soil, do you understand? I swear to you, there are times when I lie awake all night, biting my hands with rage! And instead of keeping that in mind, those scoundrels there take it into their heads to strike, to squabble among themselves! It's all the priests' doing, you know. Double-dyed rascals! Scum of all the vices! Sinks of iniquity! Quietly fanning the flames, so as to dismember Italy once again.... The Sanfedisti! The Sanfedisti! I have to keep eyes at the back of my head, because they have sworn to destroy me, and watch every step I take. But they've found their match in me.... Look here!"

And he shewed Dianella the brace of Neapolitan pistols that hung from his belt.

IN THE SHRINE.

This visit to the famous "General's room," known simply as the Camerone, was indeed a special favour conferred upon Dianella Salvo. Mauro Mortara, who kept the key of this room, never allowed anyone to enter it. And not the door only, but the shutters of the two balconies and of the other window were kept permanently closed, as though the light and air, given free access, might put to flight the memories gathered and hoarded there with such jealous veneration.

Certainly, after the old Prince's departure into exile, door and windows had been flung open time and again; but Mortara, since his return to Val-sania, had kept the shutters at least permanently closed, and was under the illusion that they had been like that always, and that those walls therefore still enclosed the very breath of the General, the atmosphere of those bygone days.

This illusion was strengthened by the sight of the furniture, which had been left untouched, except for the canopied brass bed which had been stripped of its mattress, boards and heavy curtains.

This half-light was admirably suited for the awakening of distant memories!

Mauro invariably began by making a short tour of the room; stopped in front of some decrepit piece of furniture, on which the veneering had warped and split in places; then went and sat down on the sofa covered with a green stuff, now yellow with age, with a cylindrical bolster in the angle of each end, and there, with half-shut eyes, stroking his long white beard with his stunted, muscular little hand, he would give rein to his thoughts, or more often his memories, distracted, absorbed, like a praying worshipper in church.

He was not disturbed even by the rats which at times created an infernal din on tho terrace above, the floor of which, to prevent the ceiling of the camerone from collapsing, had had to be covered with sheets of metal. This remedy had availed but little and not for long; the strips of metal had gaped and shrunk in the sun, to the great delight of the rats who had come scampering back, and concealed themselves underneath; and the ceiling had already begun to bulge, and dripped in winter from two or three cracks, while the walls even in summer retained two large patches of damp encrusted with mould.

Don Cosmo did not trouble about it: he scarcely ever set foot in the camerone; Mauro did not wish it to be restored: he had but a short time to live and was determined that everything should remain as it was; he knew that, after his death, no one would take the trouble to look after this "Shrine of Liberty"; and the ceiling might then come down altogether or be repaired. Every year, in the meantime, as autumn drew round, he would go up to the terrace and would join together and fasten down the strips of metal with big stones, and on the floor of the camerone place buckets and basins to catch the drip. The drops fell clanging into them, one by one; and by their rhythmical cadence seemed to assent to being thus collected.

Dianella, as she entered the room, received a sudden shock at the unexpected sight of a stuffed animal which, in the dim light, seemed to be alive there against the opposite wall, in the corner, with lowered tail and head turned to one side, catlike.

"What a fright it gave me!" she exclaimed with a nervous laugh, covering her face with her hands. "I never expected such a thing.... What is it?"

"A leopard," said Mauro.

"What a beauty!"

And Dianella put out her hand to stroke the dappled skin; but at once drew it back covered in dust, and noticed that the animal had lost one of its glass eyes, the left.

"I presented another one, the companion to this," Mauro went on, "to the Institute Museum, at Girgenti. Haven't you ever seen it? There's a case of my stuff in the Museum. Next to the leopard, there's a hyaena, a great big one, and above them an imperial eagle. On the case is a label: *Shot, stuffed and presented by Mauro Mortara.* Yes, indeed. But come over here, first. I want you to look at something else."

He led her across to the broken-down old sofa.

Hanging upon the wall behind it were four medals, two of silver, the others of bronze, pinned to a frayed and faded velvet shield. Over the shield was a framed letter, written in a minute hand upon a sheet of paper that had once been blue.

"Ah, the medals!" Dianella exclaimed.

"No," said Mauro, with emotion, shutting his eyes. "The letter. Bead the letter."

Dianella went nearer to the sofa and read the signature first: "Gerlando Laurentano."

"The General?"

Mauro, his eyes still shut, nodded gravely in assent.

And Dianella read:

Burmula, December 22, 1852.

My friends,

The news from France of Louis Napoleon's *Coup d'Etat* must certainly present a long and serious hindrance to the movement in support of our sacred cause, and postpone for an indefinite period our return to Sicily.

At my age, I cannot any longer endure the burden of this life of exile.

I feel that I shall no longer be fit to lend my right arm to the Country when she, in the fulness of time, shall have need of it. All the less reason, therefore, to drag out any longer an existence that is painful to myself and harmful to my children.

You, who are younger than I, have still such a reason; go on living, therefore, for the country and think sometimes with affection of

Yours,

GERLANDO LAURENTANO.

Dianella turned to look at Mortaro who, withdrawn into himself, his eyes now wide open and staring, his features contracted and his hand covering his mouth, was endeavouring to stifle the sobs that broke from him in the tangle of his beard.

"It's years since I last read it," he murmured when he was able to speak.

He stood for a long time nodding his head, then went on:

"He played me false that time. He wrote the letter and dressed himself up in his best, as if he was going to a ball. I was in the kitchen; he called me. 'Take this letter to Mariano Gioeni, at La Valletta.' The other Sicilian exiles were at La Valletta, who had all been together here, in this room, before Forty-Eight, at the time of the conspiracy. I can see them now: Don Giovanni Ricci-Gramitto, the poet, Don Mariano Gioeni and his brother Don Francesco, Don Francesco De Luca, Don Gerlando Bianchini, Don Vincenzo Barresi: all here; and myself down below, keeping guard. However! I took the letter.... How should I know what was in it? When I got back to Burmula, I found him dead."

"Had he killed himself?" Dianella asked in alarm.

"With poison," Mauro answered. "He hadn't had time even to draw his other leg up on the bed. What a handsome man he was! You've seen Don Ippolito? He was handsomer. Yes, taller, straight upright, with a pair of eyes that flashed fire: a Saint George! Even when he was an old man, the women would all fall in love with him."

He shut his eyes again and in a low tone repeated the clos-ing words of the letter, which he knew by heart:

"*You, who are younger than I, have still such a reason; go on living, therefore, for the country and think sometimes with affection of yours, Gerlando Laurentano.* You see? And I did go on living; as he wished. And here, under the letter, which I made Don Mariano Gioeni give me back, I decided to hang up my medals, by way of an answer. But I had to win them first! Sit down, sit down here; you mustn't tire yourself...."

Dianella sat down on the old sofa. At that moment, Donna Sara Alaimo, hearing the sound of voices in the camerone and see-ing the unusual spectacle of the door standing ajar, thrust in her bonneted head to inspect.

"What do you want here?" Mauro Mortara sprang upon her as the leopard, had it been alive, might have sprung. "This is no place for you!"

"Pooh!" said Donna Sara, quickly withdrawing her head. "Who spoke to you, pray?"

Mauro hastily barred the door.

"I could throttle that woman! I can't abide her, I can't endure the sight of her, that old spy of the priests! So she dares to poke her nose in here now, does she? She never did that before. It's the priests that are keeping her here, you know? Taking advantage of Don Cosmo's silliness. The Sanfedisti, the Sanfedisti..."

"But do they really exist still, these Sanfedisti?" Dianella inquired with a kindly smile.

"*Oh Marasantissima, lasciatevi servire!*" Mortara once more exclaimed. "Do they exist? They may perhaps call themselves by some other name now; but they are still the same. An infernal sect, scattered all over the world! They have spies everywhere: I came upon one in Turkey, even, just fancy! At Constantinople."

"Have you travelled as far as that?" asked I Dianella.

"As far as that? A great deal farther!" Mauro replied with a smile of satisfaction. "Where have I not been and what have I not done? Let us count up; but ten fingers aren't enough: herd boy, farm labourer, servant, ship's boy, dock labourer, able seaman, stoker, cook, bathing attendant, big game hunter, then one of Garibaldi's volunteers, orderly to Bixio; then, after the Revolution, head jailer: three hundred prisoners I had on my hands at Santo Vito, when they tried to escape; and here I am ending up as a peasant again. The story of my life? It wouldn't be believed, if anybody tried to tell it."

He stroked his beard for a while in silence, while his green eyes glowed again, at the thrill of his memories. "Cut down the trunk of a tree," he said, "and cast it into the sea, far out from the shore. Where will it drift to? I was like a tree-trunk, horn and bred up here, at Valsania. The storm came and uprooted me. First the General went with his comrades; I went off two days later, by night, in a sailing ship, as the way was then; a big boat of the kind they call tartans. I laugh at it now. If you knew how frightened I was, though, that night, on the sea!"

"The first time?"

Who had ever done such a thing before? Black, pitch black, sky and sea. Only the spread sail showed a glimmer of white. The stars, thousands of stars, high up above, looked like dust.

The sea was dashing and breaking against the tartan's sides, and the mast rocked. Then the moon came out, and the brute grew calm. The crew were smoking their pipes and chatting together in the bows; I, down in the hold, among the bales and coils of tarred rope, could see the light of their pipes; I was crying, with my eyes wide open, and never noticed it. The tears fell on my hands. I was like a child of five; and I was three and thirty! Good-bye, Sicily; good-bye, Valsania; Girgenti, that you see from far out, standing up on the hill; good-bye, bells of San Gerlando, whose hum used to reach me in the silence of the fields; good-bye, trees that I knew every one apart.... You can't imagine how, when you are far out at sea, all the precious things that you are leaving behind come back to you, and take hold of you and tear your heart! I could see certain spots here, at Valsania, just as if I had been there; better, in fact; I noticed certain things that I had never noticed before; how the blades of grass quivered in the north-easterly breeze, a stone that had dropped from the wall, a tree that had begun to lean over a bit, and could be put straight, I could count every leaf upon it.... However! At daybreak, I reached Malta. First of all you touch the island of Gozzo.... Malta, you must understand, takes in the sea, like a big bay. Every here and there is an inlet. On one of these is Burmula, where the General had taken a room. Great big harbours, forests of masts; and people of every race and nation: Arabs, Turks, Bedouins, Moroccans; besides English, French, Spaniards. A hundred tongues spoken. In Sixty there was an outbreak of cholera, brought by the Jews from Susa, who had fine women with them, oh, beauties! but, do you know, young girls of sixteen or eighteen like yourself...."

"Oh, I am older than that," said Dianella.

"Older? You don't look it. They painted their faces. With no need," Mauro went on, "just like old women. A pity! Fine girls! They brought the cholera, I was saying: a terrible epidemic! Just imagine that at Burmula, a small village, in one day, there were eight hundred deaths. They were dying like flies. But when a man is down, death has no terror for him. I used to eat egg-fruit and tomatoes, like anything: I did it on purpose. I had learned a Maltese song and used to sing it night and day, sitting astride a window-sill.

For I was in love...."

"Indeed? Out there?" Dianella asked, in surprise.

"Not there," replied Mauro. "I had left a peasant girl here, at Valsania, whom I used to court: Serafina.... She married another man, barely a year after. And I used to sing.... Would you like to hear the song? I remember it still."

He shut his eyes, threw back his head and began to hum in falsetto, pronouncing the words of the popular ditty after his own fashion:

Ahi me kalbi, kentu giani...

Dianella gazed at him in wonder, with a feeling of emotion, of bitter sweetness, which was diffused also by the plaintive rhythm of that air drawn from a far off time and place, which awakened on the old man's lips a faint echo of his adventurous youth. She had never for an instant suspected beneath the rough and hairy rind of Mortara any such store of tender memories.

"How pretty it is!" she said. "Sing it again!" Mauro, deeply moved, shook his finger in refusal.

"I can't; I have no voice.... Do you know what the first words mean? *Ah me, my heart, how it aches*. I don't remember what the rest means. The General was so fond of that song. He was always making me sing it. Eh, I had a good voice, then.... Are you looking at the leopard? Now I'll tell you about that."

And he went on to tell her how, after the General's death, left alone at Burmula, and not wishing to return to Sicily, where he had already come under suspicion, he had gone to La Valletta. There, the Sicilian exiles had wished to help him; but he, knowing in what a wretched plight they themselves were, had refused all offers of help and had taken up work in the harbour, as a ship's boy, a dock labourer, an able seaman. They were short of hands, the population having been decimated by the cholera. Then he had embarked on a British vessel as a stoker. For more than six months he had been buried alive there, in the massive, roaring belly of the ship, roasting himself at the fire that had to be fed day and night, without ever knowing whither she was bound. The English engineers would look at him and laugh--why, he could not imagine-- and one day they had taken him by force and presented him, all grimy and tattered as he was, to the captain--a little red-faced man with a big brown beard almost down to his knees--and the captain had slapped him on the back several times, praising him perhaps for his zeal. And indeed, throughout all those months, he had never given himself a moment's rest, not even to snatch a mouthful of food; he had lost his appetite: all he could do was to drink, to cool the burning heat of his body which, down below there, was tortured for want of air! His only amusement, when the ship lay in some harbour, was an old cookery book, all dog's-eared, from which he had learned to spell out the alphabet with the help of the ship's cook, also an Italian, who had long ago emigrated to Malta.

An amusement and a godsend to him, that book! Because, one day, the cook, having fallen seriously ill, had to be put ashore at Smyrna, and, failing anyone else, he, the inheritor of the book and of its culinary lore, had been put to the test of that other fire. He had flung himself with all his energy into this new calling and in a short time had managed to give the captain such satisfaction that he, seeing his new cook about to fall ill like the other, had of his own accord found him a place in the kitchen of an English family, of great wealth, who lived in Constantinople.

But the illness he had contracted on board ship had not allowed him to remain for long in this post, owing to an unfortunate accident that befell him one day. A chemist from Alcamo, established for many years there, in Constantinople, to whom he would repair now and again to hear the sound of his native dialect, had tried to poison him. Yes! Instead of a dose of the oil of sweet almonds, he had given him apparently oil of bitter almonds. Was he a spy of the priests, of the Sanfedisti, too? An unintentional error? The idea! He could well remember how one day the man had dared to rebuke him sharply over the affair of the hanged Franciscan, which he had told him, simply as a joke. Ah, but having recovered by a miracle, after about three months, from his poisoning, he had made the fellow pay dearly for his crime. With his fist (here Mauro showed his fist with a smile) he had laid him out on the floor of his shop. He had a huge iron ring on his finger, like a twisted nail, which he had bought at Smyrna, and with this--without meaning to, of course!--he had fractured the man's skull.

After the first alarming shock of seeing the man fall to the ground in a heap, before his eyes, streaming with blood, he had taken to his heels and a few hours later had set sail on board a vessel bound for a small port in Asia Minor. He could not remember the name of the little seaside town in which he had landed: it was summer and he had at once found employment as a bathing attendant.

"Have you ever heard of Grazio Antinori?" Mortara inquired at this stage.

"The explorer? Yes," said Dianella.

"He came there, one day, to bathe," Mauro went on, "with another Italian. I heard them talking, and went up to them. Antinori was engaging people to go out shooting big game in the Libyan desert. He liked the look of me, and took me on. We went out there; we sent him the beasts we shot; he stuffed them and then sent them off to the museums, London, Vienna.... When I came back from the expedition, as he had taken a fancy to me, knowing I could be trusted, I helped him to prepare his materials, and while I was doing so, quietly picked up his secrets. So I learned how to stuff animals; and when he left, I went on shooting game and sending home specimens on my own account. Let me tell you about one adventure we had. One day, we had lost our way, he and I, and were half dead with hunger and thirst. Suddenly we caught sight of some fig-trees and made a dash for them, as you can imagine. But the best figs were high up and we couldn't reach them. Then I, the peasant, what did I do? I went off and came back in a minute with a reed, a fine long one; I split it a little way at one end and set to work to gather the ripest figs from the top, oozing tears of milk: they were like honey, I can tell you! Antinori stood watching me and gnashing his teeth with rage. At length he could stand it no longer and shouted: 'What are you doing? Stop, will you? Are you going to leave me to be killed by the Turks?' I knew the answer to that. Without saying a word, I put out my arm and handed him the reed. I went off and got another, and we went on calmly stealing figs. Ah, Antinori... he liked me, and helped me a lot, even after he had gone aw-ay. I stayed there more than six years. Then I heard that Garibaldi had landed at Marsala; I flew back at once to Sicily. I landed at Messina; I joined the volunteers at Milazzo. Don Stefano Auriti died in my arms. He couldn't speak, he gave me a look begging me to take care of his son, Don Roberto, his twelve year old lion cub.... How we fought! At Reggio it was I that opened fire, do you know? The first shot fired was mine! Then Bixio took me as his orderly.... What a day that was, at Volturno! But now, after all the things I have seen and been through, I have had enough, why not! Italy is great! Italy stands at the head of the nations! She lays down the law to the world! And I can say that I too, poor ignorant wretch that I am, have done something, without making any talk about it. I can go to the King and say to him: 'Your Majesty, in the throne you're sitting on, if it's not a leg or a crossbar, there's a little peg somewhere that was stuck there by me. I've done my share for you, my lad!' And I am content. I go about Valsania here, I see the telegraph wires, I hear the pole hum, as if there was a nest of hornets inside it, and my chest swells; I say: 'The fruits of the Revolution!' I go over there, I see the railway, the train burrowing underground, in the tunnel below Valsania, which is like a dream to me; and I say 'The fruits of the Revolution!' I go and stand under the pine, there, I look towards the sea, I see Porto Empedocle, which at the time when I left for Malta had nothing but the tower, the Bastiglie, the Old Harbour and a few hovels, and has now grown to be almost a town; I see the two long breakwaters of the new harbour, which make me think of a pair of arms stretched out to all the ships of all the civilized nations of the earth, as much as to say: 'Come! Come! Italy has risen again, Italy embraces you all, offers you all the riches of her sulphur, the riches of her gardens!' Fruit of the Revolution, this too, I think, and--would you believe it?--I burst out crying like a child, for joy. ..."

So saying, he took from the open bosom of his coarse flannel shirt a big handkerchief of blue cotton, and wiped his eyes, which really were filled with tears.

Dianella felt her own eyes too grow moist. This old man who inspired such terror, who had killed one man, as though it were nothing, and had caused the death of another, simply out of an insane suspicion, who went about armed to the teeth, always within an inch of shedding fresh blood, quick to anger as he was and savage and proud; there he was crying like a child in front of her; he was crying from tenderness, from satisfaction at the work that had been accomplished, which he saw to be without fault and glorious; he cried, exalting himself in his deeds and in the greatness of his country, for which he had suffered so much and fought so well, without ever asking for any reward, generous and fierce, faithful as a dog and bold as a lion. Not his pigeons, nor the peace of the fields, nor the custody of his vineyard, nor the song of the larks could succeed in calming his spirit after all those years; this *camerone* was, so to speak, his church; and he came out of it reeling like a drunken man, and wandered up and down the solitary paths, under the almond trees and olives, talking to himself of battles and conspiracies, looking askance at the sea in the direction of Tunis, from whence he imagined a surprise attack by the French....

A jingle of bells and the sound of carriage wheels came suddenly to distract Dianella from these reflexions and Mauro from his tears.

"Your father?" he asked, his face at once darkening, as he replaced his handkerchief in the bosom of his shirt.

Dianella rose in alarm, and ran to the window to look out between the slats of the shutters. She remained there. From the carriage, which had drawn up in front of the villa, there alighted her father, home again, and Aurelio Costa--he!--in his working clothes.

"Off with you, off with you," Mauro said to her, almost thrusting her from the room. "I'll shut up and get away!"

Dianella went out into the corridor and saw at the far end of it Costa and her father, on their way to the latter's room, the door of which they shut behind them. Whereupon Mauro Mortara, like a wild animal surprised in its lair, crept stealthily away, without another word to her.

She stood there in perplexity, profoundly moved, not knowing what to make of her father's unexpected and unprecedented return. Evidently, both his return and Aurelio Costa's visit had some connection with the reports of the disturbances at Aragona. Something very serious indeed must have happened. Had Aurelio run away? No: Dianella refused even to imagine such a thing. Perhaps it was her father himself that had sent for him. With what object?

She was tempted to retire to her own room, next door to her father's, in the hope of hearing some of their conversation through the wall; but she remembered the look her father had given her, that morning, and held back; she remained, however, as though drawn in opposite directions, in the entrance hall.

"Your Papa," Donna Sara Alaimo informed her, thrusting her head out from behind the kitchen door.

Dianella nodded. "With the engineer," Donna Sara went on, in a whisper.

Dianella again nodded to shew that she knew this already, and went out to the head of the outside stair. The carriage was still there, waiting, at the foot of the steps. So her father was starting off again immediately? Perhaps he had come back to fetch some of his papers.

"Are you going to Porto Empedocle at once?" she asked the coachman.

"Yes, Your Excellency," was his answer.

And out came her father and Costa, in evident haste. Flaminio Salvo did not expect to find his daughter at the head of the steps, and, on catching sight of her, drew back a little, without stopping, smiled at her and waved his hand in farewell. Aurelio Costa, who followed him, stopped for a moment in confusion, and was about to take off his travelling cap; but Salvo called out to him:

"Come along, come along...."

Dianella, pale, hardly able to breathe, saw them get into the carriage and drive off, without turning their heads, and followed them with her eyes until they disappeared among the trees of the avenue.

How Aurelio had altered! So agitated.... He looked ill, aged, with his unshaven chin.... Dianella remembered the opinion that Nicoletta Capolino had expressed of him. She would have liked to see him more independent of her father; would have liked him, notwithstanding her father's imperious summons, to stop at the head of the steps, if only to bid her good day. Instead of at once obeying the call....

Perhaps the moment.... What could have been happening at the pit?

AN AMBUSH.

Flaminio Salvo came home late that evening, in high spirits, as he always was when he had taken an important decision.

At supper he apologized to Don Cosmo for his outburst that morning; explaining that his gorge rose at the endless worries that kept pouring upon him from those sulphur pits at Aragona, and that he had decided to close them.

"And so," he exclaimed, "those fine gentlemen can do a little striking for my amusement, and will have more time to listen to the sermons of their humanitarian priests. Let them live upon sermons! A fine thing, the humanitarian gospel, Don Cosmo, if you keep to one page! If they were to turn the page.... But you won't find them doing that! They are quite right; but their reason is here!"

And he tapped his stomach.

"Go and explain to them that the fiscal policy pursued by the Italian Government has been a regular gold mine to the industry and capitalists of Northern Italy, and an utter disaster to the South and to our poor Island; that for years past taxation and our other burdens have been steadily increasing and our output steadily falling; that with the price to which sulphur has now fallen not only is it absolutely impossible to treat them more generously, but it is sheer madness to carry on the industry at all.... I have kept the sulphur pits open for their sake, to let them have at least a crust of bread. They strike, do they? Most considerate of them! That means to say that they can get along without work. A public holiday! Cakes and ale!"

"Life!" sighed Don Cosmo, his lips drooping. "When you come to think it over.... The sulphur, of course... our industries... this tablecloth here, damask... this cut glass... the bronze lamp... all this nonsense on the table ... and in the house... and all over the place ... steamers on the sea, railways, balloons in the air.... We are mad, upon my word of honour it's mad we are.... Yes: they serve, they serve to fill up to a certain extent that supreme nonsense which we call life, to give it a certain form, a certain consistency.... Mah! I swear to you, there are moments when I don't know whether it is I that am mad, I who understand nothing about it, or the people who seriously believe that they do understand something about it, and talk and move as if they really had some definite goal in front of them, which, when they reached it, would not appear futile in their own eyes. I should begin, my dear sir, by breaking this glass. Then I should pull down the house.... To begin all over again, possibly!... You say that those poor fellows have their reason here? They are fortunate, my friend! And woe to them if they reach satiety. ... Where do you keep your reason? Where is mine?"

And he rose from the table.

A little later, Flaminio Salvo and Dianella were standing by the window. The night was dark as pitch. The profound stars, that studded and enlarged the firmament, failed to shed any light on the earth. The grasshoppers were chiming uninterruptedly in the distance, and, now and then, from the depths of the valley rose the agonising note of an owl, like a sob. The darkness, the silence round the villa was at intervals pierced here and there and set throbbing by the swift shriek of unseen bats. Then the moon rose, fiery red, where the cloister of Monserrato loomed large against the sky, and the leaves stirred faintly over the whole countryside. A dog, far away, howled.

"Have you nothing, Dianella, nothing at all to say to your father?" Salvo asked, without looking at her, in a sorrowful tone, as though in the spirit he were straying far afield beyond the window. "I?" said Dianella, puzzled and almost tongue-tied. "Nothing.... What could I have to say to you?"

"Nothing, then," her father went on. "No tiny, tiny secret... nothing, eh? I am glad of that. Because you, my poor child, have only me, alas, and I have so many worries.... And to-day ... what a day it has been!... Do you know what most people lack? The sense of what is opportune. I don't mean to imply that I should have said

144

yes, if the request had been put to me on some other day, in some other way; but I should have said no, a little more politely at least, after I had spoken to you."

Dianella was afraid, as she listened to her father's calm, slow utterance, that he might hear the violent beating of her heart, held in an agony of suspense, amid the impetuous boiling of all the blood in her veins.

"They came to me... you understand what I mean," Salvo went on, turning and gazing into her eyes. "And I, being certain that my good daughter, who is such a sensible girl, could never, even for a moment, have fixed her attention upon a young man--oh, a good young man, yes; but still, for all sorts of reasons, neither suitable nor worthy--I, caught at a really inopportune moment, refused, point blank. Let us think now, can't you guess?"

"No...." Dianella breathed rather than uttered the word, while her hosom heaved in a welter of mingled emotions.

"You can't guess, really?" her father insisted, with a smile, as though conscious of the torture he was inflicting upon her. "Come, have a try...."

"I... I couldn't..." she stammered.

"Then I shall have to tell you," her father concluded, "so that you may know where you are. De Vincentis...."

"Ah!" exclaimed Dianella, with an irrepressible peal of laughter. "That poor Nini!"

"That poor Nini," her father echoed, shaking his head and smiling himself also. "Then you expected it?"

"No, I swear to you," Dianella hastily and emphatically replied. "I had noticed, yes...."

"But you were thinking of some one else?" her father was prompt with the question, looking more sharply at her.

Dianella remained silent for a moment, meeting her father's gaze with a firm coldness.

"I have already said no."

The suspicion that her father had intended by this speech to set a trap for her had turned to certainty. Perhaps it was not even true that Nini De Vincentis had made him this proposal. And that her father should have made use of him, a penniless youth of noble birth, only too much of a gentleman, as though to bring him into derision, seemed hateful to her, knowing as she did that De Vincentis was another of her father's victims.

He said nothing more; he remained for a while at the window, looking out, then turned away with a sigh and bade his daughter good night before going off to bed.

"Good night," Dianella answered him, coldly.

As soon as her father had left the room, she buried her face in her hands and cried, cried impetuously, silently, stifling her sobs. She felt that her father had been amusing himself by lacerating her heart, like a cat playing with a mouse. Why, oh why was he so cruel, even with his own daughter, when it would have been so easy for him to be kind to everyone? If he really wished her to tell him her secret, when he reminded her that she had no one else in whom to confide but himself, why, at the very moment in which he set before her the cruel fate that had robbed her of a mother's counsel and love, did he lay a trap for her? And so, no; it was now obvious: he did not wish her to be in love with Aurelio. He had shut down the sulphur pits; perhaps he had put into effect his threat of that morning: "I'll send you all packing!" Aurelio too? Oh, Aurelio could get on without him now! If he lost that post, there were plenty more, and better, that he would at once be able to find. And this perhaps (why, surely), annoyed her father all the more, namely that he should have put the young man in a position to get on without him, and have done so because of an obligation which bound him to the young man. He wanted people to be pliable tools in his hands; instead of which, Aurelio might rise against him, where he most dreaded rebellion, in the heart of his daughter. Yes, yes, because he knew very well that she was in love with him. If Aurelio had only known it too! But what was to happen meanwhile, if her father had really shut down the pits and dismissed him? Aurelio would go away again, might return perhaps to Sardinia, without the slightest suspicion of her love for him, and there, perhaps Dianella again buried her face in her hands. In the agonizing void, fastening her attention, unconsciously, on the dense, continuous chime of the grasshoppers, it seemed to her that it, in the silence, became at every moment louder and more intense; she thought of the disturbances at Aragona and Comitini; and that fervid chorus became then to her, of a sudden, the distant, vague clamour of a populace in revolt, to whom Aurelio, turned rebel, was going, to make himself their leader and avenger. And she? and she?

She took her hands from her face: like a dream now appeared to her the desolate peace of the countryside, spread out before her in the moist pale light of the moon. And a cool, unlooked-for spring of tenderness burst from her heart; and fresh tears dimmed her eyes.

Ah, it was beautiful all the same, how beautiful, the spectacle of that profound moonlit night over the country, with those ancient trees, motionless in their sad perennial dream, raising their trunks from the earth's bosom, with those hills behind which enclosed, dark against the sky, the mystery of the most distant ages, with that tremulous limpid persistent song of the grasshoppers which, scattered among the grass of the plain, seemed to be urging forgetfulness of everything.

Between grasshoppers and trees, moon and hills, was there not perhaps a mysterious concert, from which man remained excluded? So much beauty was not created for men, who at that hour, weary, closed their eyes in sleep; it would last all night long, unseen by any eye, in the silence of the countryside, after she too had closed her window. Perhaps this was what the invisible bat wanted, that shrieked as it flitted past outside, hurt and attracted by the light: did it want her to cease from disturbing by her vigil the nocturnal mysterious concert of solitary nature?

Dianella shut the window: she left open just a chink of one of the inside shutters, and, through this breathing space, her hands clasped before her lips, prayed in silence for all that beauty which remained outside, animated of a sudden in her eyes by the spirit of God, Whom men offended with their turbulent and sordid passions. Casting a farewell glance at the avenue leading from the villa, she observed a shadow passing along it, a bald scalp that gleamed in the moonlight. Don Cosmo? It was he.

Ah, immersed, out there, in the spirit of God, he perhaps was not conscious of it! He was pacing up and down the avenue, at that hour of the night, his hands clasped behind his back, absorbed still, she might be certain, in his own dark and vain meditations.

CHAPTER VI

ON GUARD

Neither appeals to the electors printed in letters a foot high on paper of every hue, nor any unusual animation along the tortuous streets of the old city. And yet the day fixed for the parliamentary election was close at hand.

But boredom had long since yawned in the face of charlatanry, which had lost its voice. The ladder for the assault of the walls, of the bastions, had rotted in its hands, the gluepot was broken.

Charlatanry had assumed the respectable disguise of a priest, and, collected, cautious, hypocritical, went on its way, concealing amid the folds of the priestly cloak the stick of the big drum, converted into an aspergili.

The townsfolk had no difficulty in recognizing it beneath this disguise: they let it go about as it chose; they even respected it; provided, of course, that it did not weary them with too many sermons; it lent them money, besides, on the quiet--at a high rate of interest, but still it lent it; while publicly, with a large subsidy from Salvo and others from minor investors, it had opened a Catholic People's Bank--in the approved interest of Holy Mother Church.

The public offices, the Prefecture, the Customs and Excise, the national schools, the law courts, still gave a little movement, though barely more than mechanical, to the town: the tide of life was now flowing elsewhere. The industry, the trade, all the true activity in short, had transferred itself, some time since, to Porto Empedocle, yellow with sulphur, white with lime, dusty and noisy, grown in a short time into one of the busiest and most crowded marts on the island.

But even there, the superabundance of the sulphur in the primitive conditions in which the industry was carried on, people's ignorance of the uses to which the substance was applied and of the profits that could be derived from it, the absence of capital on a large scale, the need of or greed for a quick return, all brought it about that this natural wealth of the soil, which should have meant the wealth of the inhabitants, was swallowed up day by day in the holds of the British, American, French and German trading steamers, leaving all those who lived by the industry or the trade with their backs broken by hard toil, their pockets empty and their minds poisoned by the savage and insidious warfare with which they fought for the wretched sums paid as purchase money or freight for goods which their own activity had cheapened. At Girgenti, only the summary courts and the assize courts were really busy, open as they were all the year round. Up at the Culmo delle Forche the gaol of Santo Vito was always overflowing with prisoners, who sometimes had to wait three or four years before being tried. And it was a good thing that, in the majority of cases, there was no danger of innocence being injured by this enforced delay.

The town was quiet on the whole; but in the country districts and villages of the Province crimes of bloodshed, spontaneous or hired, due to sudden quarrels or to schemes of vengeance, and highway robberies and cattle stealing and kidnappings and extortion of ransom were incessant and numberless, the fruit of misery, of savage ignorance, of hard and brutalizing toil, of vast, burnt, barren tracts of land insufficiently policed.

There, to the Piazza Sant'Anna, where the law courts were, in the centre of the town, the litigants came flocking from all parts of the Province, rough, stunted folk, baked by the sun, gesticulating in a thousand vivaciously expressive ways: owners of land or sulphur at law with their tenants or with the warehousemen of Porto Em-pedocle, and brokers and agents and lawyers and messengers; there came crowding in the dazed, loutish peasants from Grotte or Favara, Racalmato or Raffadali or Montaperto, sulphur workers or farm labourers, most of them, with grimed and sunburned faces and foxy eyes, dressed in their thick holiday clothes of dark blue broadcloth with headgear of strange fashion: conical caps, of velvet; cowls, of knitted cotton; or Paduan caps;

with rings or chains of gold in their ears, come to give evidence or to visit their relatives in prison. They spoke, all of them, in deep guttural tones or with full-throated and voluble interjections. Sparks flew from the cobbled roadways at the heavy tread of their iron-shod boots, made of rawhide, high, solid and clumsy. And they brought with them their womenfolk, mothers and wives and daughters and sisters, with eyes that shrank in terror or flashed with a puzzled shy anxiety, in gowns of barracan; with short broad-cloth capes, white or black, and brightly coloured kerchiefs on their heads, tied below the chin; some of them with the lobes of their ears torn by the weight of their ornaments, rings, pendants, tear-drops; others garbed in black, their eyes and cheeks scalded by tears, the relatives of some murdered man.

Among these, when they were Unescorted, would circulate, sharp-eyed and slinking, an old bawd or two to tempt the younger and better looking of them, who flushed crimson with shame but yielded nevertheless at times and were led away, overcome by confusion and trembling, to make a surrender of their bodies, without any pleasure to themselves, so as not to return to the village empty-handed, to buy for the fatherless little ones at home a pair of shoes or a little frock. (Such bargains! A poor girl ought not to miss the opportunity. No one would ever know.... Quick, quick.... A sin, yes, but God read what was in the heart....)

The many idlers of the town strolled meanwhile up and down, up and down, always at the same pace, dropping with boredom, with the automatic gait of lunatics, up and down the principal street, the only level road in the place, bearing a fine Greek name, Via Atenea, but as narrow and tortuous as all the rest.

Via Atenea, Rupe Atenea, Empedocle... names: illuminating names, which made all the more dreary the poverty and squalor of things and places. The Akragas of the Greeks, the Agrigentum of the Romans had ended in the Kerkent of the Musulmans, and the brand of the Arabs had remained indelibly stamped on the minds and manners of the people. A taciturn slothfulness, a sensitive and jealous distrust.

>From the Bosco della Civita, the heart of the vanished ancient city, there ran up at one time to the hill on which the new town sits in squalor a long avenue of tall, austere cypresses, as

though to point the way for death. Few of these now remained; one, the tallest and darkest, still rose beneath the town's one public avenue, called Viale della Passeggiata, the only beautiful thing that the town possessed, lying open as it did to the magnificent view of the whole vast expanse of country, undulating in hills and valleys and plains, and of the sea beyond, contained in the boundless curve of the horizon. This cypress, standing out blue and majestic, after the flames of the marvellous sunsets had died down, against the lowland darkening with the blue of night, seemed to embody in itself the infinite sadness of the silence exhaled from places once so clamorous with life. Here, to-day, death sat enthroned. Commanded, from the top of the hill, by the old Norman cathedral dedicated to San Gerlando, the Bishop's palace and the Seminary, Girgenti was the city of priests and passing bells. From morning to night, the thirty churches exchanged, in long, slow peals, the note of mourning and the call to prayer, diffusing over all a horrid gloom. Not a day went by that you did not see passing in funeral procession the grey-clad orphan girls of the Boccone del Povero: pale and bent, their wasted little faces all eyes, with veils on their heads, medals on their bosoms and tapers in their hands. Anyone, for a modest fee, might secure their escort; and nothing was sadder than the sight of all that girlhood oppressed by the spectre of death, which they must follow thus, day after day, at a crawling pace, taper in hand, its flame flickering invisible in the sunlight.

Who, in such a state of mind, could take any interest in a parliamentary election? No one had any faith in institutions, nor had ever had any such faith. Corruption was borne as a chronic, irremediable evil; and he was deemed a simpleton or a madman, impostor or self-seeker, who ventured to raise his voice against it.

At that moment, the idlers were talking less of the approaching election than of the duel between the candidate Ignazio Capolino and Guido Veronica.

The violent intrusion of Roberto Auriti had complicated the question at issue. Guido Veronica had at once accepted Capolino's challenge; he had asked however for a few days' grace in order to provide himself with seconds. And there had come from Palermo the Deputy Corrado Selmi, with another gentleman, who professed to be a famous swordsman. Roberto Auriti, meanwhile, being debarred from fighting Preola and not wishing that anyone else should avenge his father's memory for the vile insult offered to it, had claimed the right to fight Capolino first. The latter's seconds, as also Veronica himself, had opposed this claim. In Capolino's name, his seconds had honourably declared their regret for Preola's article, which had found its way surreptitiously into the newspaper. The person actually responsible for the insult being thus disowned by his own party, being moreover admittedly unqualified to take the field and having in the meantime been expelled from Girgenti, Auriti was no longer in a position to demand satisfaction; and a single duel was to be fought, in order that the affair might terminate honourably: the duel between Veronica and Capolino, for the assault made upon the latter in the open street. Quite right!

This greatly debated quarrel had aroused keen excitement among the townsfolk, quite a number of whom had suddenly revealed a passionate interest in duelling; and this excitement had been raised to the highest pitch by the intervention of so notorious a person as Selmi and by the provoking, Spaniard-like airs of Veronica's other second, the swashbuckler.

But on the other side, the local champion, Ignazio Capolino, had placed himself in good hands also: in those of a certain D'Ambrosio, a distant relative of his wife, who knew how to handle a sword and was not the sort of man to let himself be imposed upon either by the reputation of Corrado Selmi or by the other gentleman's swagger. He stood alone, though, for Capolino's other second was a joke: Nini De Vincentis, just imagine! Poor Nini, he had positively been dragged in by the hair of his head! Sabres, blood--he that was a regular young lady, a lily-bearing San Luigi Gonzaga. He would be sure to faint, when it came to the fight! What on earth was that fellow Capo-lino thinking about, to go and choose Nini of all people, as though the town were not full of far more suitable men! But perhaps D'Ambrosio had chosen him deliberately, as a piece of bravado.

Nini was still unaware of the definite refusal given by Salvo to the offer of marriage which--under pressure from his brother Vincente--he had made Monsignor Montero convey. Capolino had forced him to accept this position (a terrible one to him) of second supporter at the duel, giving him to understand that Salvo would be extremely grateful to him. Perbacco, was he or was he not going to give the lie, once and for all, to the reputation for modest, girlish timidity which he had won in the town? A man! A man! He must prove that he was a man! Anyhow, paunch and presence: that was all that was required of him. Paunch, indeed? Was Nini required to shew a paunch? Thin and straight as a lath.... Go on, it was only an expression: "Paunch and presence." Calm and neat as any dandy from Paris, he was certain to cut a splendid figure.

All four seconds had assembled in the course of the morning at the Prince of Laurentano's villa, Colimbetra, where the duel was to be fought, to make the necessary arrangements and to choose the ground. No one out there would dare to interrupt the proceedings. The Prince was going, on the following morning, to Valsania, to be introduced to his bride, as had been arranged; immediately after his departure, the duel was to begin. The peripatetic idlers, from the Viale della Passeggiata, watched the four seconds drive back from Colimbetra.

Ignazio Capolino, meanwhile, was waiting for his seconds to return, strolling with the officials of the Party upon the wide marble terrace, outside the Club which, like so many other things there, was called Empedocle.

This duel, on the very eve of the election, had increased his importance and had won him friends. He made a show of not being in the least concerned, and this display of entire indifference aroused an admiring approbation in the friends who strolled by his side. He had already begun his tour of the constituency, and was now describing the enthusiastic welcome he had received the day before in the suburban district of Favara. He would have liked to go that day to the other suburb, Siculiana, where the electors were impatiently awaiting him; but D'Ambrosio, his master, his tyrant for the time being, had absolutely forbidden this, for fear of his tiring himself unduly.

He was sorry, for the sake of his friends at Siculiana, that was all. They too had prepared a great welcome for him. His victory was assured, notwithstanding the threats and high-handedness of the Government, and the Prefect's orders, and police persecution. Roberto Auriti would or might have a majority of a handful of votes only in the village of Comitini, where Pompeo Agro numbered many friends.

Capolino gave this information with genuine regret for his opponent, and this regret was genuinely shared by all that heard him. Because it was well known that Auriti had never reaped any reward from the Liberal principles for which he had fought in his boyhood, nor from his persistent loyalty to them in later life; and that it was certainly not in the hope of reaping any reward from them that he had come to ask for the votes of his fellow citizens, but almost as a duty that was imposed upon him or perhaps under the ingenuous illusion that he had a sufficient claim to those votes in the respect due to his honesty. No one denied him that respect, indeed everybody was quite prepared to do him some honour proportionate to his deserts. But the honour of electing him to Parliament, no, what an idea! That honour was not, could not be for him; and the clearest proof of this lay in the ingenuousness of such an illusion.

When his seconds arrived, Capolino withdrew with them to a corner of the big morning room of the Club.

Nini De Vincentis appeared dazed, his face mottled as though it had been pinched all over, and his eyes glistening, absent and sullen. D'Ambrosio, tall and fair, short-sighted, restless, with a horse face, arched shoulders, an enormous chest and long, bony legs, was speaking volubly, running all his words together. He was the most plain-spoken of men, and people put up with his plain speech not only because they knew him to be quarrelsome, but because he often made them laugh. His insults became blunted and lost their sting in the laughter with which they were received, and so he was able to insult everyone, and to shout the vilest abuse in people's faces without anyone's feeling offended or hurt.

"Do me a blessed favour," he began, "and tell my cousin Nicoletta to leave you alone to-night, as you have to fight for your holy devils. For your holy ideals, I should say. You're getting an old man, Gnazio, do you know that? Hold out your arm: let me see whether it shakes."

Capolino with a smile held out his arm.

"Good," D'Ambrosio went on. "We'll pump the lead into them, my boy. I mean it! First of all, pistols. Three rounds each at five-and-twenty paces. (Nini must remember not to stop his ears when he hears the bang.) Then the sabres. As far as the sabres are concerned, we're in clover; but the pistols--Gnazio, my boy, you're getting old, and I fear.... Oh, well; come along home with me. There's the courtyard. I want to see how well you can shoot."

Capolino tried to resist; but there was no way out of it; he was obliged to go, as also was Nini, to accustom his ears to the sound.

They went up the steep Via di Lena, where a brawl seemed to be in progress, a mob of people gathered round some one who was singing. It was nothing! Only the fish-hawkers who, having just arrived from the harbour, and dismounted from their loaded mules, were crying fresh fish amid the crowd, with a long and cheerful lilt. The trio proceeded by the increasingly steep ascent of Bac Bac, and came out by the highest of the city gates, that to the north, the old name of which, likewise of Arabic origin, Bab-er-rjiah (Gate of the Winds) had been corrupted to Biberia.

D'Ambrosio lived up there in an old house with its *baglio* (an immense cobbled yard) and a water tank in the middle, keeping house with his aged mother, to whom he paid a more than religious devotion. The poor old lady was deaf, and lived in constant anxiety, in a continual tremor for that hotheaded son of hers. A half-knitted stocking in her hands, she was always looking out from one of the windows. She saw the hill, on which Girgenti stands, drop precipitously to the Val Sellano, intersected by a network of dusty roads. The view to the front was vast and mountainous. To the right, rose dark and looming Monte Caltafaraci; beyond, in the background, San Benedetto; from there extended the plain of Consolida and, still looking westward, the plain of Clerici, beyond the mountain of Carapezza and the nearer Montaperto. Below, and just opposite, the chalky face of the Serra Ferlucchia shewed the cavernous mouths of the sulphur pits and the bleak white mounds of burnt refuse. Far away, at the boundary of the Province, rose cloud-capped and majestic Monte Gemini, one of the highest peaks in Sicily. The grey, arid, hard asperity of the landscape was relieved only here and there by an occasional dark carub.

D'Ambrosio left his friends to wait in the courtyard; he went upstairs and came down again a moment later with a big duelling revolver and a box of cartridges; with a stick of charcoal he sketched a few lines on the wall, by the empty stable, the form of a man, Guido Veronica; then stepped out twenty-five paces from the wall.

"Here, Gnazio! I shall clap my hands three times; at the third, you fire! Are you ready?"

Capolino had submitted to this test as to a joke, without enthusiasm. Only when he saw facing him, on the wall, the human target which now seemed with an affectation of lifelessness to be awaiting his shots, but to-morrow would be stepping out to meet him, detaching itself from the wall, with live arms and legs, pointing the muzzle of a similar pistol at himself, Capolino, his lips frozen in a smile, knitted his brows and resolutely fired.

D'Ambrosio declared himself highly satisfied with the test; then, just for fun, tried to force Nini to fire at the mark as well.

Nini proved as obstinate as a mule. But D'Ambrosio would not rest until he had compelled him to fire; whereupon he burst out in a wild peal of laughter:

"Upon my word, he shut his eyes, both of them! A glass of water! A glass of water!"

And he ran to support him, as though Nini were about to faint. But he did not prolong the joke farther. He began to speak with great fervour of Corrado Selmi:

"A charming fellow! He looks quite a young man, you know? And he was out on the 4th of April, in the affair at La Gancia.... He must be at least fifty.... He looks thirty-five, thirty-eight at the very most.... Clever as they make 'em, broad-minded, an all round man. They say he has more debts than there are hairs on his head. I can well believe it! And... oh, a game-cock! Mad on the hens. His Excellency the Minister D'Atri ought to know something about that...."

Having arranged that they should meet again on the following morning, Capolino went away with Nini De Vincentis.

"Don't forget about Nicoletta! Keep a prudent vigil!" D'Ambrosio called after him from the door of the courtyard, making a trumpet of his hands; then, as though he had caught sight of a mad dog: "Look out, Gnazio, look out, man! He's after you! He's after you!"

156

Luigi Pirandello

Capolino and Nini De Vincentis turned round to look, laughing, and saw close behind them Nocio Pigna, *Propaganda*, who was coming down by the same way, with his long arm dangling and the other balanced on his knee. *Propaganda* also turned, angrily, to face D'Ambrosio, opened his lustrous madman's eyes and, raising his arm, hurled at him the word which to him was the deepest brand of infamy: "*Ignorante!*"

PROPAGANDA AND COMPANY.

And he had a better right, now, than ever to stamp with this brand all his enemies, bourgeois and priests and nobles, had Propaganda: the *Fascio*, in spite of the Prefect and Town Council, the Police and the military authorities, had at length succeeded in establishing itself.

Yes, my friends, even at Girgenti, in the town of crows and passing bells, the Fascio.

He looked up, swelling with pride, and with an air of patronage, at those old hovels of the San Michele quarter, dens of misery; at those old lanes, crooked, filthy, deep-rutted; and his eyes blazed.

More than with his fellow men, he felt himself in harmony now with the worn, blackened stones of those hovels, the gaping cobbles of those breakneck lanes; he talked to them in his heart; said to them "Bye and bye!" It was for the honour of the town, first and foremost, that he had fought and was fighting, that it might not he said that Gir-genti alone, when the whole Island was in a ferment, remained silent and dead. Soon those houses, soon those streets would be jubilant with a new life.

It was a serious matter, however, that it must cost him so much labour to persuade other people to advance their own interests; that everyone must compel him to wear himself out, to grow so heated in that task of persuasion that he might almost he suspected of having some isecret motive or hope of profit!

Who was making him do it? Really, now! He had been thrust on one side, almost expelled from society, had become superfluous in his own home. Peaceably and forcibly people had said and proved to him that they could get on without him; that they no

158

longer had any need of him. After squeezing him like a lemon, seducing one of his daughters, befouling his grey hair with mud, after slandering and defaming him, they proposed now to fling him away, did they? Oh, no! Things of that sort were not done to Pigna. Not only was he not superfluous, he intended, by Jove, to be positively indispensable; indispensable, in spite of them all! And very soon they would realize this, the *ignoranti* who refused to acknowledge him. If other people worked to support him, all that he gained was the leisure to work in his turn for other people; with this further consideration, that the help given to him was meagre, after all, and provided only the humblest essentials of life; whereas the help that he gave to others, the work that he performed was great, and provided for the higher needs. Easy, comfortable, his work? Oh yes, a regular bed of roses, to be sure! Dashing about from morning to night, racing up and down upon that fine pair of shanks that God had given him, shouting himself hoarse, wasting his breath, anybody could imagine what a pleasant life his must be!

Like a beleagured fortress, everything in which had been used as a missile to repel the assaults from without, so that the inside was left empty, Nocio Pigna had posted, in front and in rear and all about him, reasons and sentiments, all his own misfortunes, as weapons of defence against the people who were toiling remorselessly to destroy his reputation. The more he spoke, the more the sound of his own words increased his conviction and his passion. But by dint of always repeating the same things, in the same order, he had let them become stereotyped in a form in which they lost all their efficacy; his lips, one might say, were stopped up, like guns that emitted nothing but noise, smoke and wads. Inside there was nothing left. He was a man who spoke, and nothing more.

Meanwhile, he had brought the Fascio into being. That it was really composed entirely of working men, people were inclined to doubt. Not even Propaganda himself would have made bold, perhaps, to assert that the non-working element in his membership was as yet very numerous. But the great thing was to begin; and this is how things gradually are begun.

Certainly a fine haul, a solemn enrolment with several thousand members collected in a single day would have been poss-

ible only at Porto Em-pedocle, among the men of the sea, the carters, the crews of the lighters, the lads in the warehouses, the
weighmen and porters. But at Porto Empedocle.... Hush, for the
love of God!

Nocio Pigna could not bear to hear the place mentioned:
the memory of the hot reception he had had there was like an ever
open wound in his heart, and the merest touch would set it en-
dlessly throbbing. Breed of dogs, offscourings of civilization! To
have the sea, my friends, constantly before their eyes; what are you
laughing at? the divine sea, the immensity of it! to have planted
their own homes upon the beach, in readiness for the ships of distant lands, to have placed their life, in other words, at the mercy of
foreigners; and, my friends, no spirit of human brotherhood! Of all
that sea they could behold nothing more than the beach, or rather
the filth only upon the beach, their own sewage running down the
open drains. That sea, oh, that sea ought to have boiled with rage,
with contempt, to have reared up a mighty wave and submerged it,
engulfed it, that town of carrion!

Here, at Girgenti, one had to work like the ants, with patience! He had hegnn to negotiate with the presidents of sundry
local guilds: but those linked hands, the symbol of the mutual benefit societies, hands amputated at the wrist, bloodless, that is to say
with no political colour, or hands clasping the blessed rosary and
olive branch of some Catholic club, found it hard to unlink themselves, found it hard to extend themselves in brotherly greeting to
the workers in other trades and callings, as they had done at Catania, at Palermo, to form a wider circle, a union of all the forces of
the proletariat, in short, the Fascio of Fasci.

Luca Lizio had already written to Rome to Don Lando
Laurentano (who was one of themselves, God be praised, a Prince
and a Socialist!), so that he might give the necessary impetus to all
the doubtful and wavering: a single word from him, a sign would
be ample. They were waiting from day to day for his reply, which
was perhaps being delayed by the displeasure which his father's
absurd marriage must be causing the young Prince.

Meanwhile he, Nocio Pigna, was losing no time and was
not letting himself be cast down by the obstacles in his way. He
realized that it would be foolish to attach too much importance to

those guilds: in a dead town like Girgenti, devoid of any industry, where for years past they had ceased to build any fresh houses and everything was perishing in slow and silent decay; where not only did the inhabitants never seek any expensive amusement, but everyone was trying to restrict his most modest requirements; masons and smiths, tailors and cobblers depended too much on the few so-called gentry; and the secret discontent would certainly not find in them the courage to declare itself openly, when the occasion arose. In a day or two they would all be voting for that rascal Capolino, at a nod from Don Flaminio Salvo. And yet, by joining, by enrolling in the Party, the workmen might serve as an example to the peasants; might draw them in, indeed. Like sheep, those peasants were, poor creatures! Sheep, though, that knew the cruelty of the rapacious hands that shore and milked them; sheep that, if they succeeded in acquiring a consciousness of their rights, in forming the least conception of that famous "virtue of their force," would turn in an instant into wolves.

A section of them, meanwhile, lived scattered about the country, and did not come up to the town, perched high on its hill, save on Sundays and holidays. Those of them who were called *garzoni*, the least sunken in poverty, since they drew a meagre wage throughout the year, were too much afraid of the bailiffs, or *curatoli* or *soprastanti*, savage taskmasters in the service of the landlords. There remained the day labourers, those who, after sixteen hours of toil (when they were fortunate enough to find any work) came back to the town at night shouldering their tools, with aching backs and each with fifteen soldi or so in his pocket. At these Nocio Pigna marvelled; they were the majority; but clay, clay, clay, into which God had not breathed; or else poverty had long since quenched that breath; dried clay which gave you a painful surprise if, in looking at you, it moved its eyes, or in speaking, its lips.

He had taken a lease of the huge building of a derelict cereal factory on the Piano di Gamez, next door to his own house, capable of holding five hundred members and more: a trifle damp, perhaps, a trifle dark; but what of that; by lighting two or three candles one could see fairly well in the daytime. He had fitted it up as best he could, chiefly with his own hands. Ten tablets on the walls, five a side, with the sacramental mottoes of the Party, blazoned upon some old hangings of imitation damask, which, had they been able to speak, might have been heard muttering endless Paters and Aves to themselves: once upon a time, indeed, they had served to decorate, upon festal occasions, the church of San Pietro, where Nocio Pigna had been employed as sacristan. The old incumbent had made him a present of them at the time. He had exhumed them from the chest in which for years they had been folded away with camphor and pepper, a discredited treasure, and now there they were, and--Luca Lizio might say what he pleased-- did make a splendid show. Besides, to attract the peasants, it did not seem a bad idea to Nocio Pigna that the Fascio should have a somewhat churchlike air; and on the president's table he had set a crucifix as well. Behind the table was displayed the red flag embroidered by his daughter Rita, Luca's "companion". And Luca sat there, from morning to night, studying Marx (Markis, Pigna called him), writing, corresponding with the presidents of the other Fasci of the Province and with those of the whole Island and with Milan and Rome. A stranger, passing by the open door of the Fascio, might at tunes have supposed that he was engaged in extracting a piece of dirt from his nose and then flicking it away with his fingers; but what an idea! dirt, indeed! at such moments, Luca was thinking: with that finger in his nose, he was thinking: when he was thinking, Luca became so absent-minded that he did not even notice the trumpet blasts of the five "brethren" constituting the band, who, to tell the truth, were a perfect plague. But it did not do to blow cold upon juvenile ardour. Five of the students from the Technical Institute who had been among the first to join the Party: Rocco Centura, who had taken his accountant's certificate that year, Mondino Micciche, Bernardo Raddusa, Toto Licalsi and Emanuele Garofalo, helped Luca with his correspondence. They had found a messenger who had assumed the office of secret police, a certain "Pispisa," who hung about all day long gossiping with his official brethren. The forty members, who would soon swell to four hundred, four thousand, had already elected their decurions, each with his brave red *fascia* on his collar-band. To provide against the arrest of the President, that is to say of Luca Lizio, the Council had elected a Secret President in Rocco Ventura.

For already both Pigna himself and Lizio had been summoned together *ad audiendum verbum* by Cavalier Franco, the Commissary of Police.

Oh, most polite, with his fair hair and rosy cheeks and his smile, blinking his fine languid blue eyes or stroking with a white, ladylike hand the little golden beard that forked from his chin, Cavalier Franco had made them a little speech, which Pigna never wearied of repeating to all and sundry, mimicking his voice and gestures.

The red, the red of flag and *fasce* was what had most offended the Signor Commissario. Why, yes, like bulls, the police lost their heads at the sight of anything red....

Not that Cavalier Franco had been in the least infuriated: a polite policemanship, his, outwardly at least. All he wished to know was, why red, when after all there were so many other pretty colours to choose among: orange yellow, pea green.... And one other thing he wished to know: why these two gentlemen in particular, Lizio and Pigna, had undertaken this task. What did they expect from it? What did they hope to gain? A seat on the Town Council, or higher still even, in Parliament? Nothing of that sort? Then why? From a disinterested love of their neighbour? From a sense of social justice? Fine words. Yes, he was gracious enough to admit, himself, that the condition of the farm labourer was really unjust. But were they so certain that they would be doing him a service in raising him above that condition? People who live in darkness need spend nothing on light; and light is expensive, and makes people see things that they never saw before; and the more they see the more they require, my friends! Now, in what does true wealth, true happiness consist? In having few requirements. And so... and so... in short, a little applied philosophy, and the following conclusion:

"My dear Sirs, I am not going to have you arrested, even though you wish it yourselves. You say that the conflict is bound to come, if the conditions in which your clients are living do not improve? Very good. I beg you to remember the story of the pitcher that went too often to the well.... And that is my last word!"

Cavalier Franco had been half annoyed, half irritated by Luca's silence; during his speech it was to Luca that he had turned, and he could scarcely conceal his irritation at hearing himself answered by Pigna. But how was Luca to tell him the reason of his silence?

Poor Luca, what an affliction! He would have been less to be pitied, had he been blind. A born orator, born to harangue crowds, a type of the true public character, all for other people, no thought for himself--and to have his lips sealed by a freak of destiny! He wrote, he found an outlet in writing, and struck sparks from his pen, flakes of hell fire; then raged, poor fellow, gnawed his fingers, moaned aloud, when he heard his stuff read aloud without the right tone, the proper emphasis, the fire that he had put into it. No one was satisfactory, not even Celsina, the only one of Pigna's daughters who, aflame with the new ideas, had made a religion, a regular religion of them. Rita too, yes, a little, before her baby came.... But what was Rita compared with Celsina?

Another thorn, another thorn this which made Nocio Pigna's heart bleed: that he could not send to the University this daughter who had passed out at the head of the honours list from the Technical Institute, to the amazement of everybody there, principal, professors and fellow students. To any imbecile whose father was a rich man, the way lay open and smooth; to Celsina, every way was barred; Celsina was condemned to moulder here, in this rotten town of *ignoranti*. So much for social justice!

Meanwhile, this evening, on the eve of the election, she was to make her first public appearance; to deliver an address at the headquarters of the Fascio. Nocio Pigna had been running round all morning preparing for this solemn occasion.

They were short of chairs.

If each member had brought his own chair with him, and had left it there.... For the present, he did not even expect them to pay the wretched weekly subscription with strict punctuality. But they might at least have presented a chair each, great heavens, for their own use! Nothing....

In one way and another he had managed to scrape together a score or so. He thought of all the chairs that were in the churches; of those that had been in his own custody at one time, at San Pietro; he thought of the cartloads of them that were taken down every Sunday to the semi-circle at the end of the Viale della Passeggiata, where the military band played. Chairs in abundance, for the godly in one place, for the worldly in the other! And in the Fascio, nothing! The fault of the members, though, when all was said; so much the worse, then, for them! They would have to stand.

He was making for home, when from an alley that debouched on the Piazza he heard himself softly called by somebody who was lying in wait for him there, muffled in a hood. "Pst, pst...."

A peasant! His heart gave a bound. He went towards the man eagerly.

"Your Exc'ency's servant. May I say a word to you?"

"What's that you say?" Nocio Pigna asked him, going nearer to him, dismayed by the air of suspicion and mystery with which the man approached him, speaking through his hood which left his eyes alone barely visible. "Do you wish to speak to me?"

"Yes, Sir; the other indicated the reply more by his gesture than in words.

"Here I am, my son," Pigna hastened to assure him. "Come this way.... Let us go inside."

And he pointed to the door of the Fascio.

But the man shook his head and at once drew back farther into the alley. Pigna followed him.

"Don't be frightened. There's nobody there. What do you want to say to me?"

The man in the hood hesitated still for a little before replying; glanced round him with sharp, suspicious eyes, then murmured, still through his hood: "I was told a secret.... Some one who knows.... He says...."

And he broke off again.

"Speak, my son," Pigna encouraged him. "We are alone here.... What did they tell you?"

The sharp suspicious eyes beneath the hood revealed the painful effort that the stranger was making to overcome his reluctance to speak. Finally, cowering against the wall and laying his hand, still under cover of his cloak, upon Pigna's arm, he asked in the lowest of tones:

"Is it here that they're dividing up the land?"

Nocio Pigna, half bewildered by all this mystification, stood looking doubtfully at him for a while, his mouth gaping.

"The land?" he said. "The land, no, my son."

The other thereupon tilted his chin and shut his eyes, as a sign that he understood. He sighed:

"I see. It seemed too good to be true! They were fooling me."

And he turned on his heel. Nocio Pigna caught hold of him.

"Why fooling you? No, my son.... Listen ..."

"Your Exc'ency must excuse me," said the other, stopping for Pigna to make way. "It is no use. I understand. Let me go...."

"Wait, my dear fellow, you don't give me time to explain...." Pigna made haste to add. "The land, yes, that will come too.... It is only a matter of will! If we wish it.... It all lies in that!"

The other continued to shake his head with a dark and bitter incredulity; then said:

"But what are we to wish for, we poor folk? What can we wish for?"

Pigna shook with anger: "Then I'm to give you the land, is that it? First of all there must be the will for it, in you and in everyone, without fear, you understand? There's no question of fighting, keep that well in mind! Indeed we want to sing hymns of peace, my dear man. The Fascio is like a church! And anyone who enters the Fascio..."

"Your Exc'ency, please let me go...."

"Wait, I wish to say one thing more to you: anyone who enters the Fascio enters it to form part of a corporation which embraces, as you can calculate for yourself, four-fifths of the human race, do you understand? Four-fifths, that is all I have to say."

He waved the four fingers of one hand in front of that pair of eyes: then went on:

"Give us union, good God, and we are everything, we can do everything! The law will be laid down by us: they will be compelled to come to terms with us. Who labours? Who turns the soil? Who sows? Who reaps? Give us either everything or nothing! So much for the moment. Our programme.... Come in, I can explain it all to you...."

"Your Ex'cency, please let me go.... It is not for me...."

"How is it not for you, you great donkey? When it is concerned entirely with you, your life, your rights? Keep that in mind, son! Look: the Fascio is here. You will always find me."

"Yes, Sir, I kiss your hands.... Please, will you forget I ever said a word..."

And turning on his heel he crept furtively away, peering about him as he went. Nocio Pigna followed him for a while with his gaze, shaking his head.

THE MOUSTACHIOED DOLL.

In the house, the confusion was greater than ever. A distinct advance was discernible, from day to day, towards the social revolution. There were--and their presence could at once be guessed from the street--the five students, former classmates of Celsina. There was also, but sulking and huddled in a corner, Antonio Del Re, the grandson and nephew of Donna Caterina Laurentano and Roberto Auriti. They were all talking at once in loud tones. The giant, to wit Emanuele Garofalo, and little Micciche who trembled in every limb and sprang about the room like a jack-in-the-box, and the thickset, violent Bacalmutese, Bernardo Baddusa, were shouting (but what, it was hard to make out) round his daughter Mita, the eldest of the six who were still at home, the one who worked all day long and often at night as well with Annicchia, who was the third. Bound the latter were screaming her sisters Tina and Lilla with Toto Licalsi and Bocco Ventura; Bita was trying to soothe the baby, which was wailing in terror; Celsina, in a towering passion, was quarrelling with Antonio Del Re; and, as though all this habel were nothing, 'Nzulu, the old black poodle, whiskered and half blind, crouching upon a chair with his head in the air, was giving vent to long and modulated howls of protest.

Luca Lizio, in a corner by himself, was holding his head in both hands, as though afraid that their screams might carry it off altogether.

"My dear people, what is the matter? Where are we?" Nocio Pigna shouted, as he entered the room.

They all turned, ran towards him and, in their excitement, began to answer him in chorus. Nocio Pigna stopped his ears.

"Gently! You're deafening me! One at a time!"

Luigi Pirandello

"Mita and Annicchia, as usual!" shrilled Tina.

"Putting on airs!" Lilla added.

And Emanuele Garofalo, the giant, waving his arms above his head, in a voice of thunder:

"Downstairs, everybody! Downstairs!"

"Exercise your paternal authority!" put in Mondino Micciche, twirling his stick in the air.

"I haven't the faintest idea what you're talking about! Hold your tongues!" shouted Nocio Pigna.

They all stopped speaking; but immediately, in the silence that followed, rang out a "Silly idiot!" hurled by Celsina at Antonio Del Be in such a tone of concentrated fury that the rest broke into peals of laughter.

Celsina stepped forward, balanced nimbly on her pert hips, her bosom swelling, her swarthy face aflame and her eyes flashing. Amid all that laughter, her expression of the haughtiest irritation threatened for an instant to break down, her burning lips curved in an involuntary smile, but at once she recovered herself and shouted imperiously and with scorn:

"Come along! Come along! Anyone who wants to listen, can! If he does not want to listen... I don't care two straws!"

"And now," groaned Noeio Pigna, bending his fingers and bringing the tips together, "may I be allowed to know what the devil has been happening?" And at once added, opening his eyes wide: "But let one of you speak!"

Rocco Ventura spoke, short and plump, with a bullet nose above a pair of straggling moustaches which began at the corners of his mouth and at once ended there, like a pair of commas:

"Nothing," he said, "we were simply proposing to go downstairs, to the room on the ground floor, to attend the dress rehearsal of Celsina's speech; that was all."

"And Mita and Annicchia, as usual..." added Tina, who was all dishevelled.

"Putting on airs!" repeated Lilla. "They don't want to come down; then let them stay here!" said Celsina, from the threshold. "We all know, they are the ants and I am the grasshopper. Come along, let us go down and leave them!"

Pigna looked at his daughters Mita and Annicchia, who

remained seated, dressed both of them in black, with pale cheeks and sorrowful eyes; then at Antonio Del Re, who also remained seated, a worried expression on his face, his elbows resting on his knees, biting his nails.

"Get along, get along," he said to the others, who were preparing to follow Celsina down to the room below. "I am just coming.... I have a word to say to Don Nino Del Re."

"You'll do nothing of the sort," shouted Celsina, coming back up the wooden stair and appearing in the doorway quivering with emotion. "I forbid you, Papa! I have spoken to Nino, and that is enough! Come downstairs!"

"All right! All right!" said Pigna. "What a fuss! I have another little speech to make to him. ... Gently now, gently...."

Antonio Del Re straightened himself, sprang to his feet in a sudden access of fury; but, at once repenting of his determination to leave the house, remained where he was, searching only with his eyes, which went straying round the room, for his hat.

"Oh, Holy God, how quick to take offence you are too! Don't rush away!" exclaimed Nocio Pigna.

"No, let him go, if he wants to go," put in Celsina excitedly. "I shall be only too pleased, as I've already told him! Or rather, wait..."

She ran to the next room, which was her bedroom; took from one of the drawers an old doll, the last survivor of her dolls in days gone by, which had turned up again by chance a few days earlier, and to which that beast Emanuele Garofalo, never realizing the distress it would cause her, had taken pen and ink and secretly added a pair of serjeant-major's moustaches; came back and laid it on Antonio Del Re's bosom; and lifted up his arm, so as to clasp it tightly, saying:

"There; that is for you! Something you can love!"

And she ran out of the room and downstairs.

Antonio Del Re flung the doll into the big work-basket, which stood between Mita and Annicchia. Nocio Pigna stood for a while staring at it with knitted brows; bent down to examine it more closely; asked:

"What are they, moustaches?"

Nino's only answer was to pick up the doll again and stick

it into his pocket head downwards. Its little legs, one in shoe and stocking, the other bare, remained protruding.

"You're sending the blood to her head!" was Nocio Pigna's comment. "Calm yourself, Don Nini, calm yourself! Let us discuss matters. Really, it would be better if you went away. Your position, at the present time, with your uncle in Girgenti, standing.... We people here have work to do. It is beginning now; there is little that we can do; but we ought at least to raise one voice in protest. Now I can enter into your feelings as a nephew, and I understand them. You are still a boy, brought up in your family: I know what your thoughts are; certain things cannot be agreeable to you. You ought however to enter a little into my feelings as a father also, to understand my responsibility, do you follow me? And also... Don Nini, I am a man who is exposed to criticism, as you know; a poor man stoned with calumnies from all sides: I laugh at them; but as for you and your family, and also out of respect for your... what would Don Landino Lauren-tano be to you again? Uncle? Cousin? Uncle, isn't he? Of course, yes... your mother's first cousin--also out of respect for him, as I was saying, I would not have anyone suspect.... Am I not right, Mitina?"

Mita barely raised her eyes from her work and, lowering them again at once, went on sewing. Antonio Del Re had gone across to the balcony window and was gazing out over the deserted Piano di Gamez, still biting his nails.

"Listen," Pigna went on. "This is gospel truth: has not your grandmother done a great injury to herself, to all her family and to you personally ..."

At this Del Re sprang round and came towards him, brandishing his clenched fists, and shouting:

"That will do! Stop!"

Nocio Pigna gazed at him for a minute, speechless, then said:

"But do you know that the whole lot of you seem to be mad here to-day? I was going to add that the greatest injury of all, she did to the town, by letting all the property that was hers by rights pass into the hands of that brother of hers who ... But oh, Don Nini, let us cool our passions and speak plainly! On which side are you? We get no farther, going on like this! I am not trying to force you. But it is time to make up your mind, my dear fellow: either you stand here with us, I mean with the Party, openly; or you remain with your own people. If you don't know, yourself even..."

"But she, of all people? She?" Antonio Del Re broke out, almost crying with rage, coming towards him again and clawing the air (he alluded to Celsina). "Why she? Wasn't there yourself? Weren't there all those idiots, Raddusa or Garofalo?"

"What about her?" Pigna was puzzled.

"The address," Antonio explained in an undertone.

"Ah, the address? And what has that got to do with it? Oh, I see.... But forgive me, Don Nino, dear! You're in a different boat! You're going off now to Rome with your uncle, to continue your studies, in the great city; you are going to sit down to a spread table; fees, books, everything provided for you.... But think, great God in heaven, think that my daughter here too.... Can't you imagine how it must make her blood boil, my poor child, when she thinks that all her work, all her efforts have been in vain? That all her love of study, all her passionate ambition to succeed is to end like this? Let her blow off steam! She ought to be setting the whole town on fire! Would you have her muzzled as well? And by what right, may I ask? What are you doing, what can you do for her? If I don't leave the room, I shall scream...."

And off he went, in a fury, down the wooden Stair.

Antonio Del Re had returned to the window and was gazing out. Mita and Annicchia went on working in silence, with bent heads. In that silence all three were conscious of the sound of their own troubled breath, evidence of their inward grief, exasperated by the thought that they could do nothing to prevent or remedy a state of things which was contrary to their nature, to their affections, to their aspirations.

The most troubled of the three was Antonio Del Re. All his grandmother's sombre bitterness had transfused itself, from his infancy, into his blood, which it had poisoned; the almost morbid tenderness of his mother, all shocks and terrors, caused him distress and annoyance, a humiliating sense of constraint; the submissive resignation of his uncle, crushed by the sad vicissitudes of life, left behind, after running the race in his boyhood with such dauntless ardour, who yet was determined not to appear beaten, and smiled to shew that he still had faith in an ideal which no amount of wrongdoing, no amount of error could, according to him, either damage or dim, made Antonio angry. He felt, he knew that his uncle's smile was intended to conceal an ever open sore, in a mistaken idea of what was proper. But why, instead of concealing it, did not uncle Roberto expose his sore, like his grandmother, like his friends, all the young men here at Pigna's? In one respect, however, their exposure of their sores irritated and disgusted him. The people who had worked and fought and suffered, it was they who ought to cry aloud against all their afflictions and hardships and demand justice and vengeance in the name of their work and blood and sufferings; not these boys who had done nothing, who showed no capacity for doing anything, except chatter to pass the time, and bind everyone together in a *fascio*, the honest with the dishonest, his uncle with the plotters and intriguers, with all those patriots for amusement or for reward! It was not this sense of injustice alone, however, that gave Antonio Del Re an aversion to his comrades. Bred up in the school of a proud and sombre grief, which scorned to seek an outlet in speech, of an abnegation prouder still, which scorned any base envy, if he had thrown himself into the fray, severing every ideal link with his own people, he would neither have uttered a single word, nor have sought companions: with lowered head, set teeth and armed fist, he would have sprung at once into action. The others were there merely to chatter, to amuse themselves with Pigna's daughters.

Antonio Del Re would have refused to admit that his aversion and scorn were largely due to a fierce jealousy.

With the same bottled ardour, with which he would have hurled himself into violent action, he had fallen desperately in love with Celsina, from the very first day on which she, still a little girl with her frocks ending at the knee, had made her entry into the technical school for boys. And Celsina, albeit courted by all his schoolfellows, had responded to his love, at first in secret, then letting the others see what was happening, finally making an open avowal of her feelings and defying the jeers of the disappointed. She had not however shut herself up in his love, she had not come and clung to him as he would have liked; she had re-mained where she was, in the thick of them all, her heart on her sleeve, her mind divided, prodigal of words, glances, smiles, intoxicated with her triumphs, and with her halo of glory as a rebel against every prejudice, conscious of her own value and a thirst to have it noticed, admired, applauded.

The clearer this aspect of her became, the more Antonio realized that he ought not to be in love with her, not only because she did not appeal to him when she was like this, but because, when he thought of his mother and grandmother, he realized that one would regard her with horror, while the other would dismiss her as a silly little flirt. But no: Celsina was neither bad nor silly, as he knew very well; indeed, had he listened to the secret, innermost voice of his own conscience, a voice stifled by respect, shyness, love, instead of condemning Celsina's open rebellion, he would have condemned the too exclusive pride of his grandmother, the too submissive resignation of his mother.

"Don Nini," Mita called to him in a gentle voice. "Will you come over here a minute?"

Antonio roused himself and went to her; but when he saw her hold up the article of clothing upon which she was at work, as though to take a measurement, he at once drew back shocked, writhing with discomfort.

"No!... not just at present...."

"Dear Don Nini," sighed Mita. "You must have patience! It has to he finished quickly.... You are going away.... Lucky you!"

Mita was engaged in getting ready, with her sister, the linen that he was to take with him to Rome.

All the hest families in the town, including Antonio's grandmother and mother, gave out work to these two poor sisters, who would often go and work in their houses also by the day. This was done out of consideration, or pity rather, for themselves alone; and they were fully aware of this, and hecame every day more humble, the het-ter to deserve it, to shew their gratitude and not to forfeit their employment. They realized that so many things had to be overlooked by the people who were anxious to help them, things which their father and sisters, instead of attenuating them, did everything in their power to bring into prominence, as though they deliberately set out to rouse the whole town against them and to wear out people's patience and neighbourly charity! But would not the harm recoil on these two also? What must people be saying? We, who are outsiders, are to shew consideration for you, are to help you, are we, while your own flesh and blood, those whom you maintain with our assistance, are to make war upon us? Disorders, scandals, feuds!

To find some sort of excuse for their father, Mita and Annicchia forced themselves to believe that he had really gone out of his mind after Rosa, the eldest sister's disgrace. Certainly, from that time onwards their house had been hell let loose. It was not so much of their father that Mita and Annicchia complained, with bleeding hearts, as of their sisters. How on earth could their sisters fail to understand that only by keeping silence, only by the humblest, most retiring modesty could they succeed, if not in obliterating altogether, in making less apparent the brand of infamy, with which their house was now marked? Rita, when the baby left her a moment to herself, and also Tina and Lilla did indeed help them with their sewing, basting or machining, on the all too rare days when work was plentiful; but they worked without zest, absent-mindedly, the two last especially, since they were not resigned, after the tragedy, to the abandonment of all hope and all desire. When they saw these two sisters dress up and adorn themselves every morning, they felt their hearts wrung, realizing that they were not dressing up, were not adorning themselves with any hope or desire that was honourable: they, themselves must know, alas, that no man whose in--\ tentions were honourable would care to be seen with them now. And from day to day they waited for Tina and Lilla, with all those young fellows always dangling round them, to end like Rita. But if they could only find a good young man, like Luca! Rita might have fared worse.... Because, when all was said, they were obliged to admit that Luca was good. Only they could not forgive his obstinacy in not legalizing his union with Rita before the law and the altar. He was so good to everyone, and was so fond of the baby and was no trouble at all in the house. Certainly, if he had not made so many enemies with those ideas of his, and had not been so unfortunate, he might have been of great assistance to the family, since, as far as work went, he worked all day long, and must indeed be learned to judge by the number of books he had read and still went on reading.

A little of this respect claimed by his intellect and erudition Mita and Annicchia extended also to Celsina, whose accomplishments dazzled everyone. They dared not criticize Celsina, because really she appeared to them by so many standards to be above the ordinary run, and they agreed with their father that in another place, in other conditions, she would have been sure of a triumphant success! They saw her full of contempt for men--and this was in one respect reassuring. As for men, she had gone and challenged them in their own schools and had beaten every one of them! As a matter of fact, they had not seen their way to approve of that challenge: with greater profit, albeit with less satisfaction to herself, she might have attended the girls' classes and become a teacher. As it was, she was left without a profession. But they were not afraid for the future: some outlet Celsina was certain to find for her talents, in the town or elsewhere. That poor Don Nini, meanwhile, who was in love with her, and was jealous.... So good, poor fellow! But she was not for him, Celsina. If his family should come to hear of it! They were counting the minutes until he should leave for Rome.

Annicchia laid her hand gently upon Mita's arm to draw her attention to the two legs of the doll, which were protruding from his pocket as he still stood at the balcony window. Mita responded with a wistful smile to her sister's smile; then, remembering a request which she had made up her mind the night before to put to the young man, she rose to her feet, laying down her work in the basket, and went timidly over to him.

"Don Nini," she murmured, "before you go to Rome, you must for the last time do me that great favour, and..."

"No, for heaven's sake, no, Mita, don't speak to me of it!" Antonio Del Re violently interrupted her, pressing his hands to his forehead and screwing up his eyes.

"You are ashamed, isn't that it?" said Mita sorrowfully, lowering her gaze.

"No, it's not that! It's not that!" Antonio hastened to assure her. "But now, just at the moment ... I can't hear to listen to anything, Mita!" It was a terrible thing that the poor girl wanted of him, a terrible memory recurred to him as he spoke. He looked at her, afraid lest the horror that evidently underlay his refusal might have aroused some suspicion in her. But he saw her fine eyes more sorrowful and humble than ever, eyes which all the tears that they had shed had veiled and dimmed for ever.

Almost every night, indeed, she wept with her whole heart for Rosa, her ruined sister, her fallen sister, who had sunk into the lowest depths of infamy. More than once, not being able herself to go and visit her in the house of shame in which she was at present confined, she had asked Antonio to go there instead of her. And Antonio, the last time that he had gone there, finding her half tipsy... horrible! horrible!

A din of shouting, applause, mingled with the wailing of the baby and the barking of the dog, came up at this stage from the room below; and presently 'Nzulu, the old poodle, kicked out of the other room, trembling all over, crouching on his hind legs as though he were trying to sweep the floor with the tuft of his agitated tail, came in and laid his whiskered muzzle on the knees of Mita, who had returned to her seat.

The two sisters, when they saw the poor creature come to them imploring their protection and shelter, began to cry. Whereupon Antonio Del Re, unable to contain himself any longer, crushed his hat down on his head, opened the balcony window and, bestriding the iron railing, while Mita and Annicchia cried in terror: "Oh, gracious, Don Nini... what are you doing? What are you doing?" lowered himself, holding on at first to two of the upright bars of the railing, then let himself drop on to the piazza beneath.

They could hear the thud, and then the sound of something breaking. Mita ran to the window and saw him down below, stooping, groping with outstretched hands, like a blind man, for his hat which had fallen at his feet.

"Don Nini, you haven't hurt yourself, I hope?"

"It's all right..." he answered from below. "My glasses... I've lost my glasses."

And, snatching up his hat, he made off.

"He's gone mad!" said Mita. "Can it be possible?"

And she pointed with her hand to the room below, in which Celsina was holding forth.

As he dashed along the Via di Gamez, Antonio Del Re, who without his glasses could not see an inch before his nose, ran into somebody at the corner of the Via Atenea.

"Hallo, Nino!"

He recognized the voice as Corrado Selmi's.

"Let me pass!" he shouted at him, freeing himself with an angry gesture.

A LIGHT TRAVELLER.

Corrado Selmi had left Veronica at the hotel in the company of his other second, and was now on his way back to Roberto Auriti's house, where he was staying.

For the last four days, whenever he shewed his face in the street, he had seen every eye turned upon him, had noticed that a number of curious spectators would even stop to gaze at him open-mouthed; that others emerged from the shops and planted themselves on the doorsteps, looking over one another's shoulder.

All this curiosity obliged him to assume--what was most unusual with him--a certain air of stiffness. At the same time, he could not help laughing. And he did not know where to look, so that his naturally merry eyes, the frank and open expression of a face that was always smiling might not earn him an unmerited reputation for petulance.

He was indeed and felt himself to be still quite young, in body and in spirit, notwithstanding his age, the changes of fortune and fierce struggles he had borne. He still had not a single white hair, nor had the golden brightness of his moustaches and hair began to fade. He dressed with a gentlemanly and entirely natural elegance, and exhibited in his whole person, in every gesture, every glance, a freshness and youth that were irresistible. For this persistent youthfulness Corrado Selmi of Rosabia was indebted to his keen, constant and intense love of life, and, at the same time, to his having always refused to attach the slightest value to it. He had never consented to burden himself with any excess of memories or of studies or of scruples or of clinging aspirations, unlike so many men who find that inevitably--under such a burden--their knees begin to bend and their shoulders to arch.

179

A light traveller, such was his usual definition of himself. And he had always embarked like this--light and free--upon long, adventurous and difficult journeys. Nothing to lose, and so, forward march!

On the failure of the insurrection of the 4th of April, having escaped by a miracle from the Convent of La Gancia, he had at first carried on a guerrilla warfare with the squadrons round Palermo; he had then served in the 1860 campaign with Garibaldi until Volturno--but in what fashion? Without ammunition and with an old blunderbuss that would not fire, procured from Malta for six ducats.

In the Chamber, among all his fellow-members whose brows were pregnant with great thoughts and their portfolios bulging with reports and notes and memoranda, he had served upon the most difficult Committees. Yes, but without either a pencil or a notebook. Life, to him, spelt action. And he had always managed to find something to do, of some sort or other; though without making the slightest effort in any direction. And in everything he had secured an easy and spontaneous success, never drawing back, seeking out rather and braving the gravest perils, the most difficult undertakings, the most intricate adventures.

He did not believe, he would not admit that difficulties could exist for a man like himself, always ready for anything. He did not go out to meet life; he faced it, and passed on. Passed on, disarming everyone with his convinced, gay, tranquil confidence: stripping every abstract principle, every rhetorical display from the rigid morality of the Catos, every scruple of modesty from the women's virtue.

Was he to halt, for a moment even, in his race through life, to criticize his own conduct and decide whether he had done well or ill? Of course not! He must not waste time upon criticism, any more than he must attach importance to his own actions. Wrong to-day, right to-morrow. Useless to recall his attention to consider the wrong he had done; he would shrug his shoulders, smile, and go on his way. He was bound to go ahead, at all costs, in any way, without hesitating, letting himself be purified by his incessant activity and by his love of life, and remaining always cheerful and open, lavish with his favours to everyone, holding everyone in the hollow of his hand.

Life was for him, in short, a succession of baited hooks, which drew him this way and that. To arrest him at one of these, to suspend him from it in order to criticize him, would have been a cruel injustice.

Now Corrado Selmi was afraid that such an injustice threatened him at this moment: in other words, that people hoped to hook him by the many debts which he had been forced to contract, by the many bills with his signature that were held by one of the leading banks, the shaky condition of which was already being exposed. Perhaps at the opening of the new Session of Parliament the scandal would come out. He could imagine the spectacle that would be offered by all the jealous, bristling guardians of respectability, whom the fear of committing an action that was not quite correct had always prevented from doing anything at all, apart from their insipid rhetorical chatter; feeble, peering egoists, diligent cultivators of the arid garden-plot of their own moral sense, ringed round by a dense hedge of scruples, though there was nothing for it to guard, since the garden in question had never yielded anything but blighted fruit or useless formal flowers!

Debts! Bills! Why, certainly! But he had always been signing bills, all his life! When he was eighteen, at Palermo, in the early part of 1860, the Revolutionary Committee were at their wits' end: they had hopes of Garibaldi, they had hopes of Vittorio Emanuele and Piedmont, they had hopes of Mazzini; but funds were lacking and arms and munitions. Well, he had suggested that they should take six thousand ducats from the safe of the Bank of Sicily on the signature of the wealthiest gentlemen among them. And he had been the first to sign, though he had not a carlino in his pocket, for two hundred ducats. The Provisional Government would pay in due course. How was the Fourth of April made possible? In this way alone!

And how had he contrived, single-handed, the reclamation of the marsh lands which formed a great part of his constituency? Why, by signing one bill after another! After which the constituency had been rid of malaria, and the debts--as everyone knew--had remained on his hands, because the cultivation of the reclaimed land, which he had entrusted to certain inexperienced relatives of his own, had proved a failure, and at present the fruits of his labour were being enjoyed for the most part by other people who gave him only the rinds, as and when they chose, but continued to do him the honour of returning him to Parliament.

It was quite true: apart from the sums borrowed from the Banks for this undertaking and for others equally advantageous to many, disastrous only to himself; other sums and no small ones he had taken for his own support. Live he must; he neither could nor would live a life of poverty. As a boy he had gone straight from school to take part in the Revolution. For eleven years, until Rome was taken, he had not allowed himself a moment's rest. When the armistice came, left without a profession and with no return for the expenditure of his best years in the service of others, what was he to do? Hang himself? Fortune had not chosen to smile upon him in business; it had granted him other favours, but these had cost him dear, and one--the greatest and worst of them--not in pocket alone.

Corrado Selmi forbade himself any regret for what was past. And yet, now and again, regret for his love affair with Donna Giannetta D'Atri Montalto would assail him with a sudden tightening of the heart. But stronger than any sorrow for the love he had lost was his rage at the blind abandonment of himself in the hands of that woman who for two years had made him the talk of Rome, leading him on to do things that were really mad. It seemed that she had taken a vow to compromise herself and him in every possible way, gripped by a passion for scandal. More for her sake than for his own he had tried at first to restrain her, but had soon lost all restraint himself in the fear that his scruples might give offence, his prudence appear to her as cowardice.

His heaviest debts had been contracted at this period, albeit they did not figure under his own name, out of consideration for the woman who made him contract them. Roberto Auriti had stepped in, with brotherly abnegation, to raise the money for him from the Bank, after a private arrangement however with the Governor of that institution.

The threatened exposure of the irregularities in this Bank was therefore less alarming to Corrado Selmi on his own account than on Roberto Auriti's. But his alarm was to some extent modified by his certainty that the Government had many excellent reasons for preventing any public scandal. He well knew that such a scandal would result in the failure not of one Bank only but of the national confidence. The Government's support of his own re-election, in spite of Francesco D'Atri's being in office, and their support of Roberto Auriti's candidature, confirmed him in this certainty. Before leaving Rome, he had promised Roberto that he would come down to Girgenti to help him in his campaign; summoned there in haste by Veronica's telegram, he had come at once, and had at once realized the extremely difficult position in which Roberto found himself placed by his opponents, a position aggravated now, still further, by this duel. He would have done anything in the world to liberate Roberto from all the trials by which he saw him oppressed, to draw him up where he might breathe a different air, to raise him to the position which he knew him to deserve by the qualities of his mind and heart, by all that he had done in his youth; but as soon as he had set foot in his friend's house, at Girgenti, and had met his mother and sister, he had felt his strength fail; in a flash he had seen the reason why Auriti's life had been a failure.

It had seemed like a prison to him, that house! Was it possible that two human beings could have adapted themselves to drag out their existence in that melancholy gloom of bitter and contemptuous boredom? Could have formed so grim, so horrid a conception of life?

He had been unable to resist the temptation to broach this topic with Roberto's mother, in the hope of rousing her from her lethargy.

"But if life is a mere feather, Donna Caterina! A breath, and away it goes.... Would you attach any weight to a feather?"

"Would I, dear Selmi?" had been Donna Caterina's answer. "It is not my doing.... To you, life is a feather, and flies away; for me, it has turned to lead, my dear Sir...."

"But that is just where you make a mistake!" he had promptly retorted, "turning a feather into lead! Surely, since we have to live, does it not seem to you essential to keep our spirit in a state of... shall I say, continual fusion? Why arrest this fusion and make the spirit coagulate, fix it, stiffen it in this gloomy mould of lead?"

Donna Caterina had nodded her head, her lips curved in a bitter smile.

"Fusion... yes! But to keep the spirit, as you say, in this state of fusion, we must have fire, my friend! And when, inside you, the furnace is dead?"

"We must not allow it to die, perbacco!"

"My dear Sir, when the wind is too strong, when death comes, and breathes upon us... when you look round you and cannot find so much as a handful of twigs to feed the flame..."

"But where do you look for them? Here? Always mewed up inside these four walls as in a prison?... But Signora Anna, surely... is it possible that Signora Anna... I mean to say. ..."

He had stopped short, in a sudden embarrassment, observing that Roberto's sister, finding herself drawn into the conversation when she least expected it, had turned crimson.

Ever since he first set eyes on her, Corrado Selmi had remained lost in admiration of her pure and delicate beauty and had suffered instinctively at the sight of that beauty so mortified by her persistent widow's weeds, and not so much neglected as despised.

This sudden blush made him afraid lest he had gone a little too far; but at once, overcoming his momentary embarrassment, he had gone on:

"Haven't you a son? And you are obliged, therefore, to live for him, to cherish life for his sake... aren't you? I mean to say... perhaps I am a little too emphatic in shewing you what is in my mind, when I see all this atmosphere of gloom here, which does not appear to me reasonable. What do you say about it, Signora Anna?"

She had flushed again, had made a painful effort not to lower her eyes, and with a dazed expression and a nervous smile on her lips, shrugging her shoulders slightly, had replied, alluding to her son:

"He is young, still.... He can plan his life for himself...."

"But you, then... are you old?"

This almost spontaneous question had brought their first conversation to an end.

Now Corrado Selmi was returning to Roberto's house, exhilarated by all that he had seen at the villa of Colimbetra. All those great dolls in Bourbon uniform who had presented arms to him! Sheer lunacy! But what a splendid place, that villa! The Prince--no, he had not shewn his face. Such a pity! He would so much have liked to meet him.... There was a man, now, who had taken root, in his affections, in a past epoch... and yet he went on living, outside time, outside life ... in a most curious fashion (how charming!), projecting from his own period certain images of life, which inevitably, in the reality of to-day, must appear unsubstantial, masks, toys, all those dressed-up dolls there... how charming!

"And yet those dolls out there, dear Selmi, which made you laugh," Donna Caterina told him, "to-morrow, at the election here, will defeat you, your friend Roberto, the Prefect, your Government and everybody.... Go on laughing, if you can. Shadows? Why, it is we that are the shadows!"

"I am not, if you don't mind, Donna Caterina," said Selmi, laughing and patting his chest. "Spare me this one illusion at least. Why, the Prince, when I went to find him, melted away before me like a shadow.... I would have given anything to see him come out to meet me, if only to be quits.... Roberto knows all about that ... to be quits for a certain meeting with his son in Rome, when it fell to my lot to play the shadow. Bah! Patience.... Why yes, you are quite right, Donna Caterina; we all persist in being mere shadows, here in Sicily.... Inept or discouraged or servile.... But when the sun puts the very words to sleep on our lips! I'm not just saying this for the sake of talking, you know: I have studied the question carefully, I assure you. Sicily entered the great Italian family with a public debt of barely eighty-five millions of capital and a small balance of about twenty-two millions. She brought in as well all the wealth of her church and crown property, the accumulation of centuries. On the other hand, badly off for public works, with no roads, no harbours, no irrigation, of any sort. ... How was the sale of crown property and the letting of church property carried out? It ought to have been done with an eye to social advantage, to the relief of the agricultural classes. To be sure! It was done with an eye to financial profit. And we have been obliged to buy back our church and crown lands and free the rest of our real estate with the colossal sum of something like seven hundred millions, at the expense, naturally, of the improvement of our other lands. And that famous fourth share of all church property allotted to us by the Law of July 7, 1866? What a mockery! j Why, to begin with, the value of that property was I calculated upon the deliberate understatements f made by the Sicilian clergy when assessed for the mortmain tax; and from this nominal value, remember, were deducted all the percentages due to the State and the various charges and cost of administration. And then, if you please, all these deductions were based upon actual values, with the further subtraction of the pensions due to the members of suppressed communities. So that, up to the present, nothing, practically nothing has filtered through to our Communes. Now, after all the sacrifices we have made and accepted out of patriotism, has not our Island the right to share equally with the other regions of Italy in all the benefits, the improvements of every sort, which those other regions have already secured? But if it has never proved possible, in spite of all my efforts, to collect all the Sicilian Deputies together in an effective group?... Oh, don't let us speak of it, Donna Caterina! I should only lose my temper.... I do all I can. Then I shrug my shoulders and say: 'It means that we are getting what we deserve....'"

He turned to Roberto, to change the conversation, and went on:

"I say, I saw your opponent's wife yesterday, in the street. My dear fellow, you're simply bound to lose.... Oh, what a lovely little lady! Forgive me, ladies, for speaking like this; but I really should not have the heart to win, not even in the sacred name of the Country and of Freedom, if it brought tears to those charming eyes!"

CHAPTER VII

THE MASK.

Nicoletta Capolino entered her husband's study dressed to go out, with a curious, broad-brimmed, plumed felt hat on her beautiful raven hair. Full-blooded, lively and eminently alluring, with burning eyes and lips, she exhaled from all her secretly, artfully tended person a voluptuous, intoxicating perfume.

It was a dramatic moment, an interlude in the comedy which husband and wife had been playing day after day for the last two years, even within the privacy of their own four walls, each for the other's benefit, mutually enjoying their own subtlety and daring.

They knew very well, however, both of them knew that they would never succeed in deceiving one another; nor did they attempt to do so. That they were acting from pure love of the art could not be said, seeing that they both secretly loathed the necessity for their make-believes. But if they wished to live together, without causing scandal to other people, without too much disgust at themselves, they realized that they could not do otherwise. And so there they were, eager to dress up, or rather to mask with a polite and pretty falsehood their mutual loathing; to treat the falsehood as a painful and costly work of charity. It took the form, in fact, of a duty, a competition in exquisite courtesies, by means of which husband and wife had in course of time acquired not only an affectionate regard for each other's merits, but actually a sincere mutual gratitude. And they were very nearly in love with one another.

"Gnazio, I can't bear to leave you like this!" she said as she entered the room, as though vexed at a supposed deception, which pained and alarmed her. "Swear to me that you're not going to fight this morning."

"Oh Lord, Lelle, haven't I told you that I'm going to Siculiana!" Capolino replied, raising his hands and letting them rest gently on her arms. "I was to have gone there yesterday, as you know. Don't be alarmed, dear. The duel has been put off until after the election."

"Am I to believe that, really?" she insisted, as she attempted to button her other glove with her already gloved hand.

Capolino would have liked to answer her importunity with a snort of anger; as it was, he smiled; sprang towards her; took her hand, to button her glove for her, and lingered over the task like a lover.

"I can't tell you what a bore it is having to go to Valsania!" was her next remark, almost murmured in his ear, in faint accents.

"But you must go!" he exclaimed, looking her in the face, as though to warn her that this note of tenderness--charming and delightful as it was--was, to say the least, out of place at the moment.

"I swear to you!" she replied, obstinate, but smiling back at him.

Capolino laughed aloud:

"Go! Go! Go! You will enjoy yourself no end! Think of seeing that old walrus Adelaide meet her bridegroom.... It will be a sight for the gods! You aren't serious, Lelle?"

"If my mind were at rest..." Nicoletta repeated. "Last night you stayed in here for ever so long.... I never heard you come to bed. ..."

"But all this correspondence about the election, don't you see?" he said, pointing to the writing table. "Uncle Salesio, surely to goodness, might come and help me with this at least....

"Oh, yes, Uncle Salesio!" she exclaimed. "If they were jam tarts..."

"That will do," said Capolino. "Don't waste any more time, off with you.... Or are you waiting for the carriage?"

Nicoletta raised her eyes with the air of one resigning herself to accept a statement though not convinced of its truth, and sighed:

"If you really are going to Siculiana, couldn't you, on your way home this afternoon, look in at Valsania?"

"Why of course, if I can!" he replied. "But when I'm with friends... I shan't be coming back alone.... If I can... I mean to say, if I can manage to leave them..."

He put out his lips to kiss her. She drew back her head, instinctively, afraid of his disarranging her hair.

"Why?" she said.

"Because I like you like that.... Aren't you going to give me a kiss?"

"Gently, though...."

They were interrupted by the old maidservant, who came in to announce that Salvo's carriage was at the door. Nicoletta turned at once from her husband.

"All right, I'm coming," she said to the servant; then giving her hand to her husband: "So long, then."

"Have a good time," Capolino told her.

This carriage, in a dead-alive town like Girgenti, was really too much of a good thing; a senseless display of wealth and luxury for which only a man like Salvo could be forgiven. From the suburb of Babato, in which Capolino lived, to the Viale della Passeggiata, where Salvo, a few years earlier, had built himself a charming villa, one could go on foot in half an hour.

Nicoletta had not the least doubt that her husband was going to fight that morning. But she must not be supposed to know it, if she was to be free to enjoy herself. How many other things there were that she must not be supposed to know, in order that she might he what she was, gay and in love with life! She succeeded, often, by force of will, not indeed in not knowing them, which would have been impossible, but in behaving just as though she did not know them. Surreptitiously, when her gorge rose at them, a deep sigh, and there!--she would raise her spirit above all the miseries that had always oppressed her, almost from the cradle.

She must not know, for instance, that her mother had caused the death--if not by poison, as some slanderous tongue in the town had suggested, certainly of a broken heart--of her father, in order to unite herself in a second marriage with the man whom her daughter called Uncle Salesio, a former clerk in the Spoto Bank.

She had been scarcely five years old when her father died, and yet she remembered him quite well; so much so that her mother had never been able to persuade her to address as "daddy" this second husband much younger than this wife.

He was not a bad man, Uncle Salesio, no; but fatuous, fatuity and vanity incarnate. As soon as he became the husband of Baldassare Spoto's widow, he had seriously believed that this marriage conferred upon him a sort of title of nobility; and the strangest fumes had mounted to his brain; indeed, you might say that his whole soul turned to smoke. Soon however the fuel for that smoke had begun to fail. Wild extravagance. ... And if only it had brought him any pleasure! What a Chinese torture must they have been to him, all the time, those patent leather shoes, which obliged him to hop along on tiptoe, like a bird! Evil tongues averred that beneath his waistcoat he wore stays, like a woman. Stays, no; a woollen band he did wear, wound tightly and several times about his waist, as a protection to his back, which required support. He was not so old as all that: just a year or two older than Capo-lino; but senile decay, despite all his precautions and his most loving and assiduous attentions to his person, had begun early in him. He now looked like an automatic figure: everything adjusted, everything pieced together, everything a sham: his teeth, the pink of his cheeks, the black of his waxed moustaches and his little tuft of a beard and his exiguous eyebrows and few remaining hairs; and he walked and moved as though upon springs, with a youthful gait. His eyes, however, among all these chemical applications, almost hidden behind their swollen, lymphatic lids, were eloquent of an infinite distress. For trouble had come upon him after his wife's death. Nicoletta, who might have washed her hands of him, had shewn compassion; she had, however, taken over the management of what little remained to them; she had insisted, moreover, upon keeping up appearances, and Uncle Salesio (now almost mummified) had continued to parade the streets like a little lord, a prodigy of smartness, always in silk stockings and patent leather shoes, walking on tiptoe; but at home, ah, at home the most rigid economy. So much so that, one day, Nicoletta had been seen to arrive with a parcel containing a couple of sham roast fowls, of pasteboard, under her arm. Yes, indeed: two roast fowls of pasteboard to be displayed on the meagre table beneath the flyguards of netted wire. Every day the poor old man set them before him on the table, to deceive himself: he could not do without them! And those two pasteboard fowls and a crust of stale bread (genuine enough, but hard upon his teeth which were not) now formed the whole of his daily meal for weeks on end! Because Capolino had not chosen to take him into his own home, and Uncle Salesio Marullo, left alone in the gloomy old house which Nicoletta had made over to him with what little she had managed to save from the wreck, as often as not, being incapable of limiting his expenditure, when it was a case of buying a fine necktie or a fine cane, had to fast-- unless, that is to say, he were to call at Flaminio Salvo's, towards the luncheon hour, knowing that his step-daughter would be there. And Nicoletta, who in her shame and rage would gladly have torn his heard off or his eyes out, had to welcome him with a smile.

She felt that she might have been a good woman, at heart, and that she really had shewn herself to be good at certain moments in her life; but that a perfidious fate had refused to allow her to be good. Wicked she was compelled to be! Everything, every atom of her was false, inside and outside and round about her. And a secret, continual struggle to overcome the stifling sense of disgust, not to feel the chafing of her mask, albeit by now it had grown to her face like a second skin. But she had over her brow a lock of upturned, unruly hair, and she feared at certain moments that her soul might similarly rise up one day in her bosom, in a sudden dash for freedom after all these years of suffocation.

And now, her husband was going to fight a duel? And she herself at a party!

So as not to see, not to be seen by too many people, she told the coachman not to go by the Via Atenea but to take the Santa Lucia road, which ran outside and below the town. She had long ceased to care what people might think when they saw her in Salvo's carriage. It was common knowledge now. Besides, even in this, appearances were to a certain extent saved by Capolino's former connexion with the Salvo family and by her own position with Don Flaminio's daughter.

Audacity had defied malice and, if it had not entirely conquered it, had obliged it to hold its tongue and to bow down in public places; leaving it to gossip only in private, and even then with a certain philosophical indulgence. For philosophy has this to be said for it: that in the end it always finds a justification for any form of success.

CARDS ON THE TABLE.

Villa Salvo was situated high up, on an airy perch, and commanded the road carved in the hillside from the south. You went up to it by flights of broad steps, which conquered the steep ascent by a series of easy zigzags. At each turn, on the pillars, were four statues of a barbaric ugliness, which certainly did not offer a friendly greeting to visitors, nor appear to be congratulating them on having surmounted another stage in their climb. They were rewarded, however, on reaching the top by an enchanting view over the whole countryside undulating beneath them, with the sea in the distance.

Before mounting to the upper floor of the villa, Nicoletta made straight for Salvo's study on the ground floor; but stopped short on the threshold when she saw that he was not alone.

"Come in, come in," said Flaminio Salvo, bowing, from where he stood in front of the writing table at which a young man was seated, writing busily: Aurelio Costa. "Forgive me, if..." Nicoletta began, looking at Costa, who rose from his chair.

"Nothing of the sort!" Salvo cut her short, stroking his moustaches with a cold smile, to which the slow gaze of his eyes from behind their heavy lids gave a faint suggestion of irony. "Come in... I was just having a chat with my engineer."

Then, observing the young man's embarrassment in the lady's presence, he added:

"What! Don't you know one another?"

"By name, of course," Nicoletta replied in a tone of indifference. "I don't think we have ever been properly introduced...."

"Oh, in that case," Salvo went on, "let us observe the formalities: Ingegnere Aurelio Costa, Signora Lelle Capolino-Spoto."

193

Aurelio Costa, without raising his eyes, or moving from the writing table, made a slight bow. He was well dressed, with no trace of affectation, composed and dignified in his manly beauty, which the unfamiliar setting of a new suit of town clothes made a trifle rough, perhaps, by contrast.

"Is Adelaide ready?" Nicoletta asked Salvo, after examining the young man and acknowledging his protracted bow with a faint smile.

"Just one moment," Salvo replied. "Sit down, Donna Lelle, sit down. I shall run up and see. I think Adelaide must be ready."

And he went to the door. "But it will be better if I go up too!" Nicoletta called after him.

"No, why?" said Salvo, turning round on the threshold. "Adelaide will be down directly."

He left the room.

Nicoletta refused to sit down; she wandered restlessly about the large room, furnished with a sober luxury.

Aurelio, who was still on his feet, did not know whether he ought to sit down again or not; he was afraid of committing a breach of good manners; but at the same time he was annoyed by the thought that, through a caprice on her part, he was obliged to stand there like a servant in attendance. And really she did seem to be mistress of the house: but on what terms? And he had dreamed for years of making her his, this woman! He himself, in that house, was in Salvo's service too, like her, like Capolino, like everyone; but if she had been his wife, Salvo would certainly not have dared to imagine that he could make use of her for his senile pleasures. As it was, she found herself now placed between two old men, with her blooming, voluptuous beauty contaminated. Did she relish her position? Was she making a display for his benefit of that brazen supremacy? Did she enjoy all this luxury, all the honours that were paid to her for the loss of her own honour? To be sure! In a few days her husband would be in Parliament too.... And she, the wife of a Deputy! With him, on the other hand, what would she have been, supposing her to have succeeded in overcoming her horror-- yes, horror!--at the thought of uniting herself with a man of such humble birth? Honour, youth, a pure and sacred love? But the waving plumes and the veil of her broad-brimmed hat meant more to her! Weary and ashamed, he sat down.

"Oh, of course, do, please," Nicoletta exclaimed, turning round to look at him. "Do forgive me for not telling you.... My thoughts were wandering. ..."

She came towards him; took her stand in front of the writing table, with a sudden, decided, provoking movement of her person.

"You will be staying here now, Ingegnere?" "Perhaps.... I don't know...." he answered, gazing firmly at her in his turn. "At present we are busy planning a scheme.... If it comes to anything..." "You will remain here?" "A manager will be required...."

Nicoletta stood looking at him for a little, without any definite thought in her mind; then, gently lifting her hair from her brow with one hand: "You studied in Paris, didn't you?"

"Yes," he replied, curtly, breathing in the intoxicating perfume which she exhaled from her irresistible person.

"Paris!" exclaimed Nicoletta Capolino, raising her chin and half shutting her eyes. "I was there once, on my honeymoon....What a whirl it is! A whirl of splendour.... Tell me though, couldn't you go back to government service now, if you wished?"

Aurelio looked at her, puzzled by this sudden digression. He knitted his brows; and replied:

"I don't know. I don't think so. But I should not dream of trying. I should go back on my own account to Sardinia. I am here only to oblige Signor Salvo. I should lose nothing by leaving."

"Oh, I know," she said quickly. "With your talents.... That is exactly what I meant! And Signor Salvo certainly won't allow you to escape, if, as you say, he has a scheme in his mind...."

She screwed up her eyes and laid her finger on her lips, remained for a while in thought and continued, with a change of tone:

"But I remember you quite well, d'you know, when you were here before, as a student... quite a boy... yes, I remember you perfectly now...."

Aurelio made a violent effort to resist the disturbance, the shock that her speech, uttered with so calm an impudence, had given him. What did this woman want of him? Why was she speaking to him like this?

Truly, it was difficult to guess; for Aurelio, indeed, imposs-ible. This sudden, unlooked-for meeting with him; the impression she had received of him; the thoughts that with her furtive, femi-nine glance she had read on his brow when she had taken the liberty of invading the study and afterwards during this interval of waiting; the secret humiliation of her own position, which she her-self in her heart could not help feeling, in the presence of this young man who once upon a time had asked her to marry him, honourably, because he loved her; the thought that he would now be staying on here in Salvo's house, and that Dianella was secretly in love with him, and that before long he, by force of contact, might become aware of this; and that very soon, therefore--if Di-anella persisted until she had overcome her father's opposition--she might have to suffer the indignity of witnessing his betrothal to her employer's daughter, had thrown Nicoletta Capolino into con-fusion. It would be her duty, then, to watch over the engaged couple; and that young man there, who still showed such mortifica-tion at her scornful refusal of his offer; that young man there would be amply revenged upon her: he would presently become her master, he too, as the husband of that Dianella who, she could feel, despised and loathed her. And he was good-looking too, and strong and proud! And still (as she had not failed to observe) still fascinated by herself, offended and indignant as he might be... Why, too, had Flaminio Salvo, who knew the whole story, at once hurried from the room and left her there alone with him?

She blinked her eyes again, as though to extinguish the flame of her secret thoughts, and went on with a curious smile:

"You may remember too, perhaps..."

Aurelio, at a loss what to say, raised his eyes and stared at her with a hard, grim expression.

"Don't think badly of me," she next said, with a melancholy sweetness, tilting her head sideways. "Since you are going to stay here and we shall be seeing one another constantly, let us take this opportunity of a frank discussion and clear away a misunderstand-ing which would weigh upon us both.... People say that I am a thoughtless creature; so I am, I don't deny it; but I cannot bear pre-tences or concealments of any sort or for any reason, covert thoughts.... Are we going to be friends?"

So saying, she held out to him her pretty, fragile, Vigorous, ring-studded hand; and, after he had taken it, left it lying in his hand for a moment while she added:

"I'm not saying this, believe me, from coquetry, nor am I fishing for compliments: you are still a free man; nothing lost, nothing to regret. Are we friends?"

And, hearing the breathless approach of Donna Adelaide Salvo, amid a rustle of silken garments, she clasped his hand again, hurriedly, with a definite purpose, as though to give the form and appearance of a secret treaty to their conversation.

"Off to the fair! Off to the fair!" exclaimed Donna Adelaide, running into the room waving her arms, heated and breathless. "Look, Lelle, look, Ingegnere, my boy, how they have rigged me up.... Oh, Maria Santissima, I feel like a fine filly in season, all bells and ribbons, waiting to be taken to the fair.... But it's no good arguing with Flaminio, children; you've got to play: '*Su, bubbolino, salutami il re*'; and keep on saying yes, all the time.... You're laughing at me? Laugh if you like...."

They were indeed laughing, Nicoletta Capolino and Aurelio Costa, while Donna Adelaide with her arms outstretched spun about the room like a top; they were laughing also, helplessly, with the pleasure of hearing her express so carelessly and comically their own secret impression, which they would never have dreamed not merely of expressing but even of retaining, in such crude terms, in their own consciousness. This was just what Donna Adelaide wished. She felt the absurdity of this strange and tardy marriage, and was placing her cards on the table to disarm the malice of others.

Endowed with common sense and with a certain spirit, she had decided that she might as well make the most of her own privileged position and of that of her bridegroom, which masked with an arrogant pomp all that was illegal in their marriage. But she lent herself to the task without enthusiasm, to please her brother almost rather than herself. She knew however that the Prince was an extremely handsome and well-mannered man.

She herself, already past her prime, since the coming of this charming Nicoletta, who had acquired such a hold over Flaminio (and quite rightly, oh yes, a dear girl, a dear girl, sacrificed, poor thing, by that trickster of a husband!) had grown tired of her own "terrible maiden-ladyship" as she called it, and had said yes:

"*Su bubbolino, salutami il re!*"

Without any civil ceremony; in church only. What did that matter to her? At her age she would certainly not be having any children. The priest's absolution was enough for her, it was enough for her family and friends, and so away we go, off to the fair! With a light heart!

Sulkiness was a thing that Donna Adelaide could not endure. She was troubled by one thing only: they had told her that the Prince had a long beard. A man with a long beard must of course be intensely serious, or at least look as though he were. She hoped to be able to make him trim it. Bella Madre Santissima, she would never have the patience to stroke a great long waterfall of hair! Shorter, the beard, shorter....

Short and stout, almost neckless, Donna Adelaide was not altogether ugly; indeed she had quite a good face, but her eyes were too bright, with a crude polish like discs of enamel, and dazzlingly bright the teeth all of which she exposed in her frequent peals of laughter. She was always in a state of excitement, burdened as she was and stifled by those two enormous breasts beneath her chin, "monstrous excrescences," as she called them. And hot, hot, hot; she was always hot, and must have air, air, air!

CASSOCK AND FROCK COAT.

The old barrack of Valsania could never have anticipated, in the desolate abandonment in which it had existed for so many years, all these frills and feathers, all these gorgeous trimmings, in which the decorators had been dressing it up all the morning. And it seemed to be looking round at them, sorrowful and slightly bewildered, from the innumerable cracks in its walls, in the decrepit plaster that bulged and gaped everywhere. Oh, look! They had hung up beneath the windows a long festoon of laurel, like a necklace; another necklace higher up, of myrtle, beneath the gutter, with paper rosettes which had terrified the sparrows on the roof. Poor dear little creatures, whom it, their good old hostel, loved so well! There they were, all of them, flown away, away, hiding among the leaves of the trees round about.

... And from there they sent back to it shrill cries of dismay, as much as to say:

"Good gracious, what are they doing to you, old friend, what are they doing?"

Bah! It had long been slumbering, their old friend, in the peace of the fields. Remote from the life of men which had almost abandoned it, it had gradually begun to feel itself, in its dream, a part of nature: its stones, in the dream, had begun to feel again their native mountain, from which they had been quarried and shaped; and the moisture of the deep earth had risen and diffused itself through the walls, as the sap rises to the branches of trees through their roots; and here and there in the cracks tufts of grass had sprouted, and the tiles on the roof were coated with moss. The old barrack, as it slept, rejoiced to feel itself thus reabsorbed by the earth, to feel in itself the life of mountain and plants, almost their

199

consciousness, whereby it was now better able to understand the voice of the winds, the voice of its neighbour the sea, the twinkling of the distant stars and the gentle caress of the moon.

But now, look, men were disturbing it again; were dooming it to witness and to receive more of their strange and futile innovations. And who could say what happenings it might yet have to witness in this late autumn of its life!

What a grand new carpet blazing on the old rustic stair, with two green poles for a balustrade! What an escort of potted laurels and bamboos up the steps and along the landing above! And those damask hangings on the window sills and on the eastern terrace to hide the rusty railing! The fine carpet there too, on the terrace, with rush seats and little tables and bowls of flowers.... Now they were fixing an awning overhead. The reception and mutual introduction of bride and bridegroom would take place there, since they had failed to wrest from Mauro Mortara the key of the *camerone*.

Since daybreak he had been in hiding, no one knew where.

Don Cosmo, in his shirtsleeves, was tearing about amid the disorder of his bedroom, while Donna Sara Alaimo, her hair still unkempt, bowed over, buried in an old beechwood chest, long and narrow as a coffin, was trying to find him a decent coat in which to make a fitting appearance at the solemn ceremony. There rose from this chest, filled with old garments, a strong and pungent smell of camphor.

"You might at least hold the lid up for me, good Lord!" the poor "housekeeper" moaned in a suffocated voice, as though from the nether regions.

Twice already the lid had fallen upon her back.

And Don Cosmo:

"Nothing of the sort! What's the use, I say, what's the use? We're in the country here.... Don't bother me...."

"But you must let me dress you..." Donna Sara went on wailing from inside the chest. "The Lord Bishop is coming... the bride is coming.... Do you propose to appear in a jacket? Let me find it.... I know it's here!"

"And I tell you that it's not there!"

"But I've seen it with my own eyes! It is here! It is here!"

She was looking for an old frock coat which Don Cosmo in days gone by had worn once or twice, and which accordingly had remained brand new, buried there under the camphor, of old-fashioned cut, it was true, but a "fashionable garment," all the same....

"Here it is!" Donna Sara cried at last in triumph, raising her aching back from the chest. ... and pulled and pulled and pulled-- oh, gracious, was it as long as all that?... and pulled....

Donna Sara's arms slackened. It was a cassock. The cassock Don Cosmo Laurentano had worn as a seminarist.

She drew it all out at length, gently, to fold it properly and bury it again with due reverence. She shook her head; sighed:

"A real pity! A real pity! Who knows but you might be Bishop of Girgenti at this moment instead of Monsignor Montero...."

"It would be a lively diocese!" muttered Don Cosmo. "Put it away, bury it!"

He had been disturbed by the sudden appearance of this cassock, a spectre of his fervent, boyish faith. Empty and black as the cassock itself had his soul been ever since! What anguish, what tortures it revived in him....

With drooping lips and shut eyes, Don Cosmo let himself be immersed in the remote but still painful memories of his youth, a youth tormented for years on end by the bitter struggle between faith and reason. And reason had conquered faith, but only to be engulfed, in its turn, in that dark, profound, despairing scepticism.

"Was it there or wasn't it?" Donna Sara broke in upon his musings, standing before him with the frock coat spread out on her arms.

Don Cosmo had barely time to put it on. One of the body-guard (eight of them had come over, by twos and threes, from Colimbetra, in full review order) came clattering in to announce the Bishop's arrival.

Don Cosmo groaned again; tried to raise his arms to express the annoyance that he felt at these tidings; but was unable: the frock coat...

"Perfect! It fits you exactly! You look a picture!" Donna Sara assured him.

"A picture indeed!" shouted Don Cosmo. "It's stifling me! I

can't breathe!"

And off he went. He had hoped that the Bishop would be the last to arrive, and that it would not fall to himself to receive him and to keep him company until the other guests came. The thought of them bored him too, the whole of this pompous tom-foolery bored him intensely, but more than all or than any of them the sight of the Lord Bishop, of that exalted representative of a world from which he had severed himself after so much suffering, shocked most of all by the hypocrisy of so many of his compa-nions, who, albeit secretly assailed by the very doubts that tormented him, had remained in that world. And Monsignor Montero had been one of them. Now he held out his ring to be kissed, and had the supreme charge of the souls of an entire diocese. The unconscious illusions, the spontaneous and necessary fictions of the soul, Don Cosmo could and did excuse and commiserate and felt sympathy for them; but the deliberate fictions, no, especially in that supreme office, in that ministry of life and death.

"Oh, beautiful! Lovely!" Monsignore was saying mean-while, as he alighted from the carriage and stood gazing at the scenery, between Dianella Salvo and his secretary, a young priest, tall and thin and pallid, with deep intelligent eyes. "With the sea so near... oh, beautiful! Lovely!... and the valley... and the valley... and..."

He broke off, seeing Don Cosmo coming down steps from the decorated old mansion.

"Ah, here he comes! My dear Don Cosmo..."

"Monsignore, your most humble servant," said the other, bowing awkwardly.

"My dear fellow, my dear fellow..." Monsignore repeated, almost embracing him, and laying a hand on his shoulder. "How many years can it be since we last met.... Old men now, eh! old men.... You (we can call one another *tu*, I hope, as we did in the old days) you must, if I am not mistaken, be a year or two my se-nior...."

"Possibly... yes," sighed Don Cosmo. "But who counts the years now, my dear Montero? I know that I have many behind me, and few left to come: and the past years are a burden, and the fu-ture years seem to me enormously long.... That is all that I know...."

Dianella Salvo, as she looked at Don Cosmo, could not help smiling at the sight of the old frock coat which gripped him under the arms. The pale young priest was smiling furtively also; and the eight men of the bodyguard, posted stiffly at the foot of the steps, stared with distress and mortification at the figure cut by the brother of the Prince their master at this solemn reception. Donna Sara Alaimo had tucked away her hair as best she might under her cap, and had come down to kiss the Bishop's hand, genuflecting to the ground; the two maids had come down with her, also the cook and the manservant, and the wife of the *curatolo*, Ninfa's Vanni, had come up as well with her three half-naked bandy-legged urchins. Monsignore held out his hand to be kissed and smiled at them all, bowing his head. Then he introduced his secretary to Don Cosmo and, as he climbed the steps to the villa, spoke of the visit he had just paid, in passing, to the chapel of La Seta, and of the welcome he had received from all the folk of that hamlet.

"Such good people... such good people..."

And he asked Dianella and Donna Sara if they went there on Sundays, to hear mass in the chapel.

"I know that a priest comes out specially from Porto Empedocle, and that those good villagers collect a toll from the passers-by all the week, by the roadside...."

As he entered the villa, he turned to Dianella and inquired:

"Your mother?"

Dianella replied with a disconsolate movement of her arms, turning pale and looking him sorrowfully in the face.

"How very sad!" sighed Monsignore, going and sitting down on the now decorated terrace. "But at least she is calm, eh?"

"She takes in nothing!" exclaimed Donna Sara.

"And she still prays, doesn't she?" the Bishop went on.

"All the time," Dianella answered.

"A consolation for you," observed Monsignore, nodding his head and half shutting his protuberant eyes, "that, in the darkness of her mind, only the light of faith should remain burning.... Divine mercy...."

"To lose one's reason!" Don Cosmo muttered.

Monsignore shot an angry glance at him. But Don Cosmo did not observe it: he was lost in his own thoughts.

"I mean to keep her faith, even after she has lost her reason," Monsignore explained.

"Quite so!" Don Cosmo sighed, rousing himself. "It is the other thing that is difficult, my dear Monsignore!"

"I think it would not be advisable, would it, for her to see me?" the Bishop asked, turning again to Dianella as though he had not caught Don Cosmo's words. "Let us leave her, let us leave her in peace.... With you, though," he added, softly and with a kindly smile at Don Cosmo, "I should like to resume those heated discussions we used to have long ago, but not now and not here. ... If you would care to come and see me...."

"Discussions? I'm a perfect fool!" exclaimed Don Cosmo. "I have become a perfect fool, my dear Montoro.... I can no longer put two and two together! If one person tells me that two and two make six and another tells me that they make three...."

"Here's the Prince!" broke in Donna Sara, who was keeping a watch on the avenue from the balustrade of the terrace.

Monsignore rose with Dianella and Don Cosmo to see him arrive. The last ran down to embrace his brother as soon as he should alight from the carriage. There rode upon either side of it Captain Sciaralla and another officer, in review order likewise. The blazing red of their breeches shone out gaily against the green background of the trees and beneath the blue canopy of the sky. It was a closed carriage. The secretary, Lisi Preola, eat facing the Prince.

Donna Sara withdrew from the terrace, leaving only Monsignore, Dianella Salvo and the secretary to watch from the balustrade the exchange of greetings between the brothers.

"I DO HOPE IT'S NOT GOING TO RAIN!"

Don Ippolito Laurentano sprang from the carriage with boyish agility. He was in morning dress with a loose brimmed Panama hat on his head. He kissed his brother and at once drew back to examine him.

"Cosmo, what on earth have you been putting on yourself?" he asked with a smile. "No, my dear fellow, no! Go in at once and take off that relic of antiquity..."

Don Cosmo looked at the frock coat; he had forgotten its existence, although he felt it gripping him under the arms. "Why yes," he said, "I do notice an odour...."

"An odour? Why, you stink, my dear fellow!" exclaimed Don Ippolito. "You reek of camphor a mile away!"

He smiled at Monsignore and raised his hat in greeting to Dianella Salvo on the terrace; then began to mount the steps.

"I give you the comforting intelligence that you are a great deal more stupid than I am! Far, far more!" Don Cosmo was saying presently to the "housekeeper" who, ashamed and angry, was by no means convinced that this "fashionable garment" could be out of place on an occasion like this, with a Monsignore present. "And you've given me a headache," Don Cosmo railed, "and you've made me drunk with all your camphor. ... Off with it, I tell you, take it off at once.... I can't skin myself! Give me my own coat, quickly."

When he reappeared on the terrace, Don Ippolito threw up his arms:

"Ah, heaven be praised! Now you look splendid!"

Monsignore and Dianella laughed.

"Donna Sara's ideas! What is one to do?" Don Cosmo sighed, shrugging his shoulders. "I assure you, she's even stupider than I am."

"That I can well believe!" said the Prince with a laugh. "But tell me--Mauro? Where is he? Isn't he to be seen?"

"Humph!" said Don Cosmo. "He's vanished! I've heard nothing of him now for days past, ever since we had the honour...."

"I know where he is," said Dianella, acknowledging Don Cosmo's compliment with a graceful bow, while he tried to cut her short. "Under one of the carubs down in the valley.... But, please, nobody is supposed to know! We have made friends...."

"Indeed?" Don Ippolito inquired, as his radiant eyes took in the grace and beauty of the girl. "With that bear?"

"He is mad as a hatter!" Don Cosmo announced gravely.

"No, why?" put in Dianella.

"And look who it is that says so, Monsignore!" the Prince exclaimed. "I'd give anything in the world to be able to hide behind a curtain and watch the scenes that must go on between them when they are alone together...."

Don Cosmo nodded his assent and uttered his habitual laugh, the threefold "Oh! oh! oh!"

"They must be rare fun!" Don Ippolito added.

Dianella was gazing with pleasure, with an indefinable satisfaction at this old man, to whom his manly beauty, his firm vigour, his sure mastery of himself, imparted a nobility at once so proud and so serene; she could imagine how exquisite must be his manners without the slightest effort and yet without a trace of affectation, and it pained her to think of him in conjunction with her Aunt Adelaide, a nature so different, so diametrically opposed to his: giggling, impulsive, noisy. What impression was he going to form of her?

They all left the terrace and all, except Monsignore and his secretary, who remained at the front door, went down to the foot of the steps, when the tinkle of silver bells announced the arrival of Flaminio Salvo's carriage from the avenue.

Don Ippolito stepped forward to help the ladies to alight, and caught his bride in the act of exclaiming: "Here we are!" with her arms up-stretched towards the roof of the carriage, as though she were casting them from her. He pretended not to notice this awkward gesture, by prolonging his bow, then kissed her hand; he next kissed Donna Nicoletta Capolino's, and vigorously clasped that of Flaminio Salvo, while the two ladies rapturously embraced Dianella, and Don Cosmo stood self-consciously in the background, not knowing whether or how to introduce himself.

Captain Sciaralla on his white mare was like an equestrian statue, at the foot of the steps, facing his rigid platoon.

"Ah! The soldiers! Let me look at the soldiers!" exclaimed Donna Adelaide, waddling off like a goose, without noticing that, at the head of the steps between the potted laurels and bamboos, Monsignore Montero, his features composed in a kindly, condescending smile, was bowing to her for the third time in vain.

Dianella, observing at length Don Cosmo's embarrassment, cut short Nicoletta Capolino's expansive greetings and stopped her aunt to point out and present to her her future brother-in-law.

"Oh, of course," said Donna Adelaide, laughing and squeezing his hand in a tight grip."Such a pleasure! The hermit of Valsania, isn't it? So delighted! And how nicely they have done the villa up! Oh, look! Look! Why, there's Monsignore all the time.... And nobody told me!"

She ran towards the steps; the Prince at once hastened to offer her his arm; Don Cosmo gave his to Donna Nicoletta, and Dianella went last with her father.

"Beautifully dressed, those soldiers!" Donna Adelaide remarked to the Prince, lifting up her skirt in front with her disengaged hand, so as not to trip upon the steps. "Truly charming! They look like a lot of sugar dolls! Charming!"

Then, as she reached the head of the steps:

"Most Excellent Monsignore! I thought that Your Excellency would be coming at your own convenience, instead of which here you are, punctual to the minute!"

The Bishop smiled, held out his hand for Donna Adelaide to kiss his ring, and said to her:

"To have the joy of seeing you like this, on the Prince's arm, and to bid yon welcome, Donna Adelaide, to the house of Lamentano."

"But how very kind, thank you, thank you, truly gracious, Your Excellency!" replied Donna Adelaide, going first into the villa at the Prince's bidding.

Monsignore went in, and then Donna Nicoletta, then Dianella and Salvo and the Bishop's secretary and also Don Cosmo: the Prince choosing to enter last of all. When he emerged on the terrace, he intercepted the gentle gaze of Dianella, anxiously awaiting his coming. Instinctively he responded with a faint smile.

"Fine looking man, isn't he?" Nicoletta Capo-lino whispered to Dianella. "There certainly won't be any need to clip his beard, as Adelaide says."

"Clip his beard?" asked Dianella.

"Yes," the other replied. "She kept us in fits of laughter in the carriage, with her terror of the Prince's long beard."

"What are you two talking about over there?" Donna Adelaide broke into the conversation at this point. "Are you laughing at us? They are laughing at you and me, my dear Prince. Silly girls! But we must grin and bear it: that's what we are here for; this is our day.... Like going to the fair! Flaminio, my boy, don't devour me with your eyes. Give me courage, if anything! I do everything you tell me, always.... But let me enjoy myself I I say foolish things, because I'm excited.... Come along, Nicoletta! With your permission, Prince, I am going to pay my poor sister-in-law a visit."

And off she went, followed by her niece and by Nicoletta.

At once Salvo, to remove the unfavourable impression left on the Prince's mind by his sister's outburst, explained with an air of mystery that Signora Capolino was unaware that her husband, possibly at that very moment, was fighting a duel, and that she supposed him to be at Siciliana on a tour of his constituency.

"Let us pray to God that all may be well!" sighed Monsignore, in a tone of deep distress, raising his globular eyes to heaven.

"Oh, there's no doubt about that!" smiled Salvo. "A ridiculous adversary, who has been beaten by everybody, always: short, stout and blind as a bat. Whereas our friend Capolino..."

"Just after I left the house," said Don Ippo-lito, "I could see the two carriages in the distance coming along the road towards Colimbetra."

"Why, yes," added Salvo, "by this time, they're certain to

be..."

He stopped short. They were all silent for a moment, help-less in the grip of terror, and their thoughts flew far away to the other villa where at that moment the duel was being fought. There, was a very different spectacle: two men face to face, two drawn sabres, flashing in the air; here, amid the silence of the fields, the pompous decorations, improvised for a festal occasion which now, strangely enough, appeared to them all to be almost out of place, artificial, forced.

There was indeed, from the moment of their arrival, a cer-tain awkward chill in the spirits of both the Prince and Salvo, which they were each doing his best to conceal. This chill was caused by Landino's reply, which had at last arrived, to his father's letter: the usual congratulations, the usual wishes for the future, delicately worded expressions of his pleasure at the kind and loving companionship that his father would now have; but not a word as to his own coming down to attend the wedding.

Don Ippolito, as he started from Colimbetra, had made up his mind to send Mauro Mortara to Rome, to let Landino know how displeased, how pained his father was with his behaviour, and to try to bring him back to Sicily. He knew that Landino from his earliest boyhood had entertained a deep and tender affection for old Mauro and a keen admiration for his character, for his fanatical loyalty to the memory and ideas of Landino's grandfather, for the almost contemptuous attitude which he had adopted from the be-ginning and still maintained towards the father, that is to say towards Don Ippolito himself, who for all that was his master. No other envoy was likely to prove so effective. For this savage old rustic was, so to speak, rooted in the heart of the family, the voice of the ancient Valsania, their native soil.

He thought he would seize the opportunity of the ladies' absence to go out to the head of the steps and tell Sciaralla to send Ninfa's Vanni down to the gorge to look for Mauro, as he wished to speak to him.

"When he returned to the terrace, he found there Donna Adelaide, Donna Nicoletta and Dianella. The two former had tak-en off their hats. Donna Adelaide's eyes were red with tears and Dianella was paler and Salvo darker than before.

"I did not ask you, Don Flaminio," said the Prince, in a sympathetic tone, "to present me to your wife, because I know, alas..."

"Oh, thank you, thank you," Salvo cut him short, shrinking into himself and nodding his head gently, with half shut eyes, as much as to say: "Thank you... it is just as though she were not in the house!"

Donna Adelaide had gone across to the balustrade of the terrace and, with her back turned to the party, was wiping her eyes and loudly blowing her nose, saying to Nicoletta Capolino, who was begging her to calm herself:

"I am a great donkey, I know! But how am I to help it? Whenever I see her, whenever I see those eyes of hers, they make me feel so wretched!" Suddenly, making an effort, she threw up her arms, tossed her head as though she were stifling, panted: "Ufff, that will do for the present!" and turned round smiling.

Two footmen in livery appeared on the terrace with big trays loaded with cups and cakes. After these refreshments, Monsignor Montoro took the floor to announce in a polished little discourse (which was intended, nevertheless, to give the impression of its having been improvised on the spot) the formal promise of marriage that had been exchanged, and proceeded naturally to extol the good old days in which a contract made before God was sufficient by itself, in civilized society, to fasten the bond of matrimony, which religion alone can render sacred and noble, whereas the law of man, the so-called civil law degrades it and almost makes it infamous....

All the rest listened with lowered eyes, religiously, to the Bishop's glowing words. Only Don Cosmo sat with knitted brows and fixed gaze, as though he hoped in one of those words to find the peg for a philosophical discussion. Don Ippolito, seeing him adopt this attitude, became seriously worried about him. Flaminio Salvo, for his part, with that letter from Rome upon his mind, was thinking that it was all very well, what the Bishop was saying, but that meanwhile the Prince's noble son was turning a deaf ear, that the other side were not abiding by their agreement and that his sister, without the slightest guarantee, was allowing herself to he compromised from the start. To Donna Adelaide, this little sermon was like any sacred function, almost like hearing mass: a formality, nothing more. A piece of play-acting, on the other hand, and one that was not very amusing at the moment, it seemed to Nicoletta Capolino, and disgusting to Dianella who was watching the other and could read on her brow all that was passing through her mind.

A light breeze had risen from the sea, and the awning overhead kept on swelling and rising like a balloon, while a corner of the damask hanging slapped insolently against the railing it concealed.

This slapping noise at length distracted the never very close attention that Donna Adelaide had been paying to the little sermon, which had already lasted too long, and, as a cloud borne on the breeze hid the sun for a moment, she bent down to peep out at the sky from under the awning, and could not repress a murmur of:

"I do hope it's not going to rain...."

These few words, although barely audible, had a disastrous effect, as though the entire party (Monsignore, of course, excepted) were irresistibly led to discover an immediate connexion between the threat of rain and this ponderous and interminable sermon.

Don Cosmo opened his eyes and stared; Donna Nicoletta could not repress a titter of laughter; Don Flaminio frowned; Monsignore stopped short, lost Ms thread, said:

"Let us hope not," and at once added: "And now to conclude."

He concluded, naturally, with good wishes and congratulations, and the rest of the party rose with great relief.

Donna Adelaide, feeling that she would stifle beneath that awning, suggested going down for a stroll along the avenue. The Prince gave her his arm, Nicoletta went next with Dianella, and Monsignore, Salvo, Don Cosmo and the secretary followed in their wake.

Don Ippolito Laurentano felt his tongue parched and tied by the desperate struggle that was raging within him between his chivalrous instincts, which impelled him to be courteous and attentive to the lady, and the enormous, freezing disappointment and invincible repulsion which her manners, her behaviour, her gestures, her voice, her laugh had at once aroused in him; between the instinctive, overpowering, irresistible need to free himself from her at the earliest possible moment, dismissing without more ado a project which now, when it came to the point, seemed to him to fall so lamentably short of the idea that he had formed of it, and the thought of the serious difficulty of so doing, now that he had definitely pledged himself--with his resentment to boot, secret and bitter, against his absent son, to whom he would appear to be own-ing himself beaten, after he had so far humbled himself as almost to crave his son's consent to this marriage. He was boiling, lastly, with the bitterest rage at Monsignore, who had depicted his bride to him in such deceiving colours: "Lively, a warm heart, an open nature, sincere, vivacious, submissive...." What on earth was he to say to her now? How bring himself to address her?

Fortunately, Captain Sciaralla appeared at this moment, and, standing to attention, announced that Mortara had come up from the vallone.

"Where is he?" said the Prince curtly. "Tell him to come here."

"Mauro?" Don Cosmo asked. "Oh no, let him alone, poor fellow.... You know what he's like...."

"Oh, the person they call the Monk?" exclaimed Donna Adelaide. "Let us go and see him, let us go at once, Prince, please!"

"No, aunt!" implored Dianella, who was sorry that she had revealed his hiding place. "It would hurt his feelings."

"Is he really such a bear, then?" said Donna Adelaide, puz-zled.

"A grizzly bear!" Don Cosmo assured her.

"Just fancy," put in Flaminio Salvo; "after all this time I have never yet succeeded in setting eyes on him...."

And Nicoletta inquired: "Is it true that he wears a goatskin on his head and goes about armed to the teeth?"

"Let you and me go by ourselves, Prince!" was Donna Ade-laide's next suggestion. "I do so want to see him... I can't wait, come along!"

Mauro was standing outside the door of his room in the basement, staring moodily over the vineyard to the sea. Seeing the Prince with a lady, his face darkened, but, as Don Ippolito gave him a friendly greeting, he advanced towards him and stooped down to kiss him on the breast. His kiss was followed by a sort of sob.

"My old friend," said Don Ippolito, touched by this kiss over his heart, "do you know who this lady is?"

"I can guess; may God give you happiness!" replied Mauro, gazing solemnly at Donna Adelaide, who was staring at him with wide and glistening eyes and a smile on her lips.

"I wish to give you happiness as well," the Prince went on. "Would you like to go to Rome?"

"To Rome? I?" exclaimed Mauro in amazement. "To Rome? You can ask me that? Who knows how many times I would have gone there on foot, as a pilgrim, if my legs..."

"Good," the Prince interrupted him, "you shall go there on the steamer and the train. I have a message for you to give to Landino. Come tomorrow to Colimbetra... that is to say, not tomorrow ... let me think! I shall send over for you in the course of the week. I have a lot to say to you."

"And then... straight to Rome?" Mauro faltered.

"Immediately!"

"Because I am an old man," Mauro went on. "On my two crooked sevens. [Footnote: The number 77, in Italy, is symbolical of the bent legs of an old man. So the British soldier speaks of "legs-eleven," and the Frenchman says "prendre le train onze." C. K. S. M.] And the thought of dying without seeing Rome has always worried me!"

"But will you go dressed like that, to Rome?" Donna Adelaide asked him.

"No, Signora," Mauro replied. "I have a good coat here, of broadcloth, and a black hat, like your bridegroom's."

"And that hairy cap," Donna Adelaide asked again, "how can you wear it? Oh Lord, the very sight of it makes me sick!"

"This cap..." Mauro was beginning to explain; but a sudden shout, from the other end of the house, cut him short.

"Don Ippolito, come, quickly! Capolino...."

"What has happened?" screamed Donna Adelaide.

"Wounded?" asked the Prince.

"Yes; badly, it seems...." Salvo answered. "Come!"

"But who says so?"

"One of your men has ridden over from Colimbetra....

They have carried him up to your house, wounded in the chest.... I don't know yet if it was a sabre or a pistol.... And poor Signora Nicoletta, here with us!"

When they reached the villa, Donna Nicoletta was struggling in the arms of the Bishop and Dianella, moaning incessantly:

"My heart told me so! My heart spoke to me! My hat... my hat.... The carriage, quick. ... Scoundrels, murderers.... Oh, my Gnazio!"

"The carriage is at the door!" Captain Sciaralla came in to announce.

Nicoletta dashed out without saying good-bye to anyone.

"What about you, Prince?" said Salvo.

"Ought I to go too?" asked Don Ippolito.

To which Salvo:

"It would be as well. You, Adelaide, will remain here to-night. Come along. Come along."

The carriage, with Nicoletta, the Prince and Salvo in it, set off at full speed.

"Oh Holy Mother of God, what bad luck!" Donna Adelaide was left exclaiming at the head of the steps, beating her hands together. "But what were they doing with a duel to-day, of all days? Is that fair? Leave God out of it, Monsignore! If you don't mind! What is the good of praying? ... Your Excellency must excuse me, but is this the sort of trick to play on a poor woman like me?"

CHAPTER VIII

A PHANTOM CONCLAVE.

In the house of Donna Caterina Auriti Laurentano, on the day of the election, were assembled round Roberto the few friends who had remained faithful to him, notwithstanding his having ceased to correspond with them for many years. He had found them, in the last few days, altered like himself by time and the vicissitudes of life.

For a moment, in the eyes of each of them, as they embraced their friend, there had kindled and flashed the old youthful expression of those far off days, unconscious still of what fate held in store for them; then immediately, with a slight shake of their heads, those eyes had grown misty with emotion, with agonizing regret, while their lips parted in a sad and bitter smile.

"Who would have said," that misty gaze and that smile seemed to ask, "who would have told us then that one day we should have come to this? That we should have lost so many things, which were everything in life to us then, and which we should have thought it impossible to lose? And yet we have lost them; and life has remained to us; but what a life: this!" More painful still was the spectacle of one who had not noticed, or who pretended not to have noticed his losses, and showed his unconsciousness in the care he devoted to his middle-aged person, which exhibited, in a compassionately enfeebled form, the airs and graces of another generation.

Each of them had adapted himself as best he might to his own fate, had made a niche, a position for himself. Sebastiano Ceraulo, a lawyer who had scraped through his examinations, a fervent improviser of patriotic poetry in the years of the Revolution, at that time a spirited, impetuous youth, with a forest of unkempt locks, had been appointed, by personal influence, secretary in the Provincial office, and now trained over his scalp with pitiable industry the wisp of long, carefully waxed hair that remained on it; he had grown enormously stout; had taken a wife; had had by her five children, all girls hot in pursuit of husbands. Marco Sala, sentenced to death by the Bourbon Government, who notwithstanding had returned again and again to Sicily from his place of exile, disguised as a friar, to distribute Mazzini's proclamations by stealth; had gone first of all into the sulphur business; had done very well for several years; then had come to grief; and for some time supported his family by gambling; finally he had been made keeper of a tobacco warehouse. Rosario Trigona, who on the 15th of May, 1860, at Girgenti, while Garibaldi was fighting at Calatafimi, had sallied forth alone, an act of madness, with a handful of comrades, the tricolour in one hand and a long sabre in the other, to face the three thousand men of the Bourbon garrison, and who, pursued, under a rain of bullets, had escaped by a miracle, and made his way on foot to the victorious Garibaldi, running day and night and dodging the royal army which was scouring Sicily in search of the Filibuster, who was by that time at Gibilrossa above Palermo; Rosario Trigona, crippled now by nephritis, flabby, bald, toothless and half blind, likewise burdened with a family, was dragging out a wretched existence on the meagre salary of assistant secretary in the Chamber of Commerce. And Mattia Gangi, who had flung his cassock to the winds to take part in the Revolution, now, asthmatic, irritable, his beard, hair and bushy eyebrows dyed the colour of egg-fruit, was teaching in the elementary school *alauda est laeta: the lark is blithe*. "Blithe? Not a bit of it!" he would add, to the boys who stared, open-eyed. "How is she blithe? Why is she blithe? She seems blithe to us! She sings because she is hungry, she sings to call her mate! Blithe, indeed! Don't you believe it!" In contrast to him was Filippo Noto, tall, thin and wasted, but still golden-haired and neat. Before 1860 he had fought a duel with a young officer in the Bourbon army over a woman and had been prosecuted; this amorous adventure had served him as a patriotic precedent; but he cared little for politics; by dint of hard reading he had succeeded in keeping himself afloat, in moving with the times, while remaining a lukewarm Conservative; he was regarded as one of the most experienced members of the Sicilian bar, and was often briefed to defend the most important civil cases even at Palermo, Messina, Catania.

These five friends and Canon Agrò were endeavouring to keep the conversation going, talking of impersonal matters, of remote events, recalling anecdotes which provoked an occasional forced laugh; in order simply that the weight of defeat, however clearly foreseen, might not, with the additional burden of silence, press too heavily upon their troubled minds. But as a matter of fact, gradually, after the first shock of seeing their friend again and now with their increasing emotion at renewing the old memories of their youth, the four walls of their present consciousness were beginning to melt, and they, with a sort of secret disturbance, which weakened their resistance, became aware that not only were the persons that they now were inhabiting their bodies; but that those other persons, also, which they had been years and years before, were living still and feeling and reasoning with the same thoughts, the same sentiments that they had supposed to be obscured, cancelled, extinguished by a long oblivion. There came to life at that moment in each one of them another unsuspected self, that self which each of them had been thirty years or so earlier; but so living, so present that, as they looked at themselves, they received a strange impression, sad and at the same time absurd, of their present appearance, which even to themselves seemed scarcely to be real. There was present, actually present, alive and active in each of them, the past; and the present had practically ceased to exist.

From time to time, however, there came into the room Antonio Del Re, who saw them as the elderly men that they were, and, after listening for a while to their conversation, felt an ineffable sadness, the sadness that we feel when we see in old men who have forgotten for a moment that they are old, certain passions still vigorous for things, for people that to us are dead or obsolete: passions that have their roots in a soil of which we know nothing, which is no longer ours, which was the old men's, and which we have passed beyond in our advance, dragging after us their feeble bodies, not their souls: their souls have been left behind.

"We had been sitting up playing cards at San Gerlando," Marco Sala was recounting, "until nearly midnight, at Giacinto Lumia's, poor fellow."

"Poor Giacinto!" Trigona sighed, shaking his head. "Vincenzo Guarnotta was with us, from Siculiana," Sala went on.

"Ah, Vincenzo!" said Roberto Auriti. "What has become of him?"

"Dead," replied Sala. "It must be nine or ten years ago. He had come to Girgenti on business, and was staying at the Convent of Sant' Anna, as he used always to do. Even the Convent is gone now! It was a terrible night: wind, thunder, lightning, rain, rain that seemed to be bringing the roof down. So much so that in the end Giacinto Lumia invited us all to spend the night there. We should find some sort of shakedown. The others, being bachelors, and Guarnotta, the stranger, accepted the invitation; I, in spite of his entreaties, insisted upon going home so as not to keep my mother (now with God) and my wife in suspense. Before I left the house, Guarnotta, knowing that on my way home I must pass along the Stretto di Sant' Anna, asked me to knock at the gate of the Convent and tell the Brother Porter that he would be sleeping out that night. I promised to do so, and left. I assure you that, as soon as I had started, I regretted that I had not accepted Lumia's hospitality. What a wind! It carried you off your feet! The rain came lashing down like bullets; and the cold and darkness, a darkness torn to ribbons by the ghastly streaks of lightning! All the same, as I passed along the Stretto di Sant' Anna, I remembered what Guarnotta had said, and stopped to knock at the Convent door. I knocked, and knocked again: nothing happened! Nobody heard me! It was a wonder I didn't break down the door. I was just going away, in a towering rage, when I heard a barred window open above my head and a voice shout: 'Who's there?' 'Sala,' say I, 'Marco Sala!' 'All right!' shouts the voice from above; and with that I hear the window being shut and bolted. I stood there gaping. They hadn't given me time to open my mouth, and yet it was all right? I shook with rage at the thought that simply to oblige Guarnotta, who had remained under cover, I, at the risk of catching my death of cold, had perhaps made them think me mad or drunk. Who would ever wander about at that time of night, in such weather? Well, I had gone a few yards, when I heard, echoing down the Stretto, the slow boom of a bell, which made me jump: '*Dong*!' And the wind made the sound spread, mournfully, through the night. Then, again, *dong--dong*--more slow booms; there must have been fifteen of them; I didn't stop to count. I reached my house, tore off my clothes which were clinging to me; dried myself thoroughly; jumped into bed, and went off to sleep. Next morning, I get up early, as my habit is, go to answer the door, and guess what I find there. The bearers with the bier. As soon as they catch sight of me, they throw up their arms, start back; stand there speechless: 'Don Marco! What's this? Your Exc'ency's not dead?' 'You dogs!' I shout, raising my stick. 'Yes, sir,' they go on.... 'They sent up to Sant' Anna, last night, to say that Your Exc'ency was dead!' That bell, d'you understand, had been tolling for me. And I had called there myself to report my own death."

Albeit this little tale was not a merry one, Sala's closing words were drowned in his friends' laughter.

"You laugh, do you?" he said. "And yet, who knows whether I didn't really die that night, my friends! Yes, indeed! I can honestly say that it was the last merry evening of my youth! Perhaps, with constantly thinking about it, the impression of that tolling bell has become fixed in my memory, an evil omen; but it does seem to me that just at that very time my life began to be pent in a torrent of misfortunes, became for me what the Stretto di Sant' Anna was on that night of storm, and that the *dang-dong* of that passing bell has followed me all the way."

At this point Antonio Del Re reappeared with a fresh telegram. A number of these had already come in from the various polling stations in the constituency. Canon Agro opened it, cast his eyes over the contents and flung it into a corner, on the chair by the sofa. Neither Roberto nor any of the rest took the trouble to inquire from what district it came, what result it announced. Agro's gesture and silence had been more than eloquent.

The defeat of the moment, which affected Auriti, made more evident the other, far more serious, irreparable defeat which had been inflicted upon each of them by time and life. And this defeat seemed to be symbolized, in statuesque form, in the person of Donna Caterina Auriti Laurentano, taciturn and brooding.

From time to time Roberto and his friends cast a furtive glance at her, as at a phantom of the days of which they were the futile survivors. Other voices were there in these days, which found no echo in their hearts; other thoughts which did not enter their minds; other energies, other ideals, against which their spirits were sealed in hostile aloofness.

And the proof of this was crudely obvious in that heap of telegrams, lying there on the chair.

There had come forward unexpectedly, in the last few days, but certainly after a long and secret preparation, a third candidate in the shape of one Zappala of Grotte, a mining expert: whose nomination was openly declared to be an act of protest and assertion by the sulphur workers and farm labourers of the Province, now united in Fasci.

Roberto Auriti had dropped to the third place. In almost all the districts this Zappala had received more votes than he, putting him thus out of the running, by a quick, contemptuous thrust, as one might kick out of one's path a useless piece of rubbish, a nuisance rather than an obstacle.

At one point, when the telegram arrived from Grotte, which was one of the principal centres of the sulphur industry in the Province, with the report that the voters there had been almost unanimous for Zappala, it seemed that he might even prove a serious rival to Capolino, and qualify for a second ballot, notwithstanding the enthusiastic support which the clerical champion had received in Girgenti, to console him for his serious injury in the duel.

Trigona, wishing to cloak the truth in a pious fraud, sought to ascribe their defeat principally to the result of this ill-advised duel, to the undue violence shown by Veronica, a stranger, and to the arrogant behaviour of one of his seconds, that Signor what's-his-name, the swashbuckler, which had genuinely shocked and outraged the citizens of Girgenti, in spite of the fact that Selmi, who in the mean time had returned to his own constituency, had done everything in his power to temper their indignation.

Canon Agro nodded his head in silence. He could not forgive Veronica for having ruined, by that disgraceful scene in public, the strategic plan which he had pondered and constructed with

such subtle guile. And that other Cavaliere, Giovan Battista Mattina! Sent to Grotte to support Auriti's candidature, he had played
the part of Judas, going over at the last moment to the Popular
Party.

"But who is the fellow?" Mattia Gangi demanded with his
habitual savage glare. "What does he represent? What does he live
on? What does he do? What sewer has he escaped from? Sleek and
overdressed, with the airs of a sovereign prince...."

Canon Agro shook his head gently, curling his lips in a
sneer, then said:

"Kites, my dear friends, kites! He, Veronica, and ever so
many more! They are all kites.... You see them up overhead, in the
seven heavens, you stand open-mouthed gaping at them; and all
the time who knows what hand it is that is paying out the string? It
may be the hand of some had woman; or the string may start from
the police headquarters, or from some midnight gambling den....
No one can tell! The Idte meanwhile is there, it takes the wind, flies
with it and seems to rule it. Every now and then, a blunder, a
swoop, all the signs of a headlong crash. But the unknown hand,
down below, sends it up at once with a gentle, cunning twitch or a
strong energetic tug, and gets it into the wind again and goes on
paying out more and more string. Kites, my dear friends.... How
many we see! And they all have tails, *et in cauda venenum*...."

Six heads nodded to express their approval, silently and
with intense bitterness, of this imaginative flight by Canon Agro,
who himself seemed to remain slightly dazed by it for some moments, and heaved a sigh of relief, as though he had thus eased his
spirit of the burden of defeat.

Roberto Auriti was more distressed by his mother's obstinate, brooding silence. She had spoken volubly at first (which was
unlike her), seeking to dissuade him from the venture; and weighty
had her words been then; weightier still, now, was her silence. She
intended that only the facts should speak now, in plain terms, con-
firming all that she had said.

With a feeling of irritation, he put in:

"Whatever they may be, my friends, kites or serpents... we
need not consider them! To hear you speak, one would think that
I, in coming here, was under some illusion.... Nothing of the sort,

as you know. I was sent here by One to Whom I could not say no: I should have felt that I was a deserter."

"Poor Christ!" exclaimed Mattia Gangi. "You have come here to be crucified!"

"Not crucified, surely," Roberto smiled. "It was that my offer, with whatever value it might have in the present campaign, might be rejected by my fellow-citizens; and that their answer, given in my name to the Government, might make the Government think that something else is wanted here now for a change!" "Zappala, Zappala is what is wanted!" Mattia Gangi sneered. "How I should love to see Zappala elected!"

"Mamma," Roberto added softly, laying his hand on his mother's arm, with a smile of bitter resignation, "you can't teach an old donkey..."

His mother thrust out her lip and knitted her brows, while the others shouted in chorus, echoing Mattia Gangi's wish that Zappala might be elected. One Zappala only? No! Five hundred and eight Zappalas, one for every constituency in the Peninsula! What scenes there would be in the Chamber! The first thing would be to abolish all the schools! Abolish all taxation! Abolish the army and the police! Law and order, soap and water! The frontiers levelled, and universal brotherhood! Yes, yes, cut the heads off the mountains, reduce them all to hillocks of uniform height! And Mattia Gangi, springing to his feet, began to declaim:

Al ronzio di quella lira   Ci uniremo, gira gira,   Tutti in un gomitolo. Varieta d'usi e di clima   Le son fisime di prima;   E' mutata l'aria. I deserti, i monti, i mari,   Son confini da lunari, Sogni di grografi. ...   ... E tu pur chetati, o Musa,   Che mi secchi con las scusa   Dell'amor di patria. Son figliuol dell'universo   E mi sembra tempo perso   Scriver per l'Italia.

[To the thrumming of that lyre, we join our hands and round we go, all in a ring. Differences of custom and clime are fancies of the past; we have changed the tune. Deserts, mountains, seas, are frontiers only in the almanacs, dreams of geographers. . . . And do you keep silence now, O Muse, who weary me with the plea of love of country. I am a child of the universe, and it seems to me a waste of time to write for Italy.]

They had all risen to their feet, all except Pompeo Agro,

and were applauding enthusiastically.

"Gentlemen, gentlemen," said Filippo Noto, clawing his cuffs down from under his sleeves, "let us be fair, gentlemen; do not let us find fault with them, when the wrong is all on our side! Yes, on ours! With us Christian people! When we hear them say: 'We intend that to everyone shall be given according to his work! We intend that the spirit of man shall be able to raise itself above material cares! We intend that everyone shall have bread to eat and work to do! We ignorant bourgeois, we tender-hearted Christians, are the first to applaud. ...'"

"Why, of course! Of course! Of course!" cried Ceraulo. "In the desire for universal happiness, of course! All honest minds are agreed as to that."

"Very good, so they are, and the Socialists (ahem!) open their mouths, and you drop in," Filippo Noto promptly retorted. "They give us a glimpse of an ideal humanity and justice, with which nobody can find fault, for which everybody must feel enthusiastic; and so they make proselytes to their cause among those who cannot distinguish between the poetry of the ideal and the reality of social life, my dear Ceraulo! Simpletons, simpletons who are incapable of asking themselves even whether the new methods are not calculated to increase a thousandfold the hardships and the sadness of our vale of tears; am I not right, Monsignore?"

Pompeo Agro nodded his head in approval.

"The real danger, gentlemen, lies in this," Noto went on with increasing warmth: "in the conviction at which we Christians have arrived, that the movement of the so-called Fourth Estate is inevitable, irresistible...."

"It is, it is, it is, alas!" Ceraulo again interrupted him.

"Nothing of the sort! Absolute nonsense!" shouted Filippo Noto. "The Socialist theory lacks the support of science, my dear Sir, of science, of logic, of morals, even of civilization; it cannot maintain itself, and is bound to collapse like a crazy dream, like a drunkard's nightmare! I should like to prove it to you, I should like to prove it to every one, and first of all to the men in power who make us look on at the pitiable spectacle of a State that yields, a State that goes astray and burdens itself with things with which it ought not to burden itself!"

He grew somewhat calmer, held up his hands and continued in a different tone:

"Let me explain myself, briefly. The whole procedure is a mistake, from a to z. Just consider! Making provision for the aged, for women, for foundlings, for the sick, may be a matter that really is in the public interest."

"In the interest of humanity," said Trigona.

"Precisely! I quite agree!" Noto assured him. "But from assisting actual misfortune by means of orphanages, night shelters, soup kitchens, it has been an easy, an unconscious step, my friends, to the safeguarding of the proletariat..."

"The so-called proletariat," Gangi muttered through his teeth.

"... from potential misfortunes as well," Noto went on, "thanks to compulsory insurance against the accidents arising out of employment and against the worker's future incapacitation by old age or sickness. Now does it not seem to you self-evident, my friends, given these first steps, that others will follow which will lead us ever farther in the direction of that Providential State so strongly condemned by the most eminent practical writers? Because, when the public mind has once entertained the idea that the community ought to look after those who from bodily incapacity are unable to work, it is an easy jump across the ditch that separates us from the true realm of socialism, by extending the principle to those men who are able-bodied and unemployed. And the fact must be admitted! If these men, notwithstanding their willingness to work, cannot find work, or if their labour is not adequately rewarded, are they, do you think, less to be pitied than those who by some physical defect are unable to work? The effect is the same, gentlemen, undeserved starvation! And with the proclamation of the right to work, anyone can see where we shall end; we have seen it already, for that matter, in France, in 1848..."

At this point a sudden cry of rage from Canon Agro interrupted Filippo Noto's speech, which was beginning to assume the proportions and tone of a platform oration.

There had come in from Comitini, Agro's native village, a letter reporting a fresh betrayal. Rosario Trigona's son had sold himself there to Capolino's party, and was spreading the report that

224

Roberto Auriti had laid down his arms, was retiring from the fray, and begged his supporters to vote for the Clerical candidate against the Socialist Zappala.

Agro could not contain himself: without pity for the poor, half-blind father, who was in the room with him, he heaped coals of fire upon the wretch who had brought upon him so serious an affront, there in his own stronghold.

Roberto Auriti made several attempts to stop him, then hastened to console his friend, who at first had risen to his feet, horrified, ready to fling himself upon the letter and upon Agro, then had let himself sink heavily down on his chair, and burst out sobbing, burying his face in his hands.

"But it's sure to be a slander, Rosario... a slander, you'll find that it is! Your son must have acted in good faith, believing that he was interpreting my wishes.... In fact, between the two, between Capolino and this man Zappala, why, it is better that the votes should go to Capolino. ... He has decided that I cannot keep up the struggle... and..."

"No... no..." Rosario Trigona moaned between his sobs, inconsolable. "The wretch! The wretch!"

Fortunately, they were joined by Mauro Mortara, who had gone from Valsania to Colimbetra to arrange with the Prince for his expedition to Rome. He knew nothing about the election. Welcomed with joy by Marco Sala, Ceraulo, Gangi, who had not set eyes on him for years, he thrust them all aside with his arms and almost fell on his knees before Donna Caterina, seizing her hand and kissing it again and again; he then embraced Roberto and bent down to kiss him on the breast, over his heart.

"To Rome!" he said. "Have you heard? I'm coming to Rome!"

But his jubilation aroused no echo: they were all still disconcerted and upset by Trigona's tears.

"Oh, Don Rosario!" exclaimed Mauro. "Why, what is the matter? Why?"

He looked round the circle and fastened his eyes on Canon Agro, who appeared the most sombre and disturbed of them all.

"Nothing," Roberto interposed quickly. "A report which is sure to be unfounded. Gentlemen, please! I am pained... pained by your distress ... far more than for myself. Do you wish to make me happy? Let us say nothing more about it. Let bygones be bygones! That will do! You know how fond I am of you all, and why. I do not thank you for what you have done for me, on this occasion, because I know that, if the times have changed, our hearts have not changed, and that you therefore could not help doing for me what you have done. The mistake is ours, really, my friends! And we all know it, and have known it for some time, one in one way, another in another. And so... and so that will do: why complain of things now? It has been an additional test, of which I, for my part, did not feel any need.... That is all!"

Roberto Auriti was at the end of his patience. The sight of these friends gathered round him and his mother's silence, Trigona's tears, Agro's bitter resentment, Note's frigid pedantry had become unendurable. He was in a hurry to write to Rome, to report the loss of the election without delay to his mistress, to her who for so long had lulled to sleep his aspirations and his dislikes, and with whom he, submerged now in indifference to everything that was not related directly and minutely to her person, lazy and forgetful, satisfied only the brutal appetite of his senses.

In the presence of his mother's nobility, his sister's purity, he felt himself almost instinctively obliged to conceal even from himself his passionate thraldom to this woman who knew all his sorrows. And he wrote to her at night, misrepresenting his own feelings, since to remain at peace with her and to have her docile and prompt to his wishes, he had not ventured to confess to her, before leaving Rome, the true reason for which he was engaging in this contest, but had given her to understand that it was to strengthen his position, by bringing himself--as a Deputy--more into prominence. And in his first letters he had allowed her to hope that victory was not improbable; then gradually had left her in doubt; he had written to her finally that the only thing which mattered to him now was that he should return at once to her side. He went himself to the post with these letters, whereas for all the rest of his correspondence he employed his nephew. And yet he knew that this nephew, next day, would be going with him to take up his university career in Rome and would be living in his house, and would see, therefore, and know everything. But he preferred, so long as he was there, to keep his secret. That unkempt, angular youth was not formed, certainly, to attract anybody's confidence. And Roberto resented the thought of having to take the boy with him, of letting him know, and, through him, his mother and sister, the nature of the life that he was leading in Rome. But how was he to get out of it?

Donna Caterina, meanwhile, was asking Mauro for news of her brother Cosmo, "that lunatic," and of Donna Sara Alaimo.

"Don't speak of them, for pity's sake!" exclaimed Mauro. "I am going to Rome, I tell you, and I know nothing more, I don't wish to know anything more at present!"

"My dear Mauro," Donna Caterina answered him, with a bitter smile, "if that is how it is, shut your eyes, stop your ears tight and go back this very instant to the country: take my advice!"

THE BATS ON THE AVENUE.

When, from the Badia Grande, the party came down to the Via Atenea, they found themselves caught in a stream of people who were cheering the announcement of Ignazio Capolino's election. Canon Agro's carriage was obliged to halt. The old butler-coachman with the crooked legs kept cracking his whip: "Hey, by your leave! Hey, by your leave!" How could he ever have imagined that people would be wanting in respect for his master, or that his master could shew fear? And, amid the clamour and confusion, he did not hear the voice of the Canon who was shouting to him:

"Turn back, Cola! Back! Go by the Via del Purgatorio!"

A hoot of derision, another, a third.... Sons of dogs! But Capolino was still in bed, convalescent in the Prince of Laurentano's villa, at Colimbetra, and the demonstration of rejoicing, for want of a direct outlet, was sorely tempted to change there and then into a demonstration of protest against Canon Agro. Fortunately, the section leaders managed to quell the storm which threatened to burst upon the rashly venturing carriage, showing respect not for Pompeo Agro, who deserved none; but for the cloth, that was it, the cloth which he disgraced. An occasional hoot, perhaps, as he drove past, would not come amiss; then away, everyone, to the Passeggiata, to assemble beneath Flaminio Salvo's villa!

"Viva Ignazio Capolinooo!"

"Vivaaa!"

"Three cheers for our new Deput-eee!"

"Vivaaa!" In the darkness of the night, heneath the faint glimmer of the street lamps, there passed in a tumult along the narrow street that torrent of people, who let themselves be swept on

228

without the slightest enthusiasm, like a bellowing herd, by the will of two or three interested persons.

Flaminio Salvo's villa was illuminated from top to bottom, splendidly, so that it might be visible, as a sign of triumph, from distant Colimbetra. Inside were assembled the committee of the Party, who went out in a body upon the great balcony with the balustrade of marble, as soon as the roar of the demonstration reached them from the avenue beneath.

"Viva Flaminio Salvooo!"

"Vivaaa!"

"Viva Ignazio Capolinooo!"

"Vivaaa!"

There came up to the villa a deputation from the crowd, who were received by Salvo with his habitual frigid smile, to which the slow stare of his eyes beneath their heavy lids gave a faintly ironical expression. And indeed those fifteen or sixteen excited townsfolk, newly emerging from the nameless multitude which down below in the darkness of the avenue sounded so imposing, assuming in an instant each his own name, his own appearance, standing there, timid, embarrassed, hesitating, bewildered, obsequious, their hands apparently sewn up in their sleeves, cut a sorry enough figure amid the splendours of the magnificent drawing-room.

Flaminio Salvo expressed his gratitude to the townsfolk for this solemn affirmation of the popular feeling; gave them the latest report of the Hon. Capolino's condition and, in the presence of the deputation, asked the engineer Aurelio Costa to go off at once to the Prince's villa, to report there the result of the election and this manifestation of joy by the entire population of Girgenti.

Whereupon one of the fifteen, swelling and reddening like a turkey cock, went to the balcony and, between the lamps held up by a pair of footmen, delivered an impassioned harangue to the crowd.

No one gave any thought to the discomfiture of the poor bats on the avenue, which, dazzled by the glare, dropped from above to crawl over the heads of the demonstrators, then, at the shouts, at the clapping of hands, rose again in a panic, uttering shrill cries, as though appealing for help and vengeance to the stars that twinkled merrily in the sky. The extempore orator was saying that Capolino's election was one of the most memorable events in the history of modern Italy; but no one, certainly, could have got it out of the heads of those bats that the whole town was banded together, that evening, to declare a most unprovoked war upon themselves.

The speaker was still declaiming, when Aurelio Costa, mounted upon one of Salvo's chestnuts, which had been hastily saddled, set off at a gallop for Colimhetra.

Lost in the crowd, down there, was Pigna, who had drifted down to the tail of the procession, expurgated, voided (so to speak) from its body by a succession of violent efforts along the whole of the route. Insolence! Oppression! He had been going about his own business, was preparing to cross the Via Atenea, when the crowd surged round him. He had not had time to escape, and then the people in front had thrust him back so that they themselves might pass, and so the flood had engulfed him. To escape, with those legs and that hunched back, had been impossible; furious, shouting at the top of his voice, he had begun to push in all directions with fists and feet and elbows, to clear a space round him and make his way out; but the crowd, for the fun of taking him along with them as a hostage, had fallen upon him, with shouts of: "Here's Pigna! It's Pigna! Viva Pigna! Abbasso Propaganda! No, Viva! Down with us!" and sticks had begun to fly, and blows were exchanged. More infuriated than ever, like a boar at bay among a pack of hounds, he had gone so far as to bite those nearest to him; more than once, thrusting out feet and shoulders to disengage an arm, and expecting the crowd to close up behind him, and finding instead a space left by some one who was trying to avoid him, he had been on the point of falling; but immediately some one else had propelled him forward against the back of the man in front, and there, packed tight, gasping like a fish out of water, more sticks and buffets and jeers. And, pushing and pulling, they had tossed him from side to side like a shuttle, ill-treating him in every possible way, until, overpowered, he had let himself go with the crowd, but not on his own feet, no, no! like that, carried away.... Oh, the savages! Oh, the scoundrels! Bartered consciences! What a spectacle! Oh Girgenti, disgrace to Sicily and to humanity! A name for scorn and derision! All of them in the sacristy to-morrow, yes, yes, sticking together with the sacred wafers the torn halves of five-lire notes.... Yes, up with Capolino and up with Salvo! Up with Bacchus and up with Mammon!

And, exclaiming thus, and looking round with an air of menacing contempt at the crowd assembled beneath Salvo's villa, he now straightened out his battered hat, now rubbed a bruised shoulder, now sighed or groaned, now gave a sniff of disgust; pooh, dregs of humanity! Pooh, vile *ignoranti*!

"All right, Propaga', wait till to-morrow!" some of them shouted. "To-morrow we shall all come and join the Fascio! To-night, we're here: 'Viva Capolinooo!' (You mustn't believe us, you know? We're only pretending.) 'Viva! Vivaaa!'" Was this the end of a day of battle, this his reward for all his running to and fro since daybreak between one polling station and another, alloting their duties to the comrades, giving instructions, ordering the people in one place, persuading, inciting, imploring them in another, according to circumstances, that all the votes of the workers must be given to a worker, their comrade, perdio! Angelo Zappala, who would defend their interests, who would plead their cause in Parliament!

Yes, granted that this popular candidature was to be of value only as a protest, he might after all have professed himself satisfied with the result: yes; but only of the voting in the surrounding villages! His heart bled, however, for the disgrace of Girgenti, the capital, his native city! A name for scorn, for derision....

FAREWELL, LOVE!

When, at length, Pigna, pounded and pummelled, with no voice left, ready to drop with exhaustion, returned home, to the Piano di Gamez, to swallow a mouthful of supper poisoned by bile, as he mounted the first steps of the wooden staircase which led from the big room on the ground floor to the room above, he found standing there in the darkness, eagerly conversing, Celsina and Antonio Del Re.

"Hallo, you here?"

"Go upstairs, Papa!" said Celsina. "I'm just saying good-bye to him. He leaves to-morrow."

"Oh, good-night, then," said Pigna. "I mean to say, a good journey to you.... You're going off at once, then? I envy you, my dear fellow. Oh, you are certain to see in Rome... what relation to you is Don Laudino Laurentano? Of course, yes, your uncle, you told me: give him my most humble regards, tell him that Girgenti needs him; Girgenti is a disgrace to the Island...."

"We know all that, Papa," Celsina cut him short, tartly. "Let him talk to me now! Go away!"

"A town of carrion!" muttered Pigna, dragging his crooked shanks painfully upstairs. "Rascals ... *ohi ohi... ignoranti....*"

He turned the corner. Immediately the two young people were in each other's arms again. Antonio had lost all self-control; drunken, desperate, he could not tear himself away from her; he sought her lips, as though his were parched with thirst, for another kiss, which penetrated to the inmost depths of his being; another kiss, passionate, burning, endless, in which to give her the whole of himself and to take the whole of her, in the spasm of the most intense longing.

232

"Stop," she groaned, exhausted, letting her head sink on his bosom. But he clasped her again, more ardent; quivering more than ever; he wanted her lips again.

"No, stop, Nino," said Celsina, recovering herself. "Stop... stop..."

She took his hands, pressed them tight; laid them upon her heaving bosom, still holding them; went on:

"So!... Now, listen... you will see, won't you? you will try.... You must do all you can..."

"Yes...."

"Are you listening?"

"Yes...."

"You're not listening! That will do, now, Nino! I've told you, that will do. You're not listening to me...."

"Yes, I am.... I will try...."

"What will you try? Let me alone, for heaven's sake!"

"I don't know.... I will do all I can.... You know I will! Give me another kiss...."

"No! Where will you try?"

"Why, everywhere, everywhere...."

"Yes, a post of any sort... even a humhle one... to begin with, you understand? You know that I can.... I will make myself do anything! I must, I must be in Rome, as soon as possible, are you listening?"

"Yes, love... love... my love!" he gasped; then gripping her arms, and raving: "What am I to do? Oh, my Celsina.... I shall die...."

"Hush!" Celsina warned him. "I don't want them to hear you upstairs."

"Then I'm off.... I can't..."

"Yes, go, go...it's late! They're calling me. You'll write at once, remember?"

"Yes...."

"Good-bye, good-bye."

But he still could not bring himself to let go her hand; he thrust his face close to hers, asked her:

"What will you give me?"

"What do you want?" said she.

"You, all of you! Come with me, come with me!"

"If I could! This instant!"

"Oh, my love.... What will you give me?" he repeated. "Something of your own...."

"I haven't anything, my Nino...."

"But I have something of yours, you know, that you gave me."

"I?"

"Haven't you given me anything? Not even your heart, a little?"

"Ah, that...."

"And something else as well.... Don't you remember?"

"No...."

"The doll...."

"Ah," smiled Celsina, "that one with the moustaches?"

"Don't laugh, don't laugh. I've rubbed them out, you know. I am taking it with me."

"Baby...."

"D'you know? I had it in bed with me all last night, in my arms. And I shall always..."

"Goon! I'm not the doll, you know!"

"I know; but it is yours, it has been yours. ... Haven't your lips kissed it?"

"Often, when I was little...."

"Very well, then...."

"Go, Nino, go. They're calling me. Good-bye. Don't forget, now. Write to me! Good-bye!"

Another long, long kiss at the front door, and Antonio went away. He stopped in the Piano di Gamez, where not a soul was stirring; and gazed about him, in bewilderment; he gazed up at the motionless vault of heaven, and felt a sense of stupefaction, as though he had passed into a waking dream. How brightly the stars shone! He heard the balcony window open. Celsina leaned out.

"Good-bye. Remember."

"Yes. Good-bye!"

Already she was remote; remote was her voice, remote her form; and that little house, the front of which, clear and bright against the misty blackness of the Piano, reflected the moon's rays, and the Piano itself, the chattering voice of the fountain, and those narrow alleys, crooked and dark, the whole town silent in the night, high on its hill, beneath the stars--everything seemed to him to be henceforward remote; he felt as though he from a distance, with infinite sadness, with infinite pain, were contemplating his own life which remained there, severed from himself.

LIGHT AND DARKNESS.

When Aurelio Costa arrived at Colimbetra, Don Ippolito knew already of Capolino's election; and was discussing it in the drawing-room with Don Salesio Marullo and Nini De Vincentis.

The former had come hurrying from Girgenti on hearing of the result of the duel, a most fortunate result for him; the latter, after the encounter, at which he had been present as a second, had remained at Colimbetra by the victim's bedside.

Uncle Salesio was listening to the Prince with an air of proud condescension, as though he himself were responsible for Capolino's election. And of course he was! Had he not given him his stepdaughter's hand in marriage?

During the last five days uncle Salesio had taken a new lease of life there, amid the splendours of Colimbetra, in which he took as much pride as though they had been his own property. He trod the thick carpets more on tiptoe than ever; pursed his lips at all the pretty and valuable things he saw; at table he almost fainted with pleasure at the sight of all that gleaming silver, or when Liborio, in a swallow-tail coat and white gloves, handed him the choice dishes which--it seemed to him almost impossible!--were not made of pasteboard. And at sunset, notwithstanding his aching feet, he would go down to the lawn and walk as far as the gate to enjoy the delight of receiving a military salute from the sentry in his red breeches and blue greatcoat. The sentry took an equal delight in saluting him; and each of them, after the salute, would look at the other and smile.

Nini De Vincentis seemed not to have recovered yet from the terror that had overpowered him when he saw Capolino sink to the ground, wounded in the chest by Veronica's pistol, at the second round. It had indeed been a terrible surprise to everybody, that shot. The pistols, by a tacit understanding between the seconds, had been loaded in such a way as not to inflict any injury, their intention being that the actual duel should begin with the sabres. And it was a lucky thing that the bullet, striking him without much force, had barely grazed one of his ribs and swerved aside from his heart!

But it was not only this terrifying memory that kept poor Nini still so crushed and helpless; Nicoletta Capolino had given him plainly to understand that Dianella Salvo was not and never would be his, even if her father had not met his suit with so curt a refusal.

After spending the first night by her husband's bedside, notwithstanding the doctors' assurances that all danger had fortunately been averted, Nicoletta had persuaded herself that it no longer behoved her to play the despairing wife, as she had done at Valsania when the news came that "her Gnazio" was wounded. And she had begun to alternate her loving and diligent attention to her poor wounded "paladin" with a skilful endeavour to remain there at Colimbetra, in Don Ippolito Laurentano's memory, as a most charming guest.

Ah, if only, instead of that walrus Adelaide Salvo, it had been herself that was presently to become the queen of this little realm! She felt that all the good qualities with which nature had intended to endow her and which her destiny had chosen to suppress and stifle in her would have revived spontaneously and in time have gained the upper hand in her; that she would have managed to bring happiness to the last years of that proud, magnificently handsome old man, still so fresh and vigorous!

She guessed how bitter had been his disappointment at the sight of his future bride; but knew also that no seductive art would prevail over such a man, who had made a sort of religion of loyalty to his plighted word. Not a vestige of coquetry, therefore, must she shew, but must vie with him in compliments and courtesies, during those days, without the least affectation. And what words in season to Uncle Salesio, who would not understand that there was no longer any reason at all for his remaining at Colimbetra. He knew his place, and kept it, quite--rather too much so, indeed--did Uncle

Salesio; and yet... and yet!...

And for her unrealizable dream; for her longing for a virtuous life; for the incubus which was the sight of her step-father, so polite and so preposterous, for the disgust she now felt at her long and hateful pretence of affection for that husband, that worthy companion of her own baser self, Nicoletta took her revenge in tormenting Nini De Vincentis, especially in the evenings, on the marble terrace, built out upon the columns of the porch, by speaking to him of Dianella Salvo.

She took a delight in wounding him, knowing that no affliction, no injustice, could--let alone making that uncorrupt and incorruptible young man do anything wrong--provoke a bitter word from his lips, so much was he the slave of his own goodness and resigned to it!

She spoke to him mysteriously, in broken sentences, as though not to saturate him, at any one time, with his own grief.

Nini was anxious to know on what grounds she had told him that Dianella Salvo would never be his, even if her father had given his consent. "Why? Ah, dear Nini.... There is a reason, a reason that is painful to others besides yourself!"

"What reason?"

"I cannot tell you."

"But to whom else is it painful?"

"To me too, Nini!"

"To you?" asked Nini in amazement.

And she, smiling:

"Certainly... certainly.... You don't see it; and yet there is, there really is a connexion between myself and you and... her. What connexion? What can I have in common with you? And yet there is something, dear Nini... there is, there is.... You and I are joined by something. It seems impossible, doesn't it? And yet, believe me, we are joined...."

Nini was left to ponder over this mysterious reason, and felt his heart sink within him.

When Aurelio Costa, ushered by Liborio, entered the drawing-room, Nicoletta was with her husband; but she came in presently and felt an exquisite pleasure in letting herself be seen by him there, in that princely mansion, amid the deference and respect of all the household. Don Ippolito hastened to inform her of the popular demonstration.

"He's resting just now," she said. "I'm afraid of exciting him.... But, if they want..."

"No, no," the Prince at once assured her. "We shall find an opportunity of letting him know to-morrow...."

"On the contrary, I am sure Don Flaminio," put in Aurelio Costa, "sent me galloping out here, at this time of night, so that he might let the electors know then and there that the Honourable Capolino and the Prince would at once be informed of the demonstration."

"I am sorry for your sake, Ingegnere," said Nicoletta, "that you have had such a journey. ..."

"Not at all!" Costa at once cut her short. "Indeed, it's been a pleasure...."

"Especially as, I don't mind betting," put in Uncle Salesio, "this is the first time you were ever at Colimbetra, eh? A marvellous abode, my dear. Ingegnere, marvellous! A regular earthly paradise!"

The Prince smiled, made a slight bow, and invited Aurelio Costa to stay to supper.

That evening, Nini De Vincentis was left in peace by Nicoletta; but he was not in the least grateful to her. He had grown to enjoy being tortured.

But Nicoletta had Aurelio Costa to consider. And she meant to bewitch him properly, that evening; she meant him to interpret, in his own mind, all her coaxings and glances and smiles as a compensation for the thankless task set him by Flaminio Salvo, to wit, that of coming out there to tell them of her husband's triumph; and she meant that in this compensation which she was giving him, he should detect a note of resentment against Salvo himself who, though well aware of his sentiments, had dispatched him there like a servant. Did he regard everybody as his purchased slave? It might come to pass, nevertheless, that these slaves, in the end, under such provocation, would accept the challenge and come to a mutual understanding! Had they not some such understanding already? Was there not already an agreement, a secret pact between them?

And Nicoletta Capolino's eyes, fastened upon his, now blazed out ardent and excited, now languished, misty and disturbed, as though promising an intense, profound pleasure in store. A slave, in common slavery with her! They would be avenged upon all the old men who sought to keep their two young selves enslaved! For her sake, from now onwards, he would cherish his servile state; and would think no more of becoming his own master, even if Dianella Salvo should openly reveal her love to him. A slave, in common slavery with her!

Aurelio Costa was really like a drunken man, his face radiant with joy and gratitude to the lady, when, late in the evening, he left Colimbetra.

He did not know what to think. The blood pulsed in his veins, and sang in his ears. Was she playful like that with everyone, naturally or by acquired hahit, or was it for him alone that she had shaped those smiles, perfected those glances and coaxing attentions? Ought he to wonder or to feel certain of it? And if certain, why had this woman thus suddenly made up her mind to tempt him, to provoke him, to love him, after receiving his honourable offer of marriage, years before, with a curt and contemptuous refusal? Had she repented? Weary, sickened by the infamous part that her husband had assigned to her, had she decided to rebel and to be avenged, choosing as her weapon of vengeance the man who honourably, once upon a time, had wished to make her his own, and whom she had then maltreated and perhaps laughed to scorn? Did she wish now to give him this revenge over the man for whom she had refused him then? Or was she seeking to lay a snare for him?

This suspicion, crude and unworthy as it might appear to him at that moment, had nevertheless worked its way into his mind among the welter of possible theories. He was incapable of any great respect for her.

But what sort of snare? To make him fall in love, lose his head, to the point of arousing Flaminio Salvo's jealousy and so bringing about his own dismissal? But had he not told her that he would be sacrificing nothing, now, were he to leave Salvo? Besides, what interest could she have in banishing him? How was his presence offensive to her? Did he remind her, in her present misery, of the past? But when it had been she herself who, by that strong, intimate pressure of his hand, had chosen to remind him of that past, so as to sweep away its shadow from between them? And she had seemed to him sincere! Yes, frank and sincere! And how beautiful she was! What a fascination radiated from her whole person! Oh, to be loved by her....

Coming to Flaminio Salvo's villa, now silent and dark, Aurelio Costa put his horse in the stable, and went up to the study, where Salvo was waiting for him. Salvo at once perceived the emotion, the unusual animation on the face and in the speech of the young man, as he apologized for his lateness on the ground that he had been kept to supper by the Prince. As he listened to him, Salvo scrutinized him closely; and--when Aurelio lowered his eyes--accentuated slightly his habitual smile, letting it play over every line of his face, which a trace of fatigue, that evening, made flabbier than usual.

"I expected it," he said, caressing his side-whiskers.

"I thought that..." Aurelio attempted to interpose.

"Why, yes, you were quite right," Salvo at once cut him short. "What a fine colour you've brought back with, you! It must be good for one, a ride in the country at this time of night.... A beautiful evening! In here, it's stifling.... When you are an old man you will remember...."

"I?" asked Aurelio, tempted to smile by the affectionate tone in which Salvo addressed him, albeit the words themselves, after his reflexions on his homeward ride, filled him with suspicion. "Why?"

"No... I mean to say, perhaps..." Salvo went on, with a vague wave of his hand. "Of course, you are accustomed to that sort of thing. ... Day and night, always on the go.... A busy life, yours! But perhaps this has been a special occasion. When we are old, there come back to us, in flashes, memories, distant visions of ourselves as we were at certain moments... and we don't even know why one particular moment and not another has remained stamped on our memory, and suddenly detaches itself and strays to the surface. There was perhaps a more comprehensive memory, of a whole period in our life. It has faded. A single incident is all that remains alive, a single moment, an instant.... And you will see yourself again on horseback, on a calm, exquisite night, with stars shining... and you will try in vain, perhaps, to recollect what thoughts you had in your mind on that occasion, what feelings were in your heart...."

"But that can happen without our being old," observed Aurelio.

"It is not the same thing," replied Salvo. "You will find that out for yourself."

And he sat for a while with his eyes motionless, fixed in an unseeing gaze.

There was certainly something strange about Salvo too, that evening, and even Aurelio noticed it, as though, during his absence, the other, left alone there in his austere study, had been plunged in thoughts which had bred in him an unaccustomed melancholy. What thoughts? He had evidently been sitting with his elbows on the writing table and his head in his hands, since on his head, which was bald at the top, the few remaining grey hairs on his brow, which he wore parted in the middle and trimmed short, had become disarranged.

Aurelio knew that this imperious spirit was at heart profoundly melancholy, and that Salvo's harsh manner, his violent resentments were no more than instantaneous eruptions of that inveterate, hidden, repressed, inconsolable melancholy. But why had he succumbed so to it on this evening of all evenings, when he should have been rejoicing in his victory?

"All well out there?" asked Salvo, shaking off his abstraction. "Did you see him?"

"No," answered Aurelio, dissembling his embarrassment and confusion, which were perhaps visible on his face, with the fear of having failed in part of his duty; he added, however, by way of excuse, blushing as he spoke: "Because the Signora said he was resting...."

"On his laurels, eh?" Salvo capped it, then, tilting his chin and smiling openly, asked: "And... tell me, is she... the Signora... pleased?"

Aurelio waved his hands, and, as though the point had not occurred to him, replied: "She didn't seem to be. Why?"

"She ought to be pleased," Salvo went on. "She is going to Rome...."

"Yes, now that her husband..."

"In Parliament, in Parliament," Salvo took him up, tossing his head. "It had to be! In Parliament."

With which he rose from his chair.

"You see, my dear fellow, what are our unpardonable faults? And then we complain of our lot! In a moment such as this, with an enterprise such as we have been considering, which has already cost us so much in hard work, has already exposed me to such risks, I have made them elect Capolino to Parliament. The very man I needed here, on the spot, wouldn't you say? To talk big in Rome, when the time comes, at the Ministry of Industry and Commerce.... But it had to be. You will find that Ignazio gets on splendidly in Rome: it is the right place for him. Here, he was in my way.... A clean sweep, a clean sweep. ... Should the need arise, I can go myself to Rome, to talk to the Minister. First of all, though, they must all sign an agreement here, all the producers of sulphur, great and small, I want them all in; with the stipulation that they consent to restrict their output, if necessary, and to store all their sulphur in common warehouses. Otherwise, nothing doing. I am risking my capital for the salvation of Sicilian industry. I am entitled to insist upon the adhesion and co-operation of all the interested parties, and upon some slight sacrifice, if necessary. In the meantime, whereas here we are seriously considering how to improve the present desperate state of affairs, have you heard about Grotte? They want to enforce the will of the majority.... Idiots! Enforce it upon whom, and why?... The people who have, to-day, are worse ruined than those who have not! The majority. ... What force can a majority have? Brute force; it can deal you a blow; but the avalanche, when it reaches the ground, crumbles into fragments at the same time. Oh, how sickening they are, how sickening! Take them singly, they are afraid, you understand; and so they gather a thousand strong to take a step which they could not take each by himself; take them singly, they have not a thought among them; and a thousand empty heads, crowded together, imagine that they have, and fail to observe that it is the thought of the madman or mischief-maker who is leading them. So much for them. And here? Here we have another spectacle, more sickening still. I am perhaps growing old, Aurelio."

"You?" the other asked, with a smile.

"I am growing old, yes," went on Salvo. "I am losing the desire to command. What has destroyed it is the servility that I discover in everyone. Men are what I want, men! I see round about me automata, puppets, mannikins, which I have to pose in one attitude or another, and which remain paralysed, as though to mock at me, in the attitudes I have put them in, until I give them a cuff that sends them flying. Outwardly, though, you understand; it is only outwardly that they allow themselves to be posed! Inside... ah, inside they remain hard, with their covert, hostile thoughts, alive only to themselves. What can you do with them? Docile outwardly, mild, malleable, with smiling faces, obsequious, they approve of everything you do. Oh, how revolting it all is! I should like to know why I am losing my temper like this; why and for whose sake I am doing it.... To-morrow I die. I have had command of men! Yes, indeed: I have allotted his part to this man and to that, to hundreds who can never have seen anything more in me than the part that I represent to them. And of all that other life, the life of affections and ideas, that stirs within me, nobody has ever had the remotest suspicion.... With whom would you have me discuss it? It is outside the part that I am expected to play.... Now and again, when somebody comes here to see me, to make me angry, I amuse myself by giving him a searching glance, a glance that penetrates his mask, and I see him, then, for an instant, caught and exposed before me, awkward and embarrassed; heaven knows the effort I have to make not to burst out laughing in his face. He would think I had gone mad, at the very least. Even you, my dear fellow, if you could see how you are staring at me at this moment..."

"I, no!" Aurelio at once protested, starting back.

Flaminio Salvo shook his head and laughed:

"You too, you too.... It is so; it is bound to be so.... How can I tell you what I should really like you to do? The pleasure that you would give me, were you to act as I perhaps should act in your place?"

"Why not?" Aurelio asked, rising to his feet. "Tell me...."

"Why not?" Salvo was quick to reply, shrugging his shoulders. "Because I cannot.... Can you tell me what you are thinking, what you are feeling, what sort of life you have within you at this moment?... You cannot.... You stand before me in such relations as there may be between yourself and me: you are my engineer, my dear son, whom I love, to whom this evening, before a score of marionettes, I gave instructions to ride over to Colimbetra, a messenger of triumph: and that is all! What else could I have to say to you? Only this, perhaps, for your good..."

Flaminio Salvo laid his hand on Aurelio's shoulder:

"Never trace out paths to follow, my boy; nor habits, nor duties; go ahead, always keep moving; shake off every fresh incrustation of ideas; seek your own pleasure, and do not fear the judgment of other people, or your own either, which may seem right to you to-day and wrong to-morrow. You've met Don Cosmo Laurentano? If you only knew how wise that madman is! Go along now, it is late; time we were in bed. Good night."

As he walked down the Viale della Passeggiata, under the dripping trees, in the vast stillness of the night, Aurelio Costa had the impression of being no longer able to find himself in himself, and stopped as though in search of what was missing.

The thoughts that had been agitating him as to his own future, in connexion with this colossal scheme of Salvo's; the provoking smiles, the words, the attentions of Nicoletta Capolino, out there at Colimbetra; and here, just now, Salvo's melancholy, tortuous, puzzling speech seemed to have divided his spirit piecemeal. Part of it had remained out there at Colimbetra; the rest here in the villa, bewildered, disturbed, made suspicious, stunned by Salvo's words. So Nicoletta would be going to Rome? What then? But how was this? Had Salvo wished to be rid of Capolino? Yes, he had said so distinctly: "A clean sweep." Had he been alluding perhaps to her? There had been a certain irony in the question that he put to him: "Is the Signora pleased?" Had he wished to banish her too from his house? Or was it perhaps she that had rebelled against him? Was this why he was so melancholy, in so unusual a frame of mind? And what did Salvo want with him? What meaning was he to extract from the strange things that Salvo had said to him? "How can I tell you the pleasure that you would give me, were you to act as I perhaps should act in your place?" What pleasure? What had he meant by that? A secret, unconfessable desire? Or had he been speaking generally? He had complained that he was surrounded by automata, puppets.... And those final words of advice....

Try as he might, he could find no solution. And then, as though leaving outside him, to stray where they would, thoughts and doubts and suspicions, he withdrew into the safe shell of his own consciousness, of the opinion, modest, calm and solid, that he held of himself.

By the mere accident of his having, once upon a time, almost without thinking, plucked Salvo from the jaws of death, he had been brought up to an enviable position, of which, with his exceptional natural gifts, and his determination to succeed, he had managed to render himself worthy. The extent of his good fortune, which everyone admitted to he deserved, the exaggerated reports of the honours he had won in his classes, in examinations, in his profession, had meanwhile given him an importance which he himself admitted to be excessive, and which proved at times embarrassing. The manner in which he found himself received and treated, the things that people were saying about him, were a continual proof to him that he was to others something more than to himself, a different Aurelio Costa, whom he himself barely recognized, of whom he could form no clear estimate; he always remained, therefore, in the company of other people, in an agonized state of mind, in a strange confused apprehension that he was falling short of their expectations, failing to live up to his reputation. He knew how to keep in his place, but would have preferred to remain in it quiet and secure; whereas he felt that other people, he having started to rise when a mere boy, were still pointing to a higher position as though it were his by right, and were urging him on, and refusing to leave him alone. It was not timidity on his part; it was an awkward reserve, which often irritated him with other people or with himself, a perpetual alarm, lest some shortcoming might be discovered in him, were he to stray ever so little beyond the field of his own knowledge, in which he felt himself to be secure; from the corner in which he could stand firm, at which he had arrived by his own practical merit. His irritation with himself arose also from his seeing that so many men, whom he himself regarded as his inferiors in every respect, managed to forge ahead without effort, and were allowed to pass;

whereas he, regarded by everyone as superior even to the conception that he had formed of himself, he lagged behind, and, were he thrust forward, often felt himself embarrassed in his movements, in his speech, and blushed at times like a girl.

To-night, Aurelio Costa was more conscious than ever of that feeling of unaccountable annoyance that was always caused him by his own shadow, as it stretched out before him, growing longer and thinner the farther he went from each of the lighted lamps which kept a lugubrious watch over the sleeping town, after the clamour of the popular demonstration.

Half way along the deserted Via Atenea, he caught sight of Roberto Auriti, by himself; he turned to gaze at him with profound sorrow, and followed him with his eyes, until he saw him turn aside into one of the steep alleys on the left, which led up to the Badia Grande.

GOOD-BYE.

There was no going to bed that night at Donna Caterina Laurentano's, since Roberto and his nephew had to set off in the dark, at four o'clock in the morning.

Anna Del Re was busy with a labour of love, making the final preparations for her son's departure. What an agony, for her, this parting!

Her whole world, her whole life, for years past, had been concentrated in love and care for this sole treasure. How was she to go on living, now, without him? She wept silent tears.

She had brought him up, had guarded him with her heart and soul, never heeding the reproaches of her mother, who was afraid of her spoiling him. Spoil him, indeed! No, no! She had been so worried and tormented, when she saw him grow up cold and sullen, always and entirely self-absorbed, and had endeavoured by her manner towards him, by her ever vigilant care, to thaw him (that was all!) with a mother's love, to make him more expansive and confiding.

She did not know what it was in his nature that kept him aloof from the companionship even of boys of his own age. A hard worker, indeed he had worked too hard, until his health was affected; and when he was not working, he would sit closely wrapped in certain thoughts which made his brows more bushy, his eyes harder and more repellent behind his powerful glasses.

"Good heavens, Ninuccio, if you could only see what a face you're making...."

He would reply with a shrug of the shoulders.

Perhaps he was distressed, her Ninuccio, by the family's straitened circumstances, perhaps he was thinking that his grand-

248

mother, even without any derogation from her dignity, from her sentiments, might have been a rich woman. Too sunless, certainly, had his childhood and boyhood been made by the dark shadow of all those tragedies in that huge old house, always shrouded in silence, into which the sun, when it did penetrate, never seemed to bring either light or heat.

What a house! She noticed it herself that night, imagining the melancholy aspect it would present to her on the morrow! The furniture worm-eaten, the ceilings grimy, the floors crumbling, the window frames warped and paint-less, the wall paper in all the rooms faded.... And yet it was constantly cared for and cleaned and put to rights; it seemed as though it too were in some dim way conscious of the misery of life. Corrado Selmi was right; he had accurately interpreted her own secret feeling.... Resigned long since to her own fate, she would have wished, if not for herself at any rate for this son of hers, that at length some smile of peace, even a sad smile, should lighten a little the burden, the incubus of those painful memories, that dark rancour against life, the mute, despairing bitterness of her mother.

Calm, not peace! The soul of Donna Caterina Laurentano could know no peace.

Perhaps because she no longer believed in anything? She herself, Anna, did believe, she believed fervently in God, albeit without keeping up any of the practices of religion. The women of the neighbourhood never saw her go out to mass, like her mother; and yet they made a distinction between the two, guessed that the "young lady" was religious and, when they caught an occasional glimpse of her, so beautiful and meek, always dressed in black, would point their fingers at her as at a Saint.

Anna's thoughts turned principally upon the new life, the strange customs among which her son would presently find himself, in her brother's house in Rome. She had not the least doubt that her brother would look after his nephew with the most loving care; but the woman he had with him? Her family? All the people who came to Roberto's house? That Corrado Selmi, who, with his strange fascination, had succeeded in disturbing even her equanimity? Who could tell what effect he would have upon her Ninuccio, who had spent all his life here, cooped up with his grandmother and herself!

They had, both of them, spoken frequently and volubly, with bitterness, of their Roberto's wasted life, of the irregular connexion that he had formed, going by the reports that had reached them from Giulio, the younger brother; reports that were distinctly vague, for Giulio, who had always lived in Rome, had lost all family feeling and tradition, had ceased even to resemble a Sicilian; and was inclined, perhaps, to make excuses for his elder brother; certainly he attached no weight, no importance to all manner of things, at which her mother and she could barely repress their horror.

She was a teacher of singing, the wife of a tenor who had lost his voice, Roberto's mistress. And Giulio had said, with a laugh, that this tenor, a worthy fellow, sat down every day at Roberto's table and then retired for the night to the house of his wife's brother, who kept a sort of college, a private *conservatorio*, in which the lady taught singing and her husband filled no less a post than that of censor. Roberto was a sort of boarder in this house where now and again, in their more prosperous seasons, another lodger or two were taken in, for whom there was no room in the brother's college.

So it was with people like these that her son would shortly be coming in contact.

More than once Anna had sought to persuade her mother to suggest to Roberto the removal of the family to Rome. They would sell this house, which had harboured so many tragedies, and would make shift to live as best they might in Rome, by themselves of course to begin with, by themselves or with Giulio only. Then possibly, by slow degrees, in time, their mother might succeed in detaching Roberto from his companions.... Would it not also be an economy, to combine three households in one? And to have the whole family under one roof....

"Dreams!" her mother had said. And she had refused even to discuss the suggestion.

She knew that neither would Giulio wish to forfeit his personal freedom, nor would Roberto be able to free himself from his thraldom to that woman. She herself, moreover, at her age, would not be able to stand so radical a change of life and habits.

"Dreams! Dreams! When I die, and Nino is grown up, you can go with him.... He will be responsible for giving you a new life."

"But in the meantime!" sighed Anna, looking at her son where he sat in the other room, listening to the conversation of his grandmother and uncle, his hand buried in his hair, his elbow resting on the table, beneath the lamp that hung from the ceiling.

He showed no sign either of regret at the prospect of leaving her for about a year, or of joy at that of going to Rome.

Always the same! Once only, at the beginning of the previous year, infatuated by a discovery which he thought he had made, a special device of his own for extracting (he said) the electrical energy from the waves of the sea (there had come, that year, to the Technical Institute an excellent professor of physics, who had succeeded in arousing an enthusiasm for that science in all his pupils), he had talked to her with genuine warmth, trying to induce her to prevail upon her mother to ask for a loan of a few thousand lire--not from the "Bourbon uncle," no, indeed!--but from uncle Cosmo: one thousand lire on loan, to construct as best he might the apparatus required for the experiments which he would make out there, at Valsania, upon the beach.

Poor boy! She had quickly damped his ardour. His grandmother? Ask her brothers for money? Didn't he know her?

He had at once shut himself up again in his husk of silence, and had refused even to give her a description of his famous discovery. There might have been something in it; who could say? Perhaps it was only a boyish illusion! Anyhow, all that year, he had continued his passionate study of the science, and now, when he went to Rome, proposed to devote himself to it entirely.

Other affections--youthful as he was--other interests, other desires he did not appear to have.

"Ninuccio," she called. She had finished packing his portmanteau, and required his help in shutting it. He came in at once.

"Too full?" she asked. "You would have all these books in here.... Wouldn't it be better to take them out and put them with the others in the case? We can send them after you to-morrow."

"I shall take the case with me," he said. "I don't trust it out of my sight. Heaven knows when it would reach me...."

"But it will be too much weight for you, my boy, don't you think? Impossible.... Don't worry about it, you shall have it in a few days. I shall see to that...."

"In that case leave the books here, in the portmanteau. Shall I shut it?"

"Your grandmother hasn't said anything to uncle Roberto in there?" she asked, alluding to her proposal.

"Nothing," her son replied.

"I realize too," sighed Anna, "that it is hardly possible. I should have liked it for your sake. ... Mah! Ninuccio dear, listen: you must write and tell me everything, always... if there is anything you want... how you are keeping... if you are well.... Everything! I shall be glad of a few lines even.... But not your first letters, you know. Your first letters must be long ones.... I want to know everything! And remember, Ninuccio... you must be a little more tidy! You will put away all your linen neatly in the drawers.... Don't leave it about as you do here! Uncle Roberto is a very tidy person, you know.... You must be tidy too! And that is all I am going to say to you.... I know you will do your duty and please your mother and grand-mother who will be left here... alone.... That is all.... It will soon be time...."

They went into the dining-room, where the grandmother and Roberto were seated side by side on the sofa.

"You will live to see it," Donna Caterina was saying. "I should like first to close these tired eyes of mine for ever. But it may perhaps fall to my lot too to behold this sight, if I am to make a good end. There will be some, I don't deny it, who do evil delibe-rately; but the soil has been prepared for years for an evil sowing. You live in Rome and neither hear nor see. I wish I were mistaken! But I am not."

She lifted her head to look at her daughter and grandson, saw the tears in Anna's eyes, and ex-claimed, raising her arm:

"Let him go, let him leave us! Air! Fresh air! He will be able to breathe.... Break through your shell, my boy; and let us stay here, to wait; for manna from heaven! In Sixty, dear Roberto, do you know what we were doing here? We were melting our souls in little saucers, like pieces of soap; the Government sent us down a straw each, as a present; and then we, poor fools that we were, set to work to blow into our soapy water, and oh, the bubbles, the bubbles, each one prettier and more iridescent than the last! But then the people began to gape with hunger, and when they gaped, pop went all those wonderful bubbles, one after another, and ended, my son, if you will pardon the expression, in drops of spittle. ... That is the truth!"

The maid came in to say that the carriage was at the door, and that the driver, who was behind his time, urged them to hurry. It took about half an hour to drive from Girgenti to the railway station in Val Sellano.

Anna, candle in hand, on the doorstep, by her mother's side, stood as though overcome, unsatisfied by that last hurried embrace of her son, as he ran with his uncle down the steps of the precipitous alley, in a darkness that was still unbroken.

"My son! My son!" she moaned to herself.

"You will see Ninuccio again," her mother said to her gently. "Shall I see Roberto? Who knows?"

They heard in the profound silence the rumble of the departing wheels. And Anna raised her eyes filled with tears to the sky, in which the stars, for her, were keeping a solemn vigil.

END OF PART I

PART II

CHAPTER I

MIDNIGHT, YOUR EXCELLENCY...

SEATED at the large writing table, on which lay open, scattered all round him, reports and prospectuses bristling with figures, the secretary was waiting for H.E. the Minister to remember that he had not finished dictating.

This was the third night in succession that Cav. Cao--not that he minded work, oh dear no! still, after all, a whole day spent drudging away at the Ministry; then in the evening, here, in His Excellency's palazzo; and one, two, three--why, at this rate, they would never get to the end of this financial statement, which, for all that, would have to be read to the Chamber of Deputies in a few days' time.

He could stand it no longer! It was not so much his physical exhaustion, however, that made this work an intolerable burden, as the distress that he had felt for some time past at the sight of that revered chief, for whom he still felt a deep and sincere affection, if not the admiration of earlier days.

Ah, that admiration!... Cav. Cao had seen so many things in his time, at first from a distance; others he now beheld at closer range! Still, to give the devil his due, a man does not, cannot live for seventy years and more, and perform none hut heroic actions. He must, inevitably, do some foolish things, big or little. And with one one day, another the next, they draw out in time....

So thinking, Cav. Cao drew out a stray hair from his moustache, of unnatural length. Per-bacco! It reached to the top of his head.... A single hair. Black.

To distract his attention from the weariness, the boredom

of waiting, he set his fancy to work. A pair of His Excellency's spectacles, lying there on the table, were transformed into twin lakes; a brush for wiping pens, into a dense grove of evergreen oaks; the surface of the table, where it was cleared of litter, a boundless plain, over which primitive, nomadic tribes might be imagined as roaming.

His Excellency was pacing the floor of the study, with bent head and bowed shoulders, his hands clasped behind his back. And Cav. Cao, raising his eyes to look at him, with the image of that penwiper still imprinted on his retina, was reminded that His Excellency had hair on his back. A hairy back and a hairy chest. He had seen him one day in his bath. He had looked just like a bear.

Ah, how many things, how many absurd peculiarities had he not discovered in the person of His Excellency, now that his early admiration of him had died! The nape of his neck, for instance, so thick and smooth and glossy, and all those little black spots that stippled his nose, and those eyebrows, running so, and so, like a pair of commas. Even in his eyes, those eyes that at one time had so overawed him, he had discovered certain curious little flecks, that seemed to puncture their green pupils.

How true it was: *minuit praesentia famam*! And Cav. Cao was astounded and at the same time saddened by the discovery that he could now see in this light the man who in other days had positively dazzled him, in the heat of his enthusiasm for the heroic deeds that were recounted of him, as a Garibaldino, and for the memorable political contests in which he had afterwards so strenuously fought.

Mah! Nowadays Francesco D'Atri thought only of timidly staining, with a canary yellow dye, the few hairs that still clung to his scalp and his sweeping beard which would have looked so well, if left white.

He himself also, it must be admitted, Cav. Cao, for the last year or so, had begun, just a little... only his moustaches. But simply so as not to have them partly white and partly black. That annoyed him. And besides, for him the dye he used would never produce the terrible consequences it had produced in the case of His Excellency. Moreover, although he was not yet fort... ah, yes, he had turned forty, three days ago: very well, forty, then: he would never marry. Whereas Francesco D'Atri had married, at sixty-seven; and a young wife, to boot.

An. unmistakable sign of softening of the brain.

So that finished him off, eh? Time to put him on the shelf (life has its hard and fast rules!)--on the shelf, without consideration or pity. Pity, at the most, he, personally, might feel for him, because he was fond of him, because he could see that he was suffering agony, in silence, for the enormous mistake he had made; but he felt contempt as well, aye, the bitterest contempt for the submissive attitude he saw him adopt towards that wife who, almost from the day of their wedding, had set to work to make a public holocaust of his honour.

All, or almost all of them had married late and ill, those fine heroes of the Revolution. Oh, in their young days, one knew, they had something very different to think of! They might fall in love, yes... *la bella Gigogin*... a kiss, and:

Farewell, dear heart, farewell, The Army's on the march....

After all, when you came to think of it, there was nothing that they had managed to do at the right time and well, neither their studies nor anything else.... In conspiracy, on the battlefield they had been in their element; in peace time, now, they were a little like fish out of water. In the public eye, and without any definite position; elderly, and without a family growing up round them.... They were bound, alas, to do late and ill all the silly things they had not had time to do in their youth, when their years would have been some excuse for them. And then, too...

Cav. Cao, at this stage, shook himself as though a shudder had run along his spine. For some days past he had been positively appalled by the gravity and tragedy of the situation.

Every night and every morning, the newsvendors were shouting through the streets of Borne the name of one or another Deputy in the National Parliament, coupled with the raucous announcement now of a fraud, now of a secret commission from one or another of the Banks.

In certain crucial moments, every conscientious man, who scorns to run with the herd, does what? He collects his thoughts; ponders the issue; takes one side or the other according to his own convictions, and sticks to it.

Well, this was what Cav. Cao had done. He had taken the side of the slandered party, and was sticking to it.

He could not, all the same, deny in his own mind that he was really enjoying the enormous scandal. He was enjoying it above all because--carried away by the part he had to play--he found himself endowed in these days with a mastery of words, a verbal fecundity which so to speak inebriated him, a stock of phrases, winged and scornful phrases, which seemed to him marvellous in their efficacy and filled him with stupefaction and wonder.

Why yes, indeed: the skies of Italy, in these days, were raining down mud, and people were rolling it into balls and throwing them; and the mud was sticking everywhere, on the pale, distorted faces of assailed and assailants, on the medals won in the past on fields of battle (these, at least, ought surely to have been held sacred!) and on crosses and orders and gold-laced coats and on the door-plates of Government and newspaper offices.

It rained torrents of mud; and it seemed as though all the sewers of the city had overflowed, and the new national existence of the third Rome must be swamped in that turbid, fetid flood of mire, over which hovered screaming--black birds of prey--calumny and suspicion.

Beneath the ashen sky, in the thick, smoky atmosphere, while, like gibbous moons in the raw twilight, the electric street-lamps spluttered into flame, and, jostling one another with their umbrellas, amid the incessant drizzle of a slow falling rain, the crowd pressed close about him, Cav. Cao saw in these days every street corner become a pillory; an executioner, every mud-spattered newsvendor, who brandished like an axe his grimy sheet, spawned in the dens of blackmail, and spewed forth ohscenely the vilest accusations. And no policeman thought of stopping their mouths! But, of course, the facts themselves were shouting more obscenely still.

A man of disciplined mind, Cav. Cao would fain have defended the Government at all costs against the charge of a shameful complicity of Ministers with the Banks and the Stock Exchange, through the Press and Parliament. He declined to believe that the Banks had subsidized the Government for electoral ends, and for other, baser, secret ends; and that, rewarding favour with favour, the Government had introduced measures which were privileges for the Banks, and had defended the miscreants, nominating them to Orders of Knighthood and to the Senate. But he could not deny that credit had been given to certain favoured politicians, who in Parliament and through the Press had fought to the profit of the fraudulent Banks, betraying the good faith of the country; and that these fortunate persons had tried to conceal facts that were already known or might be guessed; and that, now that charges were flying, they were prepared to strike, but with the hope that the destruction of the weaker vessels might enable the stronger to escape scot free. Certainly, the anger of the country at seeing so bespattered with mud various public characters who in the brave days of the heroic Liberation had given the strength of their arms to the country was now fiercely turning upon the glory of the Eevolution itself, was discovering mudstains even there; and Cav. Cao felt his heart bleed. This was the bank-ruptcy of patriotism, perdio!

And he raged against certain showers of abuse which were being concentrated, at this time, from the whole of Italy upon Rome, represented as a putrid carcass.

In a Neapolitan paper he had read that all strength was enfeebled by contact with the monstrous Corpse; all enthusiasm cooled; and every virtue corrupted. Better, better far the days when it lived upon indulgences and jubilees, letting rooms to pilgrims, selling blessed rosaries and images to the devout!

Cav. Cao trembled, because the Clericals, naturally, were exultant.

Accompanying His Excellency, now and again, to Montecitorio, he saw in the corridors and rooms all the Deputies, young and old, novices and veterans, friends or opponents of the Government, enveloped in a cloud of distrust and suspicion. It seemed to him that they all felt themselves spied upon, watched; that some of them laughed, in ostentation, while others, dismayed by the colour of their cheeks, pretended to be burying their heads in some absorbing book. For some of them, notwithstanding the cold weather outside, the furnaces were not properly regulated: too hot! too hot! too hot! Who could tell in how many consciences lurked the terror lest, at any moment, the eye of an examining magistrate might penetrate, to search and probe them, armed with the cruellest of glasses.

It had struck Cav. Cao, that afternoon, that certain Deputies, engaged in animated discussion in one of the rooms, had suddenly broken off their conversation when they saw His Excellency D'Atri pass. He had stopped for a moment to stare at them, frowning, and had heard one of these Deputies, who had at once turned his back on him, clearly repeat, several times, in an undertone but with a ringing accent and all the force of scorn, the name of Corrado Selmi, which at that time was on every tongue.

Cav. Cao knew very well that no one would have dared to cast any doubt on the integrity of Francesco D'Atri; but it might easily happen that, through his wife, he too was involved in Selmi's downfall, which everyone now regarded as inevitable.

However, there he was: pacing the floor of his study and evidently quite oblivious alike of the man he was keeping waiting, and of his financial statement. His Excellency seemed to be concerned only by the fretful wail of an infant which, in the silence of the house, penetrated to the study from a distant room, notwithstanding the closed doors in between. He had left the room once already to see what was wrong with his daughter.

Cav. Cao could not control his irritation any longer (because, good God, the whole of Rome knew that the child... the child....), rose, as though forced up by a spring, breathing heavily through his nostrils.

His Excellency stopped short and turned to gaze at him.

Immediately Cav. Cao screwed up his face, as though in a sudden, acute spasm of pain, and said, smiling and rubbing his leg:

"Cramp, Your Excellency..."

"Why, yes... you have been waiting.... Please forgive me, Cavaliere. I was thinking of something else.... That will do for to-night, eh? You must be tired; and I don't feel in the mood for work. It must be eleven o'clock, surely?"

"Midnight, Your Excellency! The exact time is ten minutes past twelve...."

"Indeed? And... and that theatre, when does it finish?"

"What theatre, Your Excellency?"

"Oh, I don't know; the Costanzi, I think. I mean for... for that child's sake.... You hear how she's crying. Nothing will quiet her. Perhaps, if her mother were here...."

"Would you like me to go round to the Costanzi, and tell her?"

"No, no, thank you.... She can't be much longer, now. Wait a minute, though: there is something I must tell Auriti."

"Cavaliere Giulio?"

"Yes. He is with my wife. He may not be coming in, after the theatre. You would oblige me greatly by telling him."

"To come up here? I shall go at once, Your Excellency."

"Thank you. Good night, Cavaliere. I shall see you to-morrow."

Cav. Cao made a deep bow, inhaling a long, long breath of air through his nostrils; as soon as he had shut the door behind him, he expelled it with a snort of rage, which changed at once however into a gracious smile at the sight of the footman in livery who came towards him.

IN THE WHIRLPOOL.

As soon as he was alone, Francesco D'Atri clapped both his hands to his face. His polished scalp reflected the blaze of the electric lights that hung from the ceiling. He remained for a while in the study, pacing the floor, his face lined with exhaustion, distorted by the grim thoughts in which he was wrapped, stroking with his small hand, wrinkled and hardened by the passage of years, that long, canary-yellow beard which contrasted so painfully and preposterously with the whole of his expression and his natural dignity. How in the world could he fail to see that such a beard, in the present circumstances, was a horrible disfigurement?

He failed to see it, because for some time past Francesco D'Atri had ceased to control his own actions, nor was he any longer his own sole master. The eyes through which he beheld himself were no longer his own; they were the eyes of a different Francesco D'Atri, who faced him every morning in the mirror with a sullen air of angry humiliation at seeing his eyelids swollen and discoloured, and all those wrinkles and white patches on his face. Nor was this the only Francesco D'Atri that came to life in him in the senile disintegration of his consciousness, and led him to think, feel and move as he himself could not, could not any longer, with those limbs and brain and heart enfeebled by age.

He was now a poor old man, who would gladly have crept into a corner never to leave it again; but all those other pitiless selves, that survived within him, taking advantage of his bewildered state, refused to leave him in peace; they fought for him, played with him, forbade him to complain and to say that he was tired, to admit that he no longer remembered anything; and compelled him to lie when there was no need to lie, to smile when he had no wish

264

to smile, to dress himself up, to do all sorts of things that seemed to him superfluous. And one of them it was that had dyed his beard in that ridiculous fashion; another had made him take a wife, when he was well aware that it was far too late; yet another made him hold on at all costs to his high office, which he knew to be far beyond his powers; another persuaded him to feel a tender affection for that baby, whom even he knew to be not his own, adducing the most specious of reasons, to wit that, he himself having begotten a daughter in his youth, to whom another man had given name and love and care and maintenance, it behoved him now to give to this child his name and love and care and maintenance, as though she were really his own poor little baby of long ago.

Yielding, however, to this sentiment, owning the child before all the world as his, "Ah!" he was warned by the self of the beard, armed with brush and lotion, "if, my dear fellow, you wish to be taken for a father, with that young wife by your side, you must give a touch of yellow to all those white hairs!" He would fain have turned a deaf ear to this foolish counsel, which seemed to him a profanation not only of his venerable appearance, but also, when it came to that, of his true feelings for the child; he was incapable, however, of offering more than a timid resistance. And this painful and absurd timidity was precisely reflected in the dyeing of his beard.

Caught, held fast as though in a crowd of people every one of whom appeared to be acting for himself without thought of him, he did not know which way to turn; nothing gave him any pleasure; but, if he were to turn one way or the other, he was afraid of arousing the displeasure of one or other of his cruel masters; and any decision, however trivial, meant a fatiguing effort.

He saw only too plainly the trap in which he had fallen, by no wish of his own; and he could think of no way out of it.

Everything was in confusion! Here in Rome, the indecent clamour of a vast criminal fraud; in Sicily, a ferment of revolt. Amid the uproar of the most abject passions, let loose in the decay of the national conscience, people had barely noticed the rumble of distant musketry, the first thunderclap of a terrible storm which was gathering with alarming rapidity. One voice alone had been

raised in Parliament to set before the Government the bloodstained spectre of certain peasants massacred in Sicily, at
Caltavuturo; to brandish before the world the angry threat of the
peril in store, were the pernicious belief to take root in the country
that the poor and weak might be struck down with impunity, while
the swindlers found sanctuary at Montecitorio.

Yes, that Sicilian Deputy had given a true account of the
facts: those Sicilian peasants, finding in their rage at the injustice of
others the courage to assert their own rights with violence, had
gone forth to till the Crown lands usurped by the petty tyrants of
their village, dishonest trustees of the property of the Commune:
alarmed by the arrival of the troops, they had stopped their work
and hurried to the municipal offices to demand the portioning of
those lands among them; in the absence of his chief, a subordinate
official had appeared on the balcony, and, to disperse the crowd,
had advised them to go back in the mean time to their work; but
on their way the crowd had found the road blocked by reinforce-
ments of militia; showing signs of resistance, they had found
themselves first of all attacked with bayonets; then with rifle fire,
for having brandished their tools in the air to frighten their assailants. Twelve were dead; the wounded numbered more than fifty:
among these, several children, one of whom had been pierced by at
least seven bayonet thrusts.

This ghastly detail had made so vivid an impression upon
Francesco D'Atri that for the last three days, in spite of all his own
troubles and distracting thoughts, his mind kept on turning to it
with horror. Because the ferocity of that soldier, venting itself on
the body of an innocent child, seemed to him the most precise illu-
stration of the times: he could see the same ferocity in everyone,
and the sight appalled him. No longer any respect, any reverence
for the most sacred things, a blind fury, an insane hatred, a frenzy
of dissolution, a savage delight in base revenge. He was expecting
to be seized at any moment by some madman or other, and made
to give an account of all his misdeeds, past and present. Misdeeds?
Was there a man alive who had never done amiss? But this was a
moment in which even the most trivial, those which at any other
time it was customary to overlook, leaped to the public eye, borrowed from the sinister glare in the sky a certain bold relief, a

certain mysterious colour, which at once aroused a furious desire
for investigation, for the vile satisfaction or fierce consolation of
discovering such other more serious corruptions as they might
conceal. The most balanced judgment, that of the Public Prosecu-
tor, held in check by everyone and persuaded with such a wealth of
argument not to break the bonds of patience, now that everyone
was of one mind had broken loose, had cast off all restraint, all social considerations; had become overbearing in its arrogance; and
no man's conscience could any longer feel at rest or safe.

That marriage of his to a young girl; the illusion that his
past reputation and the paramount distinctions he had won would
make up, in her esteem and in her heart, for all the youthful ardour
that must of necessity be lacking from his kind and deep affection;
the thoughtless profusion of their life; the scandal of his wife's intimacy with Selmi; and now the child... might at any moment
become a matter for public derision, a pretext for accusations and
spiteful insinuations, the source of any number of damaging suspicions. Amid the phantasms of his uncertainty, in that empty, dim
reality in which he seemed to be enveloped, Francesco D'Atri felt
his secret terror grow from hour to hour, now that a shout of rage
was going up at the forcible rescue, on the Government's part, of a
number of politicians more conspicuous and more deeply compromised than the rest. Among them was Selmi, who, for all that,
had shown a complete indifference to the scandal throughout. His
colleagues in the Cabinet had said nothing to him about it; but he
had gathered from the expression on their faces that he was being
given to understand that Selmi was escaping by his influence. It
was not true! Not by his influence, certainly; but because he was
one of them; and, at that moment, his downfall might bring them
all crashing down after him. Was not such a remedy worse than the
disease? He had been powerless to resist; how could he utter that
name? Free from any reproach, immaculate, because of a single
weakness, of that illusion he had so quickly lost, he saw himself
dragged down by his wife into the mud of the streets, where a mob
athirst for scandal were shouting his name to make a sacrifice of
him, heaping up in a bloodstained mass his body and his wife's and
Selmi's. Now, with equal vividness, he saw himself carried along
the streets, but with Selmi clinging fast to his wife and himself, and

with the whole mob clinging fast to Selmi. He pictured them bringing Selmi back to his house, with all the crowd roaring behind, mocking and insulting him. Everyone, yes, everyone would suppose that it was he who was saving Selmi, and not from generosity but from fear! Perhaps Selmi himself, as well. ... But, after all, what had he to fear? From generosity, if anything, he might have done it, because he could remember the time when the other was valiant and noble, setting life at naught in the face of danger, and aflame with the sacred ideal of the country. But no, not even in that generous impulse would he have done it: he felt too keenly, quite apart from his hatred and contempt for the betrayal (albeit he laid the blame for that more on his wife), he felt too keenly the suspicion that he was afraid.

There still remained, however, after all the papers that might have ruined Selmi had been hidden away, exposed, defenceless and compromised, an innocent party: Roberto Auriti. A debt of about forty thousand lire had been found standing in his name; and, what was worse, more than one laconic and mysterious note, in which allusion was made to a friend, who guaranteed the Governor of the Bank or promised that he would act or speak or write according to the instructions he had received. These notes were by this time in the hands of the judicial authorities, and this was what he would shortly have to tell Giulio Auriti, Roberto's brother.

He had grown used by now to the horror of the situation; he had come to look upon it almost as an inevitable destiny; and his feeling at the moment was one of growing revulsion, heavy with weariness and pain. No comfort to be found in his memories of the past: were he to recall them for a moment, they would serve only to increase the shame and misery of the present. And in this feeling of revulsion, the sight of everything, even of the ornaments in the room, became intolerably burdensome to him. Ah, darkness, darkness, a resting place: death, yes! All this warfare made it easy to overcome one's horror of death. What cruelty! Here was a man who must soon die. ... Why keep these dregs for the last days, to be drained from the stirrup-cup of life...

Francesco D'Atri stopped short, with staring, lifeless eyes. He imagined the time after his own death: time as it would be for other people.... Calm would be restored... for other people! The waves smoothed, the horror of the tempest quelled; and no pity, no regret, no memory of the man who had been where the storm broke and had perished under it.

All of a sudden, on the bracket upon which his gaze was fixed, he became aware of a little porcelain monkey which was grinning stupidly at him. He was tempted for a moment to break it; he turned his back on it; once again he caught the sound of the child's wailing cry and made off to the distant room from which it came.

THE GLOVE ON THE CARPET.

It was the nurse's room. A night light, screened by a talc shade, on the chest of drawers, shed a feeble glimmer. The old housekeeper, a lean, trim figure, was pacing up and down with the child in her arms, who, in the throes of its convulsions, seemed to be trying to slip from her hands; she managed to clasp it more tightly to her bosom, and kept on crooning to it, "Noona, noona..." as though in response to its agonized wails, keeping time with a rhythmical motion of her body, and bring her hand down gently upon its back.

The wet-nurse, with an enormous breast exposed, was crying also: she was crying in silence and swearing to the lady's maid, who was sitting beside her, that she had partaken of no obnoxious food.

Francesco D'Atri stopped for a moment to gaze at her with unseeing eyes: and his features expressed the effort which he almost instinctively, with his thoughts elsewhere, was making to understand what she was trying to say through her floods of tears. At the same time he gazed with disgust at that indecent breast, from the purple nipple of which a drop of milk was hanging. The maid discreetly drew the nurse's bodice together, so as to hide her breast. Whereupon Francesco D'Atri turned his gaze to the housekeeper; deafened by the wretched infant's screams, he blinked his eyes; then went across to the bed table and picked up a little bell, which he began to tinkle gently before the child's eyes, to distract its attention, following behind the housekeeper, who continued to pace up and down with her swaying motion.

So he was discovered, a little later, by Donna Giannetta on her return from the theatre, splendid, in a rustle of silken garments.

She raised her eyebrows and parted her lips in a faint mocking smile at this nocturnal, touching, family picture, supposing that His Excellency was amusing himself, before the servants, by making a display of his ridiculous paternal affection after shouldering the burdens of the State. But the maid, hastening to take the black scarf, glittering with little discs of silver, which her mistress threw off from her head, and to unfasten her cloak, explained to her in a whisper what had happened.

"Really? Poor little thing..." she said, with a show of indifference, but in a warm, melodious voice, and went across, fragrant with scent and powder, with her expanse of bosom, a magnificent figure, to the housekeeper. But D'Atri made a sign to her not to speak. The baby had at last been soothed.

Donna Giannetta then with a little yawn of weariness went off to her own room. At the door she turned and said, in a sing-song tone, to her husband:

"By the way, Giulio Auriti is in there."

Francesco D'Atri bowed his head; went towards her and said in a low and solemn voice, without looking at her:

"Wait for me. I have something to say to you."

"A long speech?" she inquired. "Oh Lord, can't it keep till to-morrow? I'm so tired, I'm afraid I should fall asleep. I've had such a boring evening."

"You will oblige me by waiting," he insisted.

And he returned to the study, where Auriti was expecting him.

Oh, how gladly now would he have avoided the sight of that young man, for whom he had terrible news! He had forgotten all about him.... He moved, in these days, gave orders, instructions, forced himself into actions, words, decisions, for which a moment later he could no longer see any reason, occasion, object. He shut his eyes and heaved a deep sigh, his brow darkened by a black oppression. He had just told his wife to wait for him, as he wished to speak to her. But about what? With what object? And he himself, not an hour ago, had asked his secretary to tell Auriti, as he left the theatre, to come round to the house, as he needed urgently to see him. But it was necessary, of course, that the poor young man should be informed immediately of the terrible disaster that threatened him. And nobody but himself could inform him of it.

As he drew back the curtain from the door and caught sight of the other inside, he felt a certain rancour at the pity and emotion that he was arousing in him already.

Giulio Auriti was not in the least like his brother: tall, slender, dressed in the height of fashion, he revealed by the tempered agility of his movements a vigorous energy, softened by a certain air of unconscious pride in his fine steely eyes. The hair of his head was prematurely grizzled, in contrast to the tawny hue of his thick, curling beard.

His face changed all of a sudden at the sight of the old Minister coming towards him with so disconcerted an air.

One of his gloves, which he was holding in his hand, dropped on the carpet.

"Well?" he inquired.

Francesco D'Atri lowered his eyelids to shut out the painful spectacle of the desperate anxiety which he could read on the other's face. He spread out his hands and murmured, shaking his head:

"They haven't found..."

"Oh no!" Auriti broke out, with a second instantaneons change of countenance, expressive of scorn, anger, and at the same time a firm resolve to rebel against an act of injustice without any further regard for anyone. "No, excuse me, Your Excellency, no: the document exists, and it must he found! You know that my brother Roberto..."

"I know, I know..." D'Atri attempted, coldly, to cut him short.

"Well, then!" Auriti pressed the matter. "That statement is the only thing that can save him, and it must not be allowed to vanish! Or else, everything else must vanish with it that can compromise Roberto!"

D'Atri sat down, clapped his hands again to his face and let fall from his hidden lips:

"The trouble is this: the judicial authorities ..."

"No, Your Excellency!" Auriti again protested. "The judicial authorities are in possession of only such material as the Government have chosen to let them have. Everybody knows that!"

D'Atri gazed at the speaker as though he himself, at least, did not know it; drew himself up in his chair and, setting his features, seemed to be warning him that he could not allow so scandalous a rumour to be repeated in his hearing.

But Auriti continued to rave, wringing his hands as he spoke:

"And I... I who was perfectly calm.... Why, Your Excellency! I was perfectly calm... it was you!"

D'Atri's head sank; but immediately, as though some force within him had given an impetus to his spirit, he drew himself up again and shouted angrily, with a glare of hatred at the young man:

"Where do I come in? What can I do?"

"Why!" Auriti repeated. "Selmi..."

"Selmi..." Francesco D'Atri roared, clenching his fists, as though he would have liked to hold the man in his clutch.

"Why, yes, let them save him, if they choose!" exclaimed Giulio Auriti. "In order to save him, though..."

"Of course! You imagine too that it is I who am saving him..." said D'Atri solemnly, shaking his head with the bitterest scorn.

"But Selmi himself, Your Excellency," Auriti promptly took him up, with a different kind of scorn, "you will find that Selmi himself will not allow them to save him at the price of the moral assassination of my brother. Besides, Your Excellency, if he does not speak, if Roberto keeps silence, I shall cry aloud! There's my mother to be considered, Your Excellency! Roberto arrested? It would kill my mother! And our name?"

At this cry, Francesco D'Atri's face lost its composure.

"Your mother... yes... your mother..." he murmured; and, bowing his head, buried his face once more in his hands; he remained for a while in this attitude, then his body began to heave as though with stifled sobs. As a young man he had known, at Turin, Donna Caterina Laurentano and Stefano Auriti, of whom this son now reminded him so vividly; he saw himself as he was then; saw Roberto as a boy; thought of a certain night at sea, with that boy asleep on his knee, an hour after they sailed from Quarto... ah, between that night and this, what a gulf!

Giulio Auriti, seeing the old Minister's massive shoulders

shake, felt ashamed.

At length he uncovered his face and, still stooping, with his eyes on the ground, his hands fluttering in accompaniment to his words:

"What will you cry?... what will you cry?" he asked him. "The disgrace of us all? We are all tarred with the same brush! You mean to tell me that you know why Selmi took this money in your brother's name? And you will cry aloud my disgrace as well!"

"No, Your Excellency!" Auriti at once protested, horrified at the suggestion.

"Yes indeed!" went on Francesco D'Atri, rising to his feet. "All tarred with the same brush, I tell you! All... all.... The shame of it is killing me.... Mud, up to here!"

He clutched his throat in both hands.

"It is stifling me! This... I have had to think of this! Our greatest names.... You think only of your brother! Nothing, it is true, nothing ever stayed in his hand; but he passed the money on to the other man.... And is not that a disgrace? How do you excuse it? What is it you cry aloud? Your brother promises, your most worthy brother guarantes, in those bills, the filthy traffickings of his friend..."

"Without naming him!" said Giulio Auriti through his clenched teeth, laughing with anger, shame, scorn. "That is why they have not been spirited away!"

"But when panic has seized hold of them all!" Francesco D'Atri shouted in his face, in a voice stifled by rage. "A quarrel among thieves, who steal by night, with trembling fingers, blindly; they shuffle things up, take some away, stick others in; and all the time, from their bag, from their pockets, the booty is tumbling out; and in the scuffle, crawling among their feet, there are those who rob the robbers, who fasten upon some paper or other that has dropped, and run off to do a deal in shame: 'Here you are, gentlemen, the greatest names in Italy! Here you have honour! Here you have the glories of the country!' Don't make me speak of it... I know to whom I am speaking! But now... I have had more than enough... it sticks in my teeth. It is not in human nature, I quite realize, it is not in human nature to expect Roberto to keep silence: for his own sake, for his mother's, for yours, for the name you bear..."

"Roberto?" said Auriti. "Why, Your Excellency knows Roberto, he'll be quite capable of silence. Selmi himself..."

"If Roberto keeps silence?" asked D'Atri, as though he were still in doubt.

"But I shan't, Your Excellency!" Auriti hastened to repeat. "I tell you beforehand: I shall not, for my mother's sake!"

"Wait!" D'Atri went on, as though commanding silence. "If I am speaking to you like this, it means that I have something to say to you."

Giulio Auriti gazed anxiously in his face. But D'Atri did not meet his gaze; it troubled, not to say annoyed him; he saw lying on the ground the glove that had dropped from the young man's hand at the beginning of their interview, and felt more strongly than ever the sense of intolerable oppression which the sight of any object caused him at this time. He took his eyes from it, and said darkly:

"You understand that in all this... in all this business... I cannot shew my hand...."

He looked at his hands, and drew them back with a gesture of disgust.

"Still," he went on, "for Roberto's sake I have spoken.... Only this evening; I said... I... recalled... his deserts.... Perhaps-- listen to what I am saying--these compromising papers, on the strength of which a warrant has already been issued... yes! But-- listen--these papers..."

He could not utter the word; with a swift, expressive wave of his hand he implied it: "gone!" "However," he at once continued, "since his name has already come out, to remove all suspicion of his being implicated, to leave no trace behind..."

"We must pay?" Auriti asked, faintly. "And where? How?"

D'Atri shrugged his shoulders crossly.

"Forty thousand lire, Your Excellency..."

"I cannot provide you with them.... You must find them.... And quickly! You realize, it is the only way...."

"Money taken from some one else..." groaned Auriti.

"How do you mean, taken?" asked D'Atri angrily. "You must admit...."

"For some one else!" protested Giulio.

"Are you a child?"

"No, Your Excellency: the difficulty is... Where am I to find it? How am I to find it?"

"Look for it... you have rich relatives... your cousin..."

"Lando?"

"Or your uncles..."

Giulio Auriti remained lost in thought, weighing the probability of success that this way offered, amid the obstacles that already blocked the path: in Lando's case, the hated shadow of Selmi; in his uncles', the unshakable pride of his mother. How was her will ever to be bent to ask for financial help to meet this indefinite liability of her son, from that brother? In the process of bending, she would undoubtedly be broken! He thereupon decided that he himself would apply to Lando: he himself, at all costs, to spare his mother that supreme sacrifice.

"How long?" he asked.

"Soon..." D'Atri repeated. "Let me see ... in five days, or six at the most...."

Giulio Auriti, at once losing all sense of time, carried away already by the part that he had to play, took his leave and departed in haste, frowning, as though he had to go off at once to his cousin's house.

Francesco D'Atri watched him leave the room; then sat for a while perplexed, frowning, one hand rubbing the back of the other, as though he were racking his brains to remember what he still had to do. All of a sudden, he again saw lying on the ground, on the red carpet, the white glove that had dropped from Auriti's hand.

That glove left lying there seemed to him a sign that he could not, henceforward, isolate himself altogether from the things, people, thoughts, by which he felt himself stifled: always a trace, a footprint, some vestige would remain, resurgent or ineradicable, like the recurring phantom of a dream. And as though that glove might be interpreted as a proof that he himself was compromised. Francesco D'Atri bent down cautiously to pick it up with a shudder of disgust and slipped it into his pocket, furtively.

UNSEEN TEARS.

Donna Giannetta, wearing a loose wrapper, with a becoming cap of lace and ribbons on her head, was waiting meanwhile in her bedroom, reclining in a deep and massive armchair of grey leather, with her legs crossed, teasing her lower lip with restless fingers. She kept her eyes sharply fixed on the toe of her red velvet slipper as it peeped out and disappeared beneath the hem of her skirt with the gentle rocking motion of her tilted leg.

It was the first time that her husband had informed her with that air and in that tone that he wished to speak to her. He had never said anything to her before, when he might have had a reason for speaking. What could he have to say to her, now?

She had noticed that, for some months past, he had seemed gloomier and more worried than usual: but not on her account, surely; perhaps because of some parliamentary trouble. She had never taken the least interest in politics; she had always flatly forbidden her friends to discuss politics with her or in her presence; she never read the newspapers, and gloried in her ignorance, enjoyed the laughter that had greeted certain of her confessions, such as that she did not know the names of her husband's colleagues in the Ministry. Did he now wish to inform her, as he had informed her once before, after the first year of their married life, that he was thinking of resigning his office? Oh, that would leave her neither hot nor cold, now...

But here he came.... At once Donna Giannetta relaxed her muscles, sank back with shut eyes in her armchair, pretending to be asleep; but, as D'Atri opened the door, she opened her eyes again wearily, as though she had really been asleep.

"Won't to-morrow do?" she asked him again, with a languid grace. "I'm so sleepy, Francesco! I shan't be able to follow you."

"You will follow me," he said in a broken voice, stroking his beard with a trembling hand. "However, if you wish it, I can say what I have to say briefly...."

"You are resigning?" she inquired, placidly.

Francesco D'Atri gazed at her in astonishment.

"No," he said. "Why?"

"I thought..." yawned Donna Giannetta, placing her hand over her mouth.

"No, here, it is here, of our own affairs, about the household that I have to speak to you," he went on. "Be patient for a minute. I am extremely tired myself! If, however, you wish me to be brief, you must not take offence."

Donna Giannetta opened her eyes wide.

"Offence? Why?"

"Why, because, if I must be brief, I must also be very clear, and not mince matters," he replied. "You will allow me to speak; then you will do, I hope, as I bid you, and that will be all. Listen, then."

"I'm listening," she sighed, shutting her eyes again.

Francesco held up two fingers and brandished them stiffly in the air:

"Two... two misfortunes have come to you," he began.

Donna Giannetta sat up:

"Two? To me?"

"One, of your own choosing," he went on. "An old misfortune. Myself."

"Oh," she exclaimed, sinking back again in her chair. "You frightened me!"

Smiling and clasping her hands behind her head, she continued:

"No... why?"

The loose sleeves of her wrapper slipped down, revealing her shapely arms.

"Up to the present, no," he resumed. "You have not been properly conscious of it, because, for the annoyance which I may have caused you from time to time..."

"Francesco, I'm so sleepy," she groaned.

"Please... please... please..." he said crossly. "What I mean is, that you have found a very considerable compensation for that annoyance in my... in my... shall I say, my philosophy ..."

"Tell me at once what the other misfortune is, please!" sighed Donna Giannetta, as though she were talking in her sleep.

Francesco D'Atri sat down. He was now coming to the difficult part of his speech, and was anxious to express himself with as little crudity as possible. He rested his elbows on his knees, took his head in his hands, the better to concentrate, and spoke, gazing at the floor.

"I am coming to that. Listen. I have been obliged.... obliged to make certain allowances. ... But you, I must add, are not in the least to blame. It was natural that, having to choose between your rights as a young woman and your duties as a wife, you should have preferred the former. I might have pointed out to you, long before this, that you yourself, on the day when you accepted, of your own free will, indeed with ... with enthusiasm, these duties towards an old man, had implicitly (am I not correct?) renounced those rights; but I do not blame you for this either, because perhaps you too, at the time, were under the illusion that..."

At this point Francesco D'Atri raised his head and stopped speaking.

Donna Giannetta was asleep, with one arm still folded over her head, and the other stretched out towards him, as though to implore his mercy.

"Gianna!" he called, but not too loud, controlling his anger and disgust, as though it would hurt his self-esteem were she, by rousing herself at his call, to admit that she had yielded so soon to slumber, while he was speaking to her of so grave a matter. He bowed his head again and continued his speech aloud from the point at which he had broken off:

"You were under the illusion that... yes, that you would find it easy to perform your duties."

Donna Giannetta did not stir; on the contrary, her raised arm slipped slowly down from her head, and fell heavily on her lap. Whereupon, Francesco D'Atri sprang to his feet in fury; in another moment he would have seized that bare, outstretched arm and shaken it with the utmost violence, shouting the most brutal insults in her face. But the unconscious calm of her slumber, shameless as it appeared to him and almost a defiance, restrained him. It seemed as though she, lying there asleep, were saying to him: "Look how young and beautiful I am! What claim can you, an old man, have on me?"

Ah, what claim indeed! But that beauty of hers, what had she done with it? And what was she doing now with her youth? A shameful sacrifice! Yes, after giving herself to him, an old man, first of all! But he, at least, would have worshipped those treasures with a heart trembling and overflowing with gratitude, as a heaven-sent prize! Whereas she, with an opprobrious disdain, with unconscious cruelty, had outraged them! And nothing now could reconsecrate that beauty and that youth so basely profaned!

Shaking his head, he stole quietly from the room.

At once Donna Giannetta sprang to her feet, with a yawn.

"O-o-oh!" Seriously, at that tune of night, an explanation? And why? When he ought to have spoken, mum! Now, now that she was merely bored, bored to death, did he call upon her for an explanation? The idea! Too late... too late.... When he himself, for that matter, with his cold reserve, amid the inevitable relations of the new life into which he had introduced her, in the face of the temptations to which that life exposed her, of the examples which it was continually setting before her eyes, had helped to make her dismiss as too ingenuous, too childish, and liable to provoke the derision of her neighbours the golden dream that she had cherished when she married him?

Oh yes, with absolute sincerity she had dreamed of gladdening with her radiant youth the last years of the heroic life of Francesco D'Atri, her father's old friend and comrade in arms.

Had he felt, perhaps, that she had been too precipitous, too impulsive in making up her mind to marry him, on that evening, now remote, when, the conversation in her father's house turning upon women, old men, marriage, on her asking a question he had answered, jestingly, with a melancholy smile: "Ah, if you were to marry me...."?

But perhaps too he had suspected her of the ambition to become a Minister's wife! For her family, for the position to which her birth entitled her, she was almost penniless.

280

Francesco D'Atri might have known, however, that, in her family, decisions were always made like that, precipitately, but that such precipitation had never impaired the firmness with which the family adhered to them.

Her father, in his youth, in the gay and heedless company of all those other young men of the aristocracy of Palermo, had all of a sudden, as though in a moment of pique, rebelled against the rest of his family, who were fervently devoted to the Bourbons; and had suffered not only persecution, imprisonment, exile at the hands of the tyrannical government, but also the most cruel revenge on the part of his own father: he had been disinherited in favour of his elder brother and his sister Teresa, the wife of Don Ippolito Laurentano and mother of Lando.

And had not she herself, once upon a time, simply out of pique, on the spur of the moment, fallen out with her cousin Lando, who, being resident at the time in Palermo, in the house of his uncle the Prince of Montalto, used to come by stealth to make love to her, his heretical cousin, the daughter of his heretical uncle, to whom his other uncle (the Prince!), as though it were an act of charity of which he ought to feel ashamed, was surreptitiously conveying an allowance that was barely enough to keep him alive?

And she had refused to have anything more to do with him! She had persuaded her father to leave Palermo for Rome, in the hope that, if she got him away from the island, amid a larger circle of friends less hidebound by prejudice, he would at length condescend to let her take the line to which her mother's blood was calling her. Her mother had been a Piedmontese actress, whom her father had met at Turin, during his banishment, and had married there. Her blood, it was her blood and not her example that called to her, for she had never known her mother, who had died in giving her birth; and everyone at Palermo, and most of all her father, had always taken pains not to let her discover what her mother had been. A Montalto on the stage! Appalling! And she herself even, yes, she was bound to admit it, felt in her heart of hearts a secret repulsion at the idea. All the same, to hurl defiance, to bring disgrace upon that uncle of hers, who was ashamed even to support them in secret, she would easily have managed to overcome not merely that repulsion, but any other!

Lando, shortly afterwards, had himself come to settle in Rome, and had joined with her father in trying to tame, to reform her. No, no, no! Already she had become enamoured of her dream of life with Francesco D'Atri, who, ever since their first meeting, had been dazzled by her charms.

But why then had he not deemed her capable of remaining faithful to that dream. How had he failed to understand that such a doubt, such a fear, revealed by certain piteous glances, certain wistful smiles, must bitterly offend her, as must also the liberty he conceded, nay almost enforced upon her, notwithstanding that doubt and that fear? So to him her fall was inevitable and he resigned himself to it? And if he did not trust her, what merit, what reward was there in her not falling? For her own sake? Ah yes, for her own sake! Her father had recently died. Profoundly grieved and embittered, and at the same time obliged to present a smiling face to everyone, she had seen herself, even in those days of mourning, watched by Lando with coldly contemptuous eyes. In a moment of anguish, of exasperation, in a moment of real madness, so that the contempt in those eyes might recoil upon himself as well, she had offered herself to him. Upright, magnanimous, heroic, Lando had repulsed her. Oh, and then, to avenge herself rather upon him than upon the sad and silent distrust of her old husband, she had flung herself into the arms of Corrado Selmi, and down, down, down... horribly, yes... like a drunkard, like a madwoman...

But enough! Had not the old man just told her that he had no fault to find with her for that? Why then should she feel remorse for it? Oh, she had never really enjoyed it! What did he want with her now?

Donna Giannetta shrugged her shoulders, and at once was aware of the movement, as though another woman had made it before her eyes. She had in a marked degree the strange faculty of observing herself like this, from without, even in moments of tense excitement, of seeing herself move, of hearing herself speak or laugh; and it almost terrified her at times, and often annoyed her; she was afraid lest her attitudes, her gestures, the sound of her voice, her sudden peals of laughter, might appear studied; it hurt her, this sudden freezing of the most spontaneous, least premeditated impulses of her nature, surprised at their birth by and in herself.

She passed her hand several times over her brow and tried to absorb herself in some thought which would efface that vision of herself so distraught. Why, of course. The other misfortune.

... What could that other misfortune be of which her husband wished to speak to her?

Her face darkened. Before her eyes rose the image of Selmi who, either in desperation, to check her passion for creating scandal, or from fear of losing her, now that she was beginning to tire of him, or perhaps even in revenge, had failed to prevent her from becoming a mother. Yes, there was no doubt about it: the other misfortune to which the old man had referred was her daughter, that baby....

"Two misfortunes have come to you.... One, of your own choosing..."

The other, therefore, was not. And he was right: this second misfortune had not been of her choosing.

But if he knew all, and knew that she could not feel any affection for the child, who reminded her of her hated lover, why, not an hour ago, had he let her come upon him in the room with the crying child, tinkling a bell? Why such a display of affection for the infant? Why had he sought to identify it with himself, as though to range himself by its side against her, when he said that the pair of them--he and the child--represented two misfortunes for her? What was his object?

Donna Giannetta was sorry she had pretended to be asleep. She sat for a while longer thinking, reflecting; then stole from the room on tiptoe and, in the darkness, holding her breath, cautiously, feeling her way, crept to the door of her husband's room. She listened, then stooped down and peeped in through the keyhole.

Francesco D'Atri, sitting there in his own room, as he had just been sitting in hers, with his elbows on his knees and his head in his hands, was crying!

Donna Giannetta felt a long shudder run down her spine, and drew back in confusion, overcome by a stupefaction mingled with dismay.

He was crying!

She stood there, trembling, her spirit in a tumult, incapable of framing a thought. Then, suddenly, afraid of his opening the door and catching her eavesdropping, she turned back towards her own room. But, as she passed like a thief in the night by the door of the room in which the child slept, she stopped.

The child, too, was crying! Both of them....

Without thinking, as though trying to find a place of refuge that would conceal her from herself at that moment, she opened the door and went in.

The nurse, sitting upright in bed, was in despair. The child, after a short spell of restless sleep, had begun to writhe again in convulsions and was wailing as before.

Donna Giannetta could not make out, at first, what the nurse was saying; she put out her hand to touch the agonized child, and at once drew it back with a start. How cold the child was! But she must be hushed.... This crying was unendurable. ... Didn't she want the breast? Perhaps she was bound too tightly? She began to unwind the wrappings with her own hands. Oh what poor little purple legs... and how they trembled, in the jerking spasms.... She tried to hold them still; but they were freezing! She was freezing all over, poor little creature.... How, in what could she cover her? There, the tester of the cradle.... Quick, quick.

Donna Giannetta took the child in her arms, pressed it to her bosom, firmly and gently, and began to walk up and down the room, rocking her daughter with the swaying motion of her body, a thing she had never done before. And she was amazed to find that she knew how to do it. She felt against her bosom the contractions of the aching little stomach, she could almost feel the gurgling flow of tears in that cold and tender little body. Almost unconsciously, then, she began to cry too, not out of pity for the little one, no... or rather perhaps yes, at the sight of its sufferings ... but she cried also because... she did not herself know why.

Gradually the infant, as though it felt the warmth of the mother's love which for the first time in its life was comforting it, grew quiet again. Donna Giannetta was by this time tired, dead tired, yet she continued for a while longer to pace the floor, bringing her hand down gently, at each step, on the child's back. Then she stopped; with the utmost precaution, so as not to awaken the child, she lifted it from her bosom; sat down and laid it on her lap; made a sign to the nurse to remain in bed, and, by the faint glimmer of the nightlight, began to study her daughter. She saw the little creature, quiet now by her intervention, lying there on her lap, as she had never seen it before. Perhaps because she had never done anything for it before. Poor little thing, growing up all this time without affection, without care.... As though it were to blame!

She screwed up her eyes, as though to banish a hateful feeling.... But no! How was the child to blame for having been born?

And then in an instant, as she gazed at her daughter, she realized what her husband had wished to say to her. He was and felt himself to be an old man, and knew that he could not fill her life; but she had a daughter, now; and a daughter can and must fill the life of her mother. He might have created a scandal, and had not done so; not only that, he had even given this child, which was not his own, the prestige of his name, of his position, and... yes, his love as well. Very well, she, the mother, would do well to give her own daughter affection, care, an example of blameless conduct.

This, yes, no doubt about it, this was what he had wished to say to her. And she had pretended to be asleep....

Hour after hour Donna Giannetta remained there, that night, with the child on her lap. She thought with the bitterest regret of her own sweet girlish dream; and, with disgust, of what men had offered her in exchange for that dream.... Stupid pretences, horrid vulgarities.... Then, gradually, she was overpowered by sleep.

Before daybreak, Francesco D'Atri, passing along the corridor on the way to his study, saw the door of the nurse's room standing ajar and put in his head. He was amazed to find his wife inside, asleep in an armchair, with the child in her arms. He stole softly into the room to look at her, and felt his amazement dissolve, as a tremor ran through his veins, in an unspeakable emotion. He stooped down and brushed her forehead with a kiss.

Donna Giannetta stirred; she too was amazed, at first, at finding herself there, with the child on her lap; then smiled--saw herself smile--and, holding out her hand to her husband and gazing at him with eyes full of a new joy, asked him:

"Is this what you wanted?"

CHAPTER II

IN THE GLORY OF ROME.

FOR the last three weeks, everybody, even those who were hurrying about their business with their thoughts elsewhere, had been turning round and stopping to gaze at a gnarled and weather-beaten old man, with a little knapsack on his back, four medals on his breast and a big black hat, from beneath the brim of which escaped a cataract of hair, his yellow locks tumbling over the tangled fleece of his beard. This old man walked as in a dream, his eyes glistening with tears of joy, without for a moment suspecting the extraordinary figure that he was cutting in the streets and piazze of Rome, in his comical attitude and with his awkward air of being in strange surroundings, like a tamed savage.

But, now that he had left at Valsania his shaggy cap, his hobnailed shoes and gun, and had put on the new suit of blue broadcloth and, beneath his coarse shirt of violet flannel, a second shirt of linen, which flowed out, white and soft, at his neck and wrists; with that big black hat and his polished shoes, Mauro Mortara was confident of being as smartly dressed as any of them. His jacket did, indeed, bulge a little over the hips ... but his pistols, ah, he had made a vow that he would never part company with them. The four medals, lastly, which might be seen pinned to his flannel shirt, on his breast, he had brought with him (asking the General's leave, first) simply to prove that he was a person worthy to walk the streets of Rome, that he was entitled to the privilege, had won the honour of beholding her. All his papers were in his knapsack.

How was he to suppose that those medals, in a Rome steeped in opprobium and mud in these days of party strife, could only raise a contemptuous smile on people's lips, now that the label "old patriot" had become almost a brand of infamy?

And he laughed back at all the people whom he saw laughing, without the remotest suspicion that they were laughing at him, believing indeed that they were sharing in his joy, in that joy watered with tears which, radiating round him like a beacon light, dazzled his vision of everything.

He saw nothing more of Rome than this joy in being there; and everything, in that blaze of hallucination, presented itself to him in a magical, vaporous guise; nor was he conscious of the ground beneath his feet. Three or four times, as he lengthened his pace, he had overstepped the pavement and had almost fallen.

He went about like a drunken man, without a goal, lost, drowned in his own bliss; and whenever there shimmered before him some magnificent sight, a fountain, a palace, a monument, down streamed a fresh flow of tears from eyes swollen with emotion.

Lando Laurentano would have given him a guide; a guide, indeed! He did not want to know; did not want anything explained to him; he was instinctively afraid that any information, any direction, any knowledge must diminish that vast, fluctuating image of greatness which his sentiment created for him.

Rome must remain for him, like the sea, unbounded.

And on his return at nightfall, tired but insaliate, to the villino on the Via Sommacampagna, where Lando lived, if he was asked whether he had seen the Colosseum, the Forum, the Capitol:

"I've seen, I've seen!" he would hasten to reply. "Don't tell me anything.... I've seen!"

"Saint Peter's too?"

"Oh Marasantissima! I tell you, I've seen. I don't want to know anything. One thing or another, what do I care? It's all Rome!"

What did he care to know who the horseman was with bare legs and a crown on his head, sitting on the great bronze horse, in that lofty square guarded by statues at the head of the steps, surmounted by a tower, with a portico on either side? It was in Rome? Then it must be some great one, surely, a hero of antiquity, a triumphant victor, a ruler of the world. And that statue over there, the red one, sitting over the fountain, with a ball in her hand? Rome: that was Rome, with the world in her grasp, which was enough for him.

Had there not been such a crowd of people continually passing through the square, he would have stooped down and kissed the rim of the fountain, would have gone up and kissed the pedestal of the bare-legged horseman. And why were all those people bustling about up there? They were worldng, working to make Rome greater still. They were all toiling to that end. And Rome, Rome, there she was: once again, before long, she would be holding the whole world, like that, in the hollow of her hand!

Was he really--he, Mauro Mortara--in Rome? Was it actually he that was breathing the air of Rome? Was it he whose feet were treading the pavements of Rome? Was he beholding all these grandeurs? Or was it a dream? Ah, his eyes might close now, after this crowning mercy! Having seen Rome, they had seen all that there was to see. Having set his signature there, in the Pantheon register, by the tomb of Vittorio, he might now die: he had recorded his presence in this life, had answered the roll call of history.

How astounding! They seemed to have sprung up before his eyes, those dark, towering columns. Doubtful whether it might not be a church, he had refrained at first from entering by the half-open gate in the railings, as he saw other people do. ... In coming to Rome, he had made the stipulation that he was going to give the churches a wide berth! hWorship God, yes, but in heaven. ... And indeed he had not set foot in Saint Peter's even. He put himself in the priests' hands? Marameo! With suspicion in his eyes, he had glared at the Vatican, pressing the butts of his pistols against his hips with his elbows.

Was this a church then also? He was just going to inquire when a man came up to him, selling photographs of Rome: "The Pantheon... tomb of the King...."

"In there?"

And immediately he had gone in. That round, staring eye in the cupola, through which you could see the sky, the altar opposite had somewhat disconcerted him. Where was the King's tomb?

There it was, to the right, towering up, in bronze. ... And he had gone towards it, timidly; he had seen beneath the tomb the two veterans on guard, with medals on their breasts, the register for the signature of visitors, and, with a smile in eyes glazed by tears, had opened his jacket a little way to let them see that he had the right to sign.

The two veterans had not quite understood, perhaps, what he meant, and, seeing him laugh and cry simultaneously, had perhaps taken him for a lunatic. One of them, indeed, as though to reassure himself, had inquired of him with a wave of the hand: "Sign?"

Yes, he had replied, with a nod: presently, after the rest had finished; for, what with his unpractised hand, his swimming eyes, and above all his emotion, it might take him a long time to write his name!

Finally, left alone with the veterans, after he had scrawled, as best he could, in the register, letter by letter, his name, surname and birthplace:

"Ah, from Girgenti... a Sicilian?" he had heard one of them ask, who had been following the movement of the pen with his eyes. "Did you serve in the Sixty campaign?"

"There they are!" he had answered, swelling with pride, pointing to his medals. "And this one, for Forty-Eight!"

"Ah, you're a veteran of Forty-Eight.... And are you a sufferer?"

"A sufferer? What do you mean?"

"Have you the pension for political sufferers?"

A pension! He? Why should he draw a pension? He had nothing.... He didn't even know that it existed, this pension; even if he had known, he would never have applied for it. Take money for what he had done? He would let his hands drop off first!

The other two, who were Piedmontese, had begun to laugh, exchanging a glance of merriment. They were applauding him--he supposed--of course they were. Just as he was applauded, in the villino, every evening, by Baffaele the footman and the boy Torello, after a stern rebuke from their master, who had caught them at a moment when they were fooling him to the top of his bent.

To Mauro's exclamations of joy, astonishment, enthusiasm, satisfaction, to his ingenuous reflexions as to the greatness of the country, Lando Laurentano, albeit filled in these days with anger and disgust, had made no reply; he had suppressed a smile even when his dear old man, one evening, had come in to announce to him, still exulting in the experience:

"I have seen the King! I have seen the King! Oh, my boy, my dear boy,... how could I ever have believed such a thing? Quite white... as white as I am....What it must cost him to sit there! What he must have to think of! Ay, he's the axle! And that's saying little: the axle on which the whole thing turns.... And do you know? He bowed to me! If the carriage hadn't been going so fast, I should have gone down on my knees, as sure as God's in heaven!"

Oh, to feel that heart beat in his own breast for a moment!--Lando Laurentano had thought with emotion and envy. Oh, to be able with that faith, with that purity of intention, to nourish a dream, a vaster dream; to face sterner conflicts for its sake and to win, thereby tasting a purer and greater joy than his!

As though to retemper his metal, to wash his spirit clean of all the filth that was spouting at this time from the life of the nation, he had plunged with a sense of relief, revival, refreshment into this old man's talk; strange talk, it was true, but a perfect fount of purity and faith.

The sight of him, his presence in Rome at this time, gave a filthier, a viler appearance to all those who, having had the good fortune to be born at a supreme and glorious moment, had put it to their personal profit, like covetous tradesmen and dishonest speculators.

What did he know of them, what could he know, this old man, who, after giving the best of his strong and simple nature to his country, had withdrawn into solitude to draw fantastic pictures of the fruit that his work must certainly have borne, confident that all the others had acted like himself? He did not think: he merely felt: a burning flame, that rejoiced in its own light and heat, and gave life to all around it with that light.

And, certainly, just as now he did not notice the shower of mud through which he was passing, radiant with joy and enthusiasm, so for thirty years past in Sicily he had never noticed the horrors of all sorts of injustice, the desolation of neglect, the shattering of illusions, the cries and threats of the oppressed.

Preoccupied, alarmed by the daily increasing gravity of the news that reached him from the Island, Lando would have been glad of some information from him, if only about the Province of Girgenti; but he had never so much as hinted this to him, knowing well that it would at once have spoiled all the old man's holiday to let him know that he, the General's grandson, was on the side of those whom Mauro was bound, in good faith, to regard as enemies of the country, and was accordingly an enemy of the country himself.

Instead, he had inquired after his father.

"You've got to come down there with me!" had been Mauro's curt response. "You are the thief; I'm the policeman. And you can thank God he sent me after you! He might have sent a squad of those terrible great dolls of his, with their Captain Sciaralla."

Lando's lips had parted in a pained smile. Whereupon Mauro had clapped his hand to his forehead, with:

"There I go! But how can I help it? He even sends them to me, to Valsania, dressed up like that, to his Father's house! My heart revolts within me and I see red at times, I swear to you! However, what were we saying? Oh yes... what do you think of this new freak of his? Going and marrying again, at his age, and one of that clan, too! Why, by all the saints in heaven, the man's father, I tell you, the man's father went to church for the Te Deum when your grandfather was sent into exile! And he, he, this Don Flaminio Salvo.... Corpo di Dio, do you know that I have had to put up with him for a whole month at Valsania? Oh, he's a feckless creature, your uncle Don Cosmo! He ought to have looked him straight in the face and said no. 'What!' he ought to have said. 'Flaminio Salvo at Valsania?' No, Sir! Nothing of the sort! Only too delighted! And do you know how I have been living for the last month? Like an animal that goes about everywhere searching for a hole or cranny to hide in. If I set eyes on him, sangue di... I 'Id catch him here, I tell you, by the throat, and then, mark my words, I'Id squeeze the life out of him. You know what I'm like when the fit takes me, what a wild beast I become.... However! This Don Flaminio Salvo, in Forty-Eight, what did he do? I can tell you what he did, he went straight off and reported to the Bourbon police where Don Stefano Auriti was hiding with your aunt Donna Caterina. It's a fact! And now, at Girgenti, he holds all the priests in the hollow of his hand! But God, oh, yes, God has chastised him! His wife is mad! A pity his daughter... no, she's not like him: she's good, his daughter is; and as pretty as she's good.... But don't you ever take it into your head to marry her! You, my dear boy, bear your grandfather's name, remember that! And the name Gerlando Laurentano ought to be ... what shall I say? No, my dear hoy, you mustn't laugh... these things are not to be laughed at in my presence!"

"I am laughing," Lando had informed him, "because my father has chosen a good ambassador to persuade me to come to his wedding!"

And Mauro, throwing out his hands:

"Oh, what of that? I tell him the same to his face. Besides, if I don't say things, you can read them just the same on mine.... A man must act as he feels. But you have got to come back with me, my boy, because your father's word is law. You are not going of your own accord. He has made his bed, and he must lie on it. If he has chosen to go that way, what is to be done? You will come for a few days to Valsania for a rest; you will lose your temper a bit with that fool your uncle Don Cosmo; but after all I'm there, there's the General's room, untouched, just as it was. ... Go in there, and your breast... oh, it swells, and your heart thumps.... I don't know about you, but I should think... Excuse me, let me listen to the clock."

He had come close to him, had placed his ear against his chest, over the heart, and, with a roguish laugh, had concluded:

"I see! Ladies' time."

DEEDS, NOT THOUGHTS!

Perfectly calm and cool to the outward eye, Lando Laurentano nourished within him a dark and bitter hatred of the times in
which he was fated to live; a hatred which never sought relief in
invective or reproaches, for he knew that, even if his complaints
had found an echo, as did those of so many genuine or pretended
malcontents, there was nothing to be gained by them.

His anger was like the fermentation of must that has gone
sour in a dirty barrel.

The vintage had been gathered. All the vine leaves were
now yellow; they curled and shrivelled on their stems; began to fall;
the bare canes writhed in the autumnal mist, like a man stretching
his limbs in a long yawn of boredom; over the grey expanse of the
fields, in the damp fog, nothing now remained save a slight, slow,
silent, rustle of drifting leaves.

Yes, the season had yielded its fruit. He had come when
the vintage was already over. The rich and generous juice, gathered
in Sicily with impetuous joy, blended with the dry, sharp juice of
Piedmont, then with the rough, stinging juice of Tuscany, and now
with the medicinal juice, gathered late in season and half by stealth
in the Lord's vineyard, carelessly stored in three vats and in barrels,
carelessly treated, now with bark and now with alum, had gone irremediably sour. A sterile age, of necessity, was his, like every age
that follows a period of exceptional exuberance. Nothing to do hut
look on, sad and idle, at the spectacle of all those who had lent a
hand to the task, and preferred now to put the finishing touches
unaided; some of them, however, overexcited and almost raving,
others already tired and basking with a senile smile of self-
sufficiency in the satisfaction of an arduous labour that has some-

how been finished, the defects in which they did not choose either to behold themselves or to let others behold.

A miserable fate, indeed, that of the hero who does not die, the hero who outlives his own fame!

For in truth the hero always dies with the heroic moment: the man survives, and fares ill. Alas for him if his soul does not explode with the force of that driving wind which inflates it, strains it and makes it assume in an instant a forbidding mask of greatness!... After that strain, when the wind has fallen, the outraged soul cannot settle again within its normal dimensions, does not recover its equilibrium: swollen still and distended in one place, flabby and battered in another, it collapses altogether and, like a balloon when its valve has begun to leak, stumbles and is torn by every stump on the roadside over which it had flown before.

Lando Laurentano sought no outlet for his anger, because, having been too young at first to do anything, and finding nothing now left for him to do, he scorned the too obvious course of saying that the others had done wrong. To do things ... yes, to be able to do things, without talking! The others had done things. Now it was time for talk. The others talked so much and to so little purpose, that he might as well spare his breath.

He saw that the men to whose lot it had fallen to do things, had long been hesitating between two conceptions, one vacuous, the other servile: the conceptions of a classic and of a romantic Italy: a toga-clad phantom, and a puppet to be dressed up in the livery or at the bidding of foreigners: a rhetorical Italy, composed of schoolroom memories, the same perhaps for which Petrarch had longed, which had inspired Cola di Rienzo, a Republican State; and a foreign Italy, or one wholly foreignized in soul and customs. Unfortunately, the trend of history pointed to the realization of the latter conception. And, after all, it was no more than the substitution of one form of rhetoric for another; for the pedantic imitation of the ancients, the absurd imitation of foreigners. Always imitation. "Oh Italians," Guerrazzi had cried from his cell in the Murate of Florence, "monkeys, not men!"

Its most generous impulses stifled by so-called reasons of State, the nation had been brought to being by concession and compromise, accident and coincidence. A single fire, a single flame ought to have coursed from end to end of Italy to melt and forge her several members into one living body. That the fusion had failed was the fault of those who had reckoned the open flame dangerous, and had preferred the cold light of their own limited, calculating intellects. But if the flame had let itself be quenched, was not this a sign that it had not in itself the force and heat that were required? What a blaze of bright and devouring fire from Sicily, up north as far as Naples! >From there again, in later years, the flame had shot forth to reach the walls of Rome.... Wherever it had been obliged to halt, at Aspromonte, or on the heights of the Trentino, it had left an empty gap, a severed member.

Could not Italy fashion herself in any other way? A sign that events were not yet ripe, or that someone had lacked the energy and daring to bring things to a head. Too many calculations and dark thoughts and vacillations and restraints and timidities had sterilized the creation of the country.

What was to be done now? Where there is a will, yes, there is always time to do good. But a modest, humble, patient good, Lando Laurentano felt that such was not for him. They had offered him, at the last general election, a seat in one of the divisions of Palermo: neither prayers nor pressure, nor the call of party discipline had availed to make him reconsider his refusal. He, at Montecitorio, at such a moment? Better to drown himself in a sewer!

From his boyhood he had trained himself to a strict and strenuous course of reading, not so much from the necessity or a passion for culture, as to be able to think and judge on his own initiative, and so to retain, in conversation with other people, his own spiritual independence.

He had here, in his lonely villino on the Via Sommacampagna, a well stocked library, in which he was in the habit of spending several hours every day. But, as he read, he was irresistibly led on to translate all that he read into action, into living reality; and, if he had a volume of history in his hands, he would feel an indescribable sense of discomfort at seeing, reduced to words, what had once upon a time been life; reduced to ten or twenty lines of print, uniformly arranged one after another, in precise order, what had been a disordered movement, stir and turmoil. He would fling the book from him, in a fit of disgust, and begin to pace up and down the room.

What a strange impression they made upon him then, all those books in the prison of their tall, wide shelves, which covered the four walls of the room from end to end! From the two low windows that overlooked the garden, came in the shrill, incessant, deafening twitter of the countless little birds that made their daily rendezvous there on the pine, aquiver with more wings than foliage. He compared that continuous, unwearying chorus, that frenzied tumult of living voices, with the words shut up in those dumb books, and his contempt for them increased. Artificial compositions, a fixed life, stereotyped in unalterable forms, logical constructions, mental architecture, inductions, deductions--away with them all!

Movement, life, not thoughts!

What anguish, what torture at times, did he let himself be absorbed in the thought that he too, inevitably, with the conceptions, the opinions that he sought to form of men and things, with the fictions that he created, with the affections, the desires that arose in him, was arresting, was fixing in and all around himself in definite forms the continual flow of life! But if he himself, with his body, was a definite form, a form that had motion, that could follow, up to a certain point, the flow of life, until, his body stiffening ever more and more, its motion, already slackened, should altogether cease! Well, on certain days, he would feel a strange antipathy to that body of his, so tall and slim, for his sallow brown face with its too wide forehead, its black, square-cut beard, its imperious nose in contrast to those eyes, the eyes of a drowsy, voluptuous Arab. He would gaze at them in the glass as though they did not belong to him. Within that body of his, meanwhile, in what he called his soul, the flow continued obscurely, creeping beneath the dykes, flooding beyond the limits he had set himself when forming a consciousness, constructing a personality. But it was possible also that all those artificial forms, assailed by the current in a moment of tempest, might crumble; while that part of the current which did not trickle away beneath the dykes and beyond the limits, but revealed itself plainly to him, and which he had carefully canalized in his affections, in the duties that he had set himself, in the habits that he had developed, might in a moment of flood burst its banks and sweep everything away.

Yes: and it was for such a moment of flood that he longed! It was for this that he had immersed himself in the study of the new social questions, in the criticism of those men who, armed with imposing arguments, were trying to raze to its foundations a constituted order of things convenient for some, unfair to the majority of mankind, and to arouse at the same time in that majority a will and a sentiment which spurred them on to strip, destroy, scatter all those forms, the accumulation of centuries, in which life had become ponderously set. Would that will, would that sentiment arise in the majority in sufficient strength to bring about an immediate upheaval? They still lacked the necessary consciousness and education. To make them conscious, to educate, to prepare them: there was an ideal! But when was it to be realized? A slow, long and patient task this too, alas!

On his vast estates in Sicily, in the Province of Palermo, which had come to him from his mother, he had already granted his peasants the fairest co-operative terms, expressly forbidding his chamberlain to burden with even a nominal interest the advances liberally made them for seed and for all the various outlay entailed in agriculture; he had founded, and maintained out of his own pocket a number of village schools; time and again, whenever he was asked, he had contributed largely to the reserve funds raised for the support of the peasants and sulphur workers in their resistance to the landlords and pit owners; he paid for the printing of a party newspaper: *La Nuova Eta*, which was issued every Sunday in Palermo.

His chamberlain, Rosario Piro, sent up protests, month after month, in interminable letters full of commonsense and malapropisms: protested and washed his hands of the whole affair. Poor Piro! What a state those hands of his must be in, after all that washing!

Lando, perhaps without noticing it, or even in the belief that he was leading a sober existence, was spending a great deal on himself. His experience of the emptiness and silliness of the life of people who made a profession of cutting a figure in the so-called world of fashion, in clubs, smart hotels and restaurants, gaming-rooms, on race courses, in the hunting field, he had bought not from any wish to acquire it, but so that he might not appear to be different from other people in a matter of so little importance to himself, and one that after all entailed no sacrifice, in view of his gentlemanly upbringing and social connexions; he continued to buy this experience, in instalments, and at a high price, whenever he felt an overpowering need to attach himself to the solid foundations of human beastliness so as to escape from or to resist certain strange impulses, certain caprices of the imagination, the maddening uncertainties of the brain. He would devote himself then to violent exercise with a coolness which at times repelled himself even, or to sensual pleasures, the scented and dazzling outward refinement of which was powerless to conceal their grim vulgarity.

But in his inertia he felt the gnawing tooth; amid the cravings of his enforced inactivity, he felt himself stifled, all the more in that he compelled himself to repress those cravings, rather than let himself be conspicuous, ever. And while he smiled, as he listened at the club or elsewhere to the silly chatter of his friends, dangling his foot or stroking his beard, he would coldly imagine some sudden outburst which would throw into a confusion at once ridiculous and alarming all this fatuous, artificial world, in which it seemed incredible to him that other people could seriously live and find contentment. Other people? What about himself? In what world did he live? He was not contented, it was true; but what did he gain by being discontented? Why, these cravings. No ephemeral desires, no satisfying of appetites did his senses find there: to withdraw would not have cost him any effort of will; indeed, he had to make an effort to remain there, as though to him it were the performance of an irksome duty, the payment of a penalty.

On the other hand, would it not drive him mad if he were to remain entirely by himself? So great was his discontent with his own arid existence, with no germ in it of warm, living desires. At night, sometimes, as he returned home with the blackest of black dogs on his back, he felt so strongly the impression that he was going to find, in the solitude of his villino, his own spirit, which had not stirred from the house, and would greet him presently from the mirror with a sneer on its face, and ask him if it was a fine night outside, if there was a moon, if one of the electric lamps had not spluttered at him as he passed, or if Saint Paul, tired of stand-ing, had not sat down upon the Antonine column; so strongly did he feel this impression, that he would turn back, to keep his body out of doors, and not expose it to such derision. There it was, his fine body, sleek and well-tended, smartly dressed... who was going to quarrel with it at that time of night? He would stop for a mo-ment to listen to the nocturnal silence round him; it seemed to him that this silence was burrowing backward into time, into the past history of Rome, and was becoming terrible. A shudder ran down his back. The night lay heavy upon a city thousands of years old, through which he was passing, an empty, pigmy shadow, which a breath of air would have swept away.

>From these not infrequent lapses he was invariably re-called to himself by the arrival from Palermo, uninvited and always ready for anything, of a friend, perhaps the only true friend that he had: Lino Apes, editor of the Nuova Eta: Socrates, Lando called him. And indeed, Lino Apes did remind one of Socrates, in his ug-liness and in his humour: tall, all neck and no shoulders, with arms that dangled down to his knees, a receding forehead, a pug nose, and a pair of keen, darting eyes, which began to laugh before his mouth, both eyes and mouth half hidden by his thick overhanging eyebrows and bristling moustaches respectively.

Without a penny to his name, amid incredible hardships cheerfully borne, he had supported himself during his student days, and graduated in Literature and Philosophy; devoid of ambition, he had turned to teaching on lines of his own in an elementary school, greatly to the delight of his pupils and the annoyance of the head-master, who dared not rebuke him officially. He spent the rest of the day squandering in conversation the inexhaustible treasure of his ideas, which, after a long circulation, returned to him barely recognizable, each of them stamped by the foolishness or vanity of whoever had appropriated it. His talk was a perennial fount of the most specious arguments, from which would suddenly flash a new and strange light that made everything unexpectedly simple and clear.

Lino Apes had many times proved to Lando Laurentano that, in calling himself a Socialist, he was lying with the most inno-cent sincerity; he saw himself not as he was, but as he would have liked to be. Which, he maintained, is what happens to all of us, and makes us ridiculous.

Socialist, a man without discipline? Socialist, an enemy, not of this or that order, but of order as a whole, of every definite form? A Socialist he was for the moment: for that great moment of flood for which he longed. But the majority of Socialists, for that matter, were just the same, and he might console himself with the thought, or rather feel contempt for them. In any event, he would always have one distinguishing feature: that of being the one rich man among a crowd of poor and of having his blood sucked by them all, including himself, Lino Apes, editor of the *Nuova Eta* and private inspector of the village schools endowed by H.E. the young Prince of Laurentano. Lando enjoyed listening to him. Anything that other people might say to him left him discontented and unsatisfied, as did anything that he might say himself, albeit he quite recognised that it was often to the point. He recognised also that ever so many people spoke better than himself; but what after all was the value of all those words, all those arguments, all those sound ideas, all those sensible observations? Inwardly, he uttered an exasperated cry of protest: "No, no, it is not that!" though he could not for the life of him have told what else it could be. But all the rest, the sparks, the lightning flashes that blazed in his spirit, were not to be expressed in words: he would have been thought mad, had he expressed them. Well, Lino Apes, Socrates, had this faculty: he could express them, yet he was reckoned wise.

He had received from him, of late, letter after letter, each of them urging him in the strongest language to return to Sicily. Never had the cocks in the scorched farmyards held their crests so fiery and erect, never had they hurled their clarion more defiantly across the fields to salute the rising sun, which for the first time, after an agelong night, was stirring the consciousness of the workers. Consciousness? For want of a better word. For the Church they had substituted the Fascio; and looked to it for all the miracles demanded in vain of its predecessor. But fanaticism was at its height: and so miracles were possible and the task of the spellbinders mere child's play. The floodgates were strained to bursting point, and in another moment the torrent might sweep away "the tainted seats of the bourgeois domination" unprotected now by a military garrison. He must hasten to the spot and take action before Sicily was invaded by troops and the reaction began.

Lando was stirred by the call to action, but could not tear himself from Rome at the moment. The bank scandal was like a fiery crater yawning before the steps of the national Parliament: one after another, as they emerged from its doors, the putrid carcasses of the "old patriotism" would be hurled into it; and that fire, by devouring them, would purge the country. The spectacle was quite enlivening in its obscene terror. But it might not have been so, perhaps, to Lando, had he not been waiting with fierce anxiety to see engulfed in that crater one man: Corrado Selmi.

Ah, at last!... Already he could see him like a tree half stripped by the heat of the approaching lava: perhaps even before being touched by the devouring tide of fire, he would vanish in a roaring blaze. And Lando hoped that his spirit would be illuminated by that blaze. Ah, if only for a moment! The harm that man had done him was past remedy: it had permanently clouded his life, had destroyed for ever all hope of turning back, of again approaching her who in his first manhood had made him realize eternity in a flash of light: a light that sparkled from a pair of dark eyes and a fleeting smile, one evening in May, upon the lighted sea front at Palermo, amid the rattle of carriage wheels, the odour of seaweed that rose from the water, the scent of orange-blossom that was wafted from the gardens. For the divine, ineradicable memory of that instant he would certainly have returned to his cousin; almost without remorse, at least without profanation on his part, once her old husband was dead, he could once more have made her his own. And it was for this reason that he had repulsed her, when she, in a moment of madness, had sought with a frenzied desperation to cling to him. And that other had then taken a scoundrelly advantage of her.

No, he could not leave Rome at that moment.

Now, when he was summoned so urgently, for very different reasons, to Sicily, the reason for which Mauro Mortara had come could not fail to strike him as a grotesque tomfoolery. He felt that it was certainly not for the pleasure of seeing him that his father wished him to be present at this marriage ceremony, but owing to a want of confidence on Salvo's part, which he found offensive. And, as the easiest way out of the difficulty, he decided to write him a letter, giving him full reassurance, after which the marriage might be celebrated without his having to put in an appearance.

To Lino Apes he wrote that, before moving, he would like to consult all the comrades who would be passing through Rome in the course of the next few days on their way to the Congress at Reggio Emilia. A meeting would be held in his house, at which Socrates must be present with the rest. Lando would pay the cost of the journey, as well for him as for the representatives of the principal Fasci, from whom he desired a precise statement of the circumstances in which the battle was to be engaged; and if these were really favourable, he would not hesitate for a moment to dash into the fray, to risk all, and damn the consequences.

Two days after he had posted this letter, there came to his ear the report of the Government's scandalous attempt to whitewash Selmi. This fairly turned his stomach, and in a boiling rage he decided to go off at once and set a match to the trains of powder that had been laid in Sicily. Next morning, while he was discussing his immediate departure with Mauro Mortara, he was informed that his cousin, Giulio Auriti, was at the door.

Mauro had gone twice to Roberto's house in Via delle Colonnette, but had not found him at home. Before leaving Rome, he would have liked at least to have paid him his respects. He did not know Giulio, having seen him two or three tunes only as a boy; as soon as he saw him enter the room he gave a violent start:

"Don Stefano!" he exclaimed. "Oh, my son! Don Stefano to the life.... Every inch of him! The same face... the same figure...."

Then, observing that the young man, in his acute agitation, stood gazing at him with a cold, frowning perplexity:

"Don't you know who I am?" he went on. "I am Mauro Mortara. Your father died here, in these arms, with a bullet in his breast, here, below the throat. He had a muffler round his neck, and a corner of it had been driven into the wound: he could not speak; with those eyes of yours, in his agony, while I held him up, he entrusted his son to my care, your brother, whom I was thrusting away with my elbow, screening your father's body with my own, so that he should not see it...."

302

Giulio Auriti clapped both his hands to his face and burst into sobs.

Lando, knowing his cousin's rigid fibre, his icy self-control, turned and gazed at him in wonder and dismay. He went up to him; laid a hand on his shoulder:

"Giulio!"

"You would have done better, had you let him see it!" said his cousin, turning to Mauro, recovering himself instantly at the sound of his own name. "He would have retained a more vivid impression. He was too young! And he has remained young. Young and blind. I have something to say to you," he then added, turning again to Lando, and rubbed his eyes with the back of his hand, as though to remove any trace of tears.

Mauro did not understand a word of this: his eyes fixed on the distant vision of the battlefield, he shook his head slowly, and sighed:

"A fine death! A fine death! A son may weep for it; but, when you think it over, it's a thing to rejoice at. It was a joy for us to die! What sort of death shall we have now? Old men, soiling the beds we lie on.... Enough; I am going. Is Don Roberto at home? I want to bid him goodbye. I have seen Rome, though, and even huddled away in a corner, devoured by flies, I can die content. ..."

With a careless wave of his hand he left the room.

FACE TO FACE.

All through the night after his talk with Francesco D'Atri, Giulio Auriti, instead of thinking of what he ought to say to his cousin in order to obtain the help that he was driven to ask of him, anticipating a hostile reception, had, to screw up his courage for the task, summoned up, amid incessant bursts of incoherent anger, thoughts and arguments which he would not be able to express to the other; had found comfort in saying to himself what he would not be able to say to him; had tried to convince himself that he was really entitled to such help.

And it had struck him that only in appearances had his relations with his cousin, hitherto, been cordial. What a store of undisclosed envy and rancour had necessity brought up that night from the secret depths of his being!

Until then he had been of the opinion that the lowliness of his position as a clerk in a government office, concealed, at the cost of so many sacrifices, beneath the garments of a gentleman, could not degrade him in the eyes of his rich and titled cousin, because Lando must know it was the result of his mother's proud, contemptuous act of renunciation; and that so far as nobility went, his birth was in no way inferior, in view of his father's career. But now? With Roberto unworthily compromised in this bank scandal, and himself obliged to sue for help, the foundations of his pride crumbled miserably, and with them, in an instant, those of his cordiality towards his cousin. And he had prepared himself for this talk with him as for an assault upon an enemy. An enemy, yes, for Lando would certainly refuse to help, knowing that the money in question had been taken by Selmi. He himself would be obliged to confess everything. But Lando ought to bear in mind, perdio, that

neither would Roberto have been reduced to the position of blindly doing these favours for Selmi, in return for other favours; nor
would he himself now be obliged to ask for help, had their mother
not renounced her inheritance! The money for which he would ask
him represented only a fractional part, after all, of the fortune
which his mother had contemptuously resigned to her elder brother; and he might even claim it as an act of restitution, given this
horrible necessity. His own sacrifice in asking for it would be just
as great as Lando's in giving it.

Now, Mauro Mortara having left the room, after arousing
that sudden emotion in him by recalling the heroic death of his
father, he, face to face with his cousin who was looking at him with
some dismay, waiting, anxious and friendly, for him to begin, remained for a while speechless, torn by his painful excitement. He
screwed up his face in a paroxysm of grief and, wringing his
clasped hands until the joints cracked:

"I need your help, Lando," he said. "This is a terrible moment for me, from which only you can deliver me, but... I warn you,
by a considerable sacrifice on your part also, moral and material."

Lando, confused, perplexed, pained by the sight of his cousin in such agitation and distress, gathering moreover from his
words the seriousness of what he was going to ask, murmured,
throwing out his hands:

"Speak.... Anything I can do..."

"Ah, no!" Giulio at once interrupted him, stung by the
commonplace expression. "It is difficult, difficult, for me as well as
for you, don't you know. But you must remember that my life,
Lando, my mother's life, our honour, are... are in your hands, there
you have it! Remember this, and then perhaps... I hope... you will
find the strength to make the sacrifice that I ask of you."

"You alarm me!" exclaimed Lando. "Speak; what has happened to you?"

Giulio again wrung his hands, convulsively, struck his lips
with them, still clasped, several times, keeping his eyes tightly shut.
The swollen veins on his contracted forehead showed what a tremendous effort he was making to control himself.

"If I tell you the whole story," he broke out, wildly, "will
you help me?"

"Why not?" asked Lando, in a tone of distress. "What is it? I can't until I know what it is all about."

"Myself," Giulio promptly replied. "Think that it concerns me alone, or rather my mother. Keep before your mind my mother and all, all the sorrows of our family. You do feel some regard and affection for my mother, don't you?"

"Why of course, you know I do!" Lando assured him, shewing a genuine interest. "Don't keep me in suspense, for heaven's sake!"

"Wait... wait..." Auriti begged him, as though he could not bear to strike out from this stream of tenderness into the bitter waters in which he must drown. "To us, to myself, it is everything; her pride, her sentiment... by reason of which, without a word of complaint at any time, we have been brought down to... this ... I don't know, I really don't know how to tell you; but we have nothing else, we have never had anything else except our pride... and now ... now..."

"Calm yourself, Giulio!" Lando again exhorted him, with a stir of impatience. "I don't understand. ... You need me. Speak, tell me.... Your mother..."

"I have to prevent her from dying!" cried Giulio. "At any cost! And you have got to help me, Lando; and to help me you must make the sacrifice of overcoming all resentment, every reason for hatred of a man who is the cause of all this ruin, and whom I detest and curse as heartily as you do and would like to see lying dead, by the same torture, with the same infamy that he is inflicting upon us!"

Lando at once stiffened, and knitted his brows.

"You mean Selmi?" he asked. "Roberto... with Selmi?"

Giulio nodded his head; then, briefly, concisely, explained his brother's position and the steps that must be taken to save him, omitting any reference to his conversation overnight with H.E. the Minister D'Atri.

But Lando, already forewarned, his thoughts concentrated on a single point, gathered nothing more at first from his cousin's breathless appeal than that saving Roberto from his predicament meant saving Selmi as well, and that Selmi's safety might still be dependent upon that of his cousin. He looked Giulio in the face, as though he were only now conscious of his presence in the room:

"What?" he exclaimed, in amazement. "You come to me, Giulio, and ask this? To me, of all people?"

Crushed by this question, uttered in such a tone of amazement, Giulio lost his head for a moment, and, as though his passion had melted into an envenomed bitterness:

"To whom... to whom else?" he stammered. "You know what my family.... And besides ... remember, I asked you, when I came in, to make a sacrifice...."

"A sacrifice, indeed! No!" Lando shouted. "It is not in human nature! You come to me and ask this? Why, don't you know what that man means to me?"

"That is why I told you..." Giulio attempted to interpose.

"What did you tell me? No!" Lando again broke out. "You come to me, Giulio, and say: 'Here is the weapon, the one weapon with which you can slay the enemy who still escapes your vengeance; but no! This weapon you must not use; you must rather help me to conceal it, to destroy it, so as to save him!' That is what you come and tell me!"

"Because you are thinking of Selmi, that is why, you are thinking of Selmi and are incapable of thinking of anyone else!" Auriti moaned. "I knew it! When I have told you all, will you give me your help?"

"Help?" Lando again retorted. "You call this help? On my part, it would be complicity! Do you wish me to be your accomplice in saving Selmi?"

"There you go!" cried Giulio. "Roberto! I want to save Roberto! My mother! What do I care about Selmi? I hate him, I tell you, I detest him as much as you do! But I must save Roberto...."

Lando, with a violent effort, succeeded in forcing himself to keep calm in the face of his cousin's blind, despairing obstinacy. He decided to try and reason with him.

"Excuse me," he began. "Look here, Giulio, answer me one thing. Is Roberto guilty? Do you believe him guilty?"

"Guilty or innocent," replied Giulio, quivering with rage, "that is not the point! He is compromised!"

"But he can defend himself, good God!" Lando at once retorted.

"Thank you! I know he can. But I have got to prevent his being charged, his being arrested, don't you understand?" Auriti explained. "1 know that he can defend himself! And if he should refuse to defend himself..."

"Oh, in that case... why, of course!" Lando assented. "You and I together..."

"No, thank you!" Giulio declined the offer, in a burst of scorn. "Help in words, thank you! I can manage that. I had no need to come to you."

"Pardon me," said Lando, with a note of irritation in his voice. "The only honest form of help ... the only true, the only ho-nourable defence, must be this. Payment would be complicity. Roberto ought to speak; not to make himself Sehni's accomplice, by keeping silence and paying up for him."

"And you propose, then," demanded Giulio, "that he should submit to the ignominy of arrest and imprisonment, when I can still save him from it?"

"With money?"

"With money, with money," Giulio repeated. "Honesty, dishonesty, what are you getting at now? It is enough for me to know that he is honest, in my own conscience! Who would believe in his honesty to-morrow, if he were arrested today? Who ever be-lieves in the defence, in the words of a man who has been in prison? Lando, for pity's sake, let us make the experiment... think only of Roberto! You, mark my words, you refuse me your help just now, simply and solely because you wish to make Roberto the instrument of your vengeance!"

"No, that is not true!" Lando emphatically denied the sug-gestion. "But I cannot make myself, don't you see, the instrument of Selmi's salvation? You are inflicting an inhuman torture on me! I cannot, I must not submit to it! For Roberto, I would do anything! But if Roberto is hopelessly involved with Selmi, and my help to one may be of service to the other, no, I cannot give it, nor can you ask it of me!"

Giulio Auriti remained silent for a while, brooding darkly.

"Then the answer is no?" he said at length, raising his head and looking his cousin in the face.

To this categorical question, Lando, filled with a profound

pity, was incapable of replying with another curt refusal. He clasped his hands together, went up to Auriti, and said:

"But quite apart from, any personal reason, Giulio, think... think of my associations, of my views, the ideas for which I am fighting.... I could not, after this, take my place among my comrades in this work of purifying the country which we have undertaken..."

He realized at once that he ought not to be speaking thus, and at the same time was unable to stop, albeit he noticed with dismay how his cousin's face darkened at every word that he spoke. Finally he saw him spring to his feet, convulsed with rage.

"Purifying, oh yes!" exclaimed Giulio Auriti, with a horrible sneer. "You are in a position to purify! You are the pure in heart, you people! We, I, Roberto, my father, too, if he were alive..."

"Giulio! Giulio!" Lando tried to stop him, genuinely pained.

But Auriti, beside himself, went on shouting:

"Tainted, all of us! And I would coin false money, yes, and rob a bank, to have these forty thousand lire, which you have got and I haven't. And because I haven't got them, I am tainted! You have them, and are pure! But just bear in mind that my mother, after all, could have had the money, and refused to take it, because she regarded it as tainted!"

Lando drew himself up to his full height and, standing in the middle of the room, looked his cousin up and down with a frigid dignity: "My money," he said, "is, as you know, only what came to me from my mother."

But, having uttered this retort, he at once regretted it, and his face clouded with disgust at the trivial crudity of the turn the discussion was taking. It flashed across his mind that, by an unfair arrangement, in his mother's family, too, one member had paid with a life of poverty for a warm-hearted act of rebellion; it occurred to him that among all the reasons for which, in his youthful fervour, he had wished to make Giannetta Montalto his, he had included this, namely the restoration to her of a part at least of all that had been taken from her disinherited father. He guessed that his cousin would reply to his arrogant, ill-considered assertion and would drag down the sordid squabble to lower depths still.

And indeed Giulio Auriti, contorting his worried features, striking his clenched fists together and then spreading out his hands before his eyes that were flashing with a blaze of scorn, sneered:

"Your mother's money too, for that matter!"

And Lando, under this provocation, once again could not restrain himself.

"My mother's money?" he demanded, planting himself in front of the other.

Giulio Auriti passed his hand over a brow cold with sweat, covered his eyes, collapsed miserably:

"Don't make me say any more!"

Lando stood gazing at him, or rather into him; then remarked, crudely and coldly, in a subdued tone, through his teeth, isolating each syllable:

"And even if I admitted what you think, would you have me pay a debt contracted by Selmi to pay for the whims of a woman who is in a position to object to my mother's money? Go, go, go... for goodness' sake, go away!" he broke out, screening his own eyes also. "I can never look you in the face again!"

He heard his cousin leave the room, but still remained for a long time with his hands over his face, in the horror that he felt at having touched the lurid depths of a reality to which he could never have expected to descend, and the horrible impression of which would always remain in his mind. Now, rising again from those depths, into which he had slithered for a moment, would not everything round about him seem false and vacuous and foul? In all his feelings, ideas, actions, words, would not some mark remain, the imprint of the mud he had handled?

With tight shut eyes, set teeth and lips parted, dry and bitter, he rubbed his hands vigorously. Then he opened his eyes, looked round the room; he felt himself stifling, and went across to a window that overlooked the garden.

Everything, ah, everything was the same!... Everything was disgusting at that moment! The pestilence was in the air. The whole social carcass was rotting, and with it his soul, all his thoughts, all his feelings... everything in decay, everything filthy.....

TO NO CONCLUSION.

Three days later, in the big library, were assembled the comrades who were on their way to the Socialist Congress at Reggio Emilia; the representatives of the more numerous Fasci of the Island, invited by Lando; a few Deputies, his friends, some Milanese of the Italian Labour Party, and Lino Apes.

Conspicuous among this crowd of men was a girl in a red jacket and black sailor hat, with a cock's feather boldly erect at one side: Celsina Pigna, who had come in place of Luca Lizio to represent the Fascio of Girgenti.

Everyone was determined not to shew surprise at her presence; but she did not fail to observe the rapid, furtive glances that all of them cast at her, especially the less youthful; and remarked, laughing quietly to herself, that the few who obstinately refrained from looking at her assumed for her benefit languid or haughty poses, and for her benefit, when they spoke, gave certain modulations to their voices, some plangent, others bold, all of which alike betrayed that animal excitement which a woman's presence is wont to arouse in men. She remarked further in more than one of them a different form of ostentation: namely, an almost contemptuous indifference, which betrayed their secret discomfort at finding themselves in a rich and well-appointed house.

Lando Laurentano had not yet arrived. Lino Apes, in his name, had begged the company to excuse him, promising that he would join them immediately. While they waited, several groups had formed: two by the windows overlooking the garden, one by the table set at the end of the room for the chairman of the meeting. Some were pacing the floor, wrapped in thought, others were reading the titles on the backs of the books in the shelves, straining their ears to catch what was being said in one or other of the groups. A few were keeping a stealthy watch on one of the Deputies, who, striding up and down the room with his fingers thrust into the pockets of his waistcoat, kept shrugging his shoulders from time to time, thrusting his head forward and, to indicate his surprise and sympathy, stiffening the line of his mouth beneath the shaggy red moustaches that were already turning grey.

This was the Republican Deputy Spiridione Covazza, who had recently published a disparaging criticism, in a French review, of the organization of the proletariat forces in Sicily. Seeing himself avoided by everyone, he seemed by his gesture to be saying: "Incredible!" And yet he must have known that his crime was that of seeing all manner of things which other people did not see, and of giving to them an importance which other people did not yet feel, because in the heat of passion everything seems to rise up to the level of our own feelings. Illusions: soap bubbles, which may at any moment turn into leaden bullets. As those poor peasants knew only too well who had been shot down at Caltavuturo.

He had written for that French review what he conscientiously believed to be the truth; in his usual style, rudely and crudely. But they implied that he took a savage delight in setting forth like that, at the wrong time and in the wrong place, the most unpalatable truths, in killing with the frost of his arguments all enthusiasm, every flame of the ideal, to which, notwithstanding, he was irresistibly drawn.

A beetle with the wings of a moth, so Lino Apes had defined him in the *Nuova Eta;* when he touched the flame, the moth's wings vanished, the beetle remained.

Calumny and ingratitude! The fact of the matter was that he felt it his duty to remain frigid among all these youthful flames, for, if these were not fires of straw, he himself would be kindled by them in time; and if they were, he was acting in the common interest in quenching them.

Doubtless his personal appearance, at once sleek and unkempt, the pale, glassy eyes, that peered sharply through his spectacles, his beak of a nose, the sound of his voice, combined to give people that impression of him, to arouse in everyone a repulsion all the more irritating, in that afterwards they were all bound to admit that events had almost invariably proved him to be in the right, to admit his vast and profound learning, the rectitude of his mind and conscience, the honesty of his intentions, and to respect and indeed admire his brutal and contemptuous frankness and the courage with which he challenged unpopularity.

For this hostile reception, meanwhile, Spiridi-one Covazza knew that he was indebted principally to three young Sicilians, who were surrounded at that moment by a fervent crowd of admirers: Bixio Bruno, Cataldo Sclafani and Nicasio Ingrao, who had felt themselves to be especially injured by his criticism.

Each of them formed the centre of one of the three groups that had collected in the room. Bixio Bruno, tall and slim, with his bold olive-hued face and thick, curling, negroid hair, was explaining with fluent, highly coloured eloquence, curving his full, red lips in a faint smile of self-satisfaction, how in a short time he had succeeded in uniting in a single Fascio the six-and-twenty workmen's corporations, the discordant guilds, whose discarded banners now hung side by side in the hall as trophies of victory. He appeared to be full of confidence and sure of a triumph. People were expecting at any moment a reaction on the part of the Government, dissolution of the Fasci, arrests, military occupation. But the good seed had been sown! Any suppression, any persecution would only enhance the greatness of the victory. How could anyone arrest three hundred thousand men? No. The leaders alone, a few dozen members, at the most; very well, the secret leaders had been appointed, their names still unknown to the police, and their propaganda would continue and be more effective than before.

Cataldo Sclafani, big and sturdy, with a beard like a quickset hedge, was discoursing to the second group, with prophetic inspiration; he was saying with smiling emphasis that down yonder, where the dayspring of national unity had first risen, it was fated that there should now break the redder, more fiery dawn of the deliverance of the oppressed. Yes, everyone knew, of course, that already in the Romagna, in the Modenese, in the Provinces of Reggio Emilia and Parma, in the Cremonese, the Mantuan country, the Polesine, Italian Socialism had emerged to fight its first battle; but it was a very different state of affairs to-day in Sicily! A revelation, astounding, prodigious!

Lino Apes, as he listened to him, was almost tugging out his moustaches by the roots, in his efforts to repress a smile. He, in his letters to Lando, called Cataldo Sclafani the Messiah of the Fasci.

In the third group Nicasio Ingrao, rough and stunted, with a black, warty birthmark covering half his face, was talking to the Deputies, putting such polish as he could on his native dialect, and alternating with strange gesticulations between the foulest imprecations and an innocent, childlike appeal; he was speaking of the crisis in the Sicilian sulphur industry, and of the appalling distress among the sulphur workers, who had now been locked out for some months.

One of the comrades, the head of the Fascio of Comitini, was trying to convey to the Deputies all that Ingrao, who owned land and houses at Aragona, had done and was doing for these sulphur workers, to prevent their being led on to acts of sabotage, incendiarism and bloodshed; but Ingrao flew at him and silenced him, threatening to fell him to the ground with his fist, if he said another word.

Celsina Pigna, from the corner to which she had withdrawn, burst out laughing at this comic display of violence, and Ingrao asked her, laughing himself as well:

"Shall I slay him, Signorina?"

In the three groups all the rest of the islanders, young men between twenty and thirty, as they listened to the words of these three leaders, men who were in the public eye, were swelling with pride, and almost moved to tears. They were confident, in their sincere youthful fatuity, that they were playing a part without precedent in history, even there in Rome. They had seen, at the feet of these three leaders of the Central Committee, thousands of women, thousands of peasants, whole populations of islanders, delirious, throwing flowers, falling on their faces on the ground, weeping and shouting, as in the old days before the images of their Saints.

The whole party turned as one man and moved towards Lando Laurentano as he hurried into the room. With apologies for his lateness, he shook hands with those of his guests who reached him first, asked them all to take their seats, and, as soon as silence was restored, began:

"I have kept you waiting, gentlemen, for a reason which is perhaps not unconnected with our interests, with the interests especially of so many of our comrades who, more than any of us, in my opinion, need our help at this moment, down in Sicily."

"The sulphur workers!" cried Ingrao, springing to his feet, as though he himself were their natural protector. "I understand!" he added. "You mean that the engineer, Aurelio Costa, is here? I understand. Ah, he travelled up with me, that gentleman! We had a long talk, and..."

Lando raised his hand in an appeal for silence.

"The engineer Aurelio Costa, precisely," he went on, "manager of the sulphur pits of Salvo, who, I understand, is one of the wealthiest mine-owners in the Province of Girgenti, has come to Rome to interest the Sicilian Deputies in a scheme..."

"Allow me!" Ingrao again interrupted. "Don't let us waste time, gentlemen! Let me explain to you how matters stand. Signor Salvo is shortly to be connected, through a sister of his, with the Prince of Laurentano..."

A murmur of protest rose at Ingrao's rudeness to Lando, to whom every eye now turned in apology for the discourtesy. But Lando, with a smile, hastened to interpose:

"Not with me, please! Not with me!"

Whereupon Ingrao, with an angry shrug, shouted:

"Holy Mother of God, what do you take me for? Didn't I say the Prince? Would I call our revered friend, our beloved host and comrade, Prince? Not that it makes any difference, but he knows that it adds nothing to his dignity if we call him Prince, and he knows that we do not wish to degrade him by calling him simply Laurentano. I allude to the Prince his father; and Lando Laurentano cannot take offence at my words. If he does, he's a silly idiot; I rise to speak, instead of him, because he lives in Rome, I live among the sulphur pits, and I know that the sole object of Signor Salvo's scheme is to curry favour with the Prince's son, by letting him see that he has the welfare of the sulphur workers at heart. Stuff and nonsense! Dust in our eyes! Signor Salvo knows as well as I do that his scheme is all damned rot. Yes, gentlemen, I call a spade a spade. If he really wants to do something, let Signor Salvo clear out of the sulphur pits that he owns the so-called *bot-*

teghe, the truck-shops where the workers are forced to provide themselves with the hare necessities of life, at a hundred per cent profit to him: wine, that is nothing but vinegar; bread, that is made of stones!"

Spiridione Covazza thereupon asked leave to speak, the whole company turning to face him with a hostile expression.

"Are you going to defend the truck-shops next?" Ingrao jeered.

Covazza did not turn a hair.

"I should like to know," he said quietly, "the general outlines of this scheme."

"I tell you it is all damned rot!" Ingrao again shouted.

Covazza held up his hand, still quite calm and composed.

"Really," he said, "shouting is not argument. I too have lived in the sulphur country; I have carefully studied the conditions of the industry, the complicated reasons for the crisis; and I can tell you frankly that if in present conditions the people who have least to hope for are the miners and carters, the prospects of the exploiters of the pits and the landowners are no less dismal; and if this scheme..."

He was unable to proceed. All the representatives of the Fasci sprang to their feet protesting. Lando interposed, tried to calm them, urged them to respect one another's opinions and suggested that one of their number should be appointed forthwith to preside over the discussion.

"Bruno! Bruno! Bixio Bruno!" the cry rose from different parts of the room.

And Bixio Bruno, accustomed by this time to see himself chosen in this capacity, in two strides had reached the table that stood in readiness at the end of the room.

"Gentlemen," he began. "We find ourselves, by indirect channels, carried into the heart of our discussion. The Hon. Covazza, in one of his recent articles..."

"Published abroad!" came a voice from the other end of the room.

"Abroad or in Italy, what does it matter!" retorted Bruno. "Our ideas, our party know nothing of national frontiers. In this article the Hon. Covazza has found fault with my work and with the work of my comrades."

Spiridione Covazza, his arms folded on his breast, shook his head in dissent.

"No?" Bruno queried. "How do you mean? Didn't you say that our propaganda was all a tissue of moonshine?"

"I said," Covazza replied, rising to his feet, "that your honest definitions of a liberty that shall confer, really and fully, the right to satisfy the needs of life; the explanations that you give of class warfare, the spoiled versus the spoilers, and of the programme of the Marxist school in general, with the minor programme that you have framed for yourselves must turn, inevitably and most regrettably, to moonshine, owing to the ignorance of the people to whom they are addressed. So much I did say! And I went on..."

Confused sounds of protest again rose from the meeting. Bruno thumped the table with his fist to command silence.

"Let him speak!"

"I went on to say," Covazza repeated, "that you, blinded by the fervour of your sincere and youthful faith, imagine that your definitions and explanations are really understood."

"So they are! So they are!" his listeners shouted in chorus.

"They are not! They cannot be!" Covazza was emphatic in his denial. "How do you expect them to be, if you don't understand them properly yourselves?"

A storm of shouts broke out at this assertion. Bruno, Lando Laurentano, Lino Apes, the Deputies tried for a while to subdue it. Spiridione Covazza waited with bowed head and shut eyes until they should succeed; at one point he put his hands together and, raising them to his face, bent his head lower still to hide his face in them, bowing his obese person with an effort; then spreading them out in a sweeping gesture and straightening himself again, he pleaded almost tearfully: "Do not compel me, gentlemen, by any false regard for your misconceived self-esteem, do not compel me to modify one iota of the truth by concessions which would make you and myself alike blush for shame, and might at a time like this be pernicious! How many of you really know Marx? Four, five, not more! Be honest! None of the rest of you has any real knowledge of what is required; yes, yes, I assure you!--nor of the best means of securing it, being all of you infatuated by a sentimental Socialism, which wreathes its brows with magic promises of justice and equality. But do you know what the word justice means to the peasants and sulphur workers of Sicily? It means violence! Bloodshed, that's what it means! Massacre! Because in legal justice, in the justice based upon right and reason they have never believed, seeing it invariably trampled underfoot to their hurt! I know them, a great deal better than you do, the peasants and sulphur workers of Sicily... yes, alas, a great deal better than you do! You deceive yourselves! You say to them: collectivism--they understand you to mean division of land, share and share alike! You say to them: abolition of wages--they interpret it as: we are all masters now, out with your purses, count up the money, and share and share alike."

"It is not true! It is not true!" some of his listeners shouted.

"Allow me to finish!" Covazza exclaimed, momentarily out of breath. "The other illusion that you create for yourselves concerns the numbers enrolled in your Fasci: three thousand in one place, four thousand in another, eight hundred, a thousand, ten thousand.... Where, how do you count them? They are empty shadows, gentlemen, mere names and nothing more! Yes, I know from experience; as soon as the lists are opened, they flock in like sheep: one gives the lead, all the rest follow! But do you seriously propose to attach any importance, to base anything upon this, which is the fruit of an inevitable spiritual contagion? How many, once the first enthusiasm has cooled, remain active members of your Fasci? The majority of them drop out at the first call for the paltry weekly subscription! And how many Fasci that have arisen to-day will be dissolved to-morrow? Listen to a man who is not deceived, and who is not deceiving you, gentlemen! I know that you are met here to-day to decide whether or not yon ought to support the tendency of the masses towards immediate action. I know that a number of you are opposed to the suggestion, and I think them wise, and give them my vote. A serious movement, such as you have in mind, is not yet possible in Sicily! If you think that it has already begun, and by your doing, you deceive yourselves! To my mind it is nothing more than a passing fever, a delirium of unconsciousness!"

Spiridione Covazza sat down, mopping the sweat from his congested face, while ten, fifteen of his audience rose simultaneously to demand the floor of the house.

Cataldo Sclafani spoke in a voice of thunder and apparently more in sorrow than in anger, since it was not the accusation itself that could offend him, but the thought that anyone was capable of accusing him, and with him his comrades.

"I rise, not to defend myself," he said, "but to explain!"

What was the strength of the Fasci? The heads of the more important of them were present, and each of them could inform the Hon. Covazza how his members were counted and how many there were. The Fasci, according to the latest statistics issued by the Central Committee, numbered one hundred and sixty-three firmly established, with thirty-five in course of formation. There did really exist, therefore, a great army of workers in Italy, in which one did not know whether most to admire the fervour, the intelligence or the discipline with which they acted upon a signal from the Central Committee. The head of each Fascio passed the word of command to the various section leaders, and they in their turn to the heads of districts and streets; in the twinkling of an eye, by day or night, all the members of the Fasci could receive a message. And if to-morrow the workers were to rise, the whole population of Sicily would be swept as by a tide of fire. Because for years past the fire had been smouldering in Sicily, ever since she had been seen to be lying in the sea like a stone at which the bogt of Italy was aiming a kick in return for all she had done for the so-called Unity and Independence of the country.

Why say that only in the last year had there been talk of Socialism in Sicily? Had there not been, as many as eighteen years ago, a section of the International there? And ever since then, party organs had continued to appear; and clubs, groups, centres had been formed here and there, so that, as soon as the idea of the Fasci first arose, there had been an immediate rallying and re-enlistment of old comrades in the faith.

It was not true therefore that the rapid formation of the Fasci was due solely to the persistent and vigorous propaganda carried on by the younger generation: the soil had long since been prepared; all that was lacking was unity, direction; and all that the young people had needed to do was to utter a call and point out the way, the same way that the proletariat of other countries had been treading for years past. The peasants and workers of Sicily had rallied to the young men with outstretched arms, crying: "You, you are our true friends!" and were prepared to follow them with joy in their hearts, fully conscious of what was required of them.

And, in proof of this consciousness, Cataldo Sclafani referred, with emotion, to the speeches delivered at the last congress at Palermo by certain women from Piana dei Greci and Corleone; speeches which proved in the clearest manner that it was not the artificial light of an academic culture, nor any lecture-room theory that was required to arouse the said consciousness, but the daily experience of hardship and injustice, and the simplest and most spontaneous indication of the remedy for all these evils: unity!

Sentimental Socialism? But the creative force is nothing more nor less than sentiment, not cold reason, armed with doctrine! What mattered the abstract notion of a right, when there was the immediate and overpowering sentiment of a need? That a man should feel his own right with the same force with which he feels the pangs of hunger was worth a thousand times more than any precise theoretical demonstration of that right. Not to mention that this sentiment had now become a firm and clear consciousness, and displayed itself in every possible way. A true spirit of brotherhood had diffused itself among the peasants and workers, whereby, in the frequent arrests of recent days, they had seen the comrades who remained at liberty supporting the prisoners and their families; when anyone was in distress, prompt succour from all the rest, and personal attention and loving care. Take for instance the nightly patrol by the decurions of the highways and taverns in town and country, in case the brethren be led to acts of violence, when heated with wine.

"These are your demagogues, Hon. Covazza!" Cataldo Sclaf ani exclaimed in conclusion, his eyes ablaze with excitement and with the emotion his own words aroused in him. "You should be ashamed of your accusations! There are here to-day, in Rome, two generations, face to face. Look at the spectacle that the old men present, and then look at us young men. To-morrow, from here, the Government, which protects all those who for years past have made of their love of their country, rolled up, and worn on the arm, a shield against the stones flung by a censorious populace,

320

will send an armed force to Sicily to stifle by violence this great stirring of a new life which we young men have set in motion there! Hitherto the majority of the Central Committee, of which I am a member, have been opposed to immediate action. But the day will soon come, I foresee, when the impatience so long held in check will break loose, and we leaders will not be able to control the people without immolating ourselves."

Lando Laurentano, sitting beside Lino Apes, listened to Sclafani's long speech with bowed head, pulling his beard with nervous fingers, and glancing to right and left of him in turn.

This meeting in his house reminded him of the dress rehearsal of a play. All these young men had their parts assigned to them, and he felt that, by dint of constant rehearsing, they had learned them by heart, and were repeating them with an artificial fervour. The vast chorus was lacking, being in Sicily. Oh yes, he spoke well, with a fine apostolic emphasis, that Cataldo Sclafani; he deserved in some respects the deafening roars of applause, the praise of the chorus, had it been present. In love with his part, he would play it with perfect coherence even when facing the muskets of a firing party, on the barrack square; or, were he arrested, before his judges, in a court of justice.

Why was it that only he himself had not yet succeeded in finding a part to play? Why still, still within him, did the despairing cry of protest sound: "No, this is not it!"

What did all these comrades really want? Little enough, for the moment, in Sicily. They wanted, by the unity and resistance of the workers, to induce the landlords and mineowners to agree to more humane terms, to abolish the starvation wage, usury, sweating, the burden of unfair municipal taxation, so that the workers should be assured not indeed of comfort, but at least of enough to provide for the primary necessities of life. They wanted, modestly adapting themselves to local conditions, to establish a co-operative system of production and consumption and to control the public services; after a few years, to triumph in the municipal and provincial elections of the Island; to head the poll in a few parliamentary divisions, so as to have preachers and prophets of the most crying needs of the poor in the municipal and provincial councils and in the Chamber of Deputies.

So much they wanted. And rightly. Admirable were the faith and constancy with which they were carrying on this task of protection and defence. What more did he want? There was nothing more to want or to do, for the time being. Why all this excitement, then, and all this ferment to secure what nobody, perhaps, outside the Island, would ever have imagined not to exist there already: that in every isolated little cottage in the fields the flickering oil lamp should no longer shew to the father, returning home spent with toil, the sleeping forms of his supperless children by a fireless hearth? That creatures should be put in the way of becoming and of feeling themselves to be men, whom a life of hardship had brought lower than the beasts that perish? But a sound agrarian law, a moderate reform of the conditions of tenure, a slight increase in the meagre rate of wages, partnership (*mezzadria*) upon honest terms, such as obtained in Tuscany and Lombardy, such as he himself had granted on his own estate, would be sufficient to satisfy and appease those poor wretches without all this clamour of threats, without any need to assume these airs of apostles, prophets, paladins.

Honest and modest aspirations, controlled by a sort of evangelical discipline, to be attained by degrees, in course of time and with a clear consciousness of the right that was being withheld! Could he feed his mind upon these and not think of something more? No, no: this was not enough for him! Had it been enough, then, by thunder, he would give away all his fortune, and then, perhaps, as a poor man, would find in these aspirations food for his restless spirit. But as things were, no, they could not suffice him!

All of a sudden, as he turned to look at Lino Apes, he heard ringing in his ears, like a peal of sardonic laughter, the lines from Leopardi's *Hymn to Italy*:

To arms, to arms, and I alone will fight, and I will fall alone!

And he sprang to his feet at the applause which at that moment broke out from all parts of the room to crown the eloquent ispeech of Cataldo Sclafani, nor could he help going forward with all the rest to clasp the orator's hand.

But Lino Apes, from his seat, with his Socratic smile on his lips and in his eyes, inquired in loud tones:

Luigi Pirandello

"Well, gentlemen, and what is our conclusion?"

The discussion appeared to be finished; the account settled; and everyone was feeling a sense of relief, as though rid of a heavy burden. At this challenge from Apes they looked one another in the face, surprised, pained, and drifted hack quietly to their places.

"Nature, gentlemen," Lino Apes went on, as soon as he saw them all seated, "nature, in its eternity, may fail to come to a conclusion, or rather it cannot and does not ever come to a conclusion. Man has to come to a conclusion, he must come to a conclusion; or at least must imagine that he has come to some conclusion; man! Well then, gentlemen, what is to be our conclusion? We are men, and we are met here for the purpose. But I can read the answer in your eyes. You have no desire for a conclusion, albeit you are not eternal! You have made a journey. Many among you will be continuing your journey, to Reggio Emilia. Here in Rome, those of you who are here for the first time have much to see; and time presses. Forgive me for speaking like this: you know that I see things on a minute scale, and I speak as I see. I have little faith in the conclusions of men, all of whom, at a certain point, looking hack upon the past, considering their works and their days, shake their heads sorrowfully and admit: 'Yes, we have grown rich,' or 'Yes, we have done this, that, or the other--but what conclusion have we reached in the end?' Nothing, strictly speaking, ever comes to a conclusion, because we are all part of eternal nature. But that does not alter the fact that we people here to-day, given the moment, ought to come to some sort of conclusion, if it be only illusory. I tell you that this is essential, because otherwise the workers from town and country, from the sulphur pits, will come here on their own account, without your enlightened guidance and your approval. And there will be a blind confusion, a savage tumult, when there might be an ordered movement, premeditated, sure. The consequences? Gentlemen, the man who is not born to act has to foresee them. Do you believe that we have cause for action? Let us consider the ways and means. The whole of Sicily is now ungarrisoned. Three or four companies of soldiers are stationed there to support the Offenbachian police, here to-day, gone to-morrow, wherever they may be needed. And against them, as you have said, an entire, compact army of workers. There is no need to arm them;

we have only to disarm that handful of soldiers, and we remain masters of the field. No? You say no? Wait! Let me speak... God in heaven, let me conclude!"

But he could not say another word. As with frogs squatting by the edge of a swamp, if one jumps in with a splash, all the rest, by twos and threes, diving in, make an ever increasing din; the audience, spellbound at first by Apes's clear reasoning, began finally, after a first interruption, to interrupt two or three at a time; and' almost in an instant, what with supporters and critics, a violent dispute broke out in every part of the room.

At one end, Lando Laurentano almost implored them:

"Yes, that is right, there is something to be done, my friends..."

Elsewhere Bixio Bruno and Cataldo Sclafani were shouting:

"No! No! It would be madness! The idea! Ruination!"

And challenges, invective, suggestions rang for a while through the room. Some of the party, Covazza among them, left the meeting in disgust. At a certain point, one of them, quaking with terror, dashed, calling for silence and with upraised arms, into the group in which the dispute was raging most fiercely and exclaimed:

"Gentlemen, we are being watched!"

All eyes were turned to the two windows.

Beyond the garden railings a couple of men were indeed watching, trying to hide behind the bushes. Celsina Pigna looked out of the window, and, as soon as she saw them, her face turned crimson.

"No!" she could not help breaking out. "I know them.... They are waiting for me."

Before her blushing smile and sparkling eyes the dispute subsided as though no one thought it possible to continue it, when this flower of girlhood, whose presence they had pretended not to notice, suddenly sprang up before them, as though to warn them: "I am here, stop it: there are people waiting for me!"

A little later, when everyone, except Lino Apes, had left the room, Celsina went up to Lando Laurentano and asked him, alluding to one of the two men who stood waiting for her beyond the railings:

"Don't you know him? He's your nephew...."

"My nephew?" said Lando in amazement, having no idea that he possessed such a thing.

"Why, yes, Antonio Del Re," Celsina assured him. "The son of your cousin Anna, the sister of Signor Roberto Auriti."

"Ah!" Lando exclaimed. "And why doesn'the come in?"

Celsina noticed a sudden wave of emotion passing over Laurentano's face immediately after this question, and interpreted it in her own way, to wit that he, suspecting some intrigue between her and his relative, had regretted the inopportune question, and made haste to reply:

"He is not one of us, you know! He is staying here in Rome with Signor Roberto. He is studying at the University.... But I am afraid..."

She broke off, seeing that Laurentano, absorbed in his own thoughts, was not listening to her; and at once went on:

"I bring you greetings from Lizio, the President of the Grirgenti Fascio, and from my father. I, too, believe, if I may express my opinion, that it is not time to act. We have in the Fascio of Girgenti about eight hundred members enrolled. ... But they are mere names: few of them attend, few of them pay..."

"Why, yes, of course..." broke in Lino Apes, a charming smile spreading over his hideous face, as though to convey to her that he had spoken as he did with the sole object of emptying the room. "Act? Why it would be madness! Are they joking?"

Celsina's eyes darted flames. She could have slapped him. She smiled at him. She held out her hand to Lando Laurentano and said:

"Excuse me. I shall leave you to yourselves."

WOODNOTES WILD.

The ex-tenor Olindo Passalacqua, honorary husband of the singing mistress Signora Lalla Passalacqua-Bonome, not to mention reigning censor of the *Privato Conservatorio Bonome*, had been doing everything in his power for the last two hours to bridle the silent, raging impatience of Antonio. He kept on talking, muttering in an undertone, and every now and then, stealthily, if the sighing Antonio was looking the other way, would slip his wife's watch out of his pocket and begin: "Yes, poor fellow, you're right!" with a pantomimic gesture of eyes, brows and lips, and a moment later, with a fresh pantomime: "Here they are: let us follow them; come on!" And he went on talking, talking apparently to order; but in a special, highly comic and almost incomprehensible manner of his own, being all in fits and starts and sidelong references to weird, remote vicissitudes in his haphazard existence. And each digression was accompanied by a sudden alteration of face and voice, exclamations, grimaces, gestures of rage or joy or menace or commiseration or contempt, which left any stranger gaping speechless who, knowing nothing of these vicissitudes, had succeeded for any length of time in listening to him without laughing. Such displays of astonishment gave Olindo Passalacqua great satisfaction; they were to him a measure of the effect he produced; and with his hands spread open fanwise he pulled up, and up, and up, the long grey hair waved so as to conceal the bald patch on his crown, and then with his forefingers touched the waxed needlepoints of his dyed moustaches, either to put the finishing touch to this habitual gesture or to make certain that they had not melted away in the heat of his discourse.

"A pittance, a mere pittance would be enough!" he was saying. "Listen, what does it amount to? What do two paltry lire a day amount to? And I would be content with less! A pittance.... The wretch! Think of all the money he flings away upon those rascals in there, who are staining his what do you call it, again? Oh, yes, his ancestral scutcheon! The swine! And my father-in-law, for the sake of Italy, letting the Carolino at Palermo go all to pot.... A gold mine! *Ione* by itself... poor Petrella!... My battle charger.... Everything there ruined... for these swine here! Do you hear how they're squealing? And he a Prince, yes sir.... They ought to be ashamed of themselves.... What I say is, two lire a day for a deserving cause.... God in heaven, a fortune like that! All got without working.... And what do you. know about it? Infernal contracts... lifelong slavery... I, myself, for ten years and more, a star and a slave.... Whereas here, he has only to say yes ... I would undertake, Nino, I would undertake personally to produce her within a year in the first theatres in Italy. You know me; I may break, I don't... I don't... *frangar...* what is the expression? I could say it in Latin, damn it! My word... if I give my word! What else have I left? My sole possession. We shall have to feed her a little bit better at first: that I admit! But if she comes off... if she comes off... oh, if she comes off.... And that bastard modern music..."

Olindo Passalacqua had discovered a portentous soprano voice in the throat of Celsino Pigna, immediately, the moment he heard her speak.

"And with her appearance, what more do you want? A furore, take my word for it: she'll create a furore! My brother-in-law would be quite satisfied, out of consideration for Roberto and yourself, with a mere nothing, one lira fifty a day, even, for the cost of her board. Feed her well ... and within a year... you don't agree?"

Antonio Del Re shook with rage whenever any of Passalacqua's remarks succeeded in forcing its way through the turmoil of conflicting thoughts to which he was a prey.

The day before, Celsina had suddenly called at Uncle Roberto's house, during luncheon. Bewildered, stunned by the clamorous life of the great city, by the unfamiliar sights, by the novel and strange customs, he had been wholly unable to keep the promise he had made her before leaving home, namely to find at once an opening for her in Rome. He had written, nevertheless, to tell her that presently, as soon as he began to settle down, he would begin to look for one; with the private conviction, however, that not only would he not be successful, but that he would have neither the will nor the means to try, caught as he felt, and must for some time continue to feel himself in a state of bewilderment which almost took his breath away and made everything round him appear vacillating and unreal.

This bewilderment, indeed, had not only persisted, it had steadily gone on growing, amid that precarious, eccentric, haphazard existence in his uncle's house. How on earth had his uncle ever trained himself to live like that, to arrange his life in a certain meticulous order of his own, in the midst of such disorder, to find a patch of soil in which to put down his roots?

He could place Olindo Passalacqua, Signora Lalla (Nanna, they called her) and her brother, Pilade Bonome: gipsies; the first-named, sprung from heaven knew where; the other two, children of a theatrical manager, established before 1860 at Palermo, and swept away on the Liberal tide by the young gentlemen of the Palermitan aristocracy, assiduous frequenters of the wings of the Teatro Carolino. The theatrical venture having failed a few years later, penniless, "victims of the Revolution," as Olindo Passalacqua still described them (who, immediately after his marriage to the manager's daughter, had lost his voice); they had come to Rome, soon after '70, and had settled upon Uncle Roberto, on the strength of an intro-duction from a friend in Palermo.

Setting sail upon the dark sea of fate, dashing into the most preposterous adventures, making without a moment's thought the queerest decisions, were as simple to them as drinking a glass of water. Here to-day, gone to-morrow; to-day abundance, to-morrow starvation: it was enough for them every day to arrive at hedtime, somehow, without turning back in the face of every conceivable obstacle, of the hardest sacrifices, flinging overboard all that they held dearest and most sacred, if only they could lighten the ship, a ship without compass or anchor or rudder, buffeted by incessant waves in that perpetual storm which had been their life. Nevertheless there was this about them that was wonderful and pitiful and at the same time comic, that albeit they had jettisoned everything without any reserve, they had remained pure in heart, had retained a living innocence that throbbed with finer feelings, had remained affectionate, generous, always ready to spend themselves upon other people, to comfort, to succour, to glow with enthusiasm for every noble action. Anything that was improper, bad, shameful in their lives they perhaps sincerely believed was not to be imputed to them. A necessity to which one must turn a blind eye, or, if one eye was not sufficient, both. With what dignity, for instance, Olindo Passalacqua--after dining at Uncle Roberto's table, and reminding him not to forget to make Nanna take the drops for her weak heart, or to have the centrepiece of fruit removed at once from the table, in case, if she were to touch, without thinking, the skin of one of the peaches, it might make her nose bleed, poor woman, as so often happened to her--would leave him in possession of his marriage-bed and, bidding his wife good night, wishing them all pleasant dreams, including the canaries and the blackbird in their cages, the parrot Coco, on his perch; Titi, the consumptive monkey, on her chain; Ragnetta, the cat with her collar and tie; the two old dogs, Bobbi and Piccini, both bedridden in the same basket, one blind, the other with his rump coated with tar; off he would go with his forefingers pressed to the points of his moustaches, stiffened already in the rigid severity of an unbending censor, to sleep in the private Conservatorio of his brother-in-law Bonome in the Via dei Pontefici!

And what a crazy vessel was that table, at which four or five strangers sat down every day, invited on the spur of the moment, or coming in uninvited. Parliamentary friends of Uncle Roberto and Corrado Selmi, long haired music teachers, singers of either sex! The talk that went on there, passing often to such boisterous laughter and fun! And how sad to see Uncle Roberto there among them all, Uncle Roberto whom he, in the old days at home, had imagined as holding the same ideas, the same sentiments as his grandmother and mother (nor had he been mistaken, for every day his uncle shewed him what he thought and felt by the most exquisite attentions, by a fatherly care of him), how sad to see him there among them all, joining in the talk, in the fun, and every now and then to surprise a look on his face, a pained smile, of mortification, if he caught his nephew's eye gazing at him with astonishment and grief!

What guidance could such an uncle give him? He might allow himself any licence, certain of meeting with neither prohibition nor reproof from him. He had matriculated in the Faculty of Science; but how was he to work in that house, which rang and gurgled and echoed from morning to night with trills and shakes and scales and exercises? Besides, the University, so far away, the crowds of giddy and thoughtless students, had inspired him from the first day with an insuperable aversion, gloom, discouragement, contempt, rage; and, taking any excuse that offered, he had not gone near the place again. He had imagined, and the thought at once became a certainty, that any one of those louts might take it into his head to make fun of him, so serious and different from themselves: and what would happen then? At the mere thought of it, his fingers became claws. The slightest incentive, at that stage, a spark, and his fury, which it cost him such an effort to repress, would have burst out in a terrific blaze. He had the impression that life was somehow bottled up inside him, and was boiling over, fomented by remorse at his idleness and by his overpowering need to find some sort of outlet. But how was he to escape from that idleness, if he was now quite certain that he would never be able to do anything, since everything had become tangled and confused in his brain? And where was he to find an outlet. He had run about Rome from end to end, like a madman, hardly noticing anything, wrapped up in himself, in that brooding discontent with everyone and everything and everybody, in that continual boiling over of impetuous thoughts which, before they acquired precision, evaporated in his brain, leaving him empty and dazed, his features altered, distorted, his fists clenched, his nails driven into the palms of his hands.

At length, from the dull rage that was devouring him, from that gloomy, sour inertia, a murderous, monstrous idea had begun to germinate in his spirit, and had at once begun to batten voraciously upon all the rancour against life that he had gathered and brooded over from his infancy.

The idea had flashed across his mind as he listened one evening to a discussion at table of the pattern of the bombs smuggled into Sicily by Francesco Crispi during the preparations for the Revolution of 1860 and of how they were made. Corrado Selmi had said that he had made some of them himself, by night, in the storehouse that Francesco Eiso had leased in the convent of La

Gancia. Proud of his knowledge of modern chemistry, he had burst out laughing, and had explained to them how childish the type in question was, and how nowadays one could secure a far more deadly effect with a mechanism of considerably less bulk.

"There, now!" Corrado Selmi had exclaimed. "Just to liven things up a little, you ought to throw one of these pretty little toys down from the gallery into the Chamber!"

All of a sudden he had felt himself gripped and completely dominated by the idea.

The shouts of indignation in the streets at the discovery of the fraudulent conduct of the banks, and the suspicion, growing into certainty, that Uncle Roberto too, with Selmi, was implicated in the scandal of these frauds, the news, more serious every day, that kept coming from Sicily, had made him decide to seek out the ways and means of putting this idea into practice as soon as possible. So much of life, now, was finished for him!

If Uncle Giulio, who had set off hotfoot for Gir-genti, did not succeed in obtaining the money from grandmother's brother, Uncle Roberto would be arrested; and then the crash, the abyss.... Ah, but first of all! Yes, yes, that would be the proper revenge, the outlet for all the bitterness that had poisoned his own life and the lives of his relatives; and he would show his companions down in Sicily, the chatter-boxes, that he was able to do single-handed what all of them put together could never have done.

And then, just at that moment, Celsina had turned up in Rome. When he saw her standing before him with a fiery face, laughing to conceal her embarrassment, a fierce anger had swept over him. He had the feeling now that nothing more could happen, nothing move from its place unless propelled by him; that people ought to remain at their posts, motionless; as though held in suspense and waiting for the great and terrible act that he was to accomplish. Whence, how had Celsina come, when he had done nothing to make her come? Lando's money... of course! That money he had refused to Uncle Roberto.... The Fascio of Girgenti.... What a pantomime! And how furious he had been to see Celsina receive so cordial a welcome from those Passalacqua, to whom it was the most natural thing in the world that a girl should come by herself to Rome, upon such a pretext, and should call at the house in search of her lover, firmly resolved to return no more to Sicily. He had turned all the colours of the rainbow when he saw them all staring at him with eyes that sparkled with a malicious tolerance, which seemed to say to him in so many words: "Why, what harm is there? We understand! Don't be ashamed!" And Uncle Roberto too had remained in the room, with his familiar wistful smile, beneath which he tried to conceal the annoyance that any novelty caused him: annoyance only. To him too there was nothing wrong in a girl's coming to call upon his nephew in his house, at a time like this, with the gulf yawning at their feet, into which they might all be plunged at any moment. To these Passa-lacqua the gulf was nothing: one of the many difficulties of life that had to be surmounted; and for surmounting it, they trusted blindly in Corrado Selmi. Quite sufficient, moreover, to set their minds at rest was the calm that Uncle Roberto forced himself to preserve in order not to agitate his Nanna, with her weak heart.

Enough of that "Signor Antonio" and that third person feminine, in which Celsina had begun by addressing him! Whom did she suppose she was taking in? Let them call one another "tu"! Oh, my dear child.... Yes, that's right, laugh. ... If she didn't laugh from her heart at her age, and with those eyes and that sweet little face. ... Oh, what a voice! Did you hear?... Clear as a bell. Had she never had her voice tested? Had she never sung, never even hummed a tune, like this? Never at all? But she must be tested, at once.... Impossible that there shouldn't be a voice there, with those inflexions, with those modulations.... Come along, quick, any old song would do, in the sitting-room, quick.... She'd drawn a lucky number! No better expedient could be imagined for not going back to Sicily! The means to study? Why, wasn't there Signora Lalla, and the *Privato Conservatorio Bonome*. Lessons free, music and piano free: only a trifling charge for her board. And Olindo Pas-salacqua, on learning that Celsina was one of Lando Laurentano's comrades in the Socialist faith, had at once suggested her applying to him for this allowance. No? Why not? A deserving cause! A plague on those scruples, that modesty, which restrain the conscience from doing good! She could always offer to repay the allowance to Lando out of her first earnings, but no, my friends, that is how sharpers, and money-lenders behave, all the more reason why a gentleman should refrain from following their example.... The mean stupidity of it all!

Antonio had writhed in his chair as he listened to this talk. He longed to seize Celsina by the arm and to shout in her face: "Off with you, back to the place you came from. These people are niad, dancing over the abyss. Go! Go! It is I that, am going to open the abyss! Nothing exists any longer; I myself no longer exist: all is finished!"

And yet, here he was, he had, with Passalacqua, escorted Celsina to the door of Lando's house, and was now waiting for the meeting to break up, and for her to reappear from the house. Celsina had promised him, privately, that she would not breathe a word to Laurentano of that ridiculous allowance; she would merely ask him to interest himself in her in some way, to enable her, by using his wide influence, to find some modest employment in Rome.

The allowance Celsina had privately intended to demand for him, for Antonio, instead. He had confided to her, the evening before, the terrible position in which his uncle found himself placed.

"And you?" she had asked him.

His sole reply to this question had been a furious gesture, of desperation. The suspicion had crossed her mind that he was meditating some act of violence, but against himself; and she had tried to rouse him, to give him fresh courage. She had come to Rome, her spirit ablaze with dreams and hopes, full of self-confidence, eager and prepared to overcome every obstacle. And so there would be two of them henceforward, to share and face those obstacles; she would sweep him along in her ardour. "Was it possible that he, with his family connexions, could perish? And was there not still his other uncle? Why, of course! The difficulties would lie in her path. But there, she laughed at them!

She came out of the villino, in a towering rage.

"Nothing! The idiots.... Come away! Come away!" she said, thrusting her companions forward.

"Didn't you say anything?" askedPassalaequa, in wondering dismay.

"Say anything!" Celsina shook. "They are a lot of madmen,

halfwits, idiots, imbeciles.... Chatter, chatter, chatter, speeches, or silly tittle-tattle that tries to appear clever.... Come along, come along! But I have scored one point at least, I am here, in Rome! Nino, for goodness' sake, Nino, don't look like that! Go away... yes, yes... it is just as well, go away! Go away!"

Olindo Passalacqua hurried after Antonio who, swelling with rage, his hair standing on end, had lengthened his pace; he caught hold of him, beckoned to Celsina to join them at once, with mute appeals for calm and prudence. But Celsina, smiling as she stole softly up behind them, shook her head, as much as to bid him let Antonio go.

"But this is madness, really... calm yourselves, children! You'll only blind yourselves ... and the remedy? How can you ever see the remedy, if you blind yourselves with rage? There is always a remedy, my friends; for everything there is a remedy; more or less hard, more or less bitter, more or less radical... but there is one! There is no need to be frightened.... First of all, what, you say, this? Not this! Never this! Then... oh, my friends, don't I know! It's another matter altogether!... And yet, and yet, and yet.... I mean to say, let us be quite clear about it, always respecting the laws of... of... of good.... Let us be gentlemen! You know, Nino, I may break but I do not... I do not..."

"What are you doing? What do you want?"

"What are you hanging about like that for?" Celsina asked Nino, who was still breathing heavily, with a murderous expression on his face. "Stop it! You're wasting your breath! I feel so calm and contented! Come along, which way do we go, Signor Olindo? You, now... look at me... no, no, look me fairly and squarely in the face... here, look in my eyes.... Before you left home, do you remember?"

Nino contracted his face in a tremendous spasm of rage, and sobbed through his nose, clapping his fist to his mouth.

"Come, that will do for the present! Let us go!" Celsina went on. "You, Signor Olindo, must tell me one thing only, but you must tell me the truth, on your conscience: Have I a voice?"

Olindo Passalacqua drew back a pace, his hands clasped to his breast:

"But I have sung with Pasta, do you know that? With Lucca I have sung; I have sung with the sisters Brambilla..."

"All right, all right," Celsina cut him short. "Then you are certain that I have a voice?"

"A voice of gold!" exclaimed Passalacqua. "Gold, pure gold, I tell you! And in less than a year you..."

"All right," Celsina again interrupted him. "And now listen, one more favour! Finding the money you mentioned will be my affair. I am quite capable of marching into every shop I pass, into all the hotels, offices, banks, caf es, and asking them if they need a cashier, saleswoman, interpreter, anything in the world! I have a diploma in book-keeping, with honours; I speak two languages, English and French.... But I would even go out as a dressmaker, a seamstress. I havo never had a needle in my hand; I can learn.... Schoolmistress, companion, governess.... Just leave it to me! You can go home now. Leave mo alone with this fine specimen! Good-bye."

And, taking Antonio by the arm, she made off.

"Take me to see Rome!"

See Rome, indeed! She could see nothing, with her brain in a ferment. She talked and talked, and her eyes sparkled and blazed beneath her little hat with its bold feather; her burning lips quivered, and she laughed without a trace of malevolence at all the people who turned round to stare at her.

After a while: "Listen, Nino," she murmured in his ear. "Take me right away... to some lonely spot... far away... I must sing! ... I want to hear how I sing.... If it should be true! Do you believe it? Ah, if it should be true, Nino dear! Come along, come along.... Is it far to the Tiber? Take me to see the Tiber, and I can sing there."

She continued to prattle all the way. She told him that of course, before she became a famous soprano or contralto, she simply must find a husband, to get rid of her ugly surname which distressed her so.

"Celsina is all right; but Pigna! Think of it! Impossible! Let us see now, suppose we try.... Celsina... what? Celsina Del Re? Oh, good gracious! My political views.... Del Re--the King's? I am a Socialist! Impossible, Nino! I can never be your wife, fate is against it! But anyhow, you don't want me.... Oh, oh, don't. You'll make my arm black and blue.... You do want me? Then it shall be Celsina Del Re, and we needn't say another word on the subject! Celsina of

His Majesty... silly, isn't it... of His Majesty Antonio I."

They arrived, just as the sun was setting, at a spot outside the fortifications, close to the Polygon, on the right bank of the Tiber. Monte Mario reared its cypress crest against the purple, vaporous sky, and the vast plain on one side, which serves as a training ground for the garrison, and on the other the grassy banks of the river, seemed, in the twilight suffused with violet and gold, like a painted canvas. In the awestruck silence, they could hear not so much the sound as the motion of the turgid stream, of a dead green, tinted here and there with roseate reflexions of the sky, stained here and there by some black flotsam.

"Beautiful!" sighed Celsina, looking round her, with the feeling that it was all a dream. "How beautiful it is here...."

Then, turning to Antonio, who had sat down on a stone and was gazing at the ground, stooping, his hands pressed tightly between his thighs:

"Nino, what are you doing?" she asked him. "You don't see, you don't hear anything? Lift up your head, look, listen... this silence here ... the river... and over there Rome... and I am here with you!"

She went up to him, laid her hand on his shoulder, stooped down to gaze in his face, and:

"You are not twenty yet!" she said to him. "And I am eighteen...."

Antonio shook himself free, crossly, at which she, piqued, shrugged one shoulder and moved away.

A moment later, from some way off, the sound of her singing reached Antonio:

The birds make love while leaves are on the trees....

Her voice welled up in the silence, limpid and fervid, like the light of the first star in the evening sky. And while she, from where she stood, went on singing:

Each calls his mate and waits for her to answer.... The time has come to build our nests anew....

he, where he sat, in desperation, clenching his fists in the frenzy of his jealousy, was seeing her attired as an actress, in a vast theatre, in the glare of the footlights, in the arms of a tenor.... He rose, shuddering, and went to find her.

"Come away! Come away! Come away!"

"What do you think of it?" she asked him, with a charming smile of happiness.

Antonio gripped her arm, and, glaring at her with a look of hatred:

"You will be ruined!" he growled at her between his set teeth.

Celsina broke into a laugh.

"I?" she said. "But if you don't want me, it is the people who come near me that will be ruined, my dear boy! I have wings... wings.... I shall fly!"

CHAPTER III

SOLEMN SPECTACLES.

The Hon. Ignazio Capolino was beside himself with joy. Thousands of workmen, in his constituency, driven wild by famine owing to the closing of Salvo's sulphur pits, were threatening violence and pillage, fire and bloodshed; Aurelio Costa, who had exposed himself to their wrath by the promises he had made in Salvo's name, was writhing with indignation at the sprightly chatter of H.E. the Under Secretary of State for Agriculture; he, meanwhile, was bursting with pride at the undreamed-of affability, the confidential manner, as of an old friend, with which the said Under-Excellency had received him.

When he secured this audience for Costa he had been afraid that his far-famed influence, his boasted personal friendship with the members of the Government would, when put to the test, suffer the most painful mortification; instead of which. ... Why, yes, of course, mad as March hares, quite so! Enemies of all law and order, those sulphur workers! a criminal gang, to be sure! stirred up by a handful of impostors who deserved hanging! Extreme measures? The utmost rigour of the law? "Why certainly! Of course! That was all that was required.... A stern eye, to be sure! a strong hand! Humanity... why, of course... so far as was possible.... Yes, yes, my dear Sir...but why not? Precisely!"

And he appeared, with ill concealed timidity, to be stretching out his hand to pat the Under Secretary of State on the back or on the knee, as a dog, after crawling on the ground to flatter the master whose severity it fears, ventures to raise a paw to see whether it has appeased him.

As for that scheme for the compulsory co-operation of all the producers of sulphur in Sicily, worked out by his friend the engineer whom he had the honour of introducing... oh, a most remarkable man, and so modest, formerly in government service as a mining engineer, yes, and a graduate of the Ecole des Mines in Paris--as for his scheme, well, if His Excellency the Minister would only condescend to run his eye over it.... No? Impossible, was it? Not the right moment ... quite! quite! that was just what he had remarked, himself!... this was not the right moment! Adding fresh fuel to the fire, quite so! something more was required... why, of course! Excellent! Oh, my dear Sir. L.. why not? Precisely!

He came out of the Ministry swelling like a turkey-cock, radiant. Aurelio Costa, to escape from the temptation to hit him, to spit in his face, silent, pale, quivering, lengthened his pace and let the other drop behind.

"Ingegnere!"

Costa, without looking round, replied with an angry wave of his hand.

"Ingegnere!" Capolino called to him as he overtook him, frowning fiercely. "I say, are you mad? What more did you want?"

"Leave me alone! For heaven's sake, leave me alone!" replied Aurelio Costa, seething with rage. "I am off to the telegraph office. Don Flaminio must come here himself! I am going straight home to-morrow."

"Calm yourself, man! Think what you're saying," Capolino went on, his tone a blend of arrogance and derision. "What more did you want of an Under Secretary of State? What did you expect? That he would throw his arms round your neck? He couldn't have been better. I myself never dreamed of such a reception...."

"I dare say!" sneered Costa. "If you..."

"If I what?" Capolino promptly retorted. "You wanted vague promises, did you? Moonshine? He treated me, he talked to me, like a true friend! And remember that I am an Opposition Deputy; that I was opposed by the Government, tooth and nail, at the election. As you know quite well!"

"I know nothing!" Costa groaned: "All that I know is: I had orders, definite orders, that the scheme must be taken into consideration at once by the Government. And you never said a word;

you did nothing but agree...."

Capolino interrupted him, looking him up and down as he spoke.

"Am I talking to a man or to a child? Where have you been living? Can you seriously believe that, at a time like this, in the thick of all this pandemonium, people can find time to examine your scheme? Orders, indeed! When? Wait one moment! When did you receive these orders from Flaminio Salvo? Before you started, wasn't it? But now, excuse me... look at this!"

And Capolino with a furious gesture of disdain pulled out from the bundle of papers under his arm the formal announcement of the ceremonial marriage of H.E. Prince Don Ippolito Laurentano with Donna Adelaide Salvo.

"You must have had one too!" he said. "So just keep your mouth shut, and don't think any more about orders or schemes!"

"Oh, then it's all a game, is it?" exclaimed Aurelio Costa. "With the lives of other people at stake?"

"Lives!" Capolino shrugged his shoulders.

"With my life! Mine!" Costa repeated, ablaze with anger and scorn. "With my life! I shall have to go back there, to Aragona, among the sulphur workers! And do you know the state I shall find them in, after being locked out for seven months? They'll he a pack of hyaenas! But why then did he make me promise everybody.-..up here even, tip here, just now, to Nicasio Ingrao, to the Prince's son? And all the plans I have drafted?"

"My dear Ingegnere, forgive my saying so," said Capolino soothingly, half shutting his eyes, keeping hack a smile, "you have been working all these years with Salvo, and have not yet discovered that he is not merely a business man but a politician as well. Now politics, don't you know--one has to live in a political atmosphere to understand--politics, my dear Sir, what are they chiefly? A game of promises, that is all! And you, allow me to tell you, are dashing headlong into it at this moment...."

"I?" Aurelio Costa burst out, clapping both hands to his breast. "I, headlong into it?"

"Why, yes, of course," Capolino was emphatic. "Blindfold, let me say! And I'm not referring only to this business, of the scheme. You don't see anything, you don't understand... there are so many things you don't understand! Listen to me, Ingegnere: don't have anything more to do with it! If you go back to your post.... I am grieved, believe me, sincerely grieved to see a man like yourself, whom I esteem so highly, cut a figure that is... not a pretty one, not at all a pretty one...."

This speech left Aurelio Costa at first open-mouthed, with amazement; then his face flushed crimson and he lowered his eyes for a moment; finally, unable to repress his impulse of annoyance:

"To me," he stammered, "you say these things to me? To me?... Why, I.... When did I ever.... Into what did I ever dash head-long, of my own accord? I have always been dragged in, by the hair of my head, and I'm sick of it, d'you hear? Sick of these schemes and intrigues and moods and scandals...."

"It is scandals now, is it?" put in Capolino.

"Yes, Sir, scandals!" Aurelio went on, casting restraint to the winds. "Scandals up here, and down there... and if you don't see them, I do! It is too much! I never wanted anything! I never aspired to anything, let me tell you, except to live in peace with my own conscience, and to lead a quiet life, doing the things I know how to do. And I have had enough! Let him come here himself, now, and see, after all the promises he has made, that he makes a proper settlement, for down there, I repeat, I must return, and I have no wish to lose my life at the game. Good day to you, Sir."

Ignazio Capolino followed him for some distance with his eyes; then turned up his nose in derision and stood shaking his head.

If he had only known that the true reason for which Aure-lio Costa wished Flaminio Salvo to come to Rome, was precisely that for which he wished him not to come: his wife!

The heat with which he defended the scheme, which had indeed been worked out with all the scrupulous care that he put into everything he did, and his annoyance at seeing it scrapped, tossed aside without a moment's consideration and almost in deri-sion, were generated actually by the heat of another passion, by his annoyance at another rebuff, which he, in order not to mortify his self-esteem in his own eyes, declined to admit. Sent away from Girgenti by Salvo on the pretext of this scheme, just at the mo-ment when Salvo's daughter knew that Nicoletta Capolino was in

Rome with her husband, he had hastened there like a thirsty man to a spring. He had expected to find Nicoletta as he had last seen her at Colimbetra, full of flattery for himself, ardent and provoking. Instead of which... it was only by a miracle that she had not burst out laughing when she read in his profound gaze the memory of that unforgettable evening!

Capolino, who had so much fault to find with his wife's conduct at this time, might have noticed it; but ever since, at Colimbetra, still swathed in bandages after his wound, he had felt the need of a pair of spectacles, he had been unable to see anything with his former clearness of vision, either in himself or round about him.

The trick played on him by that bullet, projected with unexpected force from Veronica's pistol, had profoundly disturbed his conception of life. Until that moment, he had supposed that it was he who played tricks upon other people, tricks that had always come off; now, all of a sudden, he had discovered that, in spite of every precaution, against all anticipation, laughing at every artifice and protection, fate, in its blindness, can and does play tricks also, inspiring intentions in other people. And Capolino had become extremely solemn.

Already, quite suddenly, whether from violent emotion or from loss of blood, his sight had weakened. The Prince, Don Ippolito, had been graciously pleased to present him with spectacles, a fine pair of solemn spectacles, with stems, rims and bridge of tortoiseshell. And life, as seen through these spectacles, and through the eyes of a Deputy, had given him a strange, unexpected impression: his hands, everything round him, his wife, his past, his future, presented themselves to his gaze in new shapes, lights and colours, in looking at which he had found himself almost compelled to assume at once a sort of frown, half grave, half frigid, which had made his wife, when she first saw it, burst out laughing:

"Oh, my poor Gnazio!"

There again, he simply could not see the last of this wife of his: his wife who kept looking for his eyes hehind his new spectacles, and could not he persuaded to take him seriously.

Having come to Rome with him for a fortnight or three weeks, for a month at the most, Lelle had stayed on there for more

than three months, and shewed not the slightest intention of returning home. Could she he out of her senses? Lelle was exultant.
At last she was in her element. With the Velia family, relatives of
Flaminio Salvo, and connected also with her hushand through his
first wife, she had at once made herself completely at home. Francesco Velia went in for display, Donna Rosa Velia was much the
same as her younger sister Donna Adelaide, always exclaiming and
giggling, and as for their son and daughter, Ciccino and Lillina, had
Nico-letta gone and ordered them to a pattern, she could not have
found them more to her liking. What a darling Lillina was! Still
unmarried, running to seed in her attractive, spicy plainness, she
was the inseparable companion of her brother Ciccino: sharper,
more daring, more vivacious than he, she helped him, defended
him, led him, apart from all their more intimate secrets. Brother
and sister had never thought of anything hut giving themselves a
good time; and Nicoletta, in their company, had in a few days become a perfect horsewoman; she had already ridden to hounds
three times; not to mention theatres, parties, excursions: a perfect
paradise! Lillina always knew exactly when to invent a slight headache or some other trifling malady, so as to leave Ciccino and their
new friend Lelle alone together.

Now Capolino, large as Rome was, as a Deputy and looking through those solemn spectacles, saw himself a by no means
unimportant figure, and was afraid lest his wife's unrestrained behaviour should make him conspicuous. Anyhow, he could not
allow it, not so much because of what other people might think, as
for his own sake. As a Deputy and with his spectacles, he wished
his wife, too, to be more serious in future. In Rome and with those
Velia hanging round her, and with the freedom he was obliged to
allow her, it did not seem to him possible. Flaminio Salvo, now
that Donna Adelaide had got married, would certainly be needing
her at Girgenti. For his daughter, that was to say; for that dear mo-
therless Dia-nella. If not to-day, to-morrow a letter would come
from him begging her to return. The Hon. Ignazio Capolino
longed for that letter to arrive! And now this imbecile Costa had
come, to smash all the eggs in his basket!

His life.... He was afraid of risking his life. Great donkey!
But of course, if he had not had sufficient intelligence in all these

years even to notice that Dianella was in love with him, that he had a fortune within his reach, and such a fortune too!--how could he have realized just now that an Opposition Deputy could not have been more cordially received by an Under Secretary of State? And he had dared to find fault with him for his approval.... Why, of course, to satisfy him one ought to stand up for the sulphur workers, just as though, in the last election, it was their votes that had carried him to the head of the poll! Placed between the Government and the Socialists, could a Conservative Deputy, a member of the Opposition, hesitate in his choice? But what was the use of trying to reason about such matters with a man to whom fortune gave bread because it knew that he had no teeth to chew it with?

Meanwhile Flaminio Salvo, hoping on the one hand to carry on the farce of his scheme and on the other to get into touch with Lando Lauren-tano, who had refused to attend his father's wedding, would doubtless hasten to obey the summons; and would be certain to bring with him Dia-nella, who could not be left alone at Girgenti. And Dianella would perhaps remain for a while in Rome, with her uncle and aunt, to amuse herself and--one never knew! Flaminio Salvo's eyes looked far ahead--Lando Laurentano called now and then at the Vella's, and... one never knew!

If Dianella remained in Rome, good-bye to any thought of Lelle's returning to Sicily.

So thinking, Capolino heaved a sigh, and his solemn spectacles with their stems, rims and bridge of tortoiseshell, grew misty.

GOOD-NIGHT, DEAR!

Before a week had passed, Flaminio Salvo was in Rome with Dianella, as Capolino had anticipated.

Dianella arrived there more dead than alive; Flaminio Salvo, as usual, sure of himself, with that cold smile on his lips, to which the slow gaze of his eyes from between their heavy lids gave an expression of faint irony.

They were to stay with the Velia family, who, with Capolino, his wife and Costa, went to meet them at the station. Donna Rosa, Ciccino and Lillina had never seen Dianella.

"Why, my child, what have you been living on? Lizards?" her Aunt Rosa began by asking her, at the sight of her waxen cheeks and pained, bewildered eyes. "But I know what it is, my dear, with a stupid man like your father in the house, you can never get what you want. Oh, I tell him straight out what I think, you know. I'm not like your Aunt Adelaide, who always gives way in everything. I am older than he is, and he's got to respect me."

"I kiss your hand, now as always," said Don Flaminio, with a bow.

"To be sure you do! Here it is: kiss it, kiss it!" replied Donna Rosa, holding out her plump little hand. "Of course you've got to kiss it! You just stay a while with us here in Rome, child, and you shall see that I shall send you back to Sicily as fine and fat and frolicsome as a lady ahbess. D'you see this lady?" she added, with a glance at Nicoletta Capolino. "What do you think of her? Nothing much to look at, one must admit; but now that Ciccino and Lillino have made her take riding exercise, d'you see her eye? It has come to life! Put yourself in your cousins' hands, my dear. Come along, now, come along! Laugh, laugh.... It's a great joke, life, I can tell you."

345

In the house, Don Flaminio told a marvellous tale to his sister and brother-in-law, nephew and niece, and their friends, of the marriage ceremony of the Prince and Donna Adelaide, celebrated by Monsignor Montoro in the chapel of Colimbetra, before the finest flower of Agrigentine society. H.E.H. the Count of Caserta had been graciously pleased to send an autograph letter of good wishes and congratulations to the happy couple.

"And who may he be?" asked Donna Rosa, looking all round the room; then, tapping her forehead: "Oh, of course, yes; I remember: Cecco Bomba.... I have a Bourbon brother-in-law, with soldiers.... Adelaide wrote and told me! How on earth could this poor child here be happy with a whole tribe of Royal Highnesses writing autograph letters about her aunt's wedding? Go on, man, go on!... Oh, if I had been there! You and your Prince of Laurentano...."

Continuing his narrative, Don Flaminio professed himself particularly gratified by the presence of Don Cosmo, the bridegroom's brother, at the illustrious gathering, and by the valuable present sent by Lando to his step-mother.

"I've seen it!" said Ciccino.

"We helped him to choose it!" added Lillina.

"Ah, so you know him quite well, then?" Don Flaminio asked in a tone of satisfaction.

And he plied his nephew and niece with questions, to find out how intimate they were with the young Prince, what he looked like and what sort of person he was, calling his daughter to listen, with loud exclamations of amazement and delight at the answers they gave him.

But Dianella's face shewed such evident consternation and her eyes so strange a bewilderment that he suddenly changed his tone and manner altogether, and pretended to be surprised, because the gravity of recent events in Sicily, in which the young Prince must, by all accounts, be more than a little implicated, did not appear to him to go with the gay humour which his nephew and niece described. And he started to relate, with an expression of grave consternation on his features, all that had been happening of late in Sicily, at Serradifalco, Catenanuova, Alcamo, Casale Fioresta, which proved that throughout the Island a great fire was smouldering, which would presently blaze out, and compared Sicily to a huge pile of timber, of trees that had died from want of moisture and for years past had been mercilessly felled, now that the rain of benefits was entirely confined to Northern Italy, and never a drop fell on the parched soil of the Island. Now the young folk had amused themselves by kindling beneath the pile the wisps of straw of their socialistic preachings, and behold, the old logs were beginning to catch fire. They were for the present little noisy flares, a crackling here and there; there shot forth now at one point, now at another, a threatening tongue of flame; but these had already condensed in the air into a suffocating smoke. And the worst of it was this: that the Government, instead of hastening to throw water, sent soldiers down to raise another kind of fire with the fire of their rifles. But if at least they had had enough soldiers to face the onslaught of the enraged populace! The scattered garrisons, stupidly incited to fire upon the unarmed crowds, found themselves at once compelled to barricade themselves in their barracks; and then the mob, maddened by slaughter, remained in command of the field and furiously assailed the municipal offices and set fire to them. Terror meanwhile was spreading through the island; mayors and prefects and chief constables were losing their heads; and where was it all going to end?

This he said for the special benefit of his brother-in-law Francesco Velia, Capolino and Aurelio Costa; he reserved for the ladies an account of a recent act of prowess performed by five hundred women in a village in the interior of Sicily, named Milocca. On the specious charge that a heap of manure had been spread, not outside but on the actual property of a landowner who had declined to agree to the new system of tenure introduced by the peasants of the Fascio, the public authorities had unjustly arrested, and committed for trial on a charge of criminal conspiracy the President and the four members of council of the Fascio itself. Whereupon the women of the village, to the number of five hundred, indignant at this injustice and tyranny, had burst upon the barracks of the carabinieri like so many furies, broken in the door and carried off the five men under arrest; then, wild with joy at the liberation of the prisoners, had borne in triumph, shoulder-high, through the streets of the village, one of the carabinieri and the weapons they had torn from their hands.

Donna Rosa, Nicoletta Capolino and Lillina loudly applauded the victory of these gallant women; but Don Flaminio held up his hands and cried:

"Gently, gently! Wait a moment! The rejoicing was brief.... The Milocchesi, I mean the men, who had not been in any way concerned in this revolt of their womenfolk, hearing that the Prefect of the Province was sending a reinforcement of troops and police and magistrates to Milocca, mounted their mules and, armed with shotguns, took to the fields. They are still scattered about the countryside, determined to sell their freedom dear. But the worthy magistrates, at Milocca, have arrested thirty-two women, including some who are expectant mothers, and others with infants at the breast, and have marched them off in handcuffs to the prison of Mussomeli."

"Brave men! Brave men!" Donna Rosa exclaimed. "But how in the world? And you, Gnazio, a Sicilian deputy, haven't raised your voice in Parliament, even to denounce the arrest of pregnant women and nursing mothers?"

Don Flaminio smiled and, stroking his moustaches, said:

"It wouldn't suit his book. They are Socialist wives and mothers. He is a Conservative. Although down there, you know, Don Ippolito Laurentano would like the Clerical Party to support the proletariat movement and make capital out of it, coming to some secret agreement with the leaders. But Monsignor Montero, you will be glad to hear, is against this; perhaps because Canon Pompeo Agro has been for the last month at Comitini carrying on propaganda, I don't know how far on Gospel principles, against myself, among the sulphur workers. However. We shall see a coolness between father and son. To-morrow I shall leave a card upon the young Socialist Prince."

Capolino accompanied Flaminio Salvo on this visit to the villino on Via Sommacampagna, and on his return. The strange impression, almost amounting to terror, that the sight of Dianella, on her arrival, had made upon him, was strengthened by what Salvo said to him on the way.

It was one of his usual winding discourses, full of hints and veiled allusions, from which Capolino thought that he could make out this: that he was in truth greatly worried not by the political state of Sicily but by the state of his daughter's mind, which gave him all the more food for thought inasmuch as her mother was insane; that he intended therefore to meet her wishes, if this visit to Rome did not produce the effect that he promised himself from it; to meet her wishes also, because, now that his sister had left his house, he, no longer having anyone to leave with his daughter, who needed attention, affectionate companionship, distraction, would be obliged to sacrifice too much of his working time, and could not (here Capolino felt he was expected to note a severe rebuke of his wife, who had dared to leave Donna Adelaide alone as well, on the occasion of her marriage); to meet her wishes, lastly, and at the same time bestow upon Aurelio Costa (who presently, in two or three days, would be returning to Sicily) a fitting reward, if he succeeded in bringing the sulphur workers to their right minds.

These quite obvious deductions from Salvo's long, hinting speech, cost Capolino so intense an effort that one of the glasses of his spectacles, which were continually being clouded by his breath, broke between his nervous fingers, under the strain of polishing. Fortunately the fragments of glass only tore his handkerchief, without cutting his fingers. But that evening he would have to speak to his wife, and to speak seriously, without spectacles.

Nicoletta knew that the unexpected arrival in Rome of Flaminio Salvo and Dianella was due to Costa; more perspicacious than her husband, she had at once foreseen that their coming would mark the end of her life of pleasure, and she was accordingly so inflamed with hatred of the responsible party that she would have killed him without hesitation, had she been able to do so with impunity. Already she had seen the first result of their coming: Ciccino and Lillina had gone off on a tour of Rome with their pale, mystified cousin, leaving her out of their plans from the first morning.

So it was an ill-chosen moment for a serious talk!

"I am to go, am I?" she at once asked, to cut the discussion short. "I can go to-morrow, if you like. Without any talk about it. But not alone, no!"

"With whom?" put in Capolino. "I..."

"You have the destiny of Italy on your hands, I know!" exclaimed Nicoletta. "How could the Chamber sit to-morrow, if you weren't there?"

"I beg of you," said Capolino, with a movement of his hands which signified restraint, prudence, on the one hand, and on the other that he disdained to roll the ball of conversation down a slope that was easy, however slippery. "I am here to do my duty!"

"So am I!" Nicoletta promptly retorted. "You don't agree? You, as a Deputy, I as a wife. The Mayor said when he married us: the wife must follow her husband. Oh, my dear man, if you're going to fly into a rage about it!... Leave your duties out of it; don't make me laugh! I've told you before: you, my dear, seem to have lost your sense of proportion! Let us talk as we used to, or rather, let us understand one another as we used to, without talking at all, for your good and mine. Bear in mind, Gnazio, you may be bored, but I am bored to death, and capable of... oh, I don't know, capable at this moment of doing the maddest things. I warn you!"

"God in heaven, but why?" Capolino groaned, clasping his hands together.

"Why?" shouted Nicoletta, advancing upon him, ablaze with anger and scorn. "You ask me why? You tell me to go, to return home, and you ask me why?"

"Please, please..." Capolino tried to interrupt her, and thrust his hands forward, as though to arrest her onslaught physically as well. "In our... in your own interest, surely! If you won't allow me to speak..."

"But what do you want to say! Let well alone!" exclaimed Nicoletta.

"I know what I have to say, don't worry," Capolino went on with intense gravity, lowering his eyes. "You don't know what Flaminio told me this morning. I have said nothing to you, up to the present, about your protracted stay in Rome? Nothing.... And you were blaming yourself for not having gone down to look after Donna Adelaide on her wedding day. Now, do you know what has been the effect of your absence from Girgenti? Simply this: Flaminio Salvo, left alone and overburdened, has decided to meet his daughter's wishes at last."

Nicoletta was taken aback by this news.

"Indeed?" she said; and bit her lip, a blind glare of hatred in her eyes.

"Do you understand?" Capolino went on. "He is afraid of her brain going, like her mother's. And it seems to me that his fear is not unfounded. Did you see her? She's a pitiful..."

"Sickening! Disgusting!" broke from Nicoletta. "She ought to be ashamed of herself!"

"Love!" sighed Capolino, raising his shoulders, half shutting his eyes. "And Flaminio thinks perhaps also that, with the shadow of her mother's insanity, a suitable match for her daughter not be easily found. Besides, he has put Costa in a most embarrassing position with the sulphur workers there, and is thinking of rewarding his devotion, his abnegation...."

"How thoughtful!... How sweet!" said Nicoletta. "And I am to go and wallow in it, am I, like a bee gathering honey?"

"You? Why?" asked Capolino.

"And who looks after his daughter, if it is not I?" Nicoletta inveighed. "Will it not fall to me to keep my eye on the loving couple? To watch their caresses, listen to their talk? To store in my bosom the confidences of the timid dove, restored to health and reason?"

Capolino shrugged his shoulders, as much as to say: "After all, why not?"

"Oh no, my dear!" his wife went on emphatically. "It would not matter in the least to me, if--in my own interest, as you say--I did not see myself obliged to play this part.... And you forget another thing! That this engineering gentleman once asked for my hand, and that I refused him, because I did not think him good enough for me! A fine revenge, now, for him, to become engaged before my eyes to Flaminio Salvo's daughter!"

"But such an encounter with you, who have already refused him," Capolino pointed out, "will be embarrassing for Flaminio Salvo's daughter, if anyone...."

"Indeed!" exclaimed Nicoletta, rising to her feet. "Because I am now the wife of the Honourable Deputy Ignazio Capolino!"

"Which is a great deal better, I would have you know!" cried he, thumping the table with his fist, and rising to his feet also, proudly.

Nicoletta measured him, calmly, from head to foot; then said:

"Oh, as far as merit goes, I should never dare to question it! Still... still, I am to go, that is all, purely in my own interest, as you say.... What would you have? Merit, my dear, is not always rewarded...."

"It infuriates me too," said Capolino, "that a fool, an idiot of that sort should rise like that, hoisted up by a lucky accident, shoved along like a stubborn animal in harness.... Because he, you know (he told me so himself), has no ambition whatsoever.... That is the beauty of it! He observes nothing, understands nothing, and fortune helps him on! In a day or two, he'll be Flaminio Salvo's son-in-law!"

"Ah, no!" Nicoletta broke out.... "That marriage shall not happen! I give you my word: *it shall not happen*!"

Capolino again shrugged his shoulders and screwed up his eyes:

"If Flaminio wishes it... how are you going to stop it?"

"How?" replied Nicoletta. "How... I don't know how! But at all costs... oh, at all costs! You may he quite sure of that!"

Capolino insisted:

"But really, do you suppose that Costa is capable of feeling revengeful, like that, for your refusal of him? No, I assure you! He is not capable even of that! I have studied him; with you he is respectful, obsequious... in fact, he is quite tongue-tied in your presence.... It will never occur to him! And if you... if you can manage to overcome your dislike of him, and to treat him... I mean to say, treat him with a sort of... polite indifference..."

Under the gaze of Nicoletta's eyes, which were fixed upon him with a cold and calm contempt, the smile that had accompanied these last words faded from his lips.

"As, for that matter, you have always treated him," he added with dignity. Then, changing the subject: "Oh, I was going to suggest that we might go out.... We might dine somewhere. ... Does that appeal to you?"

On their return home late at night, Nicoletta, as she got into bed, asked her husband:

"Hasn't Ingegnere Costa to go back to Sicily in a day or two?"

Luigi Pirandello

"Yes," replied Capolino. "Flaminio told me so this morning."

"And you might tell Flaminio," Nicoletta went on, curling up under the blankets, "that I too am ready to go; but not by myself. Since the engineer is going..."

"Why, of course!" exclaimed Capolino. "Excellent! You might travel down together...."

"Good-night, dear!"

"Good-night."

TOMORROW, FOR EVER.

Being firmly convinced that fate had always been against him, from the day of his birth, Flaminio Salvo believed that it was only by steadfastly maintaining an ever alert and unshakable resolution, and by opposing with actions which he himself considered harsh all those people who had made or were making themselves the blind instruments of fate that he had been able, up to the present, to defeat it.

But the aversion of fate, powerless to injure him, had turned with ferocity against his family, his wife, his son: now also, with that unconquerable passion, against his daughter. In these calamities he felt that there really was something akin to a vile and cruel revenge; and this feeling not only set him free from any remorse for all the harm that he knew himself to have done, it even made him ashamed of certain momentary weaknesses, and seemed almost to make it easy for him to do further harm, whether to be avenged upon fate in his turn or to save himself from being crushed by it.

He never for a moment let himself entertain the suspicion that there might after all be nothing wrong in his daughter's passion for Aurelio Costa. It was to him unquestionably wrong; and not on account of any difference in birth or social position (all moonshine!) but because it had its origin in a weakness of his own, in the gratitude he had shewn for all these years to his young rescuer. Out of good nothing could come to him but harm. This was an article of his belief. And no philosopher could have persuaded him to recognize that his reasoning, founded upon a prejudice, was at fault. Logic? What was logic compared with the experience of a lifetime? Besides, if, in a single instance, he was persuaded to recognize the flaw in his reasoning, what excuse had he left for all the harm that he had deliberately done in so many other instances?

Whenever a business deal, a transaction of any sort, seemed from the outset to be turning to his advantage, he, instead of rejoicing, would grow despondent, would at once suspect a trap set for him by fate and would prepare to defend himself.

He was none too well pleased, therefore, either by the information brought him and the suggestion made by Capolino, to wit, that Nicoletta was ready to start the next day, and that she would like to travel down with Costa; or by the message delivered by Ciccino and Lillina, that Lando Laurentano, who had been going about all that morning with Dianella and themselves, would look in that evening to see him. They had met him by accident, and although he had begun by telling them that he was greatly annoyed by something that had appeared in one of the morning papers, he had afterwards grown quite merry in their company and had been most grateful for the distraction it afforded.

Flanainio Salvo was in Francesco Vella's study, and was giving Aurelio Costa his final instructions with regard to his return to Sicily, which was fixed for the morning following, when his nephew and niece brought him this message, bursting noisily into the room and bringing Dianella with them. He at once noticed a very different change in Dianella's face from her usual expression on catching sight of Aurelio, and seemed almost stunned for a moment when, after her cousins had spoken of Laurentano's gracious affability to them, she, in a ringing voice that did not sound like her own, and with an air almost of defiance, corroborated them:

"Yes, most polite! Really most polite!"

"I am glad..." he replied coldly, looking at her over his spectacles. "But, if you don't mind, I am engaged just now...."

And he glanced at Costa, as much as to say: "I have something far more important to think about at the moment...."

This was true, as it happened. It was a question of exposing to the risk of death this worthy young man, in entire ignorance of the part he was cast to play; it was a question of flinging him as a prey to the fury of an entire populace, famished and disillusioned.

Salvo's soul was at that moment the scene of a strange play of conscious fictions. His pleasure at this announcement must be

transformed into displeasure, his hopes into misgivings; and therefore, not only must he not build upon the fortunate accident of
their meeting with Laurentano, or upon the good impression which
his daughter appeared to have formed of him, he must actually regard it as a positive misfortune, coming at a moment when he,
simply in order to meet his daughter's wishes, was giving this good
young fellow Costa a glimpse of his reward for the highly perilous
undertaking into which he was flinging him. And he continued in
this conscious self-deception, fired with anger at his daughter, who,
after compelling him to yield so far, came into the room now to let
him know, with a quite novel expression on her face, that the
young Prince of Laurentano had by no means failed to attract her!

Nor did the play of fictions in Salvo's soul stop there. He
pretended that he did not yet understand his daughter's strange
expression, which he had understood perfectly from the first; he
was positive, in fact, that Dianella, in paying that tribute to Laurentano in Aurelio's hearing, had intended to avenge herself on the
latter, and was now certain to be in her own room, crying and tormenting herself in secret. His feigned annoyance at the prize which
he was to dangle before Costa's eyes was therefore a genuine annoyance after all; so much so that, in order not to feel any remorse
at this anguish he was causing to his daughter, he went on pretending to believe in earnest that really, yes, really, if Costa should be
successful in bringing the sulphur workers in Sicily to their right
minds, he would give him Dianella as a reward. In the meantime,
he was sending him off next day, with Nicoletta Capolino.

That evening, he made himself polite, but with a certain
amount of reserve, to Lando Laurentano, who received a warm
welcome from the Velia family, especially from Ciccino and Lillina.

Dianella was as white as a sheet, and kept going by continuous spasmodic efforts, which pained and alarmed her relatives.
Her gentle eyes now glowed with strange piercing sparks, now darkened as though in a confused terror, now faded into a clouded
opacity. Nicoletta Capolino, invited to dine by the Velia on this last
evening, had let her know that she would be leaving Rome with
Costa in the morning; and now, there she was, speaking, without
any coy affectations, but with her habitual vivacious ease, to the
young Prince of Laurentano of the exquisite courtesy shewn to her

by Don Ippolito, down at Colimbetra, on the unfortunate occasion of her husband's duel.

Her husband himself appeared, a moment later, in the richly furnished drawing-room, with the engineer Aurelio Costa, who had come to say goodbye to the Velia family.

This was for Dianella and Nicoletta a moment of agonizing suspense.

Just as the Honourable Ignazio Capolino appeared composed and grave and troubled in those funereal tortoiseshell spectacles, so Aurelio Costa appeared light-headed, excited, dazzled. Plainly visible on his face was the profound emotion which the news of his immediate departure with Nicoletta had aroused in him. He no longer felt the ground under his feet; he was incapable of articulating a single word.

On seeing him enter the room, Nicoletta felt a sense of alarm: she could tell, without looking at him, that he was searching for her with his eyes, without a thought for anyone else. She breathed again, when, a moment later, she heard him engaged in animated discussion with Laurentano of the Fascist movement in Sicily.

All his consternation had vanished, vanished all consideration for the starving sulphur workers at Aragona, vanished his disgust at the destruction of his plan for compulsory co-operation: he would now have gone out, cudgel in hand, to face all those rebels down there.

Flaminio Salvo, with a prudent regard for Laurentano's presence, recalled him with a smile to milder language.

"So that they may set fire to the sulphur?" Costa asked him, in a white heat of rage. "I know them, the brutes! Never let them see you're afraid of them! You need a big stick to bring them to reason! Leave it to me.... Deserted by everyone, without even the satisfaction of seeing my plan considered worthy of a glance, I shall go down there, alone... and we shall meet face to face...."

In his excitement he did not perceive the astonishment with which this bellicose utterance was received; nor was he at all put out when at length he became aware that no one was paying any attention to him; he allowed Capolino to lead him out upon the wide balcony outside the room, while Flaminio Salvo, Francesco Velia and Lando Laur-entano went on talking quietly among themselves, and Ciccino promised Nicoletta that he would come down to Girgenti soon to pay her a visit, and Donna Rosa and Lillina showered advice on Dia-nella, that she should do this, that and the other, if she wished to recover her health and spirits quickly. Called by Salvo, Capolino returned to the room a moment later, and Aurelio Costa was left alone upon the balcony.

How long did he remain there? He gazed at the stars, gazed, as in a dream, at the gleam of the moonlight reflected from the distant windows opposite, across the piazza; gripped by a maddening, sweet desire; without any idea of where he happened to be; with a single image before his eyes, hers who now, in another moment, would surely be coming out in quest of him, to say to him: "Tomorrow! For ever!"--"Tomorrow, for ever," he repeated, clenching his fists, his eyes closed in voluptuous longing.

He had spoken to her already that morning. They had come to an understanding. Everything, she would leave everything, to follow him! Yes, even down there, amid the peril, from which he could not at that moment draw back. Anyhow, he was obliged to go back there; his home was there, and his work, which he would now place at the disposal of other employers, forsaking Salvo. What did that matter? What was the reward that she had mentioned to him? A great reward, which he would forfeit if he parted from Salvo.... What did it matter? What reward could be greater than the happiness that she would bring him, by loving him?

So Aurelio raved to himself on the balcony, as he waited, repeating from time to time, with ecstasy: "Tomorrow! For ever!"

In the drawing-room, meanwhile, Ignazio Capo-lino was speaking in a tone of distress of the hubbub with which the publication of a criminal charge in one of the morning papers had filled the lobbies of the Chamber all that day. It was a matter of the forty thousand lire for which appeared as debtor to the Banca Romana Roberto Auriti, "notoriously the cloak," said the paper, "for a well-known Southern Deputy, who until quite recently, was in the good graces, if not actually of the Government, of several of its members." And the paper went on to speak of the documents that had been abstracted, in order to save this Southern Deputy. But, in the heat of excitement, at the last moment, a certain letter had been overlooked and had fallen into the hands of the judicial authorities, a letter signed by Auriti himself, now anxiously in search of those forty thousand lire, to save himself and his friend.

Capolino said that several Deputies of the Extreme Left were going to raise the question in the Chamber, and foretold the imminent arrest of Auriti.

Lando Laurentano was on tenterhooks. All that afternoon he had been trying to discover from what source the information had reached the paper. It appeared to have been brought by somebody who had been listening at the door of the room in which Giulio Auriti was imploring his help; and he was afraid that Giulio might now suspect him of being responsible for the betrayal.

Salvo, Velia and Capolino, noticing the young Prince's emotion, began to commiserate Roberto Auriti, as an innocent victim, and Salvo let it be clearly understood that he would be quite willing to advance the money to save him; but Capolino said that it was now too late. There was nothing to be done except to take a cup of tea, which Lillina had made.

The first two cups, carried by Ciccino, had gone to Donna Kosa and Dianella. Nicoletta now handed a third to Lando Laurentano.

"Milk?"

"Yes, please. A little."

And Dianella, as she sipped hers, waited for Nicoletta to go out on the balcony with the last cup for Aurelio. But Nicoletta, seeing that she was being watched, pretended at first to have forgotten about him, and kept the cup for herself.

"Oh, what about my escort?" she then exclaimed, as though suddenly remembering his existence.

And she went out on the balcony.

As soon as Aurelio saw her appear, he drew back instinctively as far as he could into the darkness, to make her follow him. But she stood with one foot on the sill, and, holding out the cup to him, said quietly, stiffly:

"Come in, for goodness' sake: you are attracting attention. Don't be so childish."

"Only tell me..." he implored.

"Yes, I will tell you one thing: and get it firmly fixed in your mind," she added quickly, "that I have done everything to prevent your ruin and mine. Don't accuse me, to-morrow; because it has been your doing. That is all!" And she returned to the drawing-room.

CHAPTER IV

VA' FUORI D'ITALIA...

Corrado Selmi came out of the Chamber of Deputies livid, contorted, a convulsive tremor running through his whole body.

As soon as he reached the sunlight of the piazza, he made a desperate effort to recover himself, to seize within himself and restore to his own control the life that was ebbing from him in a tremendous turmoil; but abandoned the attempt, discovering that he had not even the strength to draw breath, as though his lungs, his stomach had been drawn and quartered.

A new feeling then arose in him suddenly: fear. Fear, not of other people, but of himself.

A moment ago he had challenged and assailed the others, there, in the Hall of Parliament, with extreme violence. It still made him tremble all over. No one, in there, had dared to breathe. But that silence... ah, that silence had been worse for him than any invective, than any tumultuous rising of the entire assembly.

That silence had overwhelmed him.

He still heard ringing in his ears the sound of his footsteps as he walked out of the hall. In the formidable silence, those footsteps had sounded like hammer-blows upon a coffin.

He felt a burning thirst; and a numbness in his legs, as though... as though they had been amputated.

Crushed by the accusation, he had attempted to rise again with all the impetus of the vital energies that were still potent in him; and had killed himself. There could be no doubt that the assembly, immediately upon his leaving the hall, had voted the necessary authority for proceedings to be taken against him.

And yet everybody knew that he was a poor man; knew that the money taken from the banks could not burden his conscience with shame or remorse, as in so many other cases.

After he had so often stared death in the face, at an age when to every man life is most dear, had he not earned the right to live? In the stupid complication of all those shady proceedings, the simplicity of this right seemed almost childish, and such that everyone must laughingly deny it to him.

Dead; not only that, but they wished him to die disgraced! He must die, then, and he might have been a hero to all these living men, who flung in his face now, as a crime, his having lived.

But it was not so much the accusation, after all, that seemed to him unjust, as his accusers; and, more than unjust, ungrateful and vile: vile because, after having for all these years understood that he had the right to live, they now rose to prove to him, scoffing, the childishness of his claim; after having for all these years understood his need, they now rose to fling it in his face as a reproach.

Nor would they stop at that! Next, the trial, conviction, prison.

Corrado Selmi laughed, and again remarked the effort that it cost him to relax the murderous expression on his face in that horrible laugh. The frank, light smile, that had always accompanied all the activities of his life, even the most serious and hazardous, was it transformed into this melancholy grimace, hard and bitter? Once again he felt afraid of himself: afraid of acquiring a precise consciousness of something obscure and horrible that had suddenly crept into his innermost being and was plunging him in confusion, giving him that impression of having been drawn and quartered, irremediably.

And, to recover as best he might his material solidity, to overcome his repulsion and horror at this impression, he looked round about him, as though imploring support and comfort from the familiar aspect of things. They too seemed to him changed and somehow evanescent. He felt, with terror, that it was no longer possible for him to re-establish a relation of any sort between himself and the things around him. Yes, he might look; but what did he see? He might speak; but what was he to say? He might move, but where was he to go?

He spoke, simply to hear the sound of his own voice; and it too seemed to him to have altered. He said:

"What am I doing?"

He knew very well what remained for him to do. But, as he squeezed from his palate with his tongue the double c of the word faccio, he was conscious of nothing but the dryness of his tongue and the bitter taste in his mouth; and stood there with a frown of disgust on his face.

"No," he went on. "First of all... what else?"

Anything else appeared to him futile, vain. He could only, for a little while longer, to relieve his feelings and thus find some outlet, some way of escape from himself, say and do foolish things. Think seriously, act seriously he could not, save at the cost of yielding to the obscure, violent purpose which threatened to destroy all the elements of life within him. He could amuse himself with the fragments of that life, which, from the internal tumult, kept springing to the surface of his shattered consciousness: amuse himself for a little.... Yes, at Roberto Auriti's! He must see him, tell him that for his sake, to shield him, he had voluntarily surrendered to the charge. Yes, he still had somewhere to go. He hailed a cab, so that the trembling weakness of his limbs might pass unnoticed, and gave the driver the address: Via delle Colonnette.

As soon as he was seated, he changed his mind, anticipating, in return for all that he had done, a violent scene. But no: at all costs he would manage to prevent that. His action appeared to him more than dutiful, positively generous to Roberto Auriti. And, at that moment, he could feel nothing but anger at his own generosity. He had stripped himself of all his prestige, of every privilege, to share the fate of a defeated wretch, who had not known how to make use of his talents, his deserts, to make a position for himself, to force himself, as he might have done, upon the consideration of his fellows. Roberto Auriti could inspire no pity, only anger and contempt. Even if he, steering blindly, had flung his friend with himself among these breakers, that castaway did not, surely, deserve that Corrado Selmi, when he had almost reached the shore, should dash back into the sea to perish with him: he did not deserve it, because he had never known how to live, that fellow, how to surmount even the most trifling obstacles: he was already in his own eyes a drowning man, to whom again and again Selmi had thrown a rope to help him to swim to the shore. When, once and once only, Selmi had tried to help him, why, by the very hand that he held out to him, he had dragged him down after him into the gulf, down, down, obliging him to abandon any chance of being rescued by other people. And that brother of his who had dashed off to Sicily to save them both: yes indeed! they must all wait in patience until he came back with the money! At his leisure! Without hurrying! And after he had disclosed everything to Lando Laurentano. The idiot! Yes, for this reason alone, he might have refrained from exposing himself to shield an incompetent. But now...

On reaching the Via delle Colonnette, as he climbed the dark stair, he ran into Olindo Passalacqua, who was hurrying down four steps at a time.

"Ah! The very man, Onorevole! I was coming to look for you.... Tell me, what has happened? What is in the air?"

"Wind," replied Corrado Selmi, placidly.

Olindo Passalacqua stood rooted to the ground.

"Wind? What do you mean? That infamous accusation? But how? Who was it? I should like to spit in his face! To go and create an Italy for swine like that!"

Corrado Selmi took the other's chin between his fingers:

"Bravo, Olindo! *Nobili sensi, invero*.... Come along upstairs!"

"Wait, Onorevole," Passalacqua pleaded, holding him back. "I must warn you! My Nanna knows nothing about it. We didn't know about it ourselves. Quite by chance, my brother-in-law Pilade happened to pick up a newspaper of the day before yesterday... opened it and saw... sent it up to us, marked.... Roberto was watering the flowers on the terrace... he read it, it fairly knocked him down.... But can you believe it? A man, a man in his position, not to read the paper, at a time like this! He's like that bird, don't you know... what do they call it? ... that buries its head in the sand.... And I take in three, if you please, every day: three papers! If he read one even! The moment he opens it he begins to nod; and then he says that he has read all three of them and can never sleep a wink!"

"The ostrich," said Corrado Selmi. "Allow me!"

And he raised his hands to Olindo Passa-lacqua's throat to put straight the flowing red necktie, knotted in a butterfly bow.

"The ostrich," he repeated. "That bird you mentioned.... Now you're all right!"

Again Olindo Passalacqua stared at him open-mouthed.

"Thank you," he said. "But then... is there no need for us to worry, then?"

Corrado Selmi gazed into his eyes, earnestly; laid his hands upon his shoulders, and:

"Aren't you a censor?" he asked him.

"Censor... yes," Passalacqua replied, with an air of perplexity, as though he were not quite sure of the fact.

"Very well, then, let the sky fall!" exclaimed Selmi with a gesture of contemptuous indifference. "Censor, put it in your pipe and smoke it. Come along, upstairs, now, with me."

They found Roberto prostrate in an armchair, his face turned to the ceiling, his arms drooping, the watering can by his side. As soon as he saw Selmi, he started to his feet and, sobbing convulsively, flung himself upon his breast.

"For pity's sake! For pity's sake!" Olindo Passalaequa entreated him, hastening to shut the door, and signalling to him with his hands not to make a noise, that Nanna would hear him in the other room.

Through the shut door, the sobbing of Roberto on Corrado Selmi's breast was answered by the caterwauling voice of a singing pupil.

Corrado Selmi, tottering under the weight of Roberto, stood for a while watching the signals of Passalacqua, who continued to implore pity on the delicate heart of his poor wife, pity on the ruined Roberto, pity on the household, which would be turned upside down; finally, his shoulders began to shake with an insane laugh:

"Give it here!" he said, seizing the watering can and dashing out upon the terrace. "Why are we all so solemn? You were watering, weren't you? Let us go on watering! Here... here ... so! Like this! Bain, Olindo! Kain! Rain!"

And a regular torrent of rain came showering from the rose

of the watering can upon Olindo Passalacqua, who tried to escape by the terrace, screaming and shielding his head with his hands, followed by Selmi roaring with laughter, saying:

"I take the water, thou takest the water, he takes the water, we all take the water!" [Footnote: A play upon the name Passalacqua. C.K.S.M.]

"Oh Lord! For pity's sake... no, my dear Sir... nooo... what are you doing?... Stop, for pity's sake... it's no joke, I tell you! Stop! Oooh! Stop!..."

His cries brought Nanna, her singing pupil, Antonio Del Be and Celsina upon the scene.

At once Corrado Selmi, breathless, ran to shake hands with Signora Lalla, who laughed as she looked at her husband shaking himself like a drenched chicken. The two girls laughed also.

"What, my dear Nanna," cried Selmi, "is the most useful of plants? The riso![1] Let us cultivate the riso! Let us water Olindo, who makes us laugh!"

"But I'm not laughing, I'm crying..." groaned Passalacqua.

"Precisely; because you're crying, you make us laugh!" retorted Selmi.

"Laughter often ends..." muttered Antonio Del Be, clenching his fists.

"In tears, you mean?" Selmi completed the saw. "Bravo, young man! Always serious! All the silly things you do will always be firm and solid, with sharp claws and plenty of snout. We do ours... here, censor, dancing, dancing.... Come, Nanna, into the other room, to the piano! You play and we dance! Roberto shall put his trousers on back to front, with the tail of his shirt sticking out; he shall take his toy sword and his wooden horse, the ones he played at soldiers with, in Sixty; we shall make him a paper helmet, and he can career round the room, gee-up, gee-up, while Olindo and I dance to the tune of Garibaldi's hymn....

Va' fuori d'Italia... va' fuori d'Italia Va' fuori d'Italia... va' fuori, o stranieri"

He was still singing the refrain when there appeared in the doorway of the terrace, with tears of joy in his eyes, radiating bliss-

---

[1] Riso in Italian means both rice and laughter. C.K.S.M

ful emotion, Mauro Mortara with his medals on his breast and his knapsack on his back.

As soon as he saw him, Corrado Selmi, with a horrified gesture, dashed through the other window that opened on the terrace, shouting:

"Ah, perdio, no! This is too much!"

Roberto Auriti ran after him to stop him:

"Corrado! Corrado!" Mauro Mortara, at this sudden flight, stood in bewilderment facing the stupefaction of Signora Lalla, Passalacqua and the singing pupil, the smiling wonder of Celsina and the scowling wonder of Antonio Del Be.

"I have come, no offence meant," he said, "to say good-bye to Don Roberto. I am leaving to-morrow."

"And who may you be?" Signora Lalla inquired, as though she saw before her a denizen of the moon, rained down from the sky.

"I am..." Mauro Mortara was beginning to explain; but he broke off abruptly on catching sight of Antonio Del Re. "Aren't you Donna Caterina's grandson?"

As he uttered her name he raised his hat.

"Do you tell them," he went on, "who I am. I have been here twice before; they would not allow me upstairs, because Don Roberto was not at home."

Passalacqua, dripping from head to foot, went up to him, began fingering the medals on his breast and inquired:

"A Sicilian Patriot? The Sicilian Patriots, perdio, deserve statues of gold! Sta... stat ... statues..."

A sneeze, slow in exploding, kept him for a while open-mouthed, with quivering nostrils and hands held out as though to ward it off; finally it exploded, and:

"Of gold!" Passalacqua repeated. "Curse that Selmi, he has made me catch cold! But why has he run away? He must be mad! Just look how he... has... but where has he gone?"

He was interrupted by a scream of "Roberto!" from Signora Lalla as she dashed from the terrace into the room through which Selmi had just made his escape.

They all crowded into the room after her, in terror.

A stranger, with his hat in his hand and his eyes lowered,

was standing rigid upon the threshold of the room, while Roberto, his chalky face mottled in patches, looked round the room, staggered, unable to make up his mind. At her cry, he put out his hands, but as though to check the outburst of his own emotion rather than anyone's else.

"Please, please," he said, "no fuss.... It's nothing.... A... a summons from the police."

"They're arresting him!" Antonio Del Be hissed through his set teeth, his face changing as he trembled all over.

Nanna gave a shriek, and fell in hysterics in her husband's arms.

"They're arresting him?" asked Mauro Mor-tara, stepping forward, while Roberto looked about the room for the clothes he would require, signalling to them all not to shout, not to make a fuss.

"How is this?" Mauro went on, gazing at Antonio Del Re.

Receiving no answer from anyone, he went up to the stranger and, with upraised arm, apostrophised him:

"You! You have come here to arrest Don Roberto Auriti?"

"Mauro!" the last-named interrupted him. "For pity's sake, Mauro... don't interfere!"

"But how?" repeated Mauro Mortara, turning to Roberto. "They are arresting you? Why?"

Roberto hastened to lend a hand to Passalaequa, the singing pupil and Celsina, who were unable to support Signora Lalla, who struggled and twisted amid screams, sobs, groans and hysterical laughter.

"Into the other room, for goodness' sake; take her out of here!" he appealed to them.

But it was not possible. Passalacqua, instead of availing himself of Roberto's help, thought fit to fling his arms round his neck, bursting into sobs and exclaiming:

"Scapegoat! Scapegoat!"

Roberto freed himself, with a shudder of disgust, and stopped his ears, while Passalacqua, turning again to Mauro, went on:

"You see, Patriot? This is how Italy rewards her heroes! Like this!"

"The son of Stefano Auriti!" Mauro Mortara was muttering to himself, his eyes starting from their sockets, beating his breast as he spoke. "The son of Donna Caterina Laurentano!... And I came to Rome to see this! But what have you been doing?" he demanded of Roberto, gripping both his arms and shaking him. "Tell me that you are still the same man! Yes? You are? Very well, then..."

He snatched at his medals; tore them from his breast; flung them on the ground; stepped on them and trampled them underfoot; then, turning to the police inspector:

"Tell that to your Government!" he shouted. "Tell them that an old campaigner, come on a visit to Rome, with his Garibaldi medals, when he saw them arrest the son of a hero who died in his arms at the battle of Milazzo, tore the medals from his breast and trampled on them! So!"

He turned to Roberto, took him in his arms, and, hearing him sob upon his shoulder began trying to soothe him with murmurs of "My boy! My boy!" patting him on the back.

At this stage Antonio Del Re rushed from the room, with a moan of rage, knocking a chair over in his flight. Celsina, who was keeping an eye upon him, ran after him, in alarm, calling to him by name. Mauro Mortara turned with feline stealth, as though, at this headlong exit, it had flashed across his mind that they were determined at all costs to prevent Roberto's arrest; and shewed himself prepared for any deed of violence. Freed from his embrace, Roberto stepped in front of the inspector.

"Here I am."

"No!" cried Mauro, seizing him again by the arm. "Don Roberto! Do you surrender like this?"

"Kindly let me go...." said Roberto Auriti; then, turning to the inspector: "You must excuse ..."

He beckoned to Nanna, who was now gasping for breath, with both hands pressed to her heart, and kissed her on the brow, saying:

"Courage...."

"And what shall I say to your mother?" exclaimed Mauro Mortara, waving his hands in the air.

Roberto's bosom heaved, he covered his face with his hands to dam the torrent of his emotion, and left the room, es-

corted by the inspector, while Signora Lalla, supported by her husband and the pupil, started moaning rather than shouting:

"Roberto! Roberto! Roberto!"

Mauro Mortara was left staring, crushed and senseless.
When Passalacqua informed him of all that had happened, and,
fresh from his recent perusal of the newspaper, set before him all
the misery and shame of the moment:

"This," he said, "this is Italy?"

And, seeing his great dream shattered, he thought no more
of Roberto Auriti, of his arrest; heard, saw nothing any more. He
saw only his medals lying there on the ground, trampled underfoot.

DON'T BOTHER!

As he was going down the stair from Koberto's, Corrado Selmi ran into the police inspector and his escort, on their way up to arrest the innocent man. He stopped for a moment, undecided; but at once felt his brain filled by a dense mist, and in that darkness of wrath and anguish heard a voice warning him from the depths of his consciousness that he could not by any precipitate action prevent this atrocious injustice. He went on his way down the stair; got into his cab again and felt a sense of stupor upon the driver's inquiring where he was to take him. Why, home of course; no need to tell him that. Where else could he go? What was there left for him to do?

"Via San Nicolo da Tolentino."

And, as though he were already there, he saw himself going up the stair of his own house: now, he was going into his bedroom; he crossed to the corner, where there was a hanging cabinet of green lacquer: opened it; took out a little bottle, and.... Instinctively, he had thrust his hand into his waistcoat pocket, where he kept the key of that cabinet. A strange thing: he was thinking now of the mirror, of a little oval mirror that hung beside the cabinet, from which he ought to have been keeping his eyes averted, so as not to see his own reflexion. And yet he could, he did see himself: yes, in that mirror, with the bottle in his hand: he saw the expression in his eyes, which smiled hack at him, as though they did not believe that he would do the deed. No! First of all he must write out and seal a statement for Auriti; just a few lines, stating the facts explicitly. His accusers did not deserve a final outburst on his part. A couple of lines, only, to save his friend, who by this time must be in prison.

His enemies.... But who were they? How many? The whole world! Was it possible? All his friends of yesterday. Everybody, and yet nobody, if he took them one by one. For he had never done anything to any of them that could transform the hearty welcome of yesterday into such aloofness of spirit, such hostility. It was the moment, the blind fury of the moment that was falling upon him, that was finding its prey in him, and seizing him and tearing him to pieces.

Oh, how the cab was crawling! It seemed to Corrado Selmi to be prolonging his agony with contemptuous cruelty.

"I am not at home to anybody," he said to Pietro, the old servant who had been with him for so many years.

And his first impulse, on entering his bedroom, was towards the cabinet. He checked it. He remembered the statement that he had to write. He decided, however, to secure the bottle first, and, without looking at it, took it with him to the writing table in his study. He stood there for a while, as though trying to remember something which he had intended to do, and which had passed out of his mind. Instinctively, gently, he tiptoed back to his bedroom; his eyes found their way to the little oval mirror, hanging on the wall by the cabinet. He had forgotten to look at himself in it. He shrugged his shoulders and turned back to the writing table; sat down; took from the blotting book a sheet of paper and an envelope; looked to see whether the stick of wax and his seal were on the table; rose again and returned to his bedroom to fetch the candle from his bed-table.

The statement turned out less brief than he had planned, since, as an additional safeguard to Auriti's innocence, he decided to cite as a witness the governor of the bank himself, who also was now under arrest, and with whom, before incurring the debt under another name, he had come to a secret agreement.

When he had finished writing, he looked at the bottle on the table and at once felt all desire to read over again what he had written vanish. They seemed to him enormous, all the little things that still remained to be done: folding and refolding the sheet; slipping it into the envelope; lighting the candle; melting the stick of wax in the flame; applying the seal.... He went through the whole process with irritation. He gasped for breath; his fingers slipped and fumbled, losing all sense of touch. He was just preparing to shut the envelope when from the street beneath rang out the strident, jerky strains of a barrel organ.

It seemed to Selmi that this sound, coming after all that had happened, must split his head: he stopped his ears, sprang to his feet, screwed up his face as though he were suffering unspeakable torments, was going to the window to hurl down abuse at the itinerant musician.

Ah no, perdio! Not that! At the sound of a trumpery little Neapolitan street song, no, no, no.

He felt humiliated by this outburst of rage. Or was it that he was really a scoundrel? No: quietly, at his ease, with a steady hand, without that dry feeling in his mouth; quietly, after he had soothed his nerves, and with a smile, he must kill himself, as was his duty.

He took the sealed envelope with the statement and slipped it into the blotting book; put the bottle of poison in his pocket. He wished to go out again, for a last drive, to bid farewell to life, released now from every care, rid of every burden, free from all passion, with clear eyes and a serene spirit; to bid farewell to life, to smile at it with his habitual gentle smile; to enjoy for the last time the things that remained to him, things that were rejoicing in this day of sunshine, unconscious amid the turbid flow of all these misfortunes, which presently time would have swept away. Yes, a last farewell to life, to the heautiful things which remained to him and which he had loved so well.

And he made the driver take him to the Janiculum. At first, confused by the dull roaring sound that was caused by a momentary stoppage in his ears, he was incapable of noticing, or seeing, or thinking anything; only when the carriage turned into the Via della Lungara, and passed the Regina Coeli prison, he reflected that possibly at that moment Roberto Auriti was confined there; but he refused to let the thought worry him any more. Soon enough, with the help of that statement, he would be released from prison, to carry on his precarious, tiresome, detrimental existence with that Signora Lalla of his and Passalacqua and Bonome, whereas he himself, on the other hand--ah, he would have been delivered!

When he reached the summit of the hill, it seemed to him a

real deliverance, that altitude, from which he could gaze upon Rome the divine, luminous in the sunlight, beneath the intense azure of the sky; a deliverance from all the bitter little miseries that had hurt and stifled him down below; from the shock of all the petty vulgarities of every day; from the tiresome quarrels of little men, who sought to dispute his right to move and to breathe. He felt himself, up there, free and alone, free and serene, raised above all hatred, above all passion, above and beyond time, exalted, assumed to that altitude by his great love of life, alone with and in that love, in defence of which he was going to take his life. And in it and with it he felt himself made pure, in an instant, for all time. In the eternity of that instant were cancelled, were absolved and vanished his weaknesses, his transgressions, his faults, since he had been after all a man, and subject to the law of necessity. Now, with death, he would surmount them all. There remained only, at this stage, luminous, indefeasible, immortal, his love of life, his love of the country, the fatherland for which he had fought and conquered. Yes, like all those who, down yonder, in defence of Rome had made a good death, cut off in the frenzied ardour of youth and rendered immune to all the frailties, free of all the obstacles which might, in time, have deformed and degraded them. Now, at this moment, he likewise, stripping himself of all his frailties, freeing himself from every obstacle, aflame and quivering with the old ardour, with the golden light in his eyes of the setting sun upon the houses of the great four-square city, he was preparing for himself, like them, a good death, a death that exalted him in his own eyes, without envy of those others who stood in effigy up there, handed down to posterity in a marble bust. He remembered that he had with him the bottle of poison; but no! At home! In the house! Quietly, on his bed: he must not make a scene!

He went down again to the city.

At the foot of the hill, he felt that he had left his soul up above, in the sunlight. Here, in the shadow, was his body, still alive, for a little while longer. He looked at his hands, his legs, and at once felt a thrill of horror. But, as though a voice from above were recalling him sternly to his duty, he controlled himself and in answer to the voice said yes, he would in a short time destroy that body, without hesitation.

After crossing the iron bridge, he heard several newsvendors crying a special edition of the most widely read sheet in Rome. Thinking that this must be for him, he stopped the carriage and bought a paper. Sure enough, on the front page was a report of the Parliamentary sitting and at the head of the sixth column his own name stood out in a headline

CORRADO SELMI

as the title of the principal feature of the paper. He began to read it; but soon felt a curious disgust for it: he noticed that to him all this stuff was already a vain and vacuous language, which had no longer any power to arouse any sentiment in him, as though it were composed of words that had no meaning. It seemed to him that the writer of the article had had no other object than to prove that he was alive, quite alive, and that, being so, he could and was going to play tricks with his words, so that the other living men, his readers, might say: "Isn't he a smart fellow? Isn't he clever?"

The sheet, flimsy as it was, seemed to him suddenly, with his name printed there at the top of the page, a tombstone, his own, which he himself, for some unaccountable reason, was taking with him in the carriage, straight to his grave; a strange stone, upon which, instead of the customary lying tributes, were carved accusations and insults. But what did they matter now to him? He lay beneath.

And indeed, as though to see where he did lie, he turned the page.

At once his eye was caught by a headline in huge type, spread across five columns of the second page:

THE MASSACRE AT ARAGONA IN SICILY

and beneath, in smaller type: *Revolt of sulphur workers--Attack on mining engineer Costa's carriage--Scenes of savagery--Mob kill him and wife of Deputy Capolino and set fire to their bodies.*

Corrado Selmi sat there, crushed by horror and disgust, his eyes fixed upon the account. He realized that it was for this and not for himself that the special edition had been published. The wife of the Deputy Capolino? He had seen her at Girgenti, when he went down there to support Roberto Auriti's candidature and to assist Veronica in his duel with her husband. Such a beautiful woman!... Murdered? And how did she come to be driving in a carriage, at Aragona, with this engineer? Ah, she had travelled from Rome with him..... An elopement?... He was Salvo's engineer.... The sulphur workers had marched in a body from the village to the station, determined not to let him pass, unless he brought them an assurance from Rome that the promises would be fulfilled.... What was this?... That Preda ... Marco Preola, that wretch whom Roberto Auriti had flung through the glass door in the office of that clerical rag... he was now in command of this savage horde of assassins... he had incited them to the attack on the carriage, the butchery. Oh, the cowards! To attack a woman. ... Costa fired... and then...

Selmi could read no more; he sat back in disgust with the paper lying open in his hands, stifled, poisoned by the foulness of the massacre; and seemed to feel himself assailed by the fierce breath of a whole populace turned to savages, drunken with blood. In a fit of loathing he rolled up the paper in a ball and flung it from the carriage. To-morrow, if not that very evening, in another special edition, it would be employing that huge type to announce his suicide.

As he let himself into the house, he was informed by Pietro, his old servant, that Auriti's nephew, Antonio Del Re, was in the sitting room.

"All right," he said. "Shew him into the study when I ring."

Pietro was perhaps expecting a reprimand for having admitted the young man, and had his answer ready, to wit, that the young man had forced his way into the house, notwithstanding his having definitely assured him that the master was not at home, and then done everything in his power to keep him out. He spread out his arms and bowed at Selmi's curt order; but, as his master made off in the direction of his bedroom, stood perplexed, wondering whether he ought not to warn him of the young man's threatening manner and distracted air. He shut his eyes, shrugged his shoulders, as much as to say: "An order's an order!" and withdrew to the sitting-room to keep the insolent visitor under observation.

"There," he said to him, with a glance at the door opposite. "In a minute, as soon as he rings...."

Antonio Del Re could contain himself no longer; he was fuming with rage. His face, under the terrible strain of waiting, was unrecognizable. His hand strayed restlessly in his pocket. And the old servant kept his eye on that hand which, through the cloth of his coat, seemed to be clutching a weapon.

And still the bell did not ring; and the longer the delay, the more the young man's ill-concealed impatience and the restless movement of his hand increased. The old servant, in the utmost consternation, went across to the door, took his stand in front of it, only just in time, for, at the peal of the bell, Antonio Del Re rushed at the door like a wild beast, brandishing a dagger, dragging in his wake the old man who had thrown his arms round him.

Corrado Selmi, pale as death, seated at the writing-table, with the glass still in his hand from which he had just drunk the poison, out of the bottle that lay overturned by the blotter, turned round and at once arrested, with a frigid stare and a faintly contemptuous smile that quivered on his lips, the young man's violent inrush.

"Don't bother!" he said to him. "You see? I have done it all, myself.... Let him go!" he ordered the servant. "And I forbid you to shout or to go for help."

He took the sealed envelope from the table and showed it to the young man, who stood gazing at him speechless and gasping.

"You are going the wrong way, my boy," he said to him. "You have a nasty look on your face.... But don't distress yourself: this letter is for your uncle. He will be released. Let it lie here."

He put the envelope back on the table; blinked his eyes, set his teeth; his body grew rigid, while the deathly pallor of his face became mottled with livid spots. He tried to rise; the servant hurried to his assistance.

"Help me... to bed..."

He turned to Del Re, his eyes already beginning to wander. The ghost of a smile seemed to flicker in his lifeless face. And he said in a strange voice:

"Learn to laugh, young fellow.... Go out into the air: it is a perfect day."

And he passed through the door, supported by his servant.

WOLF! WOLF!

As from the Via delle Colonnette, upon the arrest of Roberto Aurati, Antonio Del Re had escaped to Selmi's, so, but in a different mood, Mauro Mortara, picking up his trampled medals from the floor, had hastened in search of Lando Laurentano. At the villino on the Via Somma-campagna, Raffaele, the butler, had told him that his master, upon reading in the newspaper the account of the massacre there had been in Sicily, Girgenti way, had jumped into a cab and driven off to Velia's.

"And where is that? How am I going to find the way?"

"If you like, I can take a cab and go there with you."

In the cab, seeing Mauro's breathless anxiety to reach his destination, the other asked him whether he knew the lady and the engineer.

"What lady? What engineer?"

"What! Haven't you heard? Don't you know? They have murdered them at Aragona...."

"At Aragona?"

"The sulphurmen."

"Why, then..." And he had stopped short,, swinging round, to look first of all straight into the butler's face, with eyes that seemed to be; starting from their sockets, then out of the carriage at the passers-by in the street as though all of a sudden assailed by the suspicion that a great catastrophe had occurred without his knowing anything about it.

"Why, what is coming over us? Has everything gone wrong? Murder there! Arrests here! Do you know that they have arrested Don Roberto Auriti?"

"The master's cousin?"

"His cousin! His own flesh and blood! And he goes off to the Velia! They arrest his cousin, Don Roberto Auriti, one of the Thousand, who was out in Sixty, when he was only twelve years old! And his father died here, in my arms, at Milazzo.... Arrested! Before my eyes! That I should have lived to see the day!"

He had begun to raise his voice in the carriage, and to gesticulate and to weep aloud; and people were turning round, and stopping, and making remarks, seeing a man so strangely attired, with that knapsack on his back, driving along the street and shouting.

"Be quiet! Be quiet!"

Be quiet, indeed! Mauro Mortara was out for justice, and revenge for this arrest; and when Raffaele, to silence him, referred to the visit that, a few days earlier, possibly in this connexion, Don Giulio, Don Roberto's brother, had paid to his master:

"Of course!" he cried, remembering the occasion. "I was there! I was there! And I saw him weep! So this was why that poor boy was weeping? He was seeking help.... Then... then Don Landino must have refused to help him? Is it possible?"

"Perhaps because the amount was too large...."

"What do you mean, too large! When the honour of a patriot is at stake! And he a rich man! And his aunt never touched a penny of her father's fortune, every penny of it went to her elder brother.... Oh God! God! Donna Caterina ... the only one of them that is a worthy child of their father.... Now Donna Caterina will die of a broken heart.... But if this is true, by the Madonna, that he has refused to help, I will never look him in the face again, so help me God! I don't believe it! I won't believe it!"

On reaching Velia's house, however, he found such a turmoil raging there that he could no longer think of calling Lando to account for the arrest of Roberto Auriti.

Dianella Salvo, his little friend Donna Dianella, his dove, who in that month spent at Valsania had contrived to conquer and melt him with the tender charm of her eyes and voice, on seeing him enter the drawing-room frowning and bewildered, immediately sprang towards him with the neigh of a frightened filly, and clung to his bosom, trembling all over, burying her dishevelled head in his flannel shirt, as though seeking sanctuary in his heart, and shouting, with a hand stretched out behind her, towards her father:

"Wolf! Wolf!"

Mauro Mortara, thus overpowered, assailed, his breast buffeted by this girl in such a state, lifted his head in astonishment,
seeking an explanation in the eyes of the onlookers: he saw terrified, pained, weeping faces, hands raised in gestures of fear, self-
defence, sorrow and wonder. He did not realise that the girl had
gone mad. He took her head in his hands and tried to detach it
from his breast, so as to look her in the face:

"My child!" he said. "What have they done to you? What
have they done to you? Tell me! Murderers.... Your heart.... They
have torn the heart out of my bosom too!"

But, when he was able to see her eyes and her strange, altered face, her lips parted, now, in a mournful laugh, while a thread
of blood trickled between her teeth, he was horrified: he looked
again at the rest of the company and, laying her head back on his
breast and keeping his hand on her dishevelled locks as a sign of
protection and pity:

"Like her mother?" he said with a shudder, and stepped
back, driven by the girl who, repeating against his breast that horrible neighing laugh, kept urging him in a frenzy of excitement:

"To Aurelio... to Aurelio..."

Her cousin Lillina, her face bathed in tears, hastened to the
rescue, while at the other end of the room Lando Laurentano and
Don Francesco Velia tried to comfort Flaminio Salvo who, at this
outbreak, had buried his face in his hands, imploring her:

"Yes, Dianella, there's a good girl! He shall take you at
once... he shall take you wherever you want to go... there's a good
girl, dear!"

But Dianella, hearing her father's voice, overcome once
more by terror, had again buried her head in Macro's breast and
clung to him more frantically than ever, wailing:

"Wolf! Wolf!"

"You have me here! where is the wolf?" Mauro called to
her, encircling her again in his arms. "Don't be afraid! I am with
you, here!"

"You see? You have him, here, now! You have him!" Lillina repeated.

And Ciccino and Aunt Rosa gathered round her, repeating:

"He's here! Don't you see, he's come here for you? To defend you, dear?"

The poor girl lifted her face, happy and tremulous, a few inches, to shew a smile of gratitude, and continued to thrust Mauro towards the door:

"Yes... yes... to Aurelio... to Aurelio..."

Choked by his emotion, Mauro, driven hack like this, among these people whom he did not know and who were pressing round him, asked angrily:

"But tell me, what is the matter? How did it happen? What is she saying? She says Aurelio? Who is he? The son of Don Leonardo Costa? Ah, it is he... the man they have murdered?"

With their eyes, with their hands, they all bec-koned to him to he silent, and somebody answered him with a nod of assent.

"She was in love with him? Oh, my child..."

Lando Laurentano and Don Francesco Velia led Flaminio Salvo from the room.

"Tell me, tell me what they have been doing to you," Mauro went on, turning to Dianella, with an almost savage tenderness. "We are going now to Aurelio.... But tell me what they have been doing to you? Who is the wolf, tell me, and I will kill him! Who is the wolf?" he inquired of the others with a set countenance, which made it plain that if there really was a wolf, who had done any injury to this poor little lamb, he was ready to spring upon him.

But nobody knew with certainty what had happened, to whom actually Dianella was alluding by her cry. To her father, apparently; still, no one could say positively. Perhaps she mistook him for some one else. During their absence, Ignazio Capolino had been in the house. Dianella had stayed at home, by herself, because she was not feeling well; and upon her, unquestionably, Capolino, without mercy, maddened by the appalling tragedy, must have poured out the vials of his wrath. Ciccino and Lillina, who had been the first to return, had heard him shout:

"Your father! Tour own father, do you hear me?"

But, upon their entering the room, he had made off, in a fury, leaving the poor child half unconscious, as though stunned by all these pitiless blows upon her head; and, a moment later, she, showing signs of terror, had begun to wail: "Wolf! Wolf!"

What had Capolino said to her?

One person only could tell, as surely as though he had been a witness of the scene: Flaminio Salvo, who in the next room, with Lando Laurentano and his brother-in-law Francesco Velia, was feeling an overpowering need to confess his remorse, but nevertheless, unavoidably, in accusing himself, excused himself also.

Francesco Velia had asked him, whether he had ever noticed that his daughter was in love with Costa.

"If you were not aware of it!"

"I was aware of it. But could I, a father, bestow my daughter upon one of my own dependents? He, poor fellow, had never noticed it, my daughter was too modest, and also such a thought could never have entered his head; especially as for some time past he was head over ears in love with that other poor creature.... But the fault is mine, the fault is mine: I have no excuse! No one can know better than I that the fault is mine! I had been kind to that poor young man, as I had been kind to all those others who have murdered him down there! What other fruit can kindness yield? Costa had grown up in my house, like my own son; and that poor girl of mine.... Why yes, of course! And I, I saw clearly that the mistake that I had made at the start, in being kind to him, must end in their marrying; and yet, I confess, the idea repelled me, and I tried to put it off as long as possible. But, you see; in the meantime, I had called the boy back from Sardinia, and had put him in charge of the sulphur pits at Aragona; and just now, here in Rome, I had told Capolino that if Costa should succeed in taming those brutes down there, I would give him my daughter as a reward. Mark this: Capolino therefore knew, and consequently his wife must have known also that this was my intention. Yes, it is true, I had other, private, intentions, or rather, a hope.... Gentlemen, I might well have aspired to something very different for my daughter ..." (so saying, he looked Lando Laurentano in the face). "I had therefore brought her to Rome and proposed to leave her here in my sister's house, in the hope that she might be distracted from her childish obstinacy. Very well, Signora Capolino decided to take advantage of this hope and bring my plan to nothing: she decided to go off with Costa, to part him from my daughter for ever. And Signor Capolino perhaps hoped that, with Aurelio married presently to my daughter and already his wife's lover, he himself might continue to occupy a place in my household. And now, now that all his castles in the air have collapsed, he has denounced all his own machinations to my daughter as being mine! But I, I swear to you, gentlemen, I will crush him.... Crush him. ... If... ever again..."

He shrugged his shoulders, waved the threat aside with his hands, as though any definite proposal, now, filled him with overpowering nausea, choked him with disgust. And he flung himself down in an armchair, brooding darkly; he sat there, as though more and more terrified by the arid, horrid void which, after this long flow of words, he had created within himself.

Nothing: he no longer felt anything: no pity, no affection for anyone. A vast disgust, indeed physical sickness was what he felt now at everything, and especially at the part that he would have to play, of a father inconsolable at this calamity to his daughter, which as a matter of fact aroused no feeling in him hut irritation, that was it, and scorn, almost shame, yes, shame. This mad craving of his daughter for her lover revolted him as something shameful. And he asked himself with savage crudity, whether he had ever really loved his daughter, from his heart. No. From a sense of duty he had loved her. And now that this duty had become so serious and painful, he could feel nothing else for it but disgust and nausea. Yes, because his daughter too was doomed by fate! Was not her mother mad? And now, everything that could happen to him had happened. The cup was full, and overflowing! The destruction of his existence by fate was accomplished; and he, in that arid, horrid void, remained master, with nothing left to fear. Death he did not fear. Henceforward, he was raised above everyone and everything.

And he looked at the flash of the big stone in the ring upon the stunted little finger of his hairy hand, resting upon his leg. That flash, for some unaccountable reason, made him think of the white body of Nicoletta Capolino, which those brutes down there had burned. He raised his head, wrinkling his nostrils. Oh, how he longed for a cigar! But he remembered that he must not smoke, because at such a moment it would be thought improper. He heard Francesco Velia say to Lando Laurentano:

"Why, yes, it is obvious: they had eloped! They left here four days earlier, and had only just reached Aragona....Where were they during those four days?"

And he interposed, in a changed voice, with a changed face, as though he were no longer the game man:

"There can be no doubt about it," he said. "The day before yesterday a letter reached me from Naples, from Costa, in which he resigned from my service. And so he went down there to die on his own account: and for this too, therefore, I need feel no remorse."

At this moment Ciccino Velia entered the room, tongue-tied by the awkwardness of the message he brought and would have preferred not to convey.

"Lando," he said, hesitating, "I have something to tell you.... That old man..."

"Mauro?"

"Yes, that's right... came here with your servant to find you, to... he says... he says that they have arrested Roberto Auriti."

Lando turned pale, then coloured, knitting his brows as though perplexed by a thought which was forcing itself upon him against his will; he shewed signs of embarrassment at finding himself among people who had a far more serious trouble of their own.

"Go, go," Flaminio Salvo hastened to reassure him, holding out one hand and laying the other on his shoulder to escort him from the room.

"I trust," Lando said to him, "that this illness of your daughter's will be merely a passing disturbance."

Flaminio Salvo shut his eyes and shook his head:

"I am under no illusion."

And they returned to the drawing-room, so, Land in hand.

Mauro Mortara, already out of temper, choking, apart from the poor mad girl who clung to his breast, could not control himself at this spectacle: he shook himself free, with a roar in his throat, and shouted to the two women who were standing by him:

"Take her... catch hold of her.... He gives him his hand.... I cannot look on at such a thing.... Do you know what his name is? He bears his grandfather's name: Gerlando Laurentano!"

And, tearing himself from Dianella's arms, he fled from the room.

384

Flaminio Salvo's lips parted in a bitter smile, more of deri-sive pity than of anger; and, to the apologies offered him by Lando Laurentano, he replied:

"Infection.... It is nothing, Prince.... Insanity is, alas, as we know, infectious...."

CHAPTER V

IT WEIGHS NOTHING....

At Girgenti, the entire population were thronging upon the wide expanse of ground outside Porta di Ponte, where the road enters the town, waiting for the carriages to bring up from the station, down in Val Sellano, the remains, which were understood to have been collected in a single coffin, of Nicoletta Capolino and Aurelia Costa.

Amazement, grief, horror were depicted upon every face at this bestial crime, which for the past two days had kept the town and the whole of the Province in a ferment. In every eye was a close and painful attention, a cautious anxiety to gather fresh news of more precise details and not to let anything escape; for no one was satisfied with what he already knew, and everyone wished to see and, so to speak, touch with his eyes, in that coffin for which they were waiting, the proof that what had happened outside the town, and seemed, in its ferocity, to be incredible, was really true. Not having been able to witness the spectacle of that ferocity, they were determined at least to behold, so far as might presently be possible, its pitiable result.

Old considerations, in the case of one at least of the victims; others, more novel, which were now being divulged and increasing, amid stupefaction and pity, the tragedy of the event, if they restrained actual tears, could not prevent commiseration at the atrocity of these people's death, indignation at the reproach which it cast upon the Province as a whole.

Living still in the eyes of them all was the image of the beautiful lady, when, haughty and aloof, exquisitely attired, she used to drive past in Salvo's carriage, barely bowing her head in acknowledgment of their greetings with a smile of wistful gratification. Everyone saw in his mind's eye, with a strange sharpness of perception, some living detail of her person or expression, the whiteness of her teeth just discernible between her scarlet lips, when they parted in that smile; the sparkle of her eyes between their dark lashes; and they asked themselves with a vague misgiving, who could ever have imagined, then, that this was to be her end.

To resign like that, in an instant, the life of ease and honour, to which, with Salvo for a friend and her husband in Parliament, she had risen, and to elope with a man with whom, once already, she had refused to be joined in matrimony, why, to be sure, she must have been out of her mind. But perhaps it was done from spite, that was it, from spite against Dianella Salvo, who was secretly in love with Costa.... Perhaps? And was it not common knowledge already that she, poor girl, as soon as she heard of the elopement and massacre, had gone mad, like her mother?

And so, from an act of treachery, this pair, from an adventure which for one of them alone perhaps was an amorous adventure, and which had already by itself created such a scandal in the neighbourhood, had leaped into the jaws of such a death. But how, why had they made for Aragona, where he must have known that all those hyaenas were in wait for him, famished for months past by the shutting down of Salvo's sulphur pits? Because, having eloped together thus, they could not shew their faces in Girgenti. Their elopement was an insult not so much to the husband as to Salvo, and therefore they had turned to the one spot where everyone was against Salvo. Possibly he, Costa, believed, or at any rate hoped that, if he were to announce immediately upon his arrival that he too had rebelled against Salvo, they would welcome him as one of themselves and no longer hold him responsible for the broken promises. Besides, it was there, at Aragona, that his home was; perhaps he was going there merely to collect his belongings, the instruments of his profession, his books, with the intention of leaving again at once, of returning to his former employment in Sardinia. Yes; but with the lady? Ought he to have gone there, into the midst of his enemies, with the lady? He might at least have left her, first, in some place of safety! Ah, but perhaps she, she herself

387

had insisted upon facing the danger with him. She had a proud spirit, that lady, and had known how to shew it in front of that horde of savages, rising to her feet in the carriage, to shield Aurelio Costa's body with her own, and crying out that he had left Salvo's employ for their sake, because of the unfulfilled promises! But that rascal Marco Preola had raised his voice:

"Death to the whore!"

And the horde of savages, rendered powerless at first by the superb temerity of the lady, had been stirred to action. Perhaps even then Nico-letta Capolino might have succeeded in controlling them, in making them listen, had not Aurelio Costa instinctively, at that call for blood, at the vulgar insult, sprung up in her defence, pistol in hand. Then the carriage had been attacked from all sides, and both he and she, under a shower of knife-thrusts and hammer-blows, had been first stunned, then literally torn to pieces, as though by a pack of savage dogs; the carriage too, even the carriage had been shattered, broken in pieces; and when upon the pyre formed of the spokes of the wheels, the doors, the seats, had been flung the wretched, unrecognizable remains of their two bodies, a man had been seen to pour over them, from a big brass reflector lamp, purloined from the railway station near by, a stream of paraffin, and a crowd of others, with eager, breathless haste, set fire to the pile, as though to remove at once from their sight the appalling spectacle of carnage.

So, the incidents of the slaughter were in detail and with a sort of ecstasy of horror described and re-enacted, as though everyone had been present at the scene and saw it still before his eyes. They all saw that bloodstained brute pouring the oil from that brass lamp upon the limbs obscenely mutilated and heaped upon the pyre, and the others stooping eagerly to kindle the flames.

It was known that a large number, more than sixty, had been arrested, as well as Marco Freda, that abortion of nature; originally the forlorn hope of the Clerical Party, then President of that Fascio of sulphur workers at Aragona. Before long, therefore, perhaps that very day, another spectacular event: the convoy of all these miscreants, in chains, two by two, from the railway station to the prison of Santo Vito, amid a solemn escort of police, mounted carabinieri and soldiers.

Here, here at last came the carriages! There, look! Where was the coffin? Oh, what a little one! There it was! On the third carriage, there, the one with a serjeant on the box! Why, it all went on the back seat! That one, that box there! That little tin box! That one? With the chief constable on the seat facing it? Yes, yes! And who was the other man by his side? Ah, Leonardo Costa! The father! The father! Oh, poor father, with that box there, facing him!

A cry of pity, of horror, rose from the whole crowd at the sight of that father, who seemed petrified in an expression of rage, but at the same time stupefied in horror; with his eyes fixed on that box, as though he were asking how it could contain his son, the pillar of his house! But what could there be left then, of his son, if there were two bodies there, two? The heads only? Perhaps, torn off, yes, and a limb or two, charred. Oh God! Oh God!

And almost all of them wept, and many sobbed aloud.

Hearing their cries, their sobs, Leonardo Costa, as he drove past, uttered a cry also, gave vent to the ferocity of his grief in a howl, in which there was nothing human; then fell back, writhing, in the arms of the chief constable.

The carriage stopped at the corner of the piazza where the Prefecture stands, which is also the police headquarters. Two policemen took charge of the coffin; Cavalier Franco helped Leonardo Costa to alight. The poor old man, solidly built as he was, could not stand on his feet; one of his ears was bleeding, because at the station, in a paroxysm of rage, he had torn out one of his golden earrings. Other policemen formed a line in front of the gate, to prevent the crowd from breaking into the courtyard of the building. And the crowd remained there outside, irritated, cheated, unsatisfied. What was going to happen next? Was this the end of it all? Was the coffin to remain there, in the police station? Was there not to be a funeral procession to the cemetery of Bonamorone? That was where the ancestral vault of the Spoto family was. Now, there was no one left of that family. Aurelio Costa had still his father; for Nicoletta Capolino, no one: her husband could not be there; there might have been her stepfather, Don Salesio Ma-rullo; but it was common knowledge that the poor man, abandoned by everyone, had gone to seek a charitable asylum at Colimbetra, and had been living there for some months, sick. Perhaps Leonardo

Costa was claiming his son's remains for himself, to take them to the cemetery at Porto Empedocle; and judicial objections were being raised to his desire.

The crowd, by degrees, began to melt away, amid endless comments.

Leonardo Costa was demanding exactly what the crowd had imagined. The chief constable, Cav. Franco, tried to persuade him to have a little patience, since first of all the judicial procedure must, as he explained, be gone through, there in the office.... Why yes, in the course of the day; after the examining magistrate's visit. Costa, as though he did not understand, insisted, obstinately repeating, in identical words, his piteous request. And Cavalier Franco, albeit filled with pity for this poor father, groaned, he could stand it no longer. This was a terrible time for him, and he did not know where to turn, now that from all parts of the Province, from all over Sicily, reports kept coming in that grew daily more alarming; it seemed that at any moment a general insurrection must break out, and the military garrison was scattered, and more scattered still the police.

But what did he want, what more did this good man want now? He wanted... he wanted that the remains of his son--such as they were--should not remain there mixed up with those of the woman, that execrable woman! Why, why had they been gathered up like that together?

Cavalier Franco lost his patience.

"Why?" he shouted. "What do you suppose there is inside there?"

And he pointed to the box, which had been laid on a table.

"Oh, my son!"

"Everything that could be collected, out of the flames. Nothing! Practically nothing!"

"Oh, my son!"

"What do you propose to put aside, to identify? They came too late. At the station, there were no police. Before the inspector could arrive from Aragona, the fire.... Nothing, I tell you... a few scraps of bone...."

"Oh, my son!"

"You can't recognize anything.... Yes, yes, poor man, yes,

cry, cry, it's the best thing you can do.... Poor Costa, yes... yes.... It is a thing that... oh God, oh God, what a thing to happen... yes, it makes one deny humanity! But get into your mind, so as to pluck this arrow at least from your heart, get into your mind that there is not... your son is not in there: there is nothing there at all.... And besides, poor man, think that the woman, even if you hate her, he loved her; and perhaps he is not sorry now that whatever there may be in there of him should be together, mingled with her remains.... Poor woman! She may have had her faults, but there, what a fate hers has been too!"

"No... no... she... I can't... I can't speak... she... to perdition... my son... she! Don't you know, Signor Commissario, that my son was loved by his master's daughter? We know for certain... a fact, this is... the poor child has gone mad, like her mother! It has been... it has all been a plot.... That woman and that murderer of a father ... they had arranged it all between them ... to ruin this son of mine... to destroy that blessed creature's love for him.... Oh, Signor Commissario, bind me, bind my arms; Signor Commissario, lock me up, lock me up in prison, for, if I set eyes on him, that murderer who has made me lose my son like this, I shall kill him, Signor Commissario, I shan't answer for myself, I shall kill him! I shall kill him!"

Cavalier Franco clasped his hands together, wrung them and waved them in the air:

"But do you suppose," he then shouted, his eyes starting from their sockets, "do you really suppose that I can listen to such talk? I feel for you, you are mad with grief and do not know what you are saying. But, perdio, your son, your son ... at a time like this, when any trifle is enough ... a mere spark, to set the whole of Sicily in a blaze... is not content with running away, like a schoolboy, with the wife of a Deputy... but goes of his own accord, there, as much as to say: 'Here we are, tear us in pieces! Are you looking for fuel? Here it is! Take us!'--Perdio, they must have been mad, blind.... I don't know what to say! Of whom are you complaining? And we are here, and have to be responsible for everything ... even for an act of madness like that! And in addition to everything, I have to listen to you too saying: 'I shall kill him, kill him, kill him!' Whom are you going to kill? Do you suppose that Salvo, even if all your fantastic ideas are true, has any need of your punishment? His daughter's madness is sufficient punishment for him!"

Costa, after this outburst, no longer dared to raise his voice; he looked at the other, with eyes that were glazed with tears; gnawed his finger; murmured:

"If he were capable of remorse, Signor Commissario! But he is not!"

Cavalier Franco rose from his seat, and left the room.

"Go, go...." said Costa, behind his hack; then, cautiously, stole across to where the hox was lying upon the table, and tried to lift it.

A torrent of quick, silent sobs, in his throat and nose, made his head shake convulsively.

It weighed nothing, nothing at all, that box!

He fell on his knees before the table, resting his brow upon the chill surface of the metal, and began to moan:

"My son!... My son!... My son!..."

A SPIDER WITHOUT A WEB.

Two days later, there arrived at Girgenti, unexpected, in mourning attire, the Hon. Ignazio Capolino.

The position in which he had been placed, not so much perhaps by the sudden calamity as by his own violent outburst, which had deprived Dianella Salvo of her reason, was so difficult and uncertain, that he was obliged to collect all his faculties, there on the spot, to find a way out of it of some sort, as quickly as possible.

The scandal of his wife's elopement had been suppressed by the horror of her death; the tragic circumstances of that death made him immune from the ridicule which her elopement might have brought upon him. It was sufficient therefore for him to present himself to his fellow citizens, like this, funereal in aspect, but at the same time austerely reserved, to derive advantage from the general commotion, without however sharing in it, since his wife had done him an injury. And they must all see that he was suffering, shattered, crushed by the atrocious crime, and that he more than anyone deserved compassion, since by the two so greatly pitied victims themselves he had been injured, so that he could not mourn, could not even now mourn his own calamity.

And yet... how was this? Entering the house again, that house which his wife's exquisitely skilful management had made so perfect a setting for the comedy of polite and graceful falsehood, the rivalry in charming courtesies, in which they had both of them so whole-heartedly engaged, so that their life might not cause too great a scandal among their neighbours, be too distasteful to themselves; and feeling in the brooding silence of the rooms, which remained with all their furniture as though waiting, the void, the void in which from the first moment of his calamity he had seen

393

himself as lost...--how was this?--as he opened the door of her bedroom and detected, faint but still present, the sweet, voluptuous
perfume of herself, why, with an irresistible impulse, which
stunned him by its incoherence, but at the same time pleased him
as an unhoped-for consolation of melancholy, heart-broken ten-
derness--he wept, yes, wept at the thought of her, wept for the first
time since the news of her death reached him, wept as he had never wept in his life, conscious in his tears almost of a grief that was
not his own, but was that of the tears themselves, which welled
from his eyes against his will; but, precisely because he had not
willed them, with so sweet, so refreshing a savour!

But he must not, no, no, he must not... because. ... Why?
Why must he not weep? Oh, was she not, then, his necessary and
irreplaceable companion? The precious sharer in his subtle and
complicated devices, who, hurrying--more on her own account,
perhaps, that time than on his--to a place of safety, to which he,
nevertheless, had driven her--had fallen? Yes, and with so horrible,
so horrible a fall!

No... outwardly, that was it, outwardly at least he must not
weep for her.... Like this, in private like this; especially as these
tears were good for him, now. He had been left alone; and alone
now, by his own efforts, he must provide for himself, defend himself; and he did not yet know, did not see how.

Not by crying like this, though, certainly!

And Capolino rose to his feet; wiped away, first of all with
his knuckles, then slowly, carefully, with his handkerchief, the tears
from his eyes, nose and cheeks; put on his tortoise-shell glasses,
and planted himself, grim, severe, frowning, before the wardrobe
mirror.

Heavens, how his face had worn, aged, in a few days!

Grief? What grief? He could not admit that he had felt any
grief... unless at that moment, perhaps, a little. But perhaps, ah,
perhaps in his heart he had felt it, a very real grief, since at Rome,
upon hearing of the tragedy, he had been blinded by the rage
which had driven him to attack Dianella Salvo.

Ought he to repent of that outburst?

He had, by it, drawn upon himself for ever the hatred, the
mortal enmity of Salvo.

But even if he had managed to control himself in that first moment, to deny himself the fierce satisfaction of that revenge, what would he have gained? To him, left alone, without his wife by his side, would Flaminio have gone on giving help and support, impelled by his remorse at and secret complicity in her sacrifice? Possibly his daughter, already an invalid, would have gone mad even without that outburst, simply upon hearing of Costa's death. And then? Flaminio Salvo would have considered that he had already paid an ample penalty in his daughter's madness; and would have ceased to shew any consideration for him; would indeed have dismissed him from the house, as the embodiment of his remorse. So much was evident. Suppose, then, that Dianella had not gone mad, that her mind had been gradually set at rest, was Flaminio Salvo the man, once he had attained his object, to remain grateful to the memory of the person who had enabled him to attain it, at the cost of her own life; and, for her sake, to her husband, left a widower? When already, immediately, to unburden himself of all responsibility, he had proclaimed to the four winds of heaven that Nicoletta Capolino and Aurelio Costa had run away together and that Costa had resigned his post and had therefore gone down to die on his own account, there at Aragona, with his mistress!

Yes: she had run away with Costa, had his wife; but who had driven her to commit that act of madness? Who had sent Costa to Rome on the subterfuge of a plan that had to be submitted to the Ministry? Who had provoked her jealousy, or rather challenged her self-esteem, by letting her see his daughter's marriage to Costa as an immediate possibility? And he, Capolino, he, her husband, had been obliged to lend himself to all these perfidious manoeuvres, which were to end in so dire a tragedy; and then to be left like this, in the lurch, with no further claim to assistance, now that the fruit of all this treachery and crime had been gathered!

Ah no, perdio! He must not repent of that outburst. If he had lost his wife, the other had lost his daughter! They were quits now, and stood face to face. Salvo would at once withdraw all financial support. It rested with himself, therefore, to make immediate provision for even the harest necessities of life. And all his credit elsewhere must decline with Salvo's friendship.

How was he to manage? What was he to do?

As these thoughts passed through his mind, his restless fingers were playing with the Deputy's badge that hung from his watch chain. He still retained the prestige that this badge conferred. For the moment, Salvo could not wrest it from him. And with it in his possession, in the eyes of one who counted, if not for more, certainly not for less than Salvo in the district, he was still a Deputy. Don Ippolito Laurentano would never allow the man who sat in the Chamber as the paladin of his faith to be beset by paltry material difficulties.

That was the thing to do: at once, before Flaminio Salvo could reach Girgenti and go out to Colimbetra to poison the Prince's mind against him, he would hasten there himself and tell the Prince openly of the other's perfidy. After living for all these months with Donna Adelaide, the Prince would no longer be inclined to side with his brother-in-law; not to mention that Capolino would have in his favour the emotion aroused by his tragedy. Against this, it was true, Salvo might set that of his own daughter; but upon this very point he would go and forewarn the Prince, proving to him. that not he, with his natural and legitimate outburst, had been the cause of her madness; but her father, her father himself, who had taken these violent measures to prevent his daughter from marrying Costa, sacrificing the latter and destroying him together with Capolino's wife. Now, to free himself of all remorse, he was seeking to cast the blame upon him, and to be rid of him, as he had already rid himself of Costa and the wife.

There was his plan! But neither on that day nor on the day that followed had Capolino time to go to Colimbetra and put it into effect. An unbroken stream of visitors kept him at home, to his own intense satisfaction, albeit he knew and saw clearly that it was curiosity rather than pity for himself that had moved all these people, who undoubtedly, on the morrow, at a sign from Salvo, would be turning their backs on him. In any event, when he did go to see the Prince, he would be able to speak of this solemn expression of the sympathy and condolence of the entire town; not only that, in many minds which, stirred by the tragic event, were like a soil well ploughed and prepared, he could in the meantime sow the seeds of hatred of Salvo, without appearing to do so.

"Don't speak to me of it, please!" he protested, his face

cnanging at the slightest indication. "I should have to say things, things that... no, I say nothing; please, don't make me speak...."

And if some one, hesitating, persisted:

"That poor girl..."

"The girl?" he exclaimed. "Ah, yes, poor thing, she is another poor victim! Not more than the others, though, surely!... Please, don't force me to speak...."

When, at an opportune moment, the room being packed with people, there entered D'Ambrosio, the same who had been his second in the duel with Veronica, and was distantly related to Nicoletta Spoto, a scene occurred which, even if Capolino had deliberately arranged it, could not have turned out more effective or favourable to his cause.

D'Ambrosio entered, stifled by emotion, and with his arms outstretched. Standing in the middle of the room, they embraced one another, clasped one another tightly for a moment, both sobbing audibly. In a loud voice, with his habitual impetuosity, D'Ambrosio began, freeing himself from the other's embrace:

"Everybody in the town is saying that Nicoletta, my cousin, was that idiot Costa's mistress: is it true? You must know better than anyone: is it true?"

Speechless with horror, the onlookers turned to watch Capolino.

He sank down, as though he had been stabbed, in the armchair, his arms drooping limply upon his knees, and shook his head bitterly. Then with a barely perceptible gesture of his hands, he spoke:

"There are many... too many things that I ought to say, but I cannot.... Even your pity, you must understand... yes, yes... even these tears, my friends... are burning me I Because from those two, who deserve them by reason of their fate, but from you, my dear people, from you; not from me... from those two also I have suffered wrong; but most of all from him who led them on to their ruin; who held them in the hollow of his hand, and..."

"Salvo!" D'Ambrosio ejaculated. "They have arrested Marco Preola at Aragona; but he, Salvo, by the Madonna, is the man they should arrest! It was he who starved the whole village! He is the real murderer! And Grod has punished him rightly, with his daughter's madness! He will have to spend the rest of his life now with two madwomen, in spite of all his money!"

At this Capolino sprang to his feet, sublime.

"For pity's sake! No! No! I cannot allow such things to be said in my presence! Do you mean to defend the murderers? For shame! We all know that Salvo was acting within his rights in shutting down the sulphur pits there! Everyone has to provide, as he thinks fit, and as he chooses, for his own interests. Besides, has he not taken all sorts of trouble here for the revival of the industry? No, no! Don't you see, my friends? It is I who am speaking now, I, and I go so far as to say to you that he, on his part, as a father, believed that he was acting for his daughter's good! You people have no excuse for not admitting it; I might refuse to admit it, I alone, because the methods he chose to adopt have destroyed my home, shattered my existence! But he was aiming, there, at the good of all those brutes, and here, at his daughter's good!"

Ten, fifteen, a score of hands were held out to Capolino, in an outburst of admiration for such magnanimous generosity; and Capolino felt a cubit added to his stature.

"I may perhaps feel myself obliged," he went on, with melancholy gravity, "to hand back to you the mandate with which you have chosen to honour me."

"No! No! What has that got to do with it? Why?" some of his hearers protested.

Capolino, with a wistful smile, raised his hands to check this affectionate protest.

"My position," he said. "Just consider. Could I have any further relations, I do not say family ties or ties of friendship, but simply any common interest with Flaminio Salvo? Of course not. Well, then? I must provide for myself, gentlemen, whereas the mandate which I hold from you requires complete independence, the independence I derived from my post in Salvo's bank. Now ... now I shall have to begin to think seriously of my future. It is not a matter to be decided like this, on the spur of the moment...."

"Yes! Yes!" his comforters replied in chorus. "These are personal matters! Political representation ..."

"Ah, ah..."

"Why! That's got nothing to do with it...."

"Another matter altogether...."

"Besides, for the present..."

"For the present," he said, "it is enough for me, my dear friends, to have explained this to you: that I am ready for anything, and that I look upon things in general and upon my own tragedy with an equal and, so far as is possible, a serene mind. And now, I thank you all, my friends."

Later in the day, having gone to the Bishop's Palace to pay Monsignore a visit, he received from him information of such a kind with regard to Don Ippolito Laurentano and Donna Adelaide, that he decided to abandon there and then the plan he had originally prepared, feeling that it would be advisable, rather, to wait for Flaminio Salvo's return from Rome, before going to Colimbetra to try another plan, which had flashed across his mind, a plan of supreme audacity.

HAND IN HAND.

Flaminio Salvo did not wish to leave Dianella in Rome in some nursing home, as the doctors and his sister and brother-in-law advised; he said that, if anything, he might install her in some such place at Palermo, to have her nearer to himself and to be able to visit her more frequently; but his own house might now--he added--be converted into one of these private asylums, under the control of one or more doctors with the assistance of trained nurses: he was the only member of the household who still retained his reason; but he hoped that very soon, with the example of his wife and daughter and a little effort on his own part, he might manage to lose that also.

When he was upon the point of starting, however, he found himself obliged to appeal to Lando Laurentano, to let him have as a travelling companion Mauro Mortara, from whom Dianella refused to be separated, and who was perhaps the one person capable of inducing her to emerge from a dark closet, the sanctuary to which she had fled, and to start for home.

Lando Laurentano was making hasty preparations for his own departure, having been summoned to Palermo by his comrades of the Central Committee of the Party; he therefore replied to Salvo that they might all four travel together, and that he would come in the morning with Mauro and call for him at Velia's.

Flaminio Salvo detected in the face, voice and gestures of the young Prince a strange feverish agitation, and was more than once on the point of asking him the reason; but refrained.

Lando Laurentano was in this state for a reason that would never have dawned upon Salvo's mind at that moment: namely, the tremendous impression created in Rome by the suicide of Corrado Selmi.

400

Luigi Pirandello

The news had been made public that same evening, as he was on his way home from Velia's with Mauro. The cry of a newsvendor had informed him of what had happened. He had stopped his cab and bought a copy of the paper. But, instead of rejoicing him, the first effect of the sudden announcement had been to stun him. He had told the driver to stop beside a street lamp, so that he might read the paper, notwithstanding Mauro's impatience; had skipped the long obituary notice prefixed to the report of the suicide, and had let his eye run down the column. >From the statement supplied by Selmi's servant he had learned, first of all of the armed assault by Roberto Auriti's nephew, after Selmi had already swallowed the poison; then-- ah then!--of a visit, which the reporter termed "intensely dramatic," as Selmi was drawing his last breath, from "a veiled lady" whose name, for obvious reasons, was suppressed, "who had come," the report went on, "unaware of the suicide, perhaps to offer help and comfort to her friend, after the challenge launched by him, earlier in the day, at the assembled Chamber."

Lando Laurentano had felt not the least doubt that this veiled lady was Donna Giannetta D'Atri, his cousin; and had torn up the paper, in rage and disgust, shouting to the driver to take him home at once. There he had found, in an agony of distress, Celsina Pigna and Olindo Passalacqua, desperately searching for Antonio Del Be, who had been missing since midday. So inopportune at that moment had Lando felt the ridiculous appearance of the man, the girl's ravings, all this anxious appeal to himself to look for a young man whom he had never seen and who was so far from his thoughts, that he had given way (which was quite unlike him) to a violent outburst of rage. He had summoned Raffaele, his butler, to tell him to place himself at the disposal of the two visitors, and had remained alone with Mauro. The latter, interpreting this outburst as a sign of his contemptuous indifference to his cousin's arrest, had been unable to contain himself any longer; had stood before him, ablaze and trembling with fury, and shouted:

"I wish to go away, at once! This very moment! I never wish to look you in the face again!"

"Mauro! Mauro! Mauro!" Lando had exclaimed, waving his clasped hands in the air.

Mauro had thereupon plunged his hand in his pocket, and

brought out his medals:

"Do you see? From my breast I tore them, before the inspector, when I saw your cousin arrested! What sort of blood have you in your veins? Is this the youth of to-day? This?"

"The youth..." Lando had begun to answer with vehemence; but had at once stopped short, pressing his clenched fists to his lips, and sinking down on a chair, his elbows resting upon his knees and his head in his hands.

The youth? What youth? How? When the niggardly, timid, bullying jealousy of the old men was crushing it like this, under the monstrous weight of the meanest prudence and of such endless hardship, humiliation, shame? What youth? When it was held responsible for the passionate expiation, in silence, of all the mistakes that had been made, all the disgraceful transactions,--the mortifying of all pride and the spectacle of all this filth? Look, how the work of the old men, here and now, in the very centre of Italy, in Rome, was falling like sewage into a drain; while up in the North it was being entangled in a shameless coalition of sordid interests; and down in Lower Italy, in the Islands, had deliberately dwindled into vain babblings, so that the inertia of ignorance, the strain of poverty might continue there, and the pack of Deputies come up to Parliament to form the nameless, supine majority! There, there alone, perhaps, at the present time, the new youth, the youth that had been stifled, poisoned, sacrificed, might deal a blow to that vile, insolent oppression by the old men, and find at last an outlet and assert itself victorious!

Lando had sprung to his feet to proclaim this hope aloud to Mauro Mortara; but had stopped in compassion, seeing the old man weeping with those pathetic medals in his hand.

By morning, Antonio Del Re had been found. Olindo Passalacqua came to show Lando a couple of telegrams and a money order, dispatched at urgent rates from Girgenti to procure the young man's immediate return; but went on to say that Del Re obstinately refused to go back to Sicily. Lando had thereupon begged Mauro to go and find the young man and invite him to travel with them next day; and this Mauro had readily agreed to do.

But how was he to propose next to Mauro that they should travel with Flaminio Salvo?

On the following morning Ciccino Velia arrived betimes at the villino on the Via Somma-campagna to discuss the best way of getting Dia-nella Salvo out of her hiding place and inducing her to start. It would be fatal if she caught sight of her father! She must not set eyes on him throughout the journey. Uncle Flaminio and Lando would have to travel in a separate compartment of the carriage, without letting themselves be seen. There was also the young man, Del Re? Very well: all three of them must remain apart, in concealment. Mauro and Dianella would be by themselves, in the next compartment: a whole carriage would be reserved for the party.

It was less difficult, upon these conditions, to persuade Mauro to render this service to Salvo. When he understood that neither that morning, at Velia's, nor afterwards, during the whole of the journey, would he see him, and that it was a question of performing not so much a service to him as a work of charity to that poor demented girl, he frowningly consented, and went on ahead with Raffaele to Velia's house.

There was no necessity there for either entreaty or exhortation: as soon as Dianella saw Mauro again, she sprang from her hiding place, and clung to him, imploring him to let her escape with him. He was obliged, on the contrary, to make an effort to detain her, until they had made her as tidy as possible, brushed her dishevelled hair, pat a hat on her head, so that at least she might not attract undue attention driving through the streets with this old man who was himself so strangely attired.

When the pair of them, hand in hand, he with his air of a strayed savage and that knapsack upon his back, she with her eyes and lips agitated by a mournful, meaningless mirth, with her hair loosely bundled beneath the hat that sat askew on her head, passed through the drawing-room on their way out, those who beheld them saw clearly that, the two of them having come to Rome, at that time, one with her love, the other with his country in his heart, they could not go away again, save like this.

What was their conversation, during the journey?

Through the communicating door of their compartment, Salvo and Laurentano, listening by turns, heard them conversing together, at length, and imagined at first that the old man and the girl understood one another. Yes, indeed, they understood one another perfectly, because both of them, each on his own account, spoke only in the terms of his own mania. And the two manias sat there side by side and hand in hand.

"A woman... shocking! I mustn't say Aurelio. ... Signor Aurelio.... Signor Aurelio! But how can he possibly have forgotten?... Such a great big cut on your finger.... Come, come away, here, in the dark... in the passage. ... Let me suck the blood from your finger.... A woman? Shocking.... Signor Aurelio...."

"These are the young men... these! The new generation.... To behold this, oh murderers, we fought so many battles... sacrificed our lives... to behold this, Donna Dianella! And what am I going to hang up, now, beneath the General's letter in the earner one? What am I ever to hang up there again, after all that I have seen?"

"Ah, but who knows what the year will hring? The mulberry tree, in March, gathers fresh wood. ... And then, when it is in love, and ready to shoot, it is soft, as soft as dough, and you can bend it as you please.... Who knows what the year will bring?"

"The good is doubtful, but the evil is sure, my child! The good is doubtful, but the evil is sure!"

So they conversed between themselves, in the other compartment.

Neither Lando nor Flaminio Salvo paid any attention, meanwhile, to another person, in their own compartment, who said nothing, and yet, no less than the two next door, was out of his mind.

Antonio Del Re could see nothing, feel nothing, think of nothing any more. The desperate fury with which he had flung himself upon Selmi had riven his spirit like a flash of lightning. Upon leaving Selmi's house, he had remained void, suspended in a stupefying, terrifying blackness; and remembered nothing more, where he had gone, what he had done, how and where he had passed the night, if indeed the night, a night, had passed. He did not reply to any question; perhaps he did not hear. See, he could and did; at least he sat staring in front of him; but a reason he no longer saw, the reason of the appearance of things and of the actions of men....

He had objected, not indeed to returning to Sicily, but to

moving of his own accord from the spot to which his feet had led him and where he had dropped in exhaustion. He had moved, when Mauro seized him round the chest; but without hearing a word of what Mauro was telling him about his grandmother and mother. Passalacqua and Celsina had gone with him, in the morning, to Lando's villino; before he left, he had seen Celsina smile at Ciccino Velia, take his arm, get into a cab with him and Passalacqua: all this he had seen, and more still, in imagination; and nothing, nothing at all had stirred within him.

When, after crossing the Straits of Messina, Lando Laurentano left the train, to take another train for Palermo, Flaminio Salvo felt a certain dismay at the thought of being left alone in the compartment, for a whole day, until the train reached Girgenti, with this young man whom he did not know, who two days earlier had drawn a dagger to kill Selmi, and who was now fastening his eyes upon him with so fixed a stare, grim and at the same time meaningless.

Yes, he had three lunatics for his travelling companions; and perhaps no less mad than these three was the fourth who had just left the train with the intention of turning the whole Island upside down! Was he alone, therefore, by a terrible judgment, to preserve intact the privilege of not having in the slightest degree veiled, or clouded, whether by remorse, or by pity, or by any further affection, or by any further hope, or by any further desire, that lucid cruel limpidity of mind? He alone.

And, as though to savour the mockery of his fate, he stole once again to the communicating door between the compartments, and pressed his ear to the ventilator, to listen to the meaningless babble of the old man and the girl.

THE LAST TEAR.

As soon as Mauro Mortara, upon their arrival at Girgenti, was able to tear himself from the arms of Dianella Salvo, he dashed off to the house of Donna Caterina Laurentano. There he found Antonio Del Re still in the arms of his mother who, hugging and shaking him, was endeavouring frantically, but in vain, to melt him.

When Anna saw Mauro enter the room, she left her son and ran to meet him:

"What is wrong with him? Tell me, you, what is wrong with him?"

But Mortara shook off her aims and drowned her cry with:

"Your mother? Where is your mother?"

Giulio appeared, grown ten years older in a few days. In his eyes, in his outstretched arms lurked the hope of receiving from Mauro some definite information as to Roberto's arrest, Selmi's suicide, whether Selmi had indeed left any statement exonerating his brother, as the newspapers alleged. From his nephew he had been able to find out nothing, even though, when he was in his mother's arms, he had shaken him furiously to make him speak.

But Mortara shook him off too, repeating, with stubborn rudeness:

"Your mother? I know nothing! I know they arrested him before my eyes! I won't see anyone! I only want to see her!"

Giulio stood perplexed, wondering whether to admit him to his mother's bedroom, suddenly like this.

From the day on which he, driven by the urgency of the situation, overcoming all his reluctance, at first with circumspection, then resolutely, in so many words, had told her that she must appeal to her brother Ippolito to save her son, she had sunk into a sort of apathy, as though life and the things around her had suddenly been deprived of all meaning. Not a gesture, not a word. Nothing. And in this immobility and this silence there had been from the very beginning something so absolute and invincible, that it had been impossible for the others to make any gesture, to utter any word, to rouse or stimulate her.

Giulio had known that he would kill his mother, if he spoke. And so indeed it was; at once, with the almost mechanical precision of a decree of fate, he had spoken, and he had killed her. She could not have gone to her brother, to save her son: it would have been her death. And behold, she was dead.

Both he and Anna had hoped, at first, that she merely did not wish either to move or to speak; not that she was actually unable. But very soon they had discovered that she was unable. However, a faint contraction that lingered on her forehead, between the eyebrows, said plainly that, even if she had been able, she would not have wished it.

They had lifted her bodily from her chair and laid her on her bed. Her immobility, her silence were corpselike; only, as yet, she was not cold. And to prevent that coldness also from coming upon her, they had hastened to cover her well with bedclothes, with loving hands, weeping as they did so.

The last act of cruelty had thus to be wrought upon her, and, to make it more unjust, by the hands of her own children. Now, by their watching and weeping, her children were proving to her, or rather were proving to themselves, that it had not been they who wrought it. If she, by all that she had done, could not pay the penalty for her son, she must pay it in this coin, now. Giulio knew this; and, knowing it, had been unable to prevent it. He was obliged to speak, to drive her to her death, to deal the finishing blow. He had then gathered her in his arms, and was now heaping the blankets upon her, and folding the black woollen shawl about her shoulders, to shelter her from the final chill, and going about the room on tiptoe, so that no sound more should disturb her silence. Even the buzz of a fly would be too much, now, coming on the top of what he had done, because he must.

The thought that possibly even his own life was too much, his own breath, after what he had done, had even entered his mind.

Apart from this mother, away from Sicily, he had led his life from his boyhood. He had lived without memories or affections or aspirations, as it were from day to day: cold, detached, ironical, contemptuous.

Suddenly, when he least expected it, the destiny of his family had put out a tendril to involve, to envelop him, and had drawn him back to itself and planted him there, grafting him, re-attaching him to the root from which he had been torn; making him feel all that he had always refused to feel, remember all that he had always refused to remember.

The end of this mother, who had always felt everything, had always remembered everything, stricken down now by the blow which he had come home to plunge into her vitals, must it not now be his end also?

The trunk once felled, the branches must fall also.

In the melancholy gloom of the house, he had been horrified by the apparition of himself to himself imbued with all the sentiments and memories of this mother. But there had appeared to him also Anna, his sister: the branch that had never been severed from the trunk; that miserably, once only, for a short time, had blossomed, to yield the sour and poisoned fruit of that son whose husk not even a mother's love could succeed in penetrating. And brother and sister had clung to one another then, fused together in an embrace of infinite tenderness, of infinite anguish, in the shadows of the dark house, tasting the sweetness of the tears that were uniting them for the first time and yet were breaking their hearts.

He would have to live for this sister and for the boy.

The news of Roberto's arrest, now inevitable, expected at every moment, had finally arrived, together with the news of Corrado Selmi's suicide, but in vague terms, restricted to a few lines in the Sicilian papers, as a matter to which their readers would attach no importance, taken up as they all were, at the moment, by a morbid curiosity to learn even the minutest details of the massacre at Aragona.

Anna's trepidation for her son, alone in Rome, the thought of the help that might be given to Roberto, had prompted Giulio at first to return at once to the Capital. But how was he to leave his mother in her condition, alone there with Anna, who kept roaming about the house, calling her son, as though she were out of her mind? And what help could he give Roberto? The only help possible would have been the money, the repayment to the Bank of those forty thousand lire, so that everyone might suppose that the money had been taken by him, for his own requirements. Selmi's suicide, now, might perhaps unlock the prison door for Roberto, but he would remain indelibly branded, after the accusation and the arrest, with the mark of a crooked complicity. How many people would believe, to-morrow, that he had come forward disinterestedly to take on the debt, in his own name, on behalf of another man? Selmi's statement, if, as the newspapers asserted, it really existed, would not be sufficient to efface that mark.

Next door, in his mother's bedroom, was Canon Pompeo Agro, who for days past, and for hours on end daily, had never stirred from his armchair at the foot of the bed, his eyes fixed upon the spent face of the sufferer, perhaps in the hope of discovering on it some indication that she--having nothing more to say to men--desired by his means to communicate with God. More than once, in a deep voice, he had called her by name, repeatedly, but had elicited no answer.

Giulio told Mauro to wait a moment: he wished to consult Agro, to obtain a casting vote between his hope and his fear, whether the sight of Mortara, or the sound of his voice, by rousing his mother from that death-like torpor, would do her good or harm.

"I think," was Agro's reply, "that there is nothing left now either to hope or to fear. She will notice nothing. Try. It is all the same; if she keeps on like this, death is inevitable."

Mauro came stumbling like a blind man into the almost dark room, crying aloud, in a voice hoarse with emotion:

"Donna Caterina.... Donna Caterina...."

He stopped short, at the foot of the bed, at the sight of that face turned to the ceiling, on the heaped-up pillows, cadaverous, with eyes that the imagination could picture as clouded and thick with despairing anguish beneath the perpetual seal of their heavy, darkened lids, with an obstinate, absolute determination to die in the protruding cheekbones, the hollowed temples, the stiffened nostrils of the sharply pointed nose, the thin, livid lips, not only tight set, but in places even gummed together by dried saliva.

"Oh, child... child...." he exclaimed. "Donna Caterina... it is I... Mauro... your father's watchdog.... Look at me... open your eyes.... I wish you to look at me. ... Open your eyes, Donna Caterina; look at me and behold your own punishment.... Listen to me: I have something to tell you.... I have come back from Rome...."

Striking against the rigid, funereal impassibility of the dying woman, Mauro Mortara's emotion was abruptly shattered into a series of strident sobs, that were very like a peal of laughter.

Agro and Giulio, with tears in their eyes also, took hold of him and, supporting him by the arms, led him from the room.

The dying woman, left alone, in the dim light, motionless upon her mountain of pillows, heard his voice after an interval, as though it had had to make a long journey to overtake her in the profound, mysterious remoteness to which her spirit had already flown. And from those far tracts, in answer to that voice, came slowly to her closed eyelids a tear, her last tear, which no one saw. It welled from one of her eyes; ran down her cheek, fell and was lost among the wrinkles of her throat.

When Pompeo Agro resumed his seat in the armchair at the foot of the bed, neither in her eye nor upon her cheek was there any trace of it.

Donna Caterina was dead.

CHAPTER VI

WHEN SCIROCCO BLOWS...

For Donna Adèlaide and Don Ippolito Laurentano, there had begun, from the first evening when they were left by themselves in the villa of Colimbetra, a period of torture, which as they could both see would be most difficult to endure, however readily both he and she might apply themselves to the task.

As soon as the wedding guests had departed, Don Ippolito, with great courtesy, taking her hand in his, but without looking at it, so that he might not see how different it was from the hand he had once been used to hold between his own (a long, pale hand, that other, soft and tender and light!), tried to make her understand the benefit that he promised himself from her society in the loneliness of his exile, his reasons for which must, he supposed, be known to her, in part at any rate.

The speech that he made her upon the terrace, overlooking the silent countryside, already invaded by the darkness of night, had in truth been a little too long and a trifle tedious as well.

Poor Donna Adelaide, crushed by the violent shock of so many novel sensations, in the course of that day, and now by all the darkness and silence that brooded round her and rendered more suffocating than ever the suspense of what mysteriously lay in store still for her "terrible maiden-ladyship," after a certain point had been incapable, however earnestly she tried, of listening to another word of the quiet, interminable speech. She had received the impression that it, most inopportunely for her, was intended to drag her by force to the summit of a high and cloud-girt mountain, from which it would be difficult for her, if not actually impossible, to come down again in a fit state to endure further surprises, fresh emotions, which this night must certainly be holding in store for her.

Not from ill-will, but from want of air, that air which at a certain stage she felt to be lacking, she had never been able to listen to long speeches. Oh, good Lord, why did people keep on circling round a subject when in the end they must always come down to doing the same things, those which nature ordains? What a beastly habit, good Lord! And productive of no effect but exhaustion and irritation. Yes, irritation as well. Because the things that had to be done were simple, and could all be numbered upon the fingers of one hand; so that, in the end, everybody must admit that all this beating about the bush was not only useless but actually foolish and harmful, inasmuch as, afterwards, what with people's exhaustion, and their irritation at this admission, they were done late and done amiss.

She had begun by gazing, with imploring, startled eyes, at the Prince, or rather at his long, interminable beard. Then, in her stunned condition, she had felt an overpowering impulse to withdraw her hand and to breathe, to draw breath at least, since she could not groan, could not cry aloud to give some relief to her suffocation and rage. Finally, she had succeeded in conquering her stupor: her ears had come to life again for an instant, but only to escape far away, to seize hold of a thread of sound, in the obscurity of the night, that offered her some relief, a slight distraction.

There rose from the shore, far below, invisible, a dull continuous murmur. And all of a sudden, just at the point when the Prince's speech had become most pathetic, Donna Adelaide had come out with the question:

"What is it, the sea? Do you hear it like that, every night?"

Don Ippolito, puzzled at first ("The sea? What sea?") had felt his spirit quail:

"Oh, yes... it is the sea, the sea...."

And releasing her hand he had moved away from her.

Donna Adelaide, embarrassed, not knowing how to soothe the Prince's evident mortification at this inopportune question, could think of no other way than to persist:

"Does it roar like that every night?"

She had had to wait some time for an answer; when it came, it arrived from a distance, gravely:

"Not every night; when scirocco blows...."

That far-away voice of the sea was at once precious to him and sad. How often, in the profound peace of the night, had it brought him anguish and companionship. Leaning back in his long chair, he had let himself be lulled by that sombre incessant roar of the waters, which spoke to him of distant lands, of a different, a tumultuous life, which he would never know. He had felt himself plunged back of a sudden by that call into the deep recesses of his former solitude.

How could he go on with his speech, after this? And how, on the other hand, could he remain as he was, in silence, leave by herself, apart, there, on the terrace, this woman, who now belonged to him for all time and had entrusted herself to his chivalry, in this solitude which was novel to her and could not, certainly, be pleasing? He must make an effort, overcome his repugnance, and return to the charge. But, certain now that he could never enter into any intimacy with her, save that of the body, Don Ippolito had asked himself bitterly, what other effect this intimacy could have than an irreparable destruction of her respect for him.

And indeed, that night....

Ah, poor Donna Adelaide could never have imagined the possibility of such a spectacle, at once so pitiable and so alarming! The thought of it still made her cross herself with both hands. Ah, Bella Madre Santissima! A man with all that beard... a serious-minded man.... Dio! Dio! She had seen him, at a certain stage, dash from the room, like something less than human. Perhaps he had sought a nocturnal lair, in his. Museum rooms, on the ground floor. And she had spent the rest of the night, sitting up, half-dressed, by a window, listening to the sobs of a lovelorn owl, perhaps in the wood called Civita, perhaps in the other wood, beyond, the Torre-che-parla.

Fortunately, when morning came, the sight of the surrounding country, and of the exquisite appointments of the villa had to some extent consoled her and restored her to her normal spirits, in which she would willingly, were it not for the fear of making matters worse, have gone to the Prince and told him, in so many words, without stopping to weigh them, that he was not to worry or distress himself about anything, seeing that she ... she was satisfied, perfectly satisfied with things as they were....

His scowling face had genuinely distressed her! Poor man, he had not managed even to raise his eyes to look her in the face when, over the breakfast table, he began to address her again. Yes, yes, of course: theirs was an unusual situation; to find themselves placed like this, to be husband and wife, almost without knowing one another. In the course of time, to be sure, a mutual confidence would spring up between them, and... but yes, why, of course!

She had noticed however that, as he made this speech, the Prince's excitement had increased, had indeed become more and more exacerbated; and with real terror she had seen the night draw round again.

For several days in succession this terror had been renewed; at length she had secured the concession of being left in peace, to sleep alone, in a separate room.

All very well; but, the day after, there came down to Colimbetra Monsignor Montoro, to preach her a little homily in private. Whereupon she had broken out again: Oh Bella Madre Santissima! What was that?... No.... How on earth?... What?... What ought she to do? ... Gesù! Gesù!... At her time of life, airs and graces? Oh, not that! No no! No no! Not that! It was not in her nature. And besides, why should she? Could they not remain as they were? For her part, she could ask for nothing better.

The face Monsignore had made!

And poor Donna Adelaide, from that moment onwards, had not known in what world she was living, or, as she herself put it, had begun to feel herself "captured by the Turks."... But how? Was the fault on her side?

The Prince, closeted all day long in his Museum, never shewed his face, except at dinner and supper, rigid, frowning, taciturn. Air! Air! Air! Yes, there was plenty, there; but it was not air that Donna Adelaide could breathe. And the absurd thing was this: the suffocation, that she herself felt, must, it seemed to her, be affecting everything, the trees especially!

On the first of the three flowering terraces in front of the villa, there had stood for more than a century a saracen olive, the sturdy trunk of which, all gnarled and knotted by its struggles against the winds or an unfriendly soil, growing aslant, at barely a handsbreadth from the ground, seemed to be supporting with infinite pain the many branches that rose, tall and luxuriant, along it. Nobody could get the idea out of Donna Adelaide's head that this tree, bowed so low and burdened with all those branches, was suffering.

"Oh Dio, can't you see? It is suffering! I tell you, that tree is suffering!"

And she had made them cut it down. When it had gone, looking at the spot where it had stood:

"Ah!" she had breathed again. "Poor thing, now it is all right! I have set it free."

Nor had she stopped there. Further proofs of her kindness of heart she had given, on moonless evenings, at supper, to the various winged insects, which the light of the hanging lamp attracted into the dining-room.

A certain Pertichino, a boy of about thirteen, the son of the serjeant of the guard, was instructed to stand behind Donna Adelaide's chair and at once drive away these insects, as soon as they came into the room. Unfortunately, Pertichino was often lost in contemplation of the huge white cotton gloves, in which they had imprisoned his hands; and Donna Adelaide had invariably to tear him from this contemplation by her screams and starts at the jump of a grasshopper or the buzz of a flying beetle.

"It's only a moth.... Don't be alarmed! Here it is, a moth, look...."

"Poor creature, don't let it suffer: nip off its head, quickly; if not, it will come in again.... Done it?"

"Done, Excellency. Here it is...."

"No, no, what are you doing? Don't shew it to me: I can't bear to look at it! A moth, was it? Really a moth? Poor little creature.... But who told it to come into the room? With all that lovely country outside.... Ah, if I had wings, if I had wings!"

As much as to say that, without thinking twice about it, she would have flown away.

Don Ippolito, shocked and disgusted as he was, had allowed her to continue. But at length an evening came when he could contain himself no longer.

They were both sitting, some way apart, upon the terrace. He was waiting until, from the dense foliage of the olives that covered the face of the hill behind the villa, the full moon should rise, to renew in him a cherished, immemorial impression. It seemed to him, every time, that the full moon, peering from the boughs of those olives at the spectacle of the vast expanse of country beneath and of the distant sea, still, after all these centuries, halted, filled with awe and wonder, finding herself gazing down upon silent and deserted plains, where at one time rose one of the most splendid and luxurious cities in the world. The moon was just about to rise, was already visible through the tangle of silvery olive-boughs, and Don Ippolito was attuning his awed and eager melancholy to receive the familiar impression, in common with the whole countryside, from which rose a subdued, mysterious chime of grasshoppers, with from time to time the cry of a screech-owl, when, all of a sudden, from the barrack-room on the crest of the Sperone, there rang out, breaking, shattering the spell, the harsh and tuneless sound of Captain Sciaralla's reed pipe. Donna Adelaide clapped her hands, in jubilation.

"Oh, pretty! How nice of the Captain to give us a serenade!"

Don Ippolito sprang to his feet, quivering with anger and disgust, and stopped his ears, shouting in exasperation:

"Damn them! Damn them! Damn them!"

And, gripping Pertichino by the shoulders and shaking him furiously, he told him to run out and shout to the rascals from the edge of the ravine opposite, to stop their noise at once.

"And then, get out of here! Get out of my way! I never want to set eyes on you again! If people are annoyed by the flies, they can catch them for themselves! Without all this racket! I am tired, I am sick of all this vulgarity; I can't breathe for it! I've had enough, enough, enough!"

And he fled from the terrace, his eyes tight shut, his hands pressed to his temples.

GATHERING CLOUDS.

It was fortunate that, a few days later, Don Salesio Marullo had appeared at the villa, with a meagre, wasted expression, timid and troubled, to crave succour and hospitality. He had appointed himself, from the day of his arrival, gentleman in waiting to Donna Adelaide, who was convinced that God had sent him to her.

"Don Salesio, for goodness' sake, eat something! For goodness' sake, Don Salesio, you must keep up your appetite! Quick, Pertichino, another couple of eggs to Don Salesio!"

She had set to work to fatten him up like a turkey before Christmas. The poor old gentleman, wasted to a skeleton, had been powerless to resist; he had gobbled, gobbled, gobbled everything that was set before him, not to say shoved into his mouth, in handfuls; then... ah, then he had paid the penalty in tremendous colics and internal disturbances of all kinds, whereby, right in the middle of some entertainment which he had arranged with Captain Sciaralla as a distraction for the Princess, his face would turn all the colours of the rainbow and finally he would have to escape from the room, with what injury to his dignity need not be said, battered as that was already.

But Donna Adelaide rejoiced in his discomfiture. Powerless to assail the dignity of the Prince her husband, in revenge she had set herself to make havoc of every male dignity that came her way: including that of Sciaralla, the Captain. She had found by chance among the papers in the desk, in the secretary, Lisi Preola's room, some old verses in manuscript at the Captain's expense, in which occurred the lines:

Dimmi, corri, Sciarallino, all'assalto d'un molino? od a caccia di lumache vai cosi di buon mattino, con cedeste rosse brache e il giubbon chiaro turchino, Sciarallino, Sciarallino?

And one day, when it had been raining in torrents, as soon as the rain ceased, she had gone down to the level ground below the guard-room, where "the troops" were engaged in drilling, and, calling Captain Sciaralla mysteriously aside, had ordered him to send out his men with trowels in one hand and baskets in the other to collect the *babbaluceddi*, in other words the snails, which after such a downpour must be literally oozing from the soil.

The poor Captain had remained speechless at this order.

How was he to convey it, in a military word of command, to his men? For Donna Adelaide, to put him to the test, had insisted that this snail hunt should have all the appearance of a military expedition.

"But what am I to do, Your Excellency?"

"Why?"

"If we lose our prestige, Your Excellency...."

"What prestige?"

"Why... you must understand, I have to command... and at a time like this..."

"I want the *babbaluceddi*."

"Yes, Your Excellency... in a minute, when I break off the parade...."

"When you break off... what did you say?"

"The parade, Your Excellency."

"No no! Then the whole point would be gone! I want military *babbaluceddi*!"

And there had been no way of making her go back upon this capricious tyranny. With what effect upon discipline, Sciaralla confided bitterly next day to Don Salesio Marnilo, who had for some time past been allowed to share his consternation at the news that kept coming in from all parts of Sicily, of the great ferment of the Fasci, against which it appeared as though neither the police nor the military, the "real" military, could make any headway.

"If only they realized that we are against the Government here too.... But now, my dear Si-don Salesio: because they are in league, not so much against the Government, as against private property, don't you see?"

"I see, I see...."

"They want the land! And what if, driven out of the towns, they descend upon the country? We are a mere handful.... And we are all the more conspicuous, because we appear armed for battle, don't you see?"

"I see, I see."

"And being here, armed to the teeth like this, we as good as admit the danger; we challenge an attack; we are like a small country upon which they can quite well make a separate war, do you follow me? And, if we were attacked to-morrow, do you know how the Prefect would regard it? As a just retribution. He will look after the others, and will say of us: 'Ah, H.E. the Prince of Laurentano likes to play the King, does he, with his garrison? Very good, now he can defend himself!' But with what are we to defend ourselves? Can you tell me that.... What is all this stuff?"

"Gently.... Why, with your arms...."

"Arms? Don't make me laugh! You call these arms? But when a person chooses to keep people round him like this... and dressed up, I mean to say, just look at me... it requires courage, believe me, at a time like this to put on a coat that simply shouts aloud... and I feel myself turn pale when I look down at these red breeches... I tell you, Si-don Salesio, it's no joke! I mean to say, when a person makes it a point of honour not to give way to anybody..."

"Perhaps," Don Salesio suggested hesitatingly, "it would be prudent to collect..."

"More men? And whom, pray? That would be my plan! But whom? The peasants? And if they are in the league too? The enemy inside our gates?"

"True... true..."

"Of course it is! Do you know what is the only thing to be done?"

He did not express it in words: he took the lapel of his coat between his fingers; gave it a cautious twitch, made two other gestures which signified folding it up and putting it away; and followed them up at once with the query:

"What? No? You say no?"

Don Salesio shrugged his shoulders: "I say that the Prince... perhaps..."

"Of course, because he doesn't have to wear it himself! Sidon Salesio, the clouds are gathering, thicker and thicker, on all sides; and we shall be the first to attract the lightning, with all this iron in our hands; you shall see whether I'm wrong!"

The lightning did indeed strike, and with terrific force, a few days later, with the news of the massacre at Aragona. The bolt seemed to fall actually upon Colimbetra, since there, as it happened, beneath the same roof, were the father of the principal author of the crime, namely the secretary Lisi Preola, and the stepfather of the victim, poor Don Salesio. And the dismay and horror increased still further, when from Rome, like an echo of the crash overhead, came the later news that Dianella had gone mad.

Donna Adelaide, now directly affected by the tragedy, abandoned her attempt to kill Don Salesio with her eager, clamorous kindness, and began to cry aloud on her own account that, with Dianella driven mad by the murder, it was no longer possible for the murderer's father to remain in the house, there, at Colimbetra! And the Prince, to silence her, unfair as he thought it to punish further the poor old man, already stricken to the ground by his son's infamous deed, found himself compelled to send him away from the villa, with a pension. Before leaving, Preola, dragging himself painfully into the room, with the veins standing out upon his great skull-like head, which drooped over his chest, insisted upon kissing the Signora Principessa's hand also, and told her that he gladly offered to his employers, for his son's offences, the penance of leaving the house after thirty-three years of service, performed with so much love and devotion. Donna Adelaide, moved and repentant, flew into hysterics and called heaven to witness that the Prince was responsible for her remorse at the unjust punishment of this poor old man; yes, the Prince, yes, because of the continual state of excitement in which he kept her, so that she never knew what she really wanted and, simply to find some vent for her feelings, said and did things that were contrary to her nature.

Her ravings became more frenzied than ever, when she learned that her brother Flaminio and Dianella had returned from Rome. When Monsignor Montoro came down to Colimbetra to offer his condolences after the death of Donna Caterina, she asked him, her eyes red and swollen with! weeping, whether it seemed to him human to forbid her to go to visit and help her niece, to whom she had been a second mother!

Don Ippolito, at that moment, was not in the villa. He had gone to the cemetery of Bonamorone, within a short distance of Colimbetra, to pray by his sister's grave. When he entered the drawing-room, frowning darkly, he pretended not to see his wife's tears, and to the Bishop who came to meet him, with a mournful expression and outstretched hands, said:

"She died broken-hearted, Monsignore. Broken-hearted. Her son in prison, disgracefully compromised, with a lot more of these patriots, in the bank frauds. And that fellow Selmi, who came here as a second in the duel with Capolino, have you heard, he has killed himself. They are all paying now for their fine doings! There is a blight on them, Monsignore! May God have pity on the dead. I feel such a burning rage in my heart, that I find it impossible to pray. A smarting, a trembling in my knees made me rise from the grave of my poor sister, and I asked myself, was this the moment for prayer and weeping, and not rather for action, Monsignore, action, action! Ought we really to be remaining inert like this, while everything is breaking up and the people are rising? The crowds are having a fine time, incited by anarchist spoutings, they are turning out in the streets to protest against the burden of taxation, still carrying the Crucifix and the images of the Saints at the head of their processions!"

"Also those, though, of the King and Queen, Don Ippolito," Monsignore observed tartly.

"That is to disarm the troops!" Don Ippolito promptly retorted. "The proof that the heart of the people is still on our side lies in the others! Clearly! Do you know that my son is in Sicily?"

Monsignore nodded his head with melancholy gravity, supposing the Prince to have asked this question to head him off an unpleasant topic.

"He travelled down with Don Flaminio," he added with a sigh, "and with the poor girl."

Donna Adelaide broke out in further and louder sobs. Don Ippolito stamped his foot angrily.

"We must learn to subdue our own griefs," he said haughtily, "and to take a wider outlook! Know how to live for something that exists above our every-day troubles and all the afflictions that life showers upon us! I have written to my son, Monsignore, and have also sent for Capolino to suggest that he should go and discuss the situation with him, and see whether it is possible to come to some understanding...."

"What, Don Ippolito?" Monsignore exclaimed, pained and shocked. "With the people who have just foully murdered his wife?"

Don Ippolito again stamped his foot upon the carpet, clenched and shook his fists, and with an expression of disgust on his upturned face, fumed:

"Slavery! Slavery! Slavery! Oh, if I were not walled up here!"

Upon which, "But are we banished? Really banished?" Donna Adelaide inquired through her tears, turning to the Bishop. "Who is it prevents us from leaving here, from going where we choose, Monsignore?"

"Who?" shouted Don Ippolito, swinging round upon her, his face white with anger. "Do not you yet know? Monsignore, did not you make clear to her the terms of my recent unfortunate marriage? How is it that this woman does not yet know who prevents us from leaving here?"

"But in a case like this!" wailed Donna Adelaide. "Let me go by myself! He can stay here! Holy God, one has a heart in one's hosom, after all!"

Monsignor Montero implored her with his hands to be silent, to use some prudence. Don Ippolito raised his hands, pressed them to his face and held them there for a long time; then, disclosing a completely altered expression, of intense bitterness, profound abasement, said:

"See, Monsignore, try to persuade my brother-in-law to bring his daughter here, to her aunt. Possibly the quiet, the change of scene, may do her good."

"What, here? Really here? Oh, if she comes here..." Donna Adelaide broke out in a frenzy of joy, almost leaping up and down on her chair. "Yes, yes, yes, Monsignore dear. Do you hear? It was he said it! Make her come here, Monsignore, at once, here, my precious child!"

Glad of the concession, Monsignore held out his plump, white hands to arrest her onset: "Wait a moment... if you don't mind. I must tell you.... oh, a thing that has touched me so, so deeply.... Here, yes... but wait a moment ... you will see that it is better to leave the poor girl at Girgenti for the present.... Wait: perhaps we have a way of curing her. Yes, why, the night before last, do you know who came to see me at the Palace? De Vincentis, that poor Nini De Vincentis, who has been in love with the girl for years, as you know. Such a dear boy! Oh, if you had seen him! In a state, I assure you, that made one's heart bleed. He began to cry, to cry heartbrokenly, and begged me, implored me to tell Don Flaminio to trust in him and let him stay beside the girl, because he with his love, with his warm, insistent pity hoped to arouse her, to call her back to reason and life. Well, what have you to say to that?"

"Magari!" exclaimed Donna Adelaide. "And Flaminio? Flaminio?"

"I carried out the mission at once, yesterday morning," Monsignore replied. "And Don Flaminio, who knows the young man's warm heart, his gentle nature and his stainless honour, accepted the offer, promising De Vincentis that the girl shall be his if he performs the miracle of curing her. And now the young man is there in the house with the poor girl. Let us leave them together, Donna Adelaide, and join in prayer to God that the miracle may be accomplished!"

With this exhortation, Monsignor Montoro took his leave. On the stair he told Don Ippolito that he had in mind the idea of issuing a Pastoral to the faithful of the diocese, and that in a few days' time he would come again and read it to him, before sending it out. Don Ippolito spread out his arms and, as soon as the Bishop had driven away in his carriage, went and shut himself up again in his Museum.

Donna Adelaide continued to cry, first from emotion at this action on poor dear Nini's part, then in despair, because she knew only too well the opinion that her niece had held of the young man in the past. Perhaps, if she could have been by the girl's side as well, to persuade her... you never could tell!

And she flew into a rage again, torn between her conflicting emotions, and felt herself devoured by fury at this barbarity on the part of the Prince, who compelled her to remain there. And, after all, why should she? What did she represent, what part was she supposed to be playing there? No, no, no; she must get away, escape, flee, or she would go mad also!

She decided to write to her brother, imploring him to come over at once and rescue her, set her free from this prison, by fair means or foul.

TWO BLACK SHAWLS.

Delighted at being summoned by the Prince of Laurentano, Capolino was preparing to go down to Colimbetra when, in the entrance hall of his house, he heard his old servant gruffly turning away some one who was asking for him.

He went to the door, looked out, saw two women dressed in black, each with a shawl, likewise black, on her head, drawn close round her pale, weary face.

They were Pigna's two daughters, Mita and Annicchia.

Capolino, when he heard their name, invited them into the sitting-room, and after making them sit down inquired how he could be of service to them.

For shame at their own poverty, to support their affliction with dignity, they were both striving to repress their overflowing emotion. The effort that they were making not to cry, meanwhile, combined with their shyness, deprived them of speech. And each of them pressed tightly, beneath her black shawl, the thumb of her left hand against the top joint of the forefinger, blunted, hardened, soiled and punctured by the constant plying of needle and thread, as though only in the lost sensibility of that finger could she find the strength and courage to speak.

Finally Mita, barely raising her dark-rimmed eyes, managed to say:

"Signor Deputato, we have come to beg you...."

And the other at once prompted, corrected her:

"We are disturbing you... when you have such a great sorrow at home...."

"Go on, go on please," Capolino encouraged her. "I am here to listen to you."

"Yes Sir, I shall... Your Honour will know," Mita went on, her cheeks colouring swiftly, "that our father and Lizio, who is..."

"The husband of one of our sisters," Annicchia again prompted her.

Mita east a piteous glance of reproach at her sister.

"Have been arrested, Signor Deputato!"

"They are innocent, Signor Deputato, innocent!"

"We can bear witness that they knew nothing, nothing at all about the deed...."

Capolino, confused by the breathless, eager excitement with which the sisters were now speaking, asked:

"What deed?"

"Why!..." said Mita. "The deed that Your Honour, alas..."

"Oh Lord!" exclaimed Annicchia. "It makes my heart tremble to think of it."

And Mita continued:

"They have been arrested as well, here in the town, as innocent as Christ Himself.... We can bear witness that they were left speechless, it took their breath away, when the news came... they felt the earth gape beneath their feet...."

"And Your Honour may be sure," added Anniechia, "that we should not have had the courage to come here, to speak about it to Your Honour, if we were not more than certain, that they are innocent...."

And Mita, with downcast eyes, put in, trembling:

"Your lady; we have worked for her, and we know how good she was... such a friendly lady ... and beautiful, oh, how beautiful she was... it is dreadful!"

Capolino blinked his eyes, wriggled a little on his chair, and asked in a thick voice:

"Have they been to search the house?"

"Yes, Sir," both sisters replied simultaneously. Mita went on: "Police, detectives, magistrates ... like a band of devils... they turned everything upside down...."

"And what did they find?"

"Nothing!"

"Oh Maria, absolutely nothing.... A few letters ... newspapers... the list of members."

"Members in name only.... Nobody ever came to the meetings...."

"Books... papers.... They carried off everything... even a piece of linen, Signor Deputato, that had a drop of blood on it, which I had spilt myself, when I pricked my finger, here, with the needle...."

Capolino clutched his jaw in his hand, and sat for a while frowning, trying to think; then said:

"If nothing comes out that can compromise them..."

"Oh no, Sir!" Mita at once protested. "Nothing that has to do with the deed for which they have been arrested; absolutely nothing! Your Honour may be quite sure...."

"We should not have come to Your Honour ..." Annicchia repeated.

Capolino held up his hands to silence them; and collected his thoughts again.

"Do you know," he asked, after a pause, "that I am not in the good graces of the authorities? Do you know that, to excuse thirty years and more of misgovernment, they want it to be believed that all these riots in Sicily have been secretly engineered by the Clerical Party, to which I belong?"

"Oh, Your Honour... what an idea!" said Annicchia, clasping her hands. "When Your Honour has had... after Your Honour..."

"All the more! All the more!" Capolino cut her short. "They will say: 'There, can't you see it's all a plot? The heart is one thing, politics another! Here he comes in person to plead for the accused....' That is what they will say!" The sisters remained bewildered, crushed.

"And how can anyone believe such a thing?" asked Mita.

"Why, they don't believe a word of it!" Capolino replied with a contemptuous smile. "They pretend to believe it. It is their excuse. And I, if I appeared in court, you can understand, should be playing into their hands, without obtaining anything for you. That is just how things stand! It was the same in 1866, before you were born or thought of, the popular rising, due to political and administrative injustices, was put down to this scapegoat of a Clerical Party. It is the most convenient excuse, for the people in power, and one that is certain to be effective!"

The sisters sat for a while in silence, lost in thought, as though they saw the hope, that had brought them there, creep back into a wilderness of suffering, banished by an unsuspected argument, which they could not clearly understand.

"We had supposed," said Mita at length, "that if Your Honour were to say a word... not only before the authorities... but in the town as well.... We live by the work which we two do, my sister here and myself.... No one will give us any more work, now, because everyone, after this arrest, believes that our father and our brother-in-law were accomplices in the crime which has quite rightly infuriated the whole town. ... Now, if Tour Honour, who has been more wronged than anyone else, were to say a word ... their innocence..."

"And there is also this, Signor Deputato!" broke in Annicchia, unable any longer to restrain her tears, "that our sister, Signor Deputato, when the police came to arrest her husband and our father, had her baby at her breast. It poisoned her milk, Signor Deputato; and now the baby is dying, and we don't know what to do for it; and our sister seems to have gone out of her mind, what with her little boy dying, and his father in prison! There are five of us sisters left at home; try as we may, we can't do anything to help her.... That is why we have come here, to appeal to you, Signor Deputato!"

Capolino rose, as though propelled from his chair by his emotion.

"I shall see..." he said, "I shall see that something is done.... Give me a little time. ... I must think first, because of my... I mean to say, my political responsibility.... The heart, as I said just now, is one thing; politics another. ... But I shall see.... I don't bind myself. ... I shall see that something is done for you, never fear.... Calm yourselves, calm yourselves ... and courage, my dear girls, courage! This is a terrible time for everybody, believe me ... and nobody has yet managed to see a way out... nobody!"

So saying, he escorted them to the front door; refused to listen to any apologies or thanks; shut the door gently after them.

Without putting any faith in this vague promise of assistance, the sisters, as soon as they were in the street, felt a certain relief at the step they had taken, a certain excitement, a certain joy at having managed to speak, by which they felt their courage somewhat restored. But presently, when they thought of the quarter to which they had turned, they relapsed into their somhre grief, into the abasement of a burning sense of shame.

They called at the Post Office, to collect a small sum of money, which Celsina had sent them from Rome, and of which they did not know what to think.... And other money, at this time, little, oh so little, the piteous and repellent fruit of another notorious disgrace, came from their elder sister, from Rosa, to those hands worn with toil and now forced to remain idle, forced to gather up the sad burden of this unsought assistance.

THE FRESH WEB.

The thought that in the eyes of the world he figured as going to Colimbetra not of his own accord, but by invitation, was highly pleasing to Capolino.

There was there, at that moment, hanging from the bough, a pear, which at one time had remained unripened by the heat of his desire; but now, by all that he could conjecture from recent information, must be more than ripe, ready to drop, at a cautious but daring twitch from his hand.

This, ah this, would be the perfect consummation of his revenge! And everything appeared to have been marvellously preordained, so that with the greatest possible facility his revenge might be consummated in this way! Adelaide Salvo was still an unmarried woman in the eyes of the law.

Had he not felt an unreasonable secret jealousy at the time of the arrangements for her marriage to the Prince of Laurentano? What reason, indeed, could there be for this jealousy, since Adelaide Salvo could not any longer have become his wife, he being already married to Nicoletta Spoto? And yet... and yet he had felt this jealousy, which was now revealing itself to him as unreasonable not in the original sense, but in another that was just the opposite. Because, if he could have foreseen at the time, that it was only as a result of that specious wedding that Adelaide Salvo would be able one day to become his wife, it was not jealousy that he must have felt, but pleasure. But he had not foreseen it then, as he saw it now; and had accounted for his unreasonable jealousy by the fact that he could not look upon Nicoletta Spoto as a real and proper wife, but rather as a partner, a companion in adventure; the true wife for him, even though he was no longer a free man, was still Adelaide Salvo.

Now.... Oh, it would be another colossal scandal! Which, however--unlike the previous scandal, which had ended in tears--might perhaps end in laughter.... And by it he would be relieved from playing the part of victim, which had been cast for him by the former scandal, namely the scandal of poor Nicoletta's elopement with the unfortunate Costa. And Flaminio Salvo, who had plotted the other scandal of his wife's elopement, as previously he had plotted his sister's half-and-half marriage, would now be left doubly ridiculous and doubly punished: punished by the instrument of his own misdeeds, of the crime, that was to say, which had set him, Capolino, free from Nicoletta, and of the illegal marriage, which, by making life unendurable to his sister, delivered her into Capolino's hand, free to contract a perfectly regular marriage with him. Once he was Adelaide Salvo's husband, what would it matter to him if he forfeited his Deputy's badge? There was still a long time before the next dissolution.... He would persuade Adelaide to fly with him to Rome, to take refuge in the house of her sister Rosa. As a measure of prudence, to establish his rights as her deliverer, he would first put in a few days at Naples with her who, poor thing, must be so sorely in need of those diversions which only a big town like Naples could offer her. In Rome, they could without causing any stir contract the civil marriage. Francesco Velia would manage to find a place for him as counsel to the Railway Department; and it went without saying that Velia would be delighted that Capolino, become his brother-in-law once again, should keep that badge dangling from his waistcoat. In time, even Flaminio Salvo himself, by the intercession of Don Francesco and Donna Rosa, would perhaps be appeased and would refrain from putting obstacles in his way.

The important point, now, was to persuade Adelaide to brave the scandal of an elopement, at this unfortunate moment of her niece's insanity. But Monsignor Montoro had told him that the Prince absolutely forbade his wife to go to Girgenti, even if only to visit her brother's house. Another marvellously propitious circumstance was the compassionate offer of service to the poor girl made by that dear fellow, Nini De Vincentis. For if Dianella had been taken to Colimbetra, to be with her aunt, as the Prince had suggested, so far from thinking of an elopement, he would not have been able so much as to set foot in the house again! But could Adelaide be satisfied with this vague hope, this meagre consolation in absence, of knowing that poor San Luigi to be on his knees before her demented niece? If the truth were known, all that ardent longing, however sincere it might be, to visit her niece, must be merely a pretext for getting away from Colimbetra. The reasons for her discontent all persisted, exacerbated if anything by this prohibition. Nor would Flaminio Salvo ever be prevailed upon to persuade the Prince to grant this exeat to his sister. He must dwell upon this point, make it plain to Adelaide that her brother was not the man to fall short of the terms he had stipulated with the Prince, upon any consideration; so that she, losing all hope of assistance from her brother and seeing herself condemned to languish there in boredom and disgust, might see no other way of escape but in himself, and find in her desperation the courage necessary for flight.

These thoughts and memories and suggestions Capolino turned over in his mind as he drove down from Girgenti to Colimbetra. But they aroused in him neither eagerness nor warmth. He was conscious rather of a nauseating frigidity, as though his life had become congealed; he felt that this revenge of his was for things that were left behind in the past, irrevocable, and already dead in his heart, and that accordingly he would derive no pleasure from it, nor any promise of future happiness. He was avenging a man who, once upon a tune, had been rejected by Adelaide Salvo; but was he any longer that man? Too many things that ought not to have happened had (alas!) happened, things the dead weight of which he could feel in his heart, for him to take any pleasure now in his revenge. And it was just all these dead things that made it so easy for him. This was why he felt that nauseating frigidity. In Nicoletta Spoto he had been able to find a certain compensation, a solace in the nausea of his abject state; life for her and with her was almost worth the discomfort of being vile.... But to create a fresh scandal now, to insult such a man as Don Ippolito Laurentano, for Adelaide Salvo. ... Perhaps, however, taking it all in all, it would be a relief to Don Ippolito to have his wife stolen from him! At the moment, his self-esteem would be slightly injured; but it was not a

bad thing that at him, who had been able to enjoy the personal satisfaction of always holding his head erect, with so much dignity
and pride, fate itself should now, at the eleventh hour, by the hand
of Capolino, deal a blow, like this, in passing. Ah, Most Noble
Prince, you must bow to the spirit of the age! We can allow you a
bodyguard dressed in the Bourbon uniform; but you will do well to
learn that, in the present year of grace, there is a certain risk in
marrying a woman before God's altar alone....

Yet another providential coincidence, and this one really
unhoped-for, and such as almost took the wind out of his sails, he
found as soon as he arrived at the villa.

Don Ippolito, indignant on the one hand at the Bishop's
want of faith; completely disillusioned, on the other hand, by Lando's reply, which had reached him overnight from Palermo, as to
the possibility of coming to an arrangement with the Clerical Party,
had taken refuge, as upon so many other occasions, when in need
of comfort, in the study of ancient records, in his long interrupted
work upon Akragantine topography.

As in the case of the acropolis, so in that of the emporium
of Akragas, he had set himself against all the topographers, ancient
and modern, who placed it at the mouth of the Hypsas. Here, he
maintained, there had been merely a landing-place, whereas its emporium, its true emporium, Akragas, like other cities of ancient
Greece, which were not situated actually upon the sea, had established at a distance, in some bay or inlet that would offer a safe
anchorage to ships: Athens, at Piraeus; the Attic Megara, at Nisaea;
the Sicilian Megara, at Xiphonium. Now, what was the bay or inlet
nearest to Akragas? It was the so-called Cala della Junca, between
Punta Bianca and Punta del Filiere. Very well then, there, in the
Cala della Junca must have been the Akragantine emporium.

He had arrived at this conclusion with the help of an ancient Legendary of Saint Agrippina. And he was hugely delighted
with a page, which he had contrived to insert in the dry topographical discussion, describing the voyage of the three Virgins, Bassa,
Paula and Agathonica, who had brought the Saint's body by sea
from Rome after her martyrdom under the Emperor Valerian.
There was no doubt that the three Virgins had landed with the
body of the Saint on the Akragantine shore, at a spot named Lithos

in Greek and Petra in Latin, the spot that to this very day is known as Petra Patella, or Punta Bianca. Very well, in the text of the ancient hagiographer one read that, at the moment when the three Virgins landed, a monk who was leaving the monastery of Saint Stephen in the village of Tyrus, hard by the emporium, bound for Agrigentum, had stopped, attracted by the sweet savour that issued from the Saint's body, and had then hastened to the city to announce the portent to the Bishop, Saint Gregory. If, as the topographers, ancient and modern, asserted, the emporium was at the mouth of the Hypsas, and accordingly the *vicus* of Tyrus and the monastery of Saint Stephen were there also, how in the world could this monk, on his way to Agrigentum, encounter at Punta Bianca the three Virgins as they landed with the body of the Blessed Martyr? It was wholly inadmissible. The monastery of Saint Stephen at Tyrus must have been there, by Punta Bianca, and therefore the emporium must have been there also. And the most convincing proof lay in the name of this village, identical with that of the great Phoenician city: Tyrus. This name had been given it, in all probability, by the Carthaginians at the time of their thriving trade with the Akra-gantines, and came from some hill, which must have risen close to the village: *tur*, in Phoenician, signifying a hill. Was there, perhaps, a hill to be found by the mouth of the Hypsas? No; the hill, which, indeed, bears the generic title of Monte Grande, rises precisely there, by Punta Bianca and commands the Cala della Junca.

Don Ippolito had risen betimes that morning and had ridden out, escorted by Sciaralla and by four of his men, to make a careful examination of these sites, and especially the side of that Monte Grande, in the district called Litrasi, where there are certain remains, believed by some topographers to be Phoenician tombs, but, in his opinion, of far more recent origin and grouped and excavated in a style common in Sicily in the days of the Later Empire, so that they might date back to the episcopacy of Saint Gregory, in other words to the time of the landing at that spot of the three faithful Virgins Bassa, Paula and Agathonica with the fragrant corpse of the Holy Martyr Agrippina.

On his homeward journey, albeit on every side there lay spread out to enchant the eye, in the almost springlike warmth, vast carpets of velvety green, here gilded by the sun, there vaporous with deep violet shadows beneath the intense and ardent azure of the sky, Don Ippolito, as he gazed at his hands, resting upon his saddle-bow, had had but one thought in his mind, that of death, of his own departure from these scenes, which could not be much longer postponed. But, contemplated thus, beneath that sun, in the midst of all that verdure, while his body swayed rhythmically with the gentle motion of his horse, death had inspired in him no horror, but rather a lofty serenity, tinged with regret and at the same time with satisfaction, at the refinement and nobility of the thoughts and interests with which he had always interwoven his life amid these cherished scenes, to which presently he must bid a last farewell. And he had taken a long plunge into this novel sense of serenity, as though to wash himself clean of the agonizing terror which death had always given him until then, which had been responsible for this degrading second marriage, a marriage that had profaned the dignity of his old age, the austerity of his exile.

Shortly after midday, arriving at Colimbetra, tired after his long ride, he entered the drawing-room and found Capolino and Donna Adelaide engaged in earnest conversation; she, excited and in tears; he, pale and in a fervour of agitation. The Prince stopped short on the threshold, revolted rather than annoyed.

"Oh, Prince..." Capolino at once began, rising to his feet, at a loss for words.

"Don't move, don't move..." said Don Ippolito,. holding out his hand, more to prevent the other from approaching him than as an invitation to him to remain seated. "I make no apology for being late, because the Signora, I can see... has been describing me to you as such a barbarian, that you cannot have regretted the want of my company...."

"No... the... the Princess... really ..." stammered Capolino.

Don Ippolito assumed a haughty attitude and said, with a firm, frowning coldness:

"She may go, if she wishes. But with the knowledge that what prevents her to-day from going beyond the gate of my villa will prevent her to-morrow from returning. And now, will you please to continue your conversation."

He turned to leave the room. Capolino made an effort to

maintain his manly dignity in front of the lady, and addressed his retreating back, with an air almost of defiance, but one that might also be taken for an apology:

"You sent for me, Prince...."

Don Ippolito, who had by this time reached the door, barely turned round, thrusting aside the curtain with his hand:

"Oh, for a matter of no importance," he said. "Now.... Fads! Fancies!"

And he passed out, letting the curtain drop behind him.

"The answer... the answer..." Donna Adalaide at once broke out, rising to her feet; choking, her eyes swollen and bloodshot with Weeping, "I shall wait until to-morrow for his answer, or for him to come here in person, and tell me that I must stay here till I die, and let myself be trampled underfoot like this...."

"Why of course! Of course! Of course!" Capolino retorted, going towards her. "What do you expect Flaminio to say?"

"He must say it!" she interrupted him, in a frenzy, baring her teeth and clenching her fists. "He must say those words to me, with his own lips; and then yes, then yes, at once! I will do the worst! I am ready! I will do the worst!"

At this moment Liborio, the Prince's favourite servant, entered the room, alarmed and excited, and halted for a moment in perplexity, seeing the tears and agitation of his mistress.

"Your Excellency.... Your Excellency..." he said, "Signor Don Salesio..."

"What is the matter?" Donna Adelaide inquired angrily. "What does he want?"

"Nothing, Your Excellency... he appears to be..."

And Liborio raised his hand in a vague gesture of benediction.

"Ah," said Donna Adelaide at this, fixing Capolino with a hard stare, and continuing to gaze at him frowning and open-mouthed, as though to discover from him whether it was a good or a bad thing that the poor man should choose this particular moment at which to die. "It is better ... better so!" she then exclaimed, "better so, poor man.... Come, Gnazio, let us go and look at him...."

And she hurried in the wake of Liborio, followed by Capolino, disturbed and worried.

"I have kept him here with me..." she said to him as they went, "I have nursed him... looked after him.... Fine friends you have all been, to desert him like this... poor old man. ... It is the best thing that could happen... a merciful relief.... Even I have neglected him for the last few days.... Murderers! They have dealt him the final blow.... He himself though, I must say, did eat too much... too many sweet things...."

"Ah, yes, Your Excellency," sighed Liborio, "I told him so myself... too many..."

"Pick it up, Gnazio, pick it up.... I've dropped my handkerchief. Oh Bella Madre Santissima, what a horrible smell!"

And she stopped her nose with her fingers, coming to a standstill at the door of the room in which the poor old man lay dying, supported on his bed by the cook, who had come running in at Liborio's summons.

Spellbound by an instinctive horror of death, but perhaps even more by repulsion at the extreme thinness of the cartilaginous face, by the colourless hair, the eyeballs already stiffened beneath the half-shut lids, Donna Adelaide and Capolino were standing gazing in, still from the threshold, when they saw the dying man's mouth open, wider and wider, in a cavernous gape, as though his jaws were being forced apart with cruel violence by an internal spring.

"Oh Lord!" groaned Donna Adelaide. "Why is he doing that?"

She had not finished speaking when something shot out of that open mouth, something horrible.

Donna Adelaide uttered a cry of disgust and raised her hands to shelter her face.

Liborio went over to the bed, and there discovered a grinning set of false teeth.

"It is nothing, Your Excellency!" he said with a pitying smils. "He has taken his last bite..."

The cook meanwhile was arranging on the pillow the lifeless head of the poor old man.

CHAPTER VII

"YE HAVE THE POOR ALWAYS WITH YOU."

In the great echoing hall of the former chancery of the Episcopal Palace, with the fresco on its grimy ceiling covered in dust, its high walls with their yellowing whitewash, loaded with old portraits of prelates, covered also with dust and mildew, scattered about with no regard for symmetry above the blistered, worm-eaten cupboards and bookcases, a buzz of approval rose as soon as Monsignor Montoro, in his beautiful voice, with its measured inflexions, as though suffused with a pure, protecting authority, finished reading to the Cathedral Chapter and a number of other Canons and dignitaries assembled there for the purpose, his pastoral epistle to the reverend fathers of the diocese upon the lamentable events which had plunged Sicily in grief and were distressing every Christian heart.

A verse from Saint Matthew had given Monsignore the text for his pastoral: "*Ye have the poor always with you....*"

It was a freezing, blustering day in January; and more than once, as he read, the Bishop, in irritation, and his audience as well, had looked anxiously at the tall windows which seemed on the point of yielding, with a crash, to the screaming fury of the southwesterly gale. His calm reading of this gentle homily had had throughout the sinister accompaniment of sharp, shrill hisses, long sorrowful moans, which had often distracted the attention of more than one of his hearers, diffusing throughout the vast hall, watched over by those old portraits, dusty and mildewed, an intense feeling of regret for the vanity of time and life, a vague sense of terror.

Several of them had been looking out, through one of those windows, at the terrace of an old house opposite, upon which a poor lunatic seemed to be tasting some secret joy, that of flight perhaps, exposed to the fury of the wind which sent fluttering round his body the yellow woollen blanket that had been draped over his shoulders: he was laughing with the whole of his wretched face, while his keen, demoniac eyes glistened with a film of tears, and the long locks of his reddish hair floated out on either side of him like flames. The poor fellow was the younger brother of Canon Bata, who was present in the room, apparently paying the closest attention to what the Bishop was reading, but inwardly absorbed, beyond question, in wholly different thoughts, which had several times found expression in comical gesticulations. The reading at an end, those of the older Canons who were most familiar with their most excellent Bishop's weakness hastened to surround the table, at which he was seated, to make him repeat, one one, another another, among the many passages with which Monsignore, from the way in which he pronounced them, had seemed to them to be most satisfied and pleased.

"That sentence about Satan's Host, My Lord, how does it go?"

"Your Lordship was alluding to masonry, wasn't he? What was the expression?"

And Monsignore, inwardly overjoyed, but preserving an outward air of weary condescension, letting droop over his clear, oval eyes those eyelids of his as fine as layers of onion-skin, and nodding his head in assent, and raising his hand to bid them wait, looked for the passage and repeated:

"Evil and accursed sect... evil and accursed sect, which for its architect has chosen the devil, for its hierophant the Jew...."

"Ah, that was it! For its hierophant the Jew!" they exclaimed. "A stupendous expression, My Lord. Stupendous!..."

"Bold... daring..."

"Great heavens, what a gale!" the Bishop began to complain, distressed, as though it were not the reward that he merited for his pains.

Meanwhile the younger Canons, who had listened more attentively than any to the reading, were exchanging glances of disgust at these silly old flatterers, or of pained resignation to the reception that the people would give to this windy eloquence, which kept harping upon a question no less cruel than it was fatuous, which the reverend fathers were to transmit to the poor of the diocese: why it was that poverty, which had always existed and would always continue to exist, should only now be disturbing people's minds like this, upsetting social order, and leading to such deplorable excesses.

One or two of these young dignitaries felt that Monsignore might at least have paraphrased, with application to the occurrences in the Island, the recent Encyclical of H.H. Leo XIII, *De conditione opificum*, in which it was laid down that employers of labour must cease from usury, overt or covert, and from treating their workmen as slaves, and from trading upon the need of the poor, instead of shewing such hostility to those who "dared to question the ancient rigour of the Civil Law."

They were all the more distressed by the tone of their Bishop's Pastoral, in that, only the day before, in defence of the poor, Pompeo Agro had published a fierce pamphlet, in which, after comparing conditions in Sicily to those in Ireland, and drawing attention to the language used and attitude adopted by eminent Catholic prelates, British and American, towards the economic and social questions of the hour, he had--by way of a challenge--quoted the insolent reply of Fr. MacGrlynn, a Catholic priest in New York, to his Bishop's request that he would moderate his revolutionary propaganda: "I have always taught, My Lord, and shall continue to teach, so long as there is breath in my body, that the earth is by right the common property of the people, and that the right of individual property in land is opposed to natural justice, however it be sanctified by civil and religious laws!"

The whole of Agro's pamphlet was a bitter indictment of the ignorance and sloth of the Sicilian clergy. And here, within twenty-four hours, was their Bishop's pastoral, furnishing the most clear and convincing proof of the charge.

Another group was discussing whether it would not be as well to send, later on, privately, one of the more favoured of the seniors to Monsignore, to point out to him in so many words how inopportune this pastoral was, now that the report was going about that, with the storm raging everywhere, the proclamation of a state of siege throughout Sicily was imminent if not already decreed. A certain general had even been mentioned by name, as appointed Commissioner Extraordinary, with full powers; the same general who, a few days earlier, had landed at Palermo with a whole army corps. It was said that he had begun by arresting the members of the Central Committee of the Fasci, who, the night before, had issued a revolutionary proclamation to the workers of the Island.

"Yes, here it is... I have it in my pocket ... it is quite true!" said one of them, mysteriously. "We can read it in a moment, when we get outside...."

But, to baffle and enhance the eager curiosity of this group, there appeared in the hall at that moment, paler than usual and panting for breath, the Bishop's young secretary, who evidently brought the confirmation of this most serious news.

They all crowded round the table.

"Is it proclaimed?"

"Yes, yes, the state of siege is proclaimed; with orders to disarm the populace."

"To disarm them as well? Good... good...."

"And they have arrested the members of the Central Committee of the Fasci, in Palermo."

"All of them?"

"No, not all; some of them managed to escape. Including, it is said, the Prince of Laurentano's son."

"Heavens, what do I hear?" the Bishop groaned. "Yes... he was in it too!... Escaped? Escaped?"

The report was not confirmed: many people asserted that Laurentano had been arrested as well. Anyhow, the whole of Sicily would at once be placed under military occupation, down to the smallest villages, so that the fugitives too would be caught and imprisoned.

"Heavens, what do I hear? What do I hear?" Monsignore continued to exclaim. "But... have we really come to this?"

Furtively, from the young cleric's pocket, appeared the Committee's proclamation, which had been distributed broadcast on handbills through all the towns of the Island; it passed from hand to hand round the table; but many of those present did not know what it was, and every one, when he discovered its nature, refused to open it and handed it on to his neighbour, as though the folded, crumpled sheet might burn or soil his hands, until it ended in those of the young secretary, who unfolded it and began to read it aloud in the Bishop's presence, to the speechless dismay of some and amid a running commentary of derision or indignation from, the rest.

Treating with the Government on terms of equality, the Committee, in solemn tones, demanded in the name of the workers of Sicily: *the abolition of the local duties on flour* ("Ah! They go as far as that, do they?"); *an inquiry into the administrative services, in which, the Fasci should "be represented* ("Good for them! That's a clever stroke... to be sure!"); *The legal sanction of the agrarian and mineral agreements drafted at the congresses of the Socialist Party* ("What's that? Legal sanction? Yes, legal! The government stamp!"); *the establishment of agricultural and industrial centres, to manage the undeveloped property of private owners and such public prop, erty of the State and ecclesiastical tithes as had not yet been alienated* (at this a storm of protest hroke out, a confused din, over which predominated: "Spoliation!"... "Brigands"... "They have no right!" while the young secretary held up his hand to appeal for silence, implying that there was more, there was better still to come, and repeated, reading from the sheet: "*including ... including...*") *including the compulsory expropriation of large proprietors, with a temporary concession to the said proprietors of a small annuity* ("Oh, they are too kind!" "How considerate!" "What generosity!" "What condescension!"); *social legislation for the economic and moral improvement of the proletariat,* and then the final bombshell: *the inclusion in the national budget of a sum of twenty million lire to provide for the necessary outlay upon the execution of these demands, for the acquisition of the instruments of labour for both the agricultural and the industrial centres, and for the maintenance of their members and the establishment of the centres upon a sound and efficient basis,*

"But they are mad! They must be mad!" Monsignore broke out amid the general hubbub, as he rose from his chair. "Great God! What impudence! But is it confirmed, eh? Is it con-firmed that this army corps has arrived? Is it confirmed, eh? This is no laughing matter! Oh, Lord! Oh, Lord!"

The young secretary hastened to reassure him, then finished reading the proclamation which, in conclusion, recommended calm, *because from isolated and convulsive movements no lasting benefits would accrue,* and warned its readers that the *procedure to be adopted would depend upon the. Government's decision.*

But Monsignore, waving aside with both hands, as superfluous, these recommendations and warnings, told his secretary to send the pastoral immediately to the printer, as it would certainly gratify the General in command of the army corps; and dismissed the assembly in order that he might hasten to Colimbetra to comfort the Prince of Laurentano.

With a long and loud flapping of cassocks and cloaks the throng of Canons, buffeted by the wind, stepped down from the high ground of San Gerlando to mix in the hubbub of the town. The madman, on his terrace, was shouting, joyfully, waving his yellow blanket, as though in response to the fluttering of all those black cloaks.

THE VICTIMS.

As he hastened out to Colimhetra, Monsignor Montoro could certainly never have guessed that sentiments very similar to those which he himself had expressed with so much literary unction in his pastoral were agitating the mind of one of those men whom he had just described as mad.

At his first direct contact with those so-called comrades, at the repercussion, closer at hand and more frequent, of the bloodstained episodes of that popular rising which, even if widespread poverty, intolerable burdens, cruelties and tyrannies of every sort gave it ample justification, could not by any chance take shape and grow and predominate, lacking as it did a soul really conscious of its own strength and of its own rights, Lando Laurentano had found himself called upon by his friends in Sicily to answer, if not for a deliberate crime, since he could not but believe in their sincerity, certainly for a colossal piece of folly. Always arising from that external infatuation, due perhaps in great measure to the temperature of the soil: an infatuation which gave so theatrical an air, in voice and gesture, to the life of his fellow-islanders, and for which he--in his deliberate stiffness--had always felt such bitter contempt!

How could his friends have deceived themselves into thinking that they would succeed in a months, by their preaching, in breaking that hard, agelong shell of stupidity fortified by distrust and bestial cunning, which encrusted the minds of the peasants and sulphur workers of Sicily? How could they have believed in the possibility of class warfare, when all connexion and solidarity of principles, sentiments and intentions, nay, even the most rudimentary culture, any kind of consciousness were lacking?

The whole of their tactics, from beginning to end, were mistaken. It was not class warfare, impossible in the prevailing conditions, but rather a coalition of classes that was the object to be secured, since in every grade of society in Sicily there survived a deep-rooted resentment of the Italian Government, for its contemptuous indifference to the Island ever since 1860.

True that on the one hand feudal customs, the habit of treating the peasants as beasts of burden, and avarice and usury, and on the other the peasants' fierce and inveterate hatred of the gentry and absolute want of faith in the administration of justice, stood out as insuperable obstacles to the formation of any such coalition. But desperate as the attempt might appear, was that other revealed now as any less desperate which his friends had chosen to make, acting upon the principle, unconsciously and disastrously, of the inertia of the Government, which encouraged people to take risks?

The Government, plunged neck-deep at that moment, up in Rome, in the morass of the bank scandal, relying, down in Sicily, upon a policy either inept or arrogant and overbearing, without a thought for the evils that for so many years had afflicted the Island, without respect either for the law or for the liberty of the subject, had, by inertia or by provocation, favoured or stimulated the formation of those proletarian associations which, if they had promptly secured some improvement, however slight, of the conditions of labour on the land and in the pits, or if they had not been incited by bloodshed, would soon, without any doubt, have dissolved of their own accord, lacking as they did any unifying sentiment, any leaven of conscience, any trace of an ideal.

So much Lando Laurentano had realized now, when it was too late, on the spot; and the embittered spirit in which he had come in response to their invitation had remained crushed by a stupefaction filled with dark misgivings, as though his friends had stuffed his mouth with tow when it was burning with thirst.

Roused to action by the urgent necessity of finding some place of refuge under the lowering menace of a violent, crushing repression on the part of the Government, he had indignantly opposed the counsels of prudence advanced by his friends, who were bewildered and terrified by the extreme gravity of the situation.

Prudence? Now that, every few days, in the small villages of the interior, at Giardinello, for instance, with barely eight hundred inhabitants, and at Lercara, Pietraperzia, Gibellina, Marineo, the people were leaving their homes and herding together on the village greens, with no common plan, under no banner save the portraits of the King and Queen, with no weapon save a cross borne by some tattered, frenzied woman at the head of the procession, and marching blindly upon the rifles of a score of soldiers, who were impelled principally by the fear of being trampled underfoot to open fire spontaneously, without waiting for the word of command? True, no one had suggested to them these processions that ended in massacres; but for these and for all the other rash actions, and for the blood of the butchered victims, somebody must now answer, if only because these blind herds had been considered fit and ripe to welcome the demonstration of their rights. How could anyone draw back now, and counsel prudence? No, there was no other way of escape left now save in the final outbreak of that madness: the promoters must immolate themselves with their victims!

And Lando Laurentano had scornfully declined to append his signature to that manifesto of the Central Committee to the workers of the Island, which in the solemnity of its peremptory tone had struck him as positively ridiculous, because not so much of the terms and conditions it offered to the Government as of the entire absence of any real consciousness and strength in the people in whose name it offered them. The only real factor was the desperation of all those unfortunate creatures, condemned by their ignorance to a life of perpetual hardship; and the blood, the blood, the blood of the victims.

When the state of siege was proclaimed, Lino Apes had had to drag him off by main force into hiding. He had fled, not for the reasons which Apes in the excitement of the moment had shouted at him, but owing to his invincible repugnance to the idea of figuring as an apostle or a hero or a martyr, exposed in the dock of a military court to the wondering curiosity of the ladies of the Palermitan aristocracy who were known to him personally.

As companions in flight, in addition to Apes, he had had Bruno, Ingrao and Cataldo Selafani, all three in disguise.

How he had laughed, a laugh in which contempt mingled with pity, how degraded he had felt at the same time, and how disgusted, at the unrecognizable appearance of the last named, shorn of that quickset hedge which used to cover his cheeks and chin! It seemed as though his eyes and voice did not yet know of the loss, and they created a ridiculous effect of helplessness in their expressions, in which the beard that was now lacking had played so great a part. But this disguise did not, as a matter of fact, indicate any fear in any of the three; it was so to speak imposed on them by the part which the necessity of flight assigned to them at that moment; while there entered into it also, and to no small extent, the fatuous pride of the Islander in his racial cunning in escaping from the tyranny of constituted authority.

They had retired into the interior of the Island, fleeing before the troops who were preparing to invade the other Provinces from Palermo. If they should succeed in crossing it from end to end, they would take shelter at Valsania, and from there would take ship for Malta or Tunis. Lando would be glad to seek a haven in Malta, the scene of his grandfather's exile, not because he ventured to compare his own lot with his grandfather's but because he had intended for some time past to visit Burmula and trace, if possible, the spot where his grandfather was buried, with the help of Mauro Mortara's description, which, it must be admitted, was none too definite, since the burial had occurred amid the confusion of the great pestilence in Malta in 1852.

In vain had Lino Apes, taking as his text the incidents and discomforts of their headlong flight, now on foot, now in springless carts, now in broken-down carriages, up hill and down dale, in search of food and shelter, tried to prove to his friends that, after all, what they were doing was such a serious matter that a man could not laugh at it if he chose. Was the rending of their illusions, for instance, a sufficient reason for him to attach no importance to the rent he had made in his trousers, in climbing down from a cart? They were older than Tiberius Gracchus, those illusions; whereas his trousers were new! Where had Cataldo Sclafani left the clippings of his magnificent beard? A hair of that beard--he reflected philosophically--would have been the ideal thing for darning his trousers! The dreary aspect of the scenery, in its wintry desolation, the depressing effect of a laborious journey over a doubtful track, their eagerness to obtain news wherever they might of all that had happened since their flight began, made the subtleties of Lino Apes fall flat, arousing no echoing laugh.

The impressions that he managed to gather piecemeal, as they went farther and farther inland, of these exceptional measures that the Government had suddenly adopted, strengthened Lando's conviction that his friends had made a mistake. The old, profound discontent of the Sicilian people had in a moment changed everywhere to the most fiery indignation: even although the higher ranks of society had been alarmed at first by the popular agitation, now, in the face of this military aggression, of these armed forces with their air of an invading enemy, abolishing all law for everybody and suppressing every constitutional guarantee, they felt inclined, if not actually to fraternize with the lower orders, if not to make excuses for them, at any rate to admit that when all was said, they, up till then, had invariably had the worst of every encounter, nor had there ever yet been an armed rising, and that if they had been carried away to occasional excesses, these had been cruelly and stupidly provoked by the massacres. The native pride, common to all the Islanders, rebelled against this fresh insult which the Italian Government was inflicting upon Sicily, instead of making belated reparation for ancient wrongs; and everywhere there was a shudder of loathing at the reports that kept coming in, of towns surrounded by regiments of infantry, squadrons of cavalry, to arrest and carry off by hundreds, without any discrimination, rich and poor, students and workmen, town councillors here, schoolmasters and town clerks there, and women and old men and even little children; the suppression of newspapers; the subjection of private correspondence even to censors; the whole Island cut adrift from the rest of the community and handed over, bound and disarmed, to the mercies of a military dictatorship.

As a stubborn horse, driven against his will away from the obstacles that he was ready to jump, of a sudden, in a frenzied panic, takes fright and rears and backs, quivering in every muscle, so Lando Laurentano, swept by the vehemence of this general indignation, at a certain point had stopped, feeling himself suffocated by shame at his flight. Was this the time to flee? To desert the field of battle? The ground was burning under his feet; the air was all aflame. Was it possible that the Island, astir from end to end, would allow itself to be crushed, to be trampled underfoot like this, without rising in the exasperation of the hatred so long repressed and now so brutally provoked? A single rallying cry perhaps was enough! Enough perhaps that one man should step forward!

When he reached Imera, and heard that in a village close at hand, Santa Caterina Villarmosa, the populace had risen, Lando could contain himself no longer; and, notwithstanding that his friends did everything in their power to restrain him, shouting to him that there was nothing more that could be attempted, or hoped, and that he would simply be thrusting his head into the jaws of authority, he determined to go there.

Only Lino Apes accompanied him, and that in the hope of chilling his ardour and arresting him half way, assuming for the occasion, as best he might, the part of Sancho Panza, so that his friend, whom he knew to be sensitive to ridicule, might see himself as Don Quixote. And sure enough, very soon, the giants whom Lando in his excitement had imagined he saw embodied in those villagers of Santa Caterina Villarmosa, rising in defiance of the state of siege that had been proclaimed, revealed themselves to be merely windmills.

As they drew near to the village, they found that nobody there knew anything yet about the proclamation: a bill had been posted on the walls, but the ignorant folk had made nothing of it; and, in their ignorance, as usual, as elsewhere, with the portraits of the King and Queen, with a crucifix at the head of their procession, shouting: "Long live the King! Down with the taxes!" had proceeded to parade the village streets, until, turning out of the market place and into a narrow lane that debouched upon it, they had come upon eight soldiers and four carabinieri lying in wait for them. The officer in command (it was not for nothing that he was named Colleoni) had chosen this position with masterly strategy, so that the unarmed crowd, packed into this trap, should, when ordered to disband, find themselves unable to move; and there not once, but repeatedly, had given the command to fire upon them. There were eleven killed, and any number wounded, including women, old men and infants. Now, everything was quiet, quiet as the grave. Only, here and there, the cries of relatives, mourning for their dead, and the groans of the wounded.

"Have you had enough?" Lino Apes asked Lando.

The other turned to the old peasant who ha'd given them these details and who, in comparing the village to a graveyard, had pointed to a hill close by, crowned by a few cypresses; and inquired:

"Are they there?"

The old peasant, his eyes keen with hatred and big with pity, nodded his head several times, then held out the fingers of his earth-stained, misshapen hands, to indicate first ten and then one more; and, by the look in his eyes and the silence that followed this mute statement, made it clear that he had seen them.

Lando turned towards the hill.

"I see!" sighed Lino Apes. "Now I change to Horatio.... Scene two: Hamlet in the graveyard."

In the dreary little hilltop cemetery, save for its shivering sexton, who wore a light woollen shawl over his shoulders, there was no one to be seen. Seated upon a stool, to the left of the gate, he was gazing apathetically, in the desolate silence, at the coffins drawn up on the ground in front of him, like a shepherd watching his flock. He was expecting a visit from the judicial authorities, and orders for the burial. Seeing two strangers enter, he turned, then quickly rose and took off his cap, supposing them to be the magistrate and chief constable. Lino Apes described himself and his companion as journalists, and Lando asked him to let them see one or two of the bodies.

The custodian thereupon bent down over one of the coffins, which was bigger than the rest, old, painted grey, with two bands of crape crossed over it, and removed a heavy stone that was holding down the lid.

Two bodies, in this coffin, one upon the other: one with its face beneath the other's feet.

The one above was that of a boy. His legs were stretched apart; his head sunk between his companion's feet. In this inverted posture, he seemed to be protesting: "No! No!" with the whole of his lifeless little face, in which the eyes had not quite shut, still contracted in the agony of death. No, to such a death; no, to such horror; no, to that coffin for two, tainted by that crude and acrid stench of the slaughter-house.

But more appalling still was the face of the other, between the worn boots of the boy, with its great black eyes staring wide and a tawny shadow of beard beneath its chin. It was the body of a peasant in the prime of life. With those terrible eyes staring at the sky, from the supine body, it cried for vengeance for this final atrocity, the heaping of that other body upon itself.

"See, Lord," it seemed to be saying, "see what they have done!"

Neither Lando nor Apes was capable of uttering a word; and the sexton replaced the lid of the coffin and laid the heavy stone upon it.

After various other coffins, wretched things of unstained firwood, they came to one covered in a bright sky-blue cloth, a tiny coffin, so tiny that Lando in his uncertainty felt the hope rise that this at least was not connected with the massacre. He glanced at the sexton, who had stopped in front of it, and from the way in which he was gazing at it knew that, yes, this one too... this one too. ... He put the question, and the sexton, after nodding his head for a moment, answered:

"*Una 'nnucenti*...." (A little girl.)

"Can we see her?"

Lino Apes, revolted and horrified, protested:

"No, let it be, Lando! Don't you see? The Coffin has been nailed down...."

"Oh, if that's all..." said the sexton, producing an iron wedge from his pocket. "I shall have to open it for the magistrate. It's--quite easy...."

And he bent down to unfasten the flimsy lid, taking care not to damage the blue cloth. The nails slipped gently out of the soft wood, at each thrust of the wedge.

When the little coffin lay open, they saw inside it the child not yet rigid in death, her cheeks still blooming, her curly little head turned slightly to one side and her arms stretched out by her sides. But her rosy lips were wet with slaver, and from her nose trickled a bloody froth, still bubbling, at what seemed to be the regular intervals of res-piration. "But she is alive!" exclaimed Lando, with a shudder.

The sexton smiled bitterly:

"Alive?" and he replaced the lid.

"Would that mother have allowed her to set out alive on her last journey, who had combed and dressed her like that, who had so lovingly adorned the little coffin in that bright blue cloth?

"This is what they have done..." Lando murmured.

And Lino Apes and the sexton supposed that he was referring to the soldiers, who had killed the poor little girl.

Lando Laurentano was, however, referring to his own comrades, and saw in his mind's eye no longer the image of the little one, who had at least had the benefit of a mother's pitying care, but the terrible image of that other, adult victim, with the boots of another corpse over his face, and his eyes wide open, filled with a measureless anguish, staring at the sky.

THERE IS STILL HOPE.

In the old De Vincentis palazzo, its outer walls blackened by time and scarred everywhere like a ruin, its balconies and broad terrace carpeted with moss, behind their rusty railings, but inside, in the huge reception-rooms, full of light and peace, with those waxen saints and flowers beneath bells of crystal, which seemed to diffuse a monastic odour throughout, the silence, stamped upon the tiled floors by the rectangular patches of sunlight from the windows, which grew slowly longer and longer as the sun declined, followed by the slow, light swarming of motes in the sunbeams, was broken by a heavy, rhythmical sound of footsteps.

For the last week Vincente De Vincentis, oblivious of the Arabic manuscripts in the Itria library, had confined himself to one room, wrapped in an old and faded shepherd's cloak, with its collar turned up, pacing the floor from morning to night, his clawlike hands gripping each other behind his back, his head drooping and his eyes heavy with want of sleep, almost sightless, for in the house he never wore his glasses.

In the next room, by the glass door of the balcony, sat knitting, with a grey woollen shawl over her shoulders, and a black muffler, of wool also, round her head, tied beneath her chin, herself as soft and fleecy as a bale of wool, Donna Fana, the old housekeeper. Sitting half within the rectangle of sunshine, she seemed to be evaporating in the light, and the fluff of her woollen shawl, catching the sun, sparkled with the hovering motes in the beam.

Donna Fana had laid in their coffins with her own hands, first of all her master, who had died young, then her mistress, to whom she had been less a servant than a friend and counsellor, and

453

had seen come into the world and cradled in her arms her two young masters, entrusted now to her sole charge. As a girl, she had been a lay sister in the convent of San Vincenzo, and had remained "without the world," as she put it, a sort of domestic nun. From time to time she would heave, as in the convent, a burning sigh, followed by the inevitable exclamation:

"If I were there!"

But there was no one now to ask her, as was the custom among the nuns: "Where, sister?" so that she might answer with a second sigh:

"Sister, among the blessed angels!"

But, truly, in the peace of the angels she had always dwelt, in that house. The mistress: a true saint, innocent as a child even when she was a grown woman, incapable of thinking evil, and entirely devoted to religion and good works; those two boys: they too, each of them more virtuous than the other, well brought up in the fear of God.

Now, could the Lord ever abandon such a house, and let it go to ruin?

Donna Fana seemed to have an intimate knowledge of all God's wishes; and used to speak of Paradise as though she were already there, and were going on with her knitting beneath the eyes of the Eternal Father, as to Whom she could say where and how He was seated, with Jesus, Our Saviour, and Our Dear Lady. Years back, she had made ready the body linen and the robe and the cloth slippers and the silken kerchief in which to appear at the Last Judgment, confident that the Supreme Judge would number her among the elect, coming there so clean and neat; and every night she offered a special prayer to Saint Brigid, who was to announce to her in a vision, three days beforehand, the precise hour of her death, so that she might be ready and have received the sacraments.

And so there was nothing now that could distress her; and to her all this consternation shown by Vincente (whom she called Don Tinuzzo) was merely childish. She was confirmed in this opinion, not merely by her faith in God, but by her unassailable belief that the prosperity of the house could never come to an end. And she continued to manage the house with the time-honoured abundance, so that all the old pauper women of the neighbourhood came in after dinner to divide what was unused and the broken meats from the table, as had been their custom for so many years; and to lay in a store of all God's bounties, and to prepare with her own hands for her young masters the traditional cordials and sweetmeats, which she had learned to make at the convent, the *cus-cusu* of rice and pistacchi, the sweet fish of almond paste, the pine-kernel cakes, and all the preserves and quince jellies and fruits in syrup.

Perhaps it was true that Don Jaco Pacia, the agent, pocketed a little on the sly.

"But what of that?" she would inquire of Nini, after a furious outburst from his elder brother. "Crumbs, my son, crumbs!"

He a son of the Church too, Don Jaco Pacia, was it possible that he could be such a persistent robber as Don Tinuzzo made out? Did not Don Jaco continue to give her the same regular allowance for the housekeeping that he had always given her, without ever making the slightest comment? The entire control of the money was in his hands; why! the only thing was to turn a blind eye, if a trifle of it did stick to his fingers.

Donna Fana defended him, with a clear conscience, because she believed that she had a proof of the honesty of Pacia's thoughts and actions in the fact that, in the year when Don Jaco had gone to Rome, he had brought her back a blessed rosary and a snuff-box with the Holy Father's portrait.

Had she only known that, on this very day, Don Jaco, in order to raise money, in addition to the surrender of the lands of Milione to Don Flaminio Salvo, was coming to suggest a mortgage upon the palazzo itself, in which she sat so peacefully over her knitting.

This last bombshell, as a matter of fact, not even Vincente expected. Apart from the transfer of the land, he was preoccupied by another serious matter, which had given him no rest for two days, but one of a very different nature.

He had discovered in the corner of a room in which all the lumber was stowed away, an old gun, a flint-lock, smothered in rust and dust. Now that a state of siege and a disarming order had been proclaimed throughout Sicily, was it not his bounden duty to hand over this weapon?

Nini and Donna Fana said no; Nini even maintained that it would be regarded not merely as an impertinence but as an outrageous contempt of authority to surrender such a firearm as that. But what did they know about it? On what grounds did they say so? Like that, out of their heads! The order to hand over all arms, without exception, was positive and peremptory. Was this an arm, or was it not? Old it might be, indeed it was old and devoured by rust, but it was still an arm! Perhaps, too, it was loaded, and might go off at any moment.... You could see the flint; and the steel, there it was, hanging by a chain...."

"Very well, then, take it and hand it over!"

Nini had shouted at him, with a shrug of his shoulders, the day before, Nini who had something far more important on his mind at the moment, in his rare appearances in the house, completely upset and impatient to return to his torment, by the side of Dianella.

He, Vincente, had proposed that Nini should waste half the day, in the state of mind in which he was, in seeking information about the weapon. It was easy to say, take it! What if it went off? Hand it over, then, to whom, where? At the Prefecture? At the Town Hall? At the Police Station? He knew nothing about it, and if he were to go and inquire... like that, with a pretence of curiosity, there was the risk of his giving rise to suspicion and matters ending in a search of the house.

The state of siege had thrown, and was keeping Vincente De Vincentis in such a state of terror that he saw the most terrible threats and dangers everywhere. He had decided not to stir from the house, for as long as the ban should last. But what if, with Donna Fana's cursed habit of proclaiming aloud to the whole neighbourhood every trifling incident that occurred in the family, the police should come to hear about this weapon?

Suddenly, the old housekeeper saw him dash in frantic haste from the room in which he had shut himself up, waving his arms in the air and shouting:

"Let it go off! Let it kill me! I don't care a damn! I am going to take it, I am going to take it myself!"

"For heaven's sake, leave it alone, Don Tinuzzo!" exclaimed Donna Fana, running after him. "Don't let him, God, in that state.... You see how he's trembling all over? Leave it alone! I shall call somebody from the balcony. ..."

"Call whom? Don't you dare..." Vincente had begun to shout at her, his face purple, when from the front door, which always stood open in the daytime, there appeared Don Jaco Pacia, with his habitual air of a saint who had dropped from heaven into a world of sorrow and confusion, to which presently, quietly, with the help of God, he would restore order and peace.

He was long and dry, like a figure carved in wood, with a sad face, marked with the hard mourning band of his black eyebrows, a pair of circumflex accents, in contrast to the broad, foolish, blissful smile beneath his bushy white moustaches. His eyelids, straight like those of a Japanese, did not reveal the whites of his eyes, which remained opaque, as though indifferent to the hardness of those two circumflex accents and the foolish blissfulness of his eternal smile. With his arms always folded upon his breast and his big, unwashen, bony hands he would assume an attitude of resigned humility.

Having heard what the trouble was, he took into his own hands the affair of the gun, and said that Don Tinuzzo had not one but a hundred reasons for his alarm. Certainly, it was an arm! And, Heaven help us all, at a time like this.... A terrible time for the whole of Sicily! But he was here, he was here, on the spot, to look after his two dear boys, and, with the help of God, there was nothing to fear, in that direction! The trouble, the serious trouble, lay in another.

And he began to describe all the trouble he had had in tracing the title-deeds of the estate of Milione, first of all at the Record Office, then in the Chancery of the Law-courts and in the Diocesan Chancery, to find out all the dues, great and small, with which the said estate was burdened. Now the deeds were ready and in order at the lawyer's; but Don Flaminio Salvo was declining to pay the costs of the sale, and perhaps, from his own point of view, he was right, since, after all, he was doing a great favour... a banker like him...

"Oh indeed, a great favour? A great favour?" Vincente broke out in a fury. "Like Primosole, I suppose? A great favour!"

Don Jaco allowed him to finish, in one of his typical attitudes of holy martyrdom; then said:

"But you must have patience, my dear Don Tinuzzo! Has Don Flaminio other children, then, besides the daughter who is already promised to your brother Don Nini? Holy God, don't you see it is a pure formality? In a day or two they will be married, and it will all come back here in the end!"

"All, eh? Beautiful... easy... smooth as oil..." Vincente ejaculated, with furious jerks of his head. "The marriage of two lunatics! But if that is so, why does Don Flaminio refuse to pay the cost of the transfer? A proof that he doesn't believe it! Who says that this marriage is going to come off? Who says..."

"Don Tinuzzo!" the other interrupted him. "Has your brother Don Nini been received, or has he not, into Salvo's household? Or am I inventing it? Holy Name of God! He has been there for days on end, hasn't he? Well, what does that mean? It means that the girl is there! And you say that if the straw is kept by the fire ... Anyhow, here comes Don Nini himself.... He can tell you better than anyone."

Vincente hastened towards his brother as he entered the room; went close up to him, trembling with excitement; gripped both his arms in his clawlike hands, and tilted his crimson face sideways to make a close scrutiny of his brother's face, with his peering eyes. Then:

"Yes! Just look at him!" he sneered, stepping back and pointing to his brother. "Do you see his face! He looks like a corpse, your bridegroom!"

Nini, taken thus by assault, stood there in the middle of the room staring at his brother and Don Jaco and Donna Fana, as though he had lost his senses.

There was indeed depicted on his face, which as a rule expressed the gentle, courteous goodness of his nature, a troubled anguish, and his beautiful, dark, velvety eyes were tense with a black grief, unconscious though they seemed.

When he learned what was required of him and with what object, he drew himself up stiffly, waving his arms, with an expression of disgust. Don Jaco on one side of him, Donna Fana on the other, tried to calm him, to question him politely; but in vain: he wriggled from their grasp, shaking his head, a stifled cry in his throat.

"But do at least tell us if there is any hope, to set your brother's mind at rest!" Don Jaco cried to him finally, with clasped hands.

Nini gazed at him with a strange glare in his eyes. If there was no longer any hope of calling Dianella back to sanity, to life, what would he care about the ruin of his house, poverty, anything? Was it really possible that anyone could hope for Dianella's recovery, only for this, to save the house from ruin? That all his labour, his torment should, to these people, be serving this purpose? Yes, they were forcing him to fling his hope at them as a sop to placate their fear of poverty! Very well, then, yes, there was still hope, there was, there was....

And Nini, burying his face in his hands, burst out crying in shrill convulsive sobs.

TEARING UP....

Flaminio Salvo had with great difficulty deciphered the letter he had received from his sister Adelaide, whose handwriting, apart from the vagaries of her spelling, almost always illegible, this time suggested more than ever the furious scratchings of a hen.

It was all one long cry for help and threat of disaster, this letter, punctuated with imprecations and exclamations of despair. He had replied briefly and soothingly, telling her that he would soon be coming to pay her a visit at Colimbetra, and that in the meantime she must keep calm, as befitted a lady of her age and station.

A cold smile had hovered on his lips as he glanced, after perusing it, at this sheet of paper, which was still seeking to annoy him. Gently folding it up again he had begun to tear it slowly, along and across, into smaller and smaller fragments, without thinking of what he was doing, fallen into a profound abstraction of frowning gloom; finally, he had looked down at the result of his handiwork on the writing table: all that heap of tiny scraps of paper.

Who could say whether the sheet of paper had not been suffering, at being torn up like that, reduced to all those little scraps....

He had been left with a burning sensation in the balls of his forefinger and thumb, which had grown heated in this work of destruction, without his knowing it; of their own accord, from a lust for destruction.

Ah, to be able to tear to shreds, like that, without thinking, life as a whole: to fold it in four, like a sheet of paper soiled with stupid writing, and tear it along and across, ten, twenty, thirty times, piece by piece, slowly.

Luigi Pirandello

With a groan he had scattered over the writing table and floor all those scraps of paper, and had risen from his chair.

Looking out from the balcony window at the familiar, unchanging expanse of country; at the two breakwaters of Porto Empedocle in the distance, stretching out to sea, down there, like a pair of arms; at the dark blots made by steamers at anchor, and picturing to himself the industry of all those people down there in his service, loading the sulphur from his pits, heaped up on the beach, he had felt himself stifled by all the worries, all the thought that for years past had been inflicted upon him by that industry, which now was superfluous to him, necessary to so many, who derived from it the means of providing for their wretched daily needs, and of facing the hardships, the griefs that were interwoven with their lives and the life of every man. And it had occurred to him that he, a satiated and exhausted man, with the nausea of satiety and the helplessness of exhaustion, remained there, as though pinned to the ground, to let himself be devoured by all those restless, hungry creatures, none of whom mattered to him in the least degree. But could he possibly have prevented this? His work, the work of his whole lifetime, had assumed a bodily form outside himself, and lay there for the benefit of others. Could that expanse of country prevent a multitude of men from breaking its surface with hoe and plough, planting trees in it and gathering their fruit? So it was now with him. And, like the earth, he felt no joy in the work that other people were doing upon him to gather his fruit; nor could they, however much they walked over him, bear him company, penetrate, break his solitude, which had acquired the insensibility of stone.

He felt only an immense boredom with everything, which crushed in him the will to liberate himself, and was now capable only of moving his fingers, unconsciously, as they had moved just now, to do harm to a sheet of paper. But everything, now, for him, had the value of that sheet of paper; and he must allow his fingers, his fingers at least to do something, of their own accord, since his boredom set them in motion. Had they turned savagely upon himself, he would have allowed them to tear him, in the same way....

Was that really so? And was he not pretending the unconsciousness of his fingers when they tore up his sister's letter, so as to be able to assure himself that it was *in the same way* that he had torn

461

up, after his return to Girgenti, certain other letters, as soon as he caught sight of them in the drawers of the writing table, or in the pigeonholes in front of him? Certain letters that bore the signature of Nicoletta Capolino?

Actually, no: the images of Aurelio Costa and Nicoletta Capolino had never come and planted themselves in front of him, so that he might repel them with a *logical* smile, furnishing his reasons and pointing out to them the reasons that they required, if they wished to persecute him with remorse. Their persecution was more irritating than any other, because it was not apparent. It was not apparent, for this reason, as plain and solid and weighty as a tombstone: that they themselves, he in his own blindness, she from a personal motive of her own, had deliberately sought their death.

And yet.... And yet, beneath this reason, which buried them, which rendered them invisible to him, they, in a manner which he found himself unable to define, were... not present, no, never that; rather continuously absent: but by their very absence, yes, that was it, they were persecuting him. They were both of them there, with Dianella, in the absence of her reason. He did not see them, but yet he could feel them in the meaningless words, in the vacuous gaze and smile of his daughter. And then, to him. too, irresistibly, as though from his bowels wrung with exasperation, there came to his lips words devoid of meaning, unprompted by anything; strange vague words, which altered his face to suit each of the various expressions that they contained in themselves, on their own account, absolutely detached from his consciousness and hearing no relation to his actual state.

And so, to-day, to carry on the fiction of his unconsciousness, after tearing up his sister's letter, he had gone on to utter, in the same way, inconsequent words:

"What will serve... what will serve..." Except that, after a while, he had given a rational cloak to the fiction, which struck even him as too obvious:

"What will serve... yes. I have to light a cigar? I am served by a match. Here is the cigar ... there is the match: in themselves, two separate things; but made to satisfy my desire to smoke. First one, then the other, I light them and destroy them.... To think of all the matches I have struck in my life! Too many.... And all my work has gone up in smoke! A pity, because I have not attained my object... but I wanted a good marriage for my daughter, so as at least to set a crown... yes! a princely crown ... upon all my labours and struggles. 'A princely crown!... Smoke? Vanity? Ah, but that compensation at least for the death of my little boy! Vanity, of course it was, if fate chose to deprive me of all reason for thinking of more serious matters, and left me with one poor girl, with the shadow of her mother's madness brooding over her. And now... now... I suppose I am serving to satisfy somebody's desire to smoke...."

Why, of course, yes: had he not opened the door of his house to that stupid, harmless fellow De Vincentis? And had left his daughter alone with him: like that, to try the experiment! And if he should cure her, with those handsome, almond-shaped, velvety eyes, with his gentle, ladylike ways, why, Don Jaco Pacia, sitting at this very writing table, as lord and master, would in a few years have consumed in smoke all his bank notes, and his securities, and sulphur pits and land and houses and factories.

"What will serve... what will serve..."

This complaint from his sister Adelaide, however, no, it really was too much. What did she want from him? Was she not well enough off where she was? There were thorns? Oh, my dear woman! And she expected him to produce the roses? With all those "troops" providing an escort for her; with those portraits of the Bourbon Kings there to protect her, why, she ought to be happy and contented.... If only he had been in her place!

Now that he had failed in everything, the mere thought of seeing Don Ippolito again, and of talking to him, had become insufferably oppressive. How was he to endure, in the stark nakedness of his desolate spirit, without a shred of illusion left to cover it, the sight of that man so carefully composed and dressed up and adorned with the trappings of nobility? It seemed to him now incredible that he could have given a moment's serious thought to such a way of attaining his object. ... Poor Adelaide! She had been the one to suffer.... Still, after all! The villa was most comfortable, and the surroundings were charming; with a little patience and good will, she would be able to put up with the boredom of a man who was not precisely her natural affinity....

It was in this frame of mind that he went down, two days later, to Colimbetra.

The smile that rose to his lips as he passed through the gate, at the salute from the men on guard, still in military attire, though no longer armed, did not fade from them once during the whole of his visit.

With a smile he listened, beneath the columns of the porch, to the reply vouchsafed by Captain Sciaralla, that the fire-arms, no Sir, had not been handed over to the authorities, but had been put away for safety; with a smile he received Liborio's invitation to take a seat in the drawing-room, and, a moment later, the whirlwind inrush of his sister Adelaide and her first breathless questions, broken by sobs, as to Dianella.

"Mah... she is taking a love-cure," was his answer.

And he smiled at his sister's almost ferocious astonishment at this calm reply.

"You laugh?... Then she may be cured?"

"Cured.... Let us hope so! She is having good treatment...."

He smiled even more at the reproaches which Donna Adelaide heaped upon him in an aggressive outburst, and then at her description of all her troubles, all her sufferings and ill treatment, which she called "having her face trampled upon," on the part of her husband.

"Beware, Flaminio!" his sister adjured him at one point, seeing him still smile like that. "Beware! I am going to do something mad!"

He looked at her for a moment, and then spread out his arms.

"But why? If you don't mind my saying so, you look the picture of health!"

At this retort, his sister fled from the room, as though to put her threat into effect without a moment's delay.

And then, as he waited for the Prince to enter, for the second scene, he smiled at the portraits of the two Kings of Naples and Sicily, who were gazing down at him with the most serious expressions from the wall of the room.

Don Ippolito, with a clouded countenance, and inwardly in great anxiety as to the fate of his son, of whom he had heard nothing more, entered the room, equally disinclined for this encounter, from which the only good result that he could promise himself would certainly he obtained at the cost of a scandal, after the nauseating unpleasantness of vulgar explanations. But his face cleared at the sight of the smile upon his brother-in-law's lips. He interpreted it as meaning that two men, like themselves, could not and should not attach any importance to the ready tears, to the momentary impulses of a woman, whom their manly generosity could and should instinctively pity.

And so Don Ippolito smiled too, but a melancholy smile, as he shook his brother-in-law's hand; and, continuing to smile, spoke to him soothingly, and in that tone of masculine superiority, of his regret at the differences that had arisen between his wife and himself, because it was taking a long time... oh, a long time, alas, to bring their respective sentiments and thoughts into harmony, since she refused to understand the reasons for which...

"But really, Prince!" Salvo tried to interrupt him.

"No, no," Don Ippolito insisted. "Because I highly appreciate the sentiment that has moved her to ask me for what I cannot allow her. I sympathize, believe me, with all my heart, in your tragedy, and..."

"But, I tell you, it would be useless, everything else apart, for her to be there!" said Salvo, to make an end of the matter.

And greatly to the relief of each, they began to discuss another subject, namely the serious events of the day. Except that, then, the Prince was disconcerted by seeing that the smile still remained upon his brother-in-law's lips, while he was so heatedly expressing his indignation, whether at the outrageous measures adopted by the Government, or at the arrogance of the populace. What would have been his stupefaction if, suddenly breaking off the conversation and asking Flaminio Salvo why he went on smiling in that way, he had received the answer:

"Why?... Ah.... Because at this moment I am thinking that Colimbetra enjoys, among others, the great convenience of being close to the cemetery, so that you, presently, when you die, will have the signal advantage of being buried a few yards away, without having to go through the town, even in your coffin."

But he remembered that the Prince had built, in his own

grounds, and actually in the grove of oranges and pomegranates from which the estate took its name, a mausoleum comparable to that of Theron, and he felt a keen curiosity to go out and see it. As soon as he had a chance, he cut short this conversation also and suggested to his brother-in-law that they should take a stroll in the grove.

Donna Adelaide took advantage of this opportunity to send Pertichino post haste to Girgenti to deliver a note to the Honourable Deputy Ignazio Capolino: *8.P.M. (sue pregiatissime mani)*.

When, as night was falling, Flaminio Salvo returned home, upon his opening the door of the room in which Dianella spent most of her time, watched by her old housekeeper and by a trained nurse, he had the surprise of finding his daughter with her arms round the neck of Nini De Vincen-tis, her eyes, which were just visible over the young man's shoulder, sparkling with happiness, beneath her unkempt hair-, and her hands clasped tightly in the embrace.

"Dianella... Dianella..." he called to her, with a note of anxiety in his voice, hoping to learn that she was cured.

But Nini De Vincentis, turning his head with an effort and revealing a face convulsed with bitter anguish, answered him despairingly:

"She calls me Aurelio...."

CHAPTER VIII

THE LOGIC OF THE MEDALS.

On his return from that pilgrimage to Rome from which he had promised himself that he would bring back to Valsania so joyous an illumination of glorious dreams for his declining days, Mauro Mortara, after his visit to Donna Caterina Laurentano on her deathbed, moving with lowered head, without even venturing to glance to right or left, as though he were afraid of being laughed at by the trees, to which for years past he had talked of his adventures, of the greatness and power that had accrued to the country from the work of his old comrades in conspiracy, in exile, in battle, had taken refuge in his own room in the basement, as a wild beast, mortally wounded, slinks to its lair.

In vain had Don Cosmo, for about a week, tried to arouse him, to make him speak, moved by his own disconsolate pity for all those who deliberately shunned the remedy which he himself had found to cure every ill. To his insistent requests that Mauro should at least come upstairs to the villa for dinner and supper, the other had replied, with a shrug:

"Corpo di Dio, can't you leave me alone?"

"What will you eat?"

"My hands, I can gnaw them! Go away!"

In a swifter and more abrupt fashion, on the day after his return, he had replied to the pigeons, which during his absence had been assembled twice daily, at the appointed hours, by the curatolo, Ninfa's Vanni: "Bang! Bang!" a couple of shots in the air; and had dispersed them in fluttering confusion. Nor had he given any better reception to the welcome offered him by the three mastiffs, almost mad with joy at seeing him again.

The placid immobility of the old things in the room, which, steeped all of them in a sort of animal odour, seemed to be waiting for him to resume his normal existence among them, had aroused in him a fierce irritation: he would have liked to seize in both hands the straw mattress, which was rolled up in a corner, and fling it out of doors, with the boards and trestles that supported it, and out with that broken olive-press, and out with the chairs and boxes and halters and saddles and paniers. The only things that he had been glad to see again were the marks on the wallof the spittle, yellow with chewed tobacco, which, as he lay on his bed, he was in the habit of ejaculating in the faces of the enemies of his country, Sanfedisti and Bourbonists.

Again and again, the lure of old memories had tried to recapture him; again and again, seen through the open door, the long rows of vines, interspersed with the now budding poplars, in the awed silence of certain hours full of immemorial abandonment, had for a moment reconstructed the remote vision of that world, through which, until a short time ago, he used to wander on cloudless days, bursting with pride, like a god, stroking his beard. Suddenly, every time, the spirit that was already on its way, fascinated, towards that vision, had been drawn back by the harsh, angry buzz of a hornet which, coming into the room, recalled him forcibly to the present and broke the charm and shattered the vision.

What was he to do? How could he picture himself any longer in these spots that bore witness to his past exaltation? How could he hope any more for the healing peace of the country, when he knew that the whole of Sicily was turned upside down and all those vile renegades were rising to overthrow and destroy the work of their elders?

For years past, all his thoughts, all his sentiments, all his dreams had consisted in memories of that work and in satisfaction at its accomplishment. How could he find any rest, with the knowledge that it was threatened and on the point of destruction? In spite of the consideration due to his age, in spite of the seductive charm of his old, peaceful habits, he saw himself obliged by his ingenuous logic to admit that it was a debt of honour binding upon all those who like himself wore the medals on their breasts, as a reward for that work, to rally now in its defence.

"The old National Guard! The Old Guard! Fall in, all the veterans!"

And finally, in a moment of more intense excitement, he had tottered like a blind man, for shelter and for counsel, to the General's camerone, in which, hitherto, he had not had the heart to set foot.

As soon as he was inside, he had burst out sobbing, and without venturing to open the shutters of the windows and the balcony doors, which he had barred with loving care before setting out for Rome, had remained for a long time in the darkness, his face buried in his hands, weeping upon the dusty and dilapidated sofa. Gradually, the roar, the zest of the band of lions, the conspirators of Forty-Eight, who used to assemble there, in that room, round the old General, came back to him and made him ashamed of his tears; the ghosts of those lions, terribly indignant, had risen up round him and called to him to go in haste, yes, yes, to go in haste, old as he was, and prevent with the other old men who still survived the destruction of their country.

In the darkness, from a corner of that room, the melancholy stuffed leopard, minus an eye, had been unable to make him see all the cobwebs that fastened it to the wall, all the dust that had fallen upon its skin, spotted now, in addition to its natural markings, with many patches of mould! And Mauro Mortara had emerged with a terrible glare in his eyes, red and swollen with weeping, and had all but sprung upon Don Cosmo, who, happening to pass along the corridor, had stopped first of all in astonishment, seeing him in this state, and stared at him, and had then tried to restrain and calm him.

"If I didn't know that your mother was a saint, I should call you a bastard!" Mauro had shouted at him, almost clawing his face with his hands.

Don Cosmo had not moved a muscle, except to smile sadly, shaking his head, in token of commiseration; and had asked him where he proposed to go, against whom he proposed to fight at his age.

Mauro had made off without answering. And, downstairs, in his room in the basement, had actually begun to make preparations for departure. At his age? Sangue della Madonna, what had age to do with it? Who dare speak of age, to him! Where did he propose to go? He did not know. Armed to the teeth, ready for any provocation, he would go up to Girgenti, to discuss and arrange some plan of campaign with the other veterans, Marco Sala, Celauro, Trigona, Mattia Gangi, who surely, if the blood still flowed in their veins, must feel, as he did, the need to arm themselves and rally in defence of their common handiwork. If their enemies were united, banded in Fasci, why could not they unite, band themselves in a Fascio of their own, of the Old Guard? The troops were not sufficient; civilians must give them solid support, forcibly disband these Fasci, scatter all these dogs with powder and shot, if need be. The priests were certainly behind them, secretly fomenting them; and France too, France too, it was said, was sending money, on the sly, to dismember Italy and set the Pope back on his throne in Rome. And, for all one knew, once the revolution had broken out, she would try to land a force from Tunis in Sicily. How could he stay there with folded hands, without even attempting to defend the country, without even shewing his face to his old comrades and saying to them: "Here I am!" He must be off, be off at once!

Only, little by little, his zeal had become entangled, as in a spider's web, by all the relics of his adventurous life, exhumed from old boxes and drawers and threadbare, patched sacks, and parcels wrapped in faded paper, tightly tied with string. His plan was to make a selection, and to carry away with him as many as he could of the more precious. Confused, stunned, baffled by the memories that each one of them called to life, after a time his head had begun to swim and he had been obliged to stop. No, it was not possible to free himself so precipitately from all these bonds. And he had put off his departure until the following day.

All that night he had remained out of doors, wandering about, a prey to hallucinations. The voice of the sea was that of the General; the shadowy trees were the ghosts of the old conspirators of Valsania; and all alike kept on urging him to start. Yes, to-morrow, to-morrow; he would go out and face those cut-throats; they would overpower him and kill him; but yes, such was his desire, if the work of destruction was to be completed! What further value would his medals have, otherwise? He must die for them and with them! And he would pin them to his breast, to-morrow, be-fore setting out to confront the new enemies of his country. For Sicily must not be dishonoured, no, no, she must not be disho-noured in the eyes of the other regions of Italy, which had united to make her great and glorious!

On the following day, with his huge shaggy cap on his head, staggering under his load of papers and relics, his four med-als on his breast, the knapsack on his back and armed to the teeth, he had appeared before Don Cosmo to take leave of him. And he would doubtless have gone, had not Don Cosmo been supported in his efforts to detain him by Don Leonardo Costa, who had ar-rived from Porto Empedocle.

Having left Salvo's employ, after his son's death, and having relapsed to the ill paid and uncertain position of a foreman at the weighhouse, Leonardo Costa had accepted, chiefly in the hope of escaping from his own society, Don Cosmo's compassionate invita-tion to him to come over every evening from Porto Empedocle to feed and sleep at Valsania. The way was neither short nor easy, in the dark, on moonless evenings, along the railway line with its un-even ballast of rocks. Since his bereavement, a mortal weariness had made his legs as heavy as bars of lead. More than once he had seen the train bear down upon him; more than once he had been tempted to throw himself under the wheels and make an end of things. When there was no work to be found down on the shore, he would go up to the villa early, and through this channel, for some time past, news had been reaching Valsania without delay.

Had he not, that day, brought the tidings that the army corps had landed at Palermo, and would be certain, in the twin-kling of an eye, to crush and scatter the revolt, neither he nor Don Cosmo would have been able to restrain Mauro from going.

To calm him still further, there had next come the news of the proclamation of the state of siege and of the order to disarm. Never for an instant had it entered his mind that this order to hand over arms could possibly refer to himself, or that he could run the risk of being arrested, if he went up to the town armed. His arms were on the same footing as the soldiers'; the permission to bear them was conferred on him by his medals. The effect upon his spi-rit of the latest news brought by Costa had been like the effect upon a forest already swept by a tempest of a rapid alternation of sunshine and clouds. It had cleared slightly, when he learned that in Rome Roberto Auriti had been released from prison, although only upon bail, and that his brother Giulio had returned to Rome taking with him his sister and her son; and had darkened again at the unexpected revelation, that Laudino, the General's grandson, the inheritor of his name, was among the ring-leaders of the rising, and had fled from Palermo, after the proclamation of the state of siege, to escape arrest.

After this information, he had taken to eyeing Leonardo Costa with a savage frown, as soon as he saw him arrive tired and breathless from Porto Empedocle.

His thirst for knowledge had to contend with the angry fear that the man was coming, light-heartedly, to make some announcement that would once more oblige him to arm himself and set forth from Valsania. Since he had been on the point of doing so, he had known by experience what it would cost him to sever himself from the place, to tear himself away from all the memories that bound him to it, to relinquish the custody of the camerone, his vineyard, his pigeons, the trees that for so many years had listened to his discourses.

But Leonardo Costa, warned by his fury on the former occasion, knew now what news was for him, what for Don Cosmo and Donna Sara Alaimo. He had allowed the report about the Prince's son to escape him, because he supposed that Manro already knew him to be a Socialist and would naturally be pleased to hear that he had managed to escape.

The last piece of news that Costa was to bring, and brought piping hot, arrived amid the lightning, wind and rain of an infernal night.

Mauro had prepared the supper, in the place of Donna Sara, who had been in bed for the last two days with a severe chill; and he was waiting in the dining-room with Don Cosmo for their guest who, perhaps because of the bad weather, was late in coining. This delay irritated him, not so much because he was hungry as because he was afraid that the supper might be spoiled. He had always put his heart into everything that he did, and among all the many memories that gave him satisfaction was that of how he had

made the English "lick their fingers," when he was cook, first on
board ship and then at Constantinople. One of the reasons for his
hatred of Donna Sara was precisely the malicious joy that she had
displayed upon several occasions at the utter failure of sundry lessons in cookery which he had tried to teach her. Out of practice,
and with a mind confused and distracted by all his worries, he had
been venturing for the last two days with imperturbable courage
upon the concoction of the most complicated dishes, and had been
poisoning their guest and poor Don Cosmo.

"What do you think of it?"

"Oh, it's delicious," was Don Cosmo's invariable answer.
"Perhaps, though, I haven't much appetite."

"To my mind," Costa hazarded, "I feel that it might be better with a touch of salt."

"O Marasantissima," Mauro broke out, "here's the salt-cellar!"

Donna Sara had eaten nothing for two days.

Through the scream of the wind, the terrifying roar of the
sea, the lashing of the rain, they could hear her fits of coughing,
her lamentations and the prayers she repeated aloud. Evidently
overcome by a furious attack of religious mania, she had locked
herself up in her own little room and refused all offers of attention.

Now and again Don Cosmo, hearing her cough rather
louder and longer than usual, would go in haste to call to her
through the door of her room and to ask her if there was nothing
she wished. Donna Sara's sole reply was to shout back at him, as
soon as she was able, in a choking voice:

"Repent, you wicked devils!"

And she would go on shouting out Aves and Paternosters.

At length Leonardo Costa arrived, in a pitiable state, all
blown about by the wind, with the water running in streams from
his cloak and three inches of mud on his boots. He was completely
out of breath, and could not hold his head up, he was so tired. Mauro, by way of medicine, made him gulp down a tumbler of wine
immediately, meeting his resistance with the usual exclamation:

"Oh Marasantissima, lasciatevi servire!"

Don Cosmo hurried him off to his bedroom and helped
him to change his coat, making him put on one of his own, which
was extremely tight for him, but at any rate was not wet. Mean-

while Mauro had brought in the supper, and was calling from the dining-room:

"Holy devil, are you coming or aren't you?"

"When he saw them appear with their eyes starting out of their heads, he became apprehensive and asked with a frown:

"What's the matter now?"

Neither of them answered him. Don Cosmo, instead, asked Costa:

"And Ippolito? Ippolito?"

"He was asleep," was the answer. "At three o 'clock in the morning! He was asleep. But the story goes that when the sentry, who had been made to open the gate, ran up to the villa to report."

"Are you speaking of Don Landino?" Mauro interrupted him at this point, thrusting himself furiously between them. "Tell me what has happened?"

"Don Landino, no!" replied Costa, a look of melancholy gaiety appearing on his face. "They have dealt a finishing blow to that gallant gentleman, who was down here for a month trampling on your face! I know that you love him as dearly as I do!"

"Salvo?"

"The same!"

And Costa raised his foot as though to stamp on the neck of the fallen man. He went on:

"His sister, the Prince's wife, ran away, last night, with the Deputy Capolino..."

"Ban away? How do you mean, ran away?"

"How, eh? It's quite simple.... He came to fetch her in a carriage, and they went off in the middle of the night, by the three o'clock train, to Palermo. Of course they had arranged it all beforehand...."

Don Cosmo, still staring in amazement, murmured quietly to himself:

"Poor Ippolito... poor Ippolito..."

"He's all right!" Mauro shouted in his face.

"What comes of mixing himself with people of that class," added Costa with a grimace of disgust. "After all, you know, Si-don Cosmo, it is mortifying, perhaps, I don't say it isn't.... It's a terrible scandal: they are talking of nothing else at Girgenti and in the port.... But, after all ... he wasn't even treating her as a wife... people say they slept in different rooms and... if one's to listen to gossip... the rascal is getting her as she was before her marriage....

"When the sentry went up to the villa to report their escape and the servant went in to wake the Prince, they say he didn't even lift his head from the pillow, and said to the servant: 'Indeed? A pleasant journey to them! I shall remember to be annoyed about it in the morning, when I get up....'"

Don Cosmo shook his head and his raised forefinger emphatically several times, and put in:

"Ippolito never said that!"

"If you ask my opinion," Costa went on, sitting down to table with the others, and beginning his supper, "what else could you expect him to say? I am sorry for the Prince; but I am delighted, greatly delighted at the scandal to her brother. ... Ah, Si-don Cosmo, I don't know really why I go on living! I should like to save my soul, I swear to you; I should like to give it time to forget its pain, so that, at least in the hour of death, it might forgive him and rise to the throne of God.... But no, Si-don Cosmo: the pain is too strong, and it devours my soul; my hatred of him grows and becomes more furious from day to day; and then I say to myself: Why not? Would it not be better to kill first him and then myself, and to make an end?"

"Perhaps," Don Cosmo murmured, "you would be doing him a service...."

"That is just what keeps me from doing it!" exclaimed Costa. "Because I should be doing myself a service as well!"

"Eat and stop crying!" Mauro shouted at him.

"Have patience, Don Mauro," Costa turned to him, forcing himself to smile. "Your dishes, to my palate, always want just a touch of salt. A few tears give a savour to them."

Don Cosmo, meanwhile, lost in thought, gazing attentively at a morsel of meat speared on his suspended fork, was saying to himself:

"Like a pair of children...."

And amid her fits of coughing Donna Sara continued to shout from the room beyond:

"Repent, you wicked devils! Repent!"

IT WILL PASS!

Suddenly, while the three at the table were finishing their supper, from outside the house, where the wind and rain were still raging, above the continuous roar of trees and sea, they heard the furious barking of the mastiffs, which waited every evening on the steps for their master to emerge after supper.

Mauro, knitting his brows, sat upright on his chair and listened intently. The barks were a warning that there was somebody outside the villa. And who could it be at that hour, and in such vile weather? Confused shouts were heard. Mauro sprang to his feet, snatched up his gun, which was standing in a corner of the room, and went to the front door. Before opening it, he put his ear to the chink, and immediately, hearing that down below, in front of the villa, the dogs were trying to prevent several people from passing, who were shouting as they defended themselves, blew out the light, flung the door open, and through the violent hiss of the rain, in the pitch darkness, levelling his gun, bellowed from the top of the steps:

"Who's there?"

A throb of sinister light illuminated the scene, vaguely, for an instant. Mauro thought he could make out four or five men who, in spite of a desperate resistance, were retreating before the assault of the mastiffs.

"Mauro, perdio! These dogs! I shall kill one of them! I've been shouting to you for the last three hours!"

"Don Landino?"

And Mauro, trembling with excitement, dashed down the steps, into the gale, under the pelting rain.

"Where are you? Where are you?"

At the sound of their master's voice the dogs abandoned the assault, without however ceasing to bark.

"Mauro!"

"You, here?" the old man cried, taking the dogs' place now in harring the other's way. "Here? You, here? You have the audacity to seek refuge here with your companions in infamy? I shan't let you in! Away with you! This is four Grandfather's house! I shan't let you in!"

"Mauro, are you mad?"

"In the name of Gerlando Laurentano, begone! Away with you! Over there, with your father, is the hiding-place for you and your companions, not here! I shan't let you in!"

"Are you mad? Let me pass!" cried Lando, wrenching himself from the grip of Mauro, who had seized him by the arm.

A light shone out at the head of the steps, to be extinguished at once by the wind. And Don Cosmo, who had come hurrying to the door with Costa, called from above:

"Landino! Landino!"

His nephew answered:

"Uncle Cosmo!" and, turning to his companions, "Come along up!"

Whereupon, "Don Landino!" Mauro warned him in a voice broken by exasperation. "Do not set foot in your Grandfather's villa! If you do, I go away for ever! Give thanks to God, that your name is Gerlando Laurentano! It is only your name that keeps me from making a bonfire of you and these carrion, sacks of dung, that you have brought with you! Oh, indeed? So you're going in? God, for a thunderbolt, to shatter the house and destroy the lot of you! Wait, here you are, take this, complete your bold assault! I surrender the key to you!"

And the huge key of the camerone came clattering against the front door as it closed again.

"He's mad! He's mad!" repeated, in the darkness, Lando, Don Cosmo, Costa, searching in their pockets for matches with which to relight the lamp, while Lando's companions, astounded at such a reception in the sanctuary for which they had so yearned and which now at last they had reached, inquired, breathless and puzzled:

"But who is he?"

"Really mad?"

"But why?"

When the lamp had been lighted, the five fugitives, Lando, Lino Apes, Bixio Bruno, Cataldo Sclafani and Ingrao, appeared as though they had been fished out of a torrent of mud. Cataldo Sclafani, with his panic-stricken face, bristling already upon cheeks, lip and chin with the beard that was beginning to sprout afresh, was the most pitiable of them all: he looked like a terrified patient who had escaped by night from a hospital that had been blown away by the storm.

For a moment there was a fusillade of curt questions and hurried answers, interspersed with exclamations, sighs, and weary groans; and one shook himself, another stamped his feet, another looked round for a chair on which to fling himself down.

"Followed?" "No, no...." "Becognized?" "Perhaps!" "What's that? No...." "Yes. ..." "Lando, perhaps...." "On foot! How on earth?" "For three days!" "Torrents of rain!" "But how, I mean to say, you never attracted attention?"

This last exclamation came--need it be said?--from Don Cosmo. He went about repeating it to each of them in turn, struggling to concentrate his thoughts in the general confusion, which made him scratch the hair on his cheeks, with both hands.

"I mean to say... I mean to say.... How in the world? You never attracted attention?"

And he might have gone on repeating the question all night, had not the idea finally occurred to him that he ought to be offering some sort of help to these young men. What sort of help?

"I know, come along next door!" he began to invite them, seizing first one, then another by the arm. "Take your clothes off at once.... I have things... things for all of you... in here, in my bedroom... they're in the chest, come with me!"

Bixio Bruno and Ingrao, less bewildered and less tired than the others, stoutly opposed this strange insistence.

"No, no! Let us stay as we are!" cried the former. "There's no time to waste.... Is Porto Empedocle far from here?"

"Why, yes," exclaimed Lando, turning to his uncle. "Some one, a trustworthy peasant, to send to Porto Empedocle at once, to hire a boat... one of those big fishing boats..."

"Before the light comes, for heaven's sake!" pleaded Sclafani, coming forward with his panic-stricken air. "We onght to be out at sea before daybreak! We may have been recognized...."

"Go on! I tell you, no," Ingrao shouted at him.

"And I tell you, yes!" retorted Sclafani. "At Girgenti station, Lando, I could swear, was recognized. ...."

Leonardo Costa observed that the hiring of a boat, in so ticklish a situation, was not a task to be entrusted to a peasant.

"I can go myself, if you like! In fact, I will go this instant!"

"In this weather?" Don Cosmo asked, in a tone of distress. "Gentlemen, do not be in such a hurry.... Take my advice, and get your clothes off: you will catch your death.... D'you see ... here... this friend of mine... d'you see? I made him change, just now.... There are clothes... enough for everybody... in the chest, come and look!"

Costa, with a shrug of impatience, asked the young men:

"Would you like the boat to put in here, below! Valsania?"

"Yes, yes, here!" replied Lando. "No, uncle, for goodness sake, leave me alone!"

"Take your things off, I tell you...."

"It is not prudent," Lando went on, turning to Costa, while his uncle forcibly stripped him of his greatcoat, "it is not prudent to shew ourselves at Porto Empedocle. By this time all the seaports are certain to have received orders from Palermo for our arrest."

"But it will be difficult," Costa pointed out, "for a tartan to put in below here, at night, in this heavy sea.... However; I am not backing out.... We can try...."

And he went to fetch from the hall his big hooded cloak, still soaked with the rain.

"Friends!" shouted Ingrao, "would it not be better to go with this gentleman, while it is still night and no one can see us? We can remain in hiding just outside the town, until he has hired the boat!"

This suggestion was overruled by a wise observation from Lino Apes:

"What do you mean? Do you suppose that a tartan can be hired in five minutes, in the middle of the night and on a night like this? He will have to find the skipper...."

"I know him!" Costa interrupted. "I know one who is a friend of mine, absolutely to be trusted."

"And the crew?" asked Apes. "The skipper by himself is no use."

"Certainly! I shall have to find the crew as well," Costa admitted, "and get the boat ready ... It can't be done before daybreak."

"In that case, no!" Sclafani at once shouted, again stepping impetuously forward. "At Porto Empedocle, by daylight, no! We shall have to embark here!"

"In the meantime, I'm off!" said Leonardo Costa, who was already in his cloak.

"My poor friend!" groaned Don Cosmo. "Must you really?"

Costa refused to listen to a word of either commiseration or thanks, and ventured forth into the tempestuous darkness.

When Lando heard that he was the father of Aurelio Costa, who had been barbarously murdered with the wife of the Deputy Capolino by the sulphur workers of the Aragona Fascio, he looked darkly at Ingrao and the rest. Misinterpreting this look, Bruno expressed, albeit hesitatingly, the suspicion that he might be going to Porto Empedocle to avenge himself, by denouncing them. Whereupon Don Cosmo, shaping his lips, emitted his habitual laugh, a triple "Oh! Oh! Oh!"

"He?" he said; and explained the attitude and devotion of his poor friend, who, laying the blame for his son's death entirely upon Flaminio Salvo, had never given a moment's thought to the members of the Aragona Fascio.

"Oh, by the way!" he went on, reminded by the name Salvo which had come thus by chance to his lips. And he drew Lando aside to inform him of Donna Adelaide's elopement.

"Like a schoolgirl, don't you know? At three o'clock in the morning!"

In the general hubbub, no one had paid any attention to the voice of Donna Sara Alaimo who, imagining perhaps a genuine invasion by devils on this night of tempest, kept repeating more furiously than ever, from her little room far away at the end of the corridor:

"Repe-e-ent, you wicked devils!"

The strange cry rang out with a most startling effect in this momentary silence, and everyone, except Don Cosmo, was staggered by it; including Lando, staggered already on his own account by what his uncle had just told him.

"Who is it?"

"Oh, nothing, Donna Sara!" was the answer, as though Lando and his companions had known the old housekeeper of Valsania for years. "She's driving me out of my wits, upon my word.... She has shut herself up in her room for the last two days, shouting like that.... She is ill, poor woman. Here, too...."

And he tapped his forehead.

Lando's four companions looked one another in the face. In what sort of place had they landed after three days of desperate flight? The old man had been declared mad, who had given them that warm welcome to begin with; now this other old woman had been declared mad too; and that the third was completely in his right mind who so confidently declared the other two to be mad did not, in truth, appear to them any too evident. Up to that moment, this uncle of Lando's, except for their wet and muddy clothes, had shewn no anxiety.

Sure enough, "Haven't you changed yet?" Don Cosmo exclaimed in surprise, after giving them this explanation of Donna Sara's cry; and he hastened to open the chest in which his cast-off garments were stored. "Here, here... take what you want.... I tell you, there's enough for you all!"

The four young men could control their laughter no longer, and set to work to help one another out of their rain-soaked garments.

"The only thing that matters just now, I assure you," said Don Cosmo, "is, that you should not catch a chill. Laugh at me if you like, but change your clothes."

That there was enough for them all proved, however, to be an over-estimate. Lino Apes, not finding any garment left in the chest for himself, came forward with the seminarist's cassock spread out on his arms, as though he were carrying a child to the font:

"May I take this?"

"Why not? Ah, what is it, the cassock? Yes...if it fits you...."

And he smiled at the laughter of the other four, who were awkwardly struggling into the other garments, all of which emitted a pungent smell of camphor. Cataldo Sclafani had arrayed himself in the frock coat, and, as his head was aching, had tied round it, carter fashion, a fine big yellow cotton handkerchief, with a red check.

Gradually youth took the upper hand. None of them thought any longer of their defeat, of the uncertainty of the future. Jostled and chaffed by his companions, Lino Apes, strait-jacketed in the seminarist's cassock, hobbled to the kitchen to light the fire. They were hungry! thirsty! But here Don Cosmo found himself at a nonplus: he barely knew where the larder was; and as for the key, Mauro probably had it on him....

"The key?" cried Ingrao. "I know where it is!"

And he ran to pick up from the top of the steps outside the key that Mauro had flung against the door, which had been left lying there.

Don Cosmo studied it thoughtfully.

"This?" he said. "No.... Why, what has happened? This is the key of the camerone! Where did you find it?"

In the confusion he had not heard Mauro's final cry; and, when he learned that the key had been hurled at Lando, he at once grew pensive, and turning to his nephew:

"But in that case you will find... oh per Dio!" he exclaimed, "if he threw the key at you, you will find that he really is going.... Perhaps he has gone already!"

"Gone? Where?" asked Lando, echoing the alarm and regret of his uncle.

"Who can tell?" sighed Don Cosmo. And he recounted briefly the difficulty he had in keeping Mauro at home; then, as the other four young men were laughing at the crazy ideas and sentiment of this strange old man, he was obliged to tell them who Mauro was, what he had done; what the camerone meant to him and what it contained.

"Indeed? A stuffed leopard too?"

And, stirred by curiosity, Lino Apes, Ingrao, Bruno, Sclafani, as soon as Don Cosmo and Lando had gone in search of Mauro, retrieved the key and went into the camerone.

Immediately below it was Mauro Mortara's room.

Don Cosmo and Lando, candle in hand, had gone into a secret chamber, in the floor of which was a trap door communicating with the basement of the villa; taking care to make no noise they had lifted the trap, and gone down by the steep wooden stair, none too sound underfoot, to the cellar; from it they had passed into the flour store; they had next crossed two large, empty storerooms, a dark closet heaped with piles of old farming implements, and had arrived at an inner door leading to Mauro's room.

As he bent down to look in, Lando saw a gleam of light beneath the door.

"Mauro!" Don Cosmo called, "Mauro!"

There was no reply.

Lando stooped again, to look through the keyhole.

There reached them from above the noise made by the other four, who were chasing Lino Apes about the camerone in his seminarist's cassock, and shouting and laughing.

Mauro Mortara, seated in front of a chest, which he had pulled out from under his bed, was resting his arms upon the rim of the raised lid, his face being hidden between them.

"What is happening? What is he doing?" Don Cosmo asked.

Lando shook his fist angrily at the ceiling, which rang with the din that his friends were making. He felt, together with a bitter resentment at them and at himself, a keen remorse for the wounding insult to the sentiments of his dear old man, and a heartrending grief at not being able at that moment to add his own affectionate appeal to his uncle's.

"What is he doing?" the latter again inquired, lowering his voice.

What it was that Mauro was doing, with his face hidden thus between his arms, was indicated unmistakably by the medals which, pinned to his breast and left dangling by the position in which he was sitting, could be heard shaking every now and then. He was crying... yes... that was it... he was crying... and he had on his shoulders that absurd knapsack, which Lando had seen him wearing in Rome.

"Mauro!" Don Cosmo called to him again.

At this repeated summons, Lando, his eye still pressed to the keyhole, saw him raise his head and remain for a while listening, without however turning to face the door; he then saw him rise and dash across to the table.

"He has put out the light," he told his uncle, as he rose from his stooping posture.

They both stood there for a while listening, wondering when they would hear Mauro open the door. They realized then that they were so to speak prisoners: they had not the keys either of the store-rooms, or of the flour store or of the cellar, and would therefore be obliged to return upstairs, if they were to prevent him from going; they must act quickly, so as not to give him time to get out of reach. But not a sound came from his room.

Don Cosmo made a sign to his nephew to go upstairs again, in silence. When they were in the nearer of the two store-rooms, he stopped and said in a whisper:

"In any case, if he is determined to go, neither you nor I can prevent him by force. Perhaps he will come back, when you people are gone, and his anger has cooled."

Lando looked at his old uncle, whom he barely knew, in that huge store, over which the light of the candle projected, monstrously enlarged, the shadows of their bodies, and received the impression that a strange, unimagined reality was suddenly presenting itself to his gaze, with the queer inconsequence of a dream. For some time past he had ceased to perceive any reason for his actions, all of which left behind them a train of discomfort, a bitter taste of humiliation; but now more than ever, face to face with the reality, so strangely distinct, of this uncle of his, detached from life, in this lonely old house in the country, standing before him, in this empty store-room, with that candle in his hand. He was tempted to blow it out, as Mauro, a moment ago, had blown out the light in his own room, on the other side of the closed door. He heard the sound of the wind, the roar of the sea: outside was tempestuous darkness; including that of the fate which lay in store for him. It was essential that he should, in that darkness, at all costs, absolutely, find a reason for action, in which all his uneasiness should be set at rest, all the uncertainties of his intellect should cease to torment him. But what? When? Where?

"It will pass," said Don Cosmo a little later, the corners of his mouth drooping, his brow furrowed as though by waves of thought driven inwards by the ebb tide of his disconsolate wisdom, and with that look in his eyes which seemed to banish and scatter in the void of time all the bitter and irritating contingencies of life. "It will pass, my dear people... it will pass...."

The four young men had discovered the larder by themselves, and, since the door was open, had brought to the table all that they required; now, after they had eaten and quenched their thirst, they were making desperate efforts to struggle against the longing for sleep that had suddenly descended upon their eyelids.

Don Cosmo's exclamation was a reply to the account they had given, some with brooding bitterness, others with angry resentment and Lino Apes with his customary wit, of the recent tumultuous happenings. Looking upon them as already far remote in time, Don Cosmo was unable to discern either their meaning or their object. His aspect, to Lando's eyes, suggested the same feeling that we derive from the inanimate objects that look on, impassive, at the transience of human affairs.

"Did you see the leopard?"

"Yes, a beauty... a beauty..." growled Ingrao, burying his face, with the deformity of his dark birthmark, between his arms, which were resting upon the table.

"That was a live leopard once!"

Lino Apes opened his eyes and inquired, with a show of terror:

"A man-eater?"

"I tell you," Don Cosmo went on, "because now, my dear friends, it is stuffed with wadding. And that letter from my father? Did you read it? A faded sheet of paper.... And a living hand wrote it, like this hand of mine, like yours. ... What is it now? That poor madman has put it in a frame.... Louis Napoleon... the *Coup d'Etat*... events in France..."

He pressed his finger-tips together and waved his hands in the air, as much as to say: "What is left of them now? What meaning have they?"

"Realities of a moment... nonsense..."

He rose; went across to the balcony window, which for

some time now had been making no noise, and turned to his nephew:

"Do you hear how still it is?" he said. "I give you the comforting intelligence that the wind has ceased...."

"Ceased?" asked Cataldo Sclafani, raising with a jerk from his arms, for he too had been sprawling over the table, his panic-stricken face, like a sick man's in convalescence, with the yellow handkerchief pulled down over his forehead. "That's good.... We shall embark here.... Good night!"

And he settled down again to sleep.

"So it is with everything..." sighed Don Cosmo, beginning to pace up and down the room; and went on, coming to a standstill at intervals: "One thing only is sad, my friends: to have understood the game! I mean the game played by that frolicsome devil whom each of us has inside him, and who diverts himself by representing to us outside ourselves, as reality, what, a moment later, he himself reveals to us as our own illusion, laughing at us for the efforts we have made to secure it, and laughing at us also, as has been my case, for not having had the sense to delude ourselves, since outside these illusions there is no other reality.... And so, do not complain! Wear yourselves out and torment yourselves, without thinking that all this never comes to any conclusion. If it does not come to a conclusion, that is a sign that it ought not to come to a conclusion, and that it is idle therefore to seek a conclusion. We must live, that is to say delude ourselves; allow the frolicsome devil to play his game in us, until he grows tired of playing it; and remember that all this will pass... will pass...."

He looked round the table and drew Lando's attention to his sleeping companions.

"In fact, you see? It has passed already...."

And he left him there by himself, at the table. Lando gazed at the awkward uncomfortable attitudes of his friends, their ludicrous attire, their tired and worn faces, and envied them their ability to sleep and at the same time despised it. They had been able to joke; now they were able to sleep, forgetting that the disorders provoked by their preaching to a people oppressed by so many acts of injustice, but still deaf and blind, were now furnishing the Government with an excuse to trample once again upon this land, which alone, without making terms, with a generous impulse had given itself to Italy and in reward had received nothing but poverty and neglect. They were able to sleep, these friends of his, forgetful of the blood of all their victims, forgetful of their comrades who had fallen into the hands of the police, who undoubtedly, in the course of the next few days, would be sentenced by the military courts.

He rose from the table also; went out to the entrance hall, meaning to emerge into the open, to breathe a mouthful of fresh air, to free himself from his painful oppression, now that the wind and rain had ceased. But with his hand on the door he stopped, overcome by the odour of immemorial life that brooded over this villa, in which his grandfather had lived, in which with that desolate sense of precariousness this uncle of his allowed his joyless days to pass to no profit, in which Mauro Mortara.... Suddenly, at the thought of his old friend, whom he had cruelly uprooted, in his declining days, from this dwelling, which the cult of so many memories rendered sacred to him, he started: nothing else made him feel such contempt and shame for his own work and the work of his comrades as this latest effect of it: the driving away from Valsania of its old guardian, he who for some time past had impressed him as the purest incarnation of the old Island spirit; and he ran down the steps to try to placate him, to cry aloud to him that he was sorry, and to force him to remain.

The door of Mauro's room stood open; the room itself was in darkness and empty.

On the threshold the three mastiffs stood hesitating and bewildered. They did not bark. In fact, they gathered anxiously round him, pricking their pointed ears, wagging their stumpy tails, as though they were asking him why their master, whom they had followed as they followed him every night, after a certain distance had turned and driven them back, had rudely dismissed them: why?

From a balcony at the end of the house came Don Cosmo's voice:

"Has he gone?"

"Yes," said Lando.

Don Cosmo said nothing more. In the black darkness, solemn and portentous, of the still troubled night, he stood listening to the crashing of the sea against the cliffs of Valsania and the barking of dogs, near and far; then, placing his hand on his bald head, he fixed his gaze upon a few stars, nailheads of the mystery, as he called them, that appeared in a clear patch of sky, among the ragged clouds.

THE REWARD.

Without heeding the mud on the road, in which his iron-shod boots floundered and splashed; his eyes overshadowed by his beetling brows and almost closed; his whole face contorted with anger; a burning pain in his heart and his mind possessed by a darkness blacker than that of the night through which he was trudging, Mauro Mortara was, by this time, more than a mile from Valsania.

He was walking through a night still troubled by the last mutterings of the storm, buffeted now and again by an icy squall, which splashed in his face the drops that fell from the trees over-hanging the walls on either side of the road. He stooped as he went, walking with bowed head, his gun slung over his shoulder, the brace of pistols at his hips, a dagger with a leather sheath in his belt, his knapsack on his back, his fleecy cap on his head and his medals on his breast.

He was going up in the direction of Girgenti; but he meant to go farther, to leave the road at a certain point and take to the railway line; to pass through a short tunnel, come out in Val Solla-no, and there, just before he reached the station, turn off along another road to Favara, where, on a small farm beyond the village, lived a peasant nephew of his, the son of his sister who had died years before, who had more than once offered him a home in the event of his being obliged by ill-health to retire from Valsania,

He was going there, to this nephew,--but he preferred not to think about it.

His head, his heart were still battered, crushed and torn by the trampling feet of those young men who, as a supreme outrage, had gone in to profane the General's camerone, while he, in his own room below, was preparing for his departure. He refused to think or to feel anything more; to form any picture in his mind of the days that remained to him.

Gradually, however, his battered heart, stung by the gadfly thought that perhaps this nephew had offered him a home because he expected to inherit untold wealth from him, began to stir within him and to swell with injured pride.

Only in his young days, and from the hands of the General, before his departure into exile at Malta, had he received a Avage. Since his return to Valsania, after the storm-tossed vicissitudes of his roving life, at sea, in Turkey, in Asia Minor, in Africa, and after the campaign of 1860, he had always given his services there, disinterestedly.

And now, at seventy-eight, he was leaving the place as poor as a church mouse, without a penny in his pocket, his sole wealth those medals on his breast.

But just because this was all the wealth that he had amassed by the work of a lifetime,--"Fool," he could say to this nephew, "you are the owner of three rods of land; and if you take one step beyond them you are no longer upon your own ground; I, on the other hand, stand here, always on my own ground, wherever I set my foot, throughout the length and breadth of Sicily! Because I have scoured the Island from end to end to liberate her from the tyrant who was keeping her enslaved!"

Given this start, his exaltation increased every moment, fomented on the one hand by his grief at having severed himself for ever from Valsania, and on the other by the need to fill up, by recalling all the memories that could bring him comfort, the void that he saw before him.

He laughed and talked to himself aloud and waved his arms, without heeding where he was going: he laughed at the metals of the railway line, at the telegraph poles, fruits of the Revolution, and beat his breast and said:

"What do I care? I... I... Sicily... Oh Marasantissima... I tell you Sicily.... If it had not been for Sicily.... If Sicily had not chosen... Sicily moved and said to Italy: 'Here I am! I am coming to join yon! Do you move down from Piedmont with your King, I shall come up from here with Garibaldi, and we shall join forces in

490

Rome! Let us see who can get there first!' And who would have got there first? Oh Marasantissima, I know; Aspromonte, reasons of State, I know! But Sicily wished to be the first, from here... always Sicily.... And now a handful of scoundrels have tried to dishonour her. ... But Sicily is here, here, here with me.... Sicily, who does not let herself be dishonoured, is here with me!"

He found himself, of a sudden, at the mouth of the short tunnel that comes out in Val Sellano, and was amazed that he had reached it so quickly, without knowing how; before entering the tunnel, he looked up at the sky to see by the stars what o 'clock it was. It appeared to be about three. By daybreak perhaps he would be at Favara.

Having passed through the tunnel and come within sight of Girgenti station, at the point where the road turns off to the big village among the sulphur pits, he was obliged to halt, to wait for the passing of two companies of soldiers who, silent, breathless, at a forced pace, were making a night march in that direction. From the railwayman on duty he learned that, notwithstanding the proclamation of the state of siege, at Favara all the members of the disbanded Fascio, earlier in the evening, had arranged a meeting in the market place and had attacked and set fire to the Municipio, the nobles' club, the toll houses, that the fires and rioting still continued, and that already several people had been killed and many injured.

"Indeed? Indeed?" Mauro muttered. "Still?"

And he tore himself from the arms of the railwayman, who was trying to hold him back, seeing him thus armed, to save him from the risk to which he was exposing himself of being arrested by the soldiers.

"I, by the soldiers of Italy?"

And he ran on to overtake them.

An impetuous, frantic joy restored his strength, which was beginning to flag; gave back their youthful vigour to his old legs that had marched with Garibaldi; his excitement turned to delirium; he actually felt at that moment that he was Sicily, the old Sicily that was uniting herself with the soldiers of Italy, in the common defence, against her new enemies.

His feet ate up the road, keeping a few paces in rear of the two companies, who at a certain point, at a word from certain messengers whom they encountered on their way, had broken into a run.

When, in the first glimmer of daylight, plastered with mud from head to foot, breathless, roused to a frenzy by the march, his brain fogged; by exhaustion, he burst into the village with the soldiers, he had no time to see anything, to think of anything; hurled, amid a dense volley of stones, into a furious street fight, he received a medley of impressions so rapid and violent, that he could take in nothing, except the terrified flight of a compact mass of people, who ran away screaming; a tremendous roar; a stunning blow and...

The market place, as though it too were shattered and put to flight in the wake of the screaming populace who were deserting it, as soon as the smoke from their rifles melted in the livid glimmer of the dawn, seemed to the eyes of the soldiers to be held down by the weight of five lifeless bodies, scattered here and there.

A strange, unconquerable impulse obliged the captain to give an order at once, of any sort, to his men. Those five bodies that lay there, sprawling awkwardly on their faces, in a horrible immobility, in the mud of the market place, furrowed by the flight of the mob, formed a spectacle unendurably grim. And a serjeant and corporal, at their captain's order, advanced with hesitating steps across the market place until they came to the first of these bodies.

The serjeant bent down and saw that the body, which had fallen with its face on the ground, was armed like a brigand. He took the gun from its shoulder, and displayed it at arm's length to the captain; then handed the gun to the corporal, and bent down again over the body to take from its belt first one then a second pistol, which likewise he shewed to his captain. Upon which the captain, stirred by curiosity, although he still felt one of his legs trembling violently and was afraid that the soldiers might notice this weakness, went up to the corpse himself, and ordered them to turn it over so that he might see its face. When moved, the corpse revealed on its bloodstained breast four medals.

The three soldiers stood gazing at one another, stupefied and awed.

Who was this that they had killed?

THE END

About the Author

The Church That Had Too Much
Anita Mathias
Benediction Books, 2010
52 pages
ISBN: 9781849026567

Available from www.amazon.com, www.amazon.co.uk

The Church That Had Too Much was very well-intentioned. She
wanted to love God, she wanted to love people, but she was both
hampered by her muchness and the abundance of her possessions,
and beset by ambition, power struggles and snobbery. Read about
the surprising way The Church That Had Too Much began to resolve her problems in this deceptively simple and enchanting fable.

About the Author

Anita Mathias is the author of *Wandering Between Two Worlds: Essays
on Faith and Art*. She has a B.A. and M.A. in English from Some-
rville College, Oxford University, and an M.A. in Creative Writing
from the Ohio State University, USA. Anita won a National En-
dowment of the Arts fellowship in Creative Nonfiction in 1997.
She lives in Oxford, England with her husband, Roy, and her
daughters, Zoe and Irene.

Anita's website:
    http://www.anitamathias.com, and
Anita's blog Dreaming Beneath the Spires:
    http://dreamingbeneaththespires.blogspot.com